Abby Richardson

Familiar Talks on English Literature

A manual embracing the great epochs of English literature from the English

conquest of Britain, 449, to the death of Walter Scott, 1832

Abby Richardson

Familiar Talks on English Literature
A manual embracing the great epochs of English literature from the English conquest of Britain, 449, to the death of Walter Scott, 1832

ISBN/EAN: 9783337394028

Printed in Europe, USA, Canada, Australia, Japan

Cover: Foto ©Andreas Hilbeck / pixelio.de

More available books at **www.hansebooks.com**

FAMILIAR TALKS

ON

ENGLISH LITERATURE

FAMILIAR TALKS

ON

ENGLISH LITERATURE

A Manual

EMBRACING THE GREAT EPOCHS OF ENGLISH LITERATURE
FROM THE ENGLISH CONQUEST OF BRITAIN, 449
TO THE DEATH OF WALTER SCOTT, 1832

By ABBY SAGE RICHARDSON

In literature we have present, and prepared to form us, the best which has
been taught and said in the world. Our business is to get at this best, and
to know it well. — MATTHEW ARNOLD.

NEW AND REVISED EDITION

CHICAGO
A. C. McCLURG AND COMPANY
1892

PREFACE.

A S the title of my book suggests, this is a history of English literature told in familiar style. Its first and overruling purpose is to create a desire, on the part of those who read it, to know the best works of our best authors. I do not believe in anything said or written about English literature that shall serve as a substitute for literature itself, or that does not lead directly to the reading of the best books. For my own part, I would rather know thoroughly half-a-dozen English classics than all the works on literature ever written.

Although for several years I have been talking to classes, principally of young women, on the subjects this book includes, this is in no way a report of those talks, but has a unity and sequence which is not quite possible in detached lectures. I have endeavored to show the growth of English literature from its beginning down to the end of the first third of this century. From that time the great names that appear are the names of living men, or of men but lately dead, whose place in the archives of literature is not yet assigned. It is time only which tries the value of an author and sets him among his peers.

In a small volume like this, where I have made the attempt to combine brevity with a certain amount of detail about the author spoken of, together with an extract from his works, it has been impossible to mention every great name in the annals of English literature. What I have tried to do has been to touch on the salient points in the growth of literature; to mention the names of those who have had any marked influence upon it; to show briefly the cause of this influence; and, where it was possible, to quote sufficient from the author to excite a desire to know more of him. To carry out this plan in small space required that much should be left unsaid which I should like to say, and that many names should be omitted which are worth more than a mere mention; it also required that I should keep strictly within the limits of pure literature, — poetry, essays, fiction, — and leave the writings of historians, divines, and scientists out of my plan of work, except where they are associated with elegant literature.

As this is in no wise a cyclopedia of literature, I have not given biographical sketches of these writers, and have purposely omitted all facts about them except those facts of character or life which bear upon their work, sometimes adding incidents which would give interest or vividness to the story. I have always felt it unjust to literature to associate too closely the external life of an author with his productions, and I have tried to avoid that injustice. Handbooks of literature, especially those used in schools, have been too much like graveyards, where a series of stones record the life, death, and principal events relating to an author, ending with a few lines from his work as a sort of epitaph. I think this method has made the study of literature uninteresting. Therefore, if my treatment of the facts about a writer is desultory, and leaves unsaid what the cyclopædias say, it is to be understood as part of my method.

The style I have used may be regarded as sometimes too familiar for the subject. But I hope my book may be read largely by young people; I hope it may be read aloud in classes devoted to the study of literature; and I have therefore used a colloquial tone, hoping by this means more easily to gain the interest and the ear of the reader.

I have used the words " *our* literature," " *our* English authors," all through the book with intention. Writing as I do for American readers, for the young people of our country, I have endeavored to impress on them a pride in the works written in their language; I want them to feel that they have as much share and as much cause for pride in the glorious names of Shakespeare and Milton as if their grandfathers had not crossed the ocean to settle in Massachusetts or Virginia. English literature to the year 1800 is as much *our* literature as it is that of any girl or boy born in London or in Yorkshire. Let us lay hold of and claim this grand inheritance.

A. S. R.

CONTENTS.

———

PART I.

ENGLISH LITERATURE BEFORE CHAUCER. 449 TO 1350.

PART II.

FROM CHAUCER TO SPENSER. 1350 TO 1550.

PART III.

FROM SPENSER AND SHAKESPEARE TO MILTON.
1550 TO 1608.

PART IV.

THE CIVIL WAR AND THE RESTORATION. MILTON TO DRYDEN. 1608 TO 1700.

PART V.

FROM POPE TO WORDSWORTH. 1700 TO 1790.

PART VI.

THE LAKE SCHOOL AND ITS CONTEMPORARIES.
1790 TO 1832.

English Literature.

———•———

PART I.

BEFORE CHAUCER.

449 TO 1350.

FAMILIAR TALKS

ON

ENGLISH LITERATURE.

———•———

INTRODUCTORY.

A GREAT preacher of the past, writing many hundred
years before the invention of printing, said: "Of
making many books there is no end." I often wonder
what he would think of this century in which we live.
More than any other since the world began, this is an age
of books. Every year the great printing-presses turn out
thousands of volumes and innumerable magazines and
newspapers. Every year books become more and more a
factor in the education of all classes of people, the poor as
well as the rich. In days when there were no printing-
presses, when everything had to be copied with tedious
labor upon parchment or paper, the knowledge of books
was confined to few. Now the boys and girls in our common schools can know more books, and can easily own a
larger number, than could the kings and nobles of early days.
This does not prove that the man without books need be
ignorant, or the man with them altogether learned. There
is a great deal of culture to be gained outside a printed
page, and a man may be a narrow-minded pedant with his
head stuffed with book-learning; a great poet has told us
about —

> "The bookful blockhead, ignorantly read,
> With loads of learned lumber in his head."

But the man who combines the largest knowledge of good
books with breadth of thought, wide experience, and prac-

tical knowledge of the world, is likely to be a man of the highest and best culture.

Since we believe, therefore, that books are among the most important tools with which we are to carve out our lives, we want to know something about the best books in the world. Among the great quantities of matter which come day after day from our printing-presses there must, of course be a great deal of rubbish ; and the books preserved to us from the past are likely to be the best, because time has sifted much of the chaff from the wheat, and preserved only the wisest and wittiest things that have issued from men's minds. In the old books of the past we find a record of the best thoughts of the greatest minds that have ever lived. And in the books written by men of the past who spoke the language that *we* speak, we shall find a record of the thoughts and deeds of that race from which we are descended. See, then, what an influence these deeds and thoughts of the great Englishmen of the past must have on us to-day. Picture in your imagination this stream of thought, like a great river, flowing down through hundreds of years, bearing in its bosom so much to fertilize and enrich the age in which we live, and bearing onward to the future, from our own time, all that is noblest and greatest. This wonderful river of thought, flowing down to us and beyond us, is ENGLISH LITERATURE. And if you can feel how interesting is the knowledge of the books that keep a record of this thought, written in our English speech from the earliest days, and how important it is to know something about it, we can begin together, with real interest and sympathy, these *Talks on English Literature.*

In one sense literature comprises all the books ever written, — books on philosophy, science, text-books on all subjects, as well as poetry, essays, and fiction. But by general understanding there has come to be a division in the world of books ; and the department of poetry, fiction, and the elegant classics is separated from the more profound and scientific order of writing. This first department is sometimes called pure literature, or " polite literature." The

French say *belles lettres*, — meaning beautiful literature. It is this beautiful literature — the writings of the poets, the essayists, and the novelists — that these Talks are designed to touch upon.

Among these writers the poet is the chief, and it is the poet to whom in this book we shall give the most attention. Of all writers the poet has done most in all ages to refine and elevate. There is something in the melodious arrangement of words, richly clothing a beautiful thought, that has been able to influence the mind in all ages. The poet makes even common things seem rich, and if he puts a noble spirit in his verse, he makes life seem purer and higher. As Sir Philip Sidney says: "Now therein, of all sciences is our poet the monarch. He cometh to you with words set in delightful proportion, either accompanied with, or prepared for, the well-enchanting skill of music, and with a tale, forsooth, he cometh unto you, — with a tale which holdeth children from play, and old men from the chimney-corner. And pretending no more, doth intend the winning of the mind from wickedness to virtue, even as the child is often brought to take most wholesome things by hiding them in such other as have a pleasant taste." Therefore, although we intend in these Talks to follow the whole course of English literature, we shall dwell longest upon the poets and their works.

I have thus given you in brief the plan of our Talks. I hope, as we go on together, you will find such an interest in literature, and so feel its worth and richness, that from such brief accounts of the great authors and their works as I can give you, you will be led to know them more thoroughly, and to make them your friends. "And the love of books," says a French writer, "is one which, having taken possession of a man, will never leave him; a book is a friend which never changes."

I.

TELLING ABOUT THE ENGLISH PEOPLE, WHO THEY WERE, AND
HOW THEY FIRST CAME TO THE ISLAND OF BRITAIN.

BEFORE we begin to talk of English literature, we naturally want to know something about the people from whom the name of "England" and "English" is derived, since from their language our modern speech has been formed, and it is they whom we are proud to call our forefathers. Let us first ask, then, who these people were that have stamped their name and speech so powerfully on the world's history.

We find them, first, as a union of tribes known by the names of Saxons, Jutes, and Angles, or "English," dwelling in that part of Europe which borders the North Sea, and in the islands close to this mainland. Whence they came thither, and how long they had possessed that soil, we are not certain. We are told that most of the nations of Europe have sprung from a great mother-race called the Aryan race; that this Aryan race has many branches; and that the Teutonic branch of the family is among the strongest of them all. Wherever we find these fair-haired, blue-eyed, strong-limbed men, who speak in Teutonic tongues,[1] we find them playing an important part in history. It was a tribe of these Teutons, the Goths, who in the fourth and fifth centuries swooped down on the great Roman empire and trampled it under their feet. It was another band of these strong heroes, called Franks, or "free-men," who conquered what was formerly known as Gaul, and gave it its modern

---

[1] The languages derived from the Teutonic branch of the Aryan are: 1st, Gothic; 2d, Scandinavian; 3d, High-German; 4th, Low-German. The Gothic is the oldest of these. From the High-German comes modern German; from the Scandinavian, the languages of Denmark, Sweden, Norway, and Iceland; from the Low-German, English and Dutch.

name of France. It was the Scandinavian division of these peoples who, spreading from Denmark to Norway and Sweden, became the sea-kings of the North, — sending their ships to colonize Iceland, and sailing over the Northern Atlantic to Greenland more than four hundred years before Columbus discovered America. And it was still another horde of these Teutons who, settling all along the moist, uninviting shores of the North Sea, finally became the conquerors and holders of the British Isles. Angles, or " English," was the name common to the tribes inhabiting the various settlements along the coasts of the North Sea and in its islands ; so that of all the names which could have been given to this great nation, none is so appropriate as the *English*.

Adventurous and bold as they were by nature, and living on the borders of the North Sea, or in the islands surrounded by its waters, they naturally became daring sailors, holding stern rule over the waves they claimed as their rightful domain. Their power was soon felt among neighboring nations, and they were heard of in the island of Britain, separated from it only by the seas on which they ranged.

This island of Britain was then inhabited by a people who belonged to the Keltic branch of the great Aryan family. These were the Kymry, the Ancient Britons of history. Long before the coming of the English the country of the Britons had been invaded by Roman legions under the great Cæsar, and the Roman empire had kept up a sort of rule through the reigns of several emperors. The Romans had built military roads, camps, and walls on British soil ; and as they were the best road-makers in the world, you may find many traces of their work in England to this day. The Romans, too, had brought Christianity to Britain, and the new religion was adopted there ; so that the Britons felt their superiority over other peoples, and looked on their neighbor Teutons across the North Sea as barbarous and heathen men who knew not the true God and were outside the pale of religion and civilization. You will find it hard to believe that the Britons could have invited a people

whom they so looked down **upon to come and live among
them.**   Yet **in** the middle of the fifth century such **an** invitation was given, and a band of English, led by Hengist and Horsa, took advantage of it.   The Britons
were led to make this invitation by a mixture of fear and prudence.   **They had at their backs** in Scotland, and across the
Irish Sea in Ireland, bands of savage enemies, the Picts and
the Scots, who were constantly overrunning and devastating
Britain.   **These enemies** were dreaded by the British, who
dreaded almost equally the savage rovers of the North Sea.
But they thought, by making friends with the latter and
inviting them to come to Britain, they might get their aid
against Scot **and Pict.**   Therefore Vortigern, a British king,
introduced **Hengist and Horsa** into the land **as his** allies.
And after coming thither, Hengist made a marriage between
his daughter Rowena and the king, so that an English
woman became a queen in Britain.

Having once set foot in the British domains, the English
people, with that tenacity which is a part of their character,
prepared **to stay there.**   They called the Britons *Welsh*, —
which means *foreigner*, — and began to treat them as if they
were really interlopers and foreigners on **their own lands.**
The Britons, **no less** obstinate than the English, refused to
surrender, and were driven, inch by inch, westward and
southward into the strongholds in the mountains of Wales
and to the rocky peninsula of Cornwall.   Here their language, **their** literature, and their religion were fostered as
they had been **before** the hated English landed in Britain.
Meanwhile the English grew and spread over the island **now**
called England, on which they had fought for their **place till**
they were **firmly established as the** rightful owners of the
land.   And thus, by the right of conquest, the *English*
people became possessors of *England*.

449

II.

TELLING HOW LETTERS AND LEARNING FIRST CAME TO ENGLAND.

YOU will readily guess that these warlike English, when they landed on the shores of England, were not a literary people. The Britons, who were such savages in the eyes of the cultured Romans, were much more advanced in learning and religion than their English conquerors. Yet the Teutonic peoples did have a system of writing, in characters called Runes, which **they claimed had been** taught them by their **god Odin,** or Woden. These Runic letters were carved on stone or wood, which had been used by all ancient **peoples before paper or parchment** was discovered. Egypt wrote her hieroglyphics on stone, **just as the** North American Indian cut upon the bowlders of **his native country the rude** picture-writing which preserves the memory of **his** battles. Thus the Teutons had engraved their **Runes,** doubtless on the stones and **trees of** their various dwelling-**places. Our** word *book* is from *boc*, the Early English for beech-tree, — probably because the beech is a hard wood, which could easily be used by the **early book-makers.** Still, with only stone and wood in place of pen, ink, and paper, we cannot expect to find any works of literature among our English when they came to their new home in Britain.

The want of pen, ink, and paper, however, or even of written characters, does not prevent a people from having its poetry or history. We do not know a tribe so barbarous that they have not had among them a story-teller or minstrel, — the earliest historian or poet of a people. **These men repeat** the traditions of the past **or the deeds of the men around them ; and** these stories, rehearsed from mouth to **mouth, or handed down from** generation to generation, before the time of book-making, might in later times get written down, and so become the first history or the earliest

poem of a nation. The Britons had their *bards*, who sang
to harps songs of war and praises of heroes. The Scandinavians had a *sagaman* and *scald*; the English their *scop*
and *gleeman*. The chiefs honored these men as princes
honor poets. They had them at their feasts, they took
them to the field of battle; and the court of these old rulers
would not have been complete without its minstrel. These
singers or story-tellers would keep alive the traditions of
their tribes, and it is probable that they preserved from
father to son the old stories which had been told among the
Teutonic branch of the Aryan family, before they broke up
into different tribes; for among the Germans, Scandinavians, and English there is a great likeness in some of the
earliest literary remains, which most likely comes from the
fact that the root-stories or myths were the same, and dated
back to the time when they were one people. What is
more natural than to suppose that when these migrating
hordes separated, each carried away the early traditions, to
embellish them over again with deeds of more recent heroes
and the scenery of their new dwelling-places?

How many such myths our English forefathers brought to
Britain, we do not know. It was not until long after they
had been settled in their new homes that any verses of their
singers were written down; and only after it is committed
to writing can we fairly begin the study of literature. First,
they were obliged to seek less clumsy means for the writing
of poetry than the side of a flat bowlder or the wood of a
tree, and for characters more generally understood than the
Runic letters. Let us see, then, how the use of parchment
and our modern kind of letters first came into England.

It was hardly a hundred and fifty years after the English
had conquered Britain that a Roman priest, passing along
the streets of his city of Rome, saw some blue-eyed, handsome youths exposed for sale in the slave-market. Their
beauty attracted him so much that he stopped, and asked
who these strangers were. "They are Angles," was the
answer. "Not so," said the priest; "not Angles, but
angels, for they have angels' faces, and it becomes such

to be co-heirs with the angels in heaven." A few years later, when this same Roman priest had become Pope Gregory, and was all-powerful over the Roman empire, he remembered these Angles, or English, whose faces had so impressed him, and would not rest till he had sent Christian missionaries to England to snatch these people from heathenism. The English had received no teachings of Christianity from their conquered foes, the Britons. There were only bloody instructions on both sides, and the Britons, with pride in their superior religion, called their conquerors " heathen " and " barbarians," while the English took fierce delight in burning the religious houses and putting to death the holy men among the Britons. So the religion which taught peace and good will among men did not spread from one to the other people.

It was in the year 596 that the ship sent by Pope Gregory landed the good father Augustine, with forty monks, on the shores of Kent. Ethelbert, king of Kent, heard of the coming of this little band of strange men, clad in long robes, bearing aloft a silver cross with the image of Christ painted on a board. The English monarch, not knowing what to think of men who came without weapons, feared they were magicians, and sat under a spreading tree to receive them ; because if they tried to use any evil arts of witchcraft, their spells would be less powerful in the free air. Instead of spears and battle-axes, these monks bore rolls of parchment written all over with letters unknown to the English king. These parchments were the Bible, a book of the four Gospels, a Psalter, and a history of the Christian Martyrs.

You will see that the most important book which the Roman priests brought to England was the Old Testament. This was a sacred book of the Hebrew people, who were not related to the Teutonic peoples, from whom our English sprang. The Hebrews belong to another family of mankind, — the Semitic family ; and from them we derive our religion and that wonderful book, the Old Testament, which is made up of the writings of their inspired men, their poets and prophets. And if we believe that literature, like everything else, grows rich, the greater the number and variety of things that are added to form it, then we must regard **it as a great** good fortune to English literature to have this rare old book of the Hebrews so early brought to England.

I want you to think of the Old Testament now only as a great literary work, full of wonderful poetry and rich imagination, coming from an entirely different race, to be grafted upon the rude poetry and traditions of **this our** Northern people. Imagine this poetry of the South, with **its odors of spices, its** music of sounding harp and tinkling cymbal, its visions of green pastures and still waters, all at once mingled with the songs of the gleemen who sang **at** barbaric feasts where warriors, clothed in skins, spilled mead to the memory of dead heroes, and celebrated **the** glories of bloody warfare. Think of the unmelodious rhythm of this English singer blending all at once with the melody of the harp-strings that the Hebrew bard had struck by the rivers of Judæa, under the glowing skies of the Orient. Picture how the kindling imagination of the Northern poet, who had hardly known the language of tenderness or love, would be inspired by such ardent strains as these, from the Songs of the great Solomon : —

> " Behold, thou art fair, my love,
> Behold, thou art fair.
> Thou hast dove's eyes within thy locks,
> **Thy** hair is like a flock of goats
> That appear from Mount Gilead ;
> **Thy lips are like a thread of scarlet,**
> **And thy speech is comely.**
> **Set me as a seal upon thine** heart,
> **As a seal upon thine arm,**
> **For love is strong as death,**
> And jealousy is cruel as the grave.
> The coals thereof are coals of fire,
> A most vehement flame."

If you are able to imagine all this, you will see what a rich flood of poetry and imagery this great book of this Eastern

people added to the rude and unformed literature that
was to be nursed under the cold, wintry skies of Northern
Europe.

With these Hebrew books **the** Christian priests also
brought the Roman letters, which have ever since been the
letters used by the English. Thus all at once upon the
English soil came the CHRISTIAN RELIGION, the HEBREW
LITERATURE, and the WRITTEN CHARACTERS OF THE ROMANS,
— three great gifts to the future of our English race.

III.

THE BEGINNINGS OF ENGLISH LITERATURE.

IN the British Museum in London, where are collected the
largest number of English books **to** be found **together**
in one library, there is a time-stained and time-eaten manuscript known as the *Beowulf.* This manuscript is probably
almost a thousand years old, although its exact age **is not**
certain. Let everybody who speaks the English language
and has a reverence for English literature **look at** this old
manuscript with admiration. It is the oldest epic in the
language, the oldest *entire* poem in our literature.

The *Beowulf* is written **in the Roman** letters which were
introduced into England by Christianity, and is in the earliest English spoken on the island **of** Britain. It has been
several times translated into modern English and into other
languages, and there have been many guesses as to whence
it first came, when it was written, and to what people it
related. Some learned men have thought it was of German,
others of Scandinavian, origin ; others hold that the scenery
and character of the poem are wholly English. We shall
most likely never know all the facts about it, or anything
about its unknown author ; but one thing seems certain to my
mind, — that the traditions or story on which it is founded
are far older than the hand that first wrote it. Why may

not this time-encrusted old poem of *Beowulf* have celebrated the deeds of some Teutonic hero in a prehistoric
past? When it was first written down by the old poet, a
thousand years ago, he might easily have embellished an
older story with incidents of his own time and the scenery
of the more modern dwelling-place of the Teutons, but he
could not entirely lose, in telling the story, that atmosphere
of antiquity which carries us back, as we read it, to the time
when western Europe was filled with fens and waste places
peopled by men living in caves and lake-dwellings, with
whom the Teutons may have battled when they were wandering through Europe before they had fixed their homes
on the borders of the North and Baltic Seas.

But let me tell you here simply and briefly the story of
the poem. Beowulf is a chief of the Goths, — a "deed-
bold" warrior, the old poem calls him, accustomed all his
life to war. At the opening of the poem he is going to the
help of Hrothgar, a chief of the Danes, who is "old and
hairless" when the poem begins. Hrothgar has built a
great hall, or "folkstead," in which he sits at feast with his
warriors. It is probably much such a hall as that in which
the ancient gleeman or scald first sang the deeds of
Beowulf.

Imagine a long room, fifty by two hundred feet, with nave
and side aisles formed by two rows of pillars. Down the
centre of the hall is the great stone hearth on which burn
huge fires of wood. Between the pillars curtains of skins
or rudely woven tapestry are sometimes hung, and then
they form sleeping-places for the warriors. In others of
these alcoves are set great vats, from which the mead and ale
are dealt out to the drinkers. On a raised dais at the
upper end of the hall sits the chief with his wife, at a table
placed transversely to the long tables that run lengthwise
through the hall on each side the central hearth. At the
chief's tables are the most favored guests, or those of highest rank. The apartments of the women, when there were
women in the household, were behind the dais, shut off by
thick hangings. If you will read the description in Scott's

Ivanhoe of the hall of Cedric the Saxon, you will see that it was a hall similar to this, with appliances of a more advanced civilization, in which the English chiefs held revel and counsel as late as the coming of their Norman conquerors. Such a hall, adorned with barbaric pomp, Hrothgar the Dane built for himself and his warriors, and called *Heorot.* There the gleeman sang, the warriors feasted, the mead flowed in the cups, and all went happily, until a " grim guest called Grendel " came up from his dismal dwelling in neighboring fens, — where lurked giants, dwarfs, and all sorts of misshapen creatures, — and each night seized and bore off his prey from among Hrothgar's dearest warriors. On this account Beowulf had been summoned to subdue Grendel. He embarked, therefore, on his " wide-bosomed " ship, and went to the help of the old thane ; or, to quote the most poetical translation of the old poem, —

> " Departed then o'er the wavy sea,
>   by wind impelled,
>   the floater foamy-necked
>   to a bird most like,
>   till that about one hour
>   of the second day
>   the twisted prow
>   had sailed,
>   that the voyagers
>   saw land ;
>   the ocean shores shine ;
>   mountains steep ;
>   spacious sea-nesses;
>   then was the sea-sailer
>   at the end of his watery way."

When they had landed, the " sea-weary men " marched straight for the hall of Hrothgar. Leaning their round shields of hard wood against the wall, they entered. The Danes asked who they were and whence they came. Beowulf answered proudly that he was a chieftain, the " board sharer of the king of the Goths." On this he was made welcome ; and as soon as he was rested and refreshed, he entertained them with tales of his prowess. "The women," says the old poem, "liked the Goths' proud speeches," and the wife of Hrothgar came to sit by her lord and listen.

At night Beowulf waited sleepless for the time when Grendel, the grim guest, should come to seize another warrior. When he heard him enter, he rose and grappled with him. Then —

> "Bodily pain endured
> the fell wretch ;
> on his shoulder was
> a deadly wound manifest ;
> the sinews sprang asunder,
> the bone-casings burst ; "

and off went Grendel, leaving his hand and arm in the strong grasp of Beowulf. He died on his return to the watery fens, where —

> " Was with blood
> the surge boiling,
> the dire swing of waves
> was mingled
> hot with clotted blood ;
> it welled with fatal gore.
> Grendel had dyed it
> after he, joyless,
> in his fen-shelter,
> laid down his life."

After this fight is over and Beowulf has been honored as a victor, the giant mother of Grendel comes to avenge her son, and carries away at night Hrothgar's favorite warrior. Beowulf says consolingly to the bereaved chieftain, —

> "Sorrow not, sage man ;
> better 't is for every man
> that he his friend avenge
> than that he greatly mourn ;
> each of us must
> an end await
> of this world's life ;
> let him who can,
> work high deeds ere death."

Beowulf then goes to the watery fens and attacks the giantess in her lair, which still reeks with the gore of Grendel, and finally returns with the two heads of these giant foes. Then he rests in the great hall Heorot.

> " Rested him, the ample-hearted;
> the mansion towered,
> vaulted, and golden-hued,
> the guest slept therein
> until the black raven,
> Heaven's delight,
> blithe of heart, announced
> the bright sun coming."

At the close of the poem Beowulf returns to his home, where, as his last act of prowess, he slays a huge dragon which devastated the land, and in doing it receives his death-wound. Before his death he divides among the young warriors his shield, his war-shirt of "ringed iron," and his other weapons of war. After his death his people make a great pyre, put all his riches on it, and burn them, with their chief's body.

This is a bare outline, with scanty extracts, from the oldest entire poem which wears the dress of our earliest English speech. If from this you have caught any of its spirit, you may be able to fancy, with me, that there is something Homeric about this rude epic. But it is a Homer of the North, not of the South, who sings. A blast of the north wind seems to blow through and through these lines. The beauty and grace of Homer's heroes are not seen in this Gothic chieftain. It is the brute strength of the Northern peoples that we find in him. Yet some of the characteristics of poetry are not lacking to this early poetry. Night is called "the shadow-covering of creatures;" death is "the terrible life-devourer;" the door is the "hall's mouth." Although generally bare of ornament, and not rich in imagination, it has a few touches that show the genuine poetic spirit. Bare and bald as it is, I think you may be able to hear in it the birth-cry of our English Muse, — a true nursling of the Northern peoples, cradled under the skies of a rugged and wintry clime.

There are a number of specimens of early English poetry

which are **almost as** old as the *Beowulf,* **and one or two**
fragments which may have been committed to **writing even
earlier.**   One such collection of poetry, **called the " Exeter
Book,"** was given by **a good** bishop **to the library** of Exeter
Cathedral some **time in the** eleventh century.   Most of
these **poems are on** religious subjects, **although** two or three
of the **most poetical in the book have an air of** even greater
antiquity than the Christian religion on English soil.   Let
me give you a few lines from one of these old poems, " The
Sea-farer," which might have been sung by some old viking
in the earliest times that the ships of the Northmen sailed
the seas.   He begins, —

" I of myself can
 a true tale relate,
 my fortunes recount,
 how I in days of toil,
 a time of hardship,
 oft suffered
 bitter breast-cares,
 have endured,
 proved in the ship,
 strange mishaps many.
 The fell rolling of the waves
 has me oft drenched,
 an anxious night-watch
 at the vessel's prow
 when on the cliff it strikes.
 Pierced with cold
 were my feet,
 *bound with frost
 with cold bonds.*

*There cares sighed
hot round my heart,
hunger tore me within,* —
the sea-wolf's rage ;
that the man knows not
to whom on land
all falls out
most joyfully ;
how I miserable and sad
on the ice-cold sea
a winter passed
with exile traces,
of dear kindred bereft.
Hung o'er with icicles,
the hail in showers flew,
where I heard naught
save the sea roaring.
the ice-cold wave."

Note the atmosphere of this old poem, — the icy coldness, which almost makes one shiver in reading it, —
and you will feel that the unknown poet knew something
of the poetic art.

IV.

ON THE FORM OF EARLY ENGLISH POETRY, AND THE OLD POEM OF CÆDMON.

BEFORE going farther, I want you to glance at the construction of this early poetry, and to note in what way it differs from the poetry of other peoples. Its most marked difference is its *alliteration*, or the use of the same initial letter to begin a certain number of words in a line of poetry. The verses were written like prose; for a long time they were not supposed to be cast in poetical form, as there was no use of capital letters at the beginning of lines. There was, however, a little mark, like a colon or semicolon, dividing the poem into lines; and these lines consisted usually of two important and two unimportant syllables. Of such a pair of lines the two most important words of the first, and the most important of the second, had the same initial; thus : —

> " The *g*rim *g*uest
> *G*rendel hight."

> " An un-*w*insome *w*ood,
> *w*ater stood under it.
> The *w*ater *w*elled blood;
> the *w*arriors gazed
> on the *h*ot *h*eart's blood,
> while the *h*orn rung
> a *d*oleful *d*eath-note."

This system of alliteration, which was used by the Scandinavians as well as the English, is the distinguishing mark of the poetry of the North. Probably this use of consonant initials was as natural to these Northern peoples as the music of rhythm and the jingling of rhyme were to the nations of the South of Europe, where the language was so rich in vowels and so soft in sound. Certainly the use of a recurring consonant seems natural to the poets of the North, and we shall see that alliteration is much used by poets in later

3

English, and that it often crops out in our poetry even at the present day.

The first noted poetical outcome of the English Muse after the land was Christianized was the work of Cædmon, of whom very little is known, except that he lived near the convent of Whitby, which was presided over by the Abbess Hilda, — one of that long line of saintly women who are found in the early annals of the Christian Church.

This Cædmon, according to the earliest account, was present at some convivial party, where it was the custom, as from the earliest times among all Teutonic peoples, to sing or recite, while the others feasted, and each was called upon in turn to perform his part. But when it came to him to sing, Cædmon got up and went out, he was so ashamed of his ignorance. Going out into the stable among the cattle, the care of which was that night committed to him, he fell asleep there. In his dream he heard a voice saying, "Cædmon, sing to me." He answered, "Thou knowest I cannot sing." Then the voice replied, "However, you *shall* sing." "What shall I sing?" asked Cædmon, meekly. "Sing thou the beginning of created things." And on this he began to praise God in verse, and to utter a long poem in his dream. On waking he was still inspired by the influence he had felt in his sleep, and continued to sing the Creation, the Fall of Man, and the whole story of Paradise Lost. Taken before the Abbess Hilda, she persuaded him to enter the monastery, and he lived and died there in great holiness, leaving as his work this first English epic which Christianity inspired in England.

The poem opens with a description of the revolt of Lucifer in Heaven, the Creation, the Temptation and Fall, and goes on through nearly all the dramatic incidents of the Old Testament. Here are the lines that follow the account of Satan's conspiracy and rebellion : —

> "Then was God angry,
> and wroth with that host
> whom he erst had honored
> with beauty and glory;

> he formed for these false ones
> an exile home,
> anguish for reward,
> the groans of hell.
> hard punishment;
> bade the torture-house
> await the victims."

After he has banished Lucifer and his rebels, God
creates the earth and man to re-people the sky, empty of
the angels he has banished to hell. Of the earth the old
poem says, —

> "There had not here as yet
> save cavern shade
> aught been;
> but this wide abyss
> stood deep and dim,
> strange to its Lord,
> idle and useless."

Satan's speech of discontent has a shadowy likeness to
Milton's Satan : —

> "'Why shall I toil,' said he.
> 'To me it is no whit needful
> to have a superior.
> I can with my hands
> as many wonders work;
> I have great power to form
> a diviner home,
> higher in heaven.
> Why shall I for his favor serve?
> bend to him in such vassalage?
> I may be a god as he.
> Stand by me, strong associates,
> who will not fail me in this strife.
> Heroes strong in mood,
> who have chosen me for chief,
> renowned warriors!
> I may be their chieftain,
> sway in this realm.
> To me it seemeth not right
> that I in aught need cringe
> to God for any good.
> I will no longer be his vassal.'"

The following lines are from the description of the deluge :

> "The Lord sent
> rain from heaven,
> and also amply let
> the well brooks
> throng on the world
> from every vein.
> The torrent streams
> dark-sounded ;
> the sea rose
> o'er their shore-walls.
> Stern and strong was he
> who o'er the waters swayed,
> covered and overwhelmed
> the sinful sons
> of middle earth
> with the dark waves."

Cædmon flourished in the seventh century, somewhere in the period from 657 to 680. His successors were a line of worthy monks, who for centuries kept alive in monasteries the faint flame of learning and literature. In the early part of the eighth century appeared the first English biography, that of Bishop Wilfrid, who built York Minster, written by his pious chaplain, Eddius ; about this time, too, came the first autobiography known to our literature, written by Bishop Egwin. Text-books in the various sciences began to appear. Aldhelm, a learned monk of the seventh century, was both a musician and a poet, and assumed the garb and character of a glee-man, singing his verses in English, that it might thus attract and teach the people. Unfortunately, for a very long time the language of books and of learning was Latin, and the good every-day speech of our forefathers, the homely English, was crowded out of use. This was partly because English was not much esteemed, and partly because Latin was the language of scholars all over Europe ; and being thus a universal tongue, it was the most convenient one for authors. But it was a misfortune for the English language and literature that a foreign speech should for centuries have held such a sway over the speech of the people.

700-710

V.

TELLING OF THE VENERABLE BEDA AND OF KING ALFRED THE GOOD, AND OF THE WORK THEY DID IN LITERATURE.

BEDA, a good and pious priest, whose epitaph gave him the name of "The Venerable Beda," comes next to Cædmon as one of the great writers of this early time. Like the rest of his learned brethren, he wrote almost wholly in Latin. His best-known work is a church history of England. He wrote also text-books on natural philosophy, grammar, astronomy, music, and many other branches, which would be very amusing in this age of new-fashioned school-books and modern discoveries. All these were in Latin; but in his last days he began the translation of the Gospels into English, and died just as he finished dictating the translation of Saint John's Gospel. There is a beautiful account of his death by his favorite scholar, Cuthbert, who wrote down from his master's dictation this English version of a portion of the New Testament. As they drew near the last chapters of John, Beda ordered Cuthbert to write with all speed; but his breath came so painfully that the good old priest had to pause frequently in his dictation. As the day drew near its close, the writer said, "Most dear master, there is yet one chapter wanting: do you think it troublesome to be asked any more questions?" He answered: "It is no trouble; take the pen, make ready, and write *fast*." In the evening Cuthbert said: "Dear master, there is yet one sentence unwritten." Beda said: "Write it quickly." Soon after the boy said: "It is written." "It is well," answered Beda; and sitting upright on the floor of his cell, he breathed his last in a song of rejoicing.

673–735

A little more than a century after the death of Beda, Alfred the Great was born,—one of the best and noblest of English kings, who for the work he did in literature alone, deserves a high place in our remem-

849–901

brance. He did all he could to make the spoken language of England also its written language, when no one but a king could so easily have set the fashion of putting literature into an unfashionable garb, and so have drawn others into following it.

It is said that Alfred, at the age of twelve, could not read, but that his stepmother one day showed him and his brother a book of poetry, saying, "Whichever of you shall soonest learn this volume shall have it for his own." Attracted by the beautiful colored letters, Alfred mastered the book, and so his love for literature began. When he became king, although his hands were always full of affairs of government, to say nothing of wars constantly carried on against him by the Danes, he still made book-making one of his pursuits, and kept several literary men in his court, carrying out his plans and aiding him in his writing. An account of a voyage along the coast of Norway, and another from Denmark through the Baltic Sea, which Alfred wrote down from the lips of the narrators, are the earliest voyages written in English. One of the most famous works of Alfred was the translation of *The Consolation of Philosophy,* a book written by the Latin writer Boethius when he was shut up in prison. It is a series of conversations between the Mind, cast down by imprisonment, and Wisdom, who plays the consoler, and in doing so, utters many wise maxims that are as good to read to-day as ever they were. In this translation are many fables, which Alfred has told in the simplest words, as we should tell a story to a little child, — which proves that Alfred hit on the true way of interesting the childlike and uncultured people. This is the way he tells the story of Orpheus and Eurydice : —

"Happy is the man who can behold the clear fount of the highest good, and can put away from himself the darkness of his mind. We will now from old fables relate to thee a story. It happened formerly that there was a harper in a country called Thrace, which was in Greece. This harper was inconceivably good. His name was Orpheus. He had a very excellent wife, who

was called Eurydice. **Then began men to say** concerning the
harper that he could harp so that the wood **moved, the stones**
stirred themselves at the sound, **and** wild **beasts would run**
thereto and stand as if they were tame,— so **still that** though men
or hounds pursued them they shunned them not. **Then** said they
that the harper's wife should die, and her soul should be led to
hell. Then should the harper become so sorrowful that he could
not remain among men, but frequented the wood and **sat on the**
mountains both day and night, weeping and harping so that
the woods shook and the rivers stood still, and no hart shunned
any lion, and no hare any hound, nor did cattle know any hatred
or fear of others for pleasure of the sound. Then it seemed
to the harper that nothing in the world pleased him. Then
thought he that **he would** seek the gods of hell and endeavor
to allure them with his **harp, and pray that** they should give him
back his wife. When **he came thither, then** there should come
to him the dog **of** hell, whose name was Cerberus; he should
have three heads, and began to wag his tail and play with him
for his harping. . . . Then he went farther, until **he** met the
fierce godesses whom the common people call Parcæ, of whom
they say that they know no respect for any man, but punish
every man according to his deeds. Then began he to implore
their mercy. Then began they to weep with him. Then went
he farther, and all the inhabitants of hell ran to **him, and led**
him to their king; and all began to speak with him, and to pray
that which he prayed. . . . And all the punishments of hell
were suspended while he harped before the king. When he
long and long had harped, then spoke the king of the inhabitants of hell, **and** said: 'Let us give **this** man his wife, for he
has earned her by his **harping.'** He then commanded him that
he should well observe that **he never** looked backwards after he
departed thence, and **said if he** looked backwards he should
lose the woman. But men can with great difficulty, if at all,
restrain Love! Well-a-way! What! Orpheus led his wife till
he came to the boundary **of** light and darkness. When he
came forth into the light, then looked he behind his back to-
wards the woman. Then **was** she immediately lost **to** him.
This fable teaches every man who desires to fly the darkness of
hell and to come to the light of the true good, that **he look** not
about him to his old vices."

By such stories, so simply told, and by many translations
from the Bible and other great books, did Alfred seek to
educate his subjects.

There were, however, many influences hostile to literary work in his reign. But no matter what disturbances went on outside, within the quiet convent walls the monks wrote and copied the books which keep the thread of history through that past time. It was the habit in both British and English monasteries to keep the record of all the events of the year in a chronicle, the form of which was modelled upon the Hebrew chronicles. Every year the monks of different religious houses would meet and compare these annals, and then form a general record. One of the oldest of these, known as the "Anglo-Saxon Chronicle," was edited by Alfred and his scribes, and is valuable as history.

Alfred died just on the brink of the tenth century. After him there is no very great name for many years. There are men of learning and a few unknown poets, but little has come down to us in English, or of English origin. The invasions of the Danes interrupted literary labor, and early in the eleventh century the Danes conquered

1017 England, and King Cnut, or Canute, took the throne. But the great event in English history in this eleventh century which had an effect on language and literature was the Norman Conquest, of which I shall tell you in the next Talk.

VI.

Telling how William the Norman came to the Conquest of England.

I HAVE already spoken of the invasions of the Danes, who for so many years were attempting the conquest of England. You can guess something of their power and activity from the fact that they placed a king on the English throne in the early part of the eleventh century. Remember that these Danes, with Swedes and Norwegians, made the Scandinavian division of the Teutonic peoples, and that they are thus close cousins by race to the English. In the ninth, tenth, and eleventh centuries these Scandinavians showed such a wonderful spirit of adventure, and their deeds had so great an effect on history, and hence on literature, that I cannot make my story complete without giving a brief sketch of them.

In spreading out from Denmark to Sweden and Norway, the Scandinavians (whom I will hereafter call by their shorter name of Northmen) had become, by force of their position on peninsulas girt about by Northern seas, the most daring sailors in the world. In the year 876 a band of these Northmen, coming principally from Denmark, but swelling their number as they went along with a mixture of Jutes and Angles, who joined them readily in this marauding march, went to invade France. Led by a famous Danish chieftain, Rolf, also called Rou and Rollo, they sailed up the river Seine, devastating the country all along its borders, and prepared to besiege Paris. The French made treaties with these powerful invaders, gave Rolf a princess of royal blood to wife, induced him to be baptized a Christian, and gave him a tract of land on the borders of the English Channel, since called Normandy, from these Northmen, or Normans. They spread over their new home, marrying with the natives, increasing rapidly in numbers, and adopting the language of the people among whom they lived. In a century they had almost forgotten whence they came and the language they spoke at their coming, using wholly the *Romance* tongue, which afterwards became the modern French.

Meanwhile the Danes, overrunning England, had put King Cnut in power. He seems to have been a good king, who made fair laws, for those days. He was something of a poet too, and a little song of his is still preserved, which he made one day as he was going down the river Ouse in a boat, and heard from the open windows of the monastery the monks singing their hymns : —

"Merrily sang the monkes in Ely,
　When Cnut the king rowed by;
Row, knightes, near the land,
　And hear ye the monkes' song."

When Cnut got the throne, the English king, whose unfortunate name in history is Ethelred the Unready, fled to Normandy, where the descendants of Rolf were flourishing. Probably the reason he went there was because his wife, Queen Emma, was a Norman woman, a great-granddaughter of the famous Rolf. And the son of this unfortunate Ethelred and Emma, the gracious young prince Edward, exiled from his English home during the reign of Cnut, spent all his youth in the Norman court, spoke its language, and took on the manners and polish of its best society, — esteemed in those days a very polished and elegant society indeed. For you must understand that the rough Normans who came to Northern France one hundred and fifty years before the time of Prince Edward, had been wonderfully improved during this lapse of time. The French among whom they settled had imparted to them their civilization. Southern Europe, especially Italy, had sent to them pious pilgrims, who carried learning and religion to foreign lands. These wandering scholars had been hospitably received in Normandy, and one of them, the celebrated Lanfranc, had established a school there, which became one of the most famous in Europe.

Another people, who greatly aided in the spread of learning in Europe, were the Arabs, who had overrun Italy, conquered a large part of Spain, and made incursions into France during the century before Rolf came to Normandy. These Arabs were far in advance of the Europeans in all kinds of knowledge. They had instituted splendid libraries in Spain, had opened schools there, and their systems of teaching had an influence all over Europe. These Arabians, too, were great story-tellers, — the *Arabian Nights' Entertainments* bears testimony to that, — and among them were also musical poets. When the Norman mercenaries, following their taste for adventure, went into Southern Europe to help the Italians in battle against these Arabs, they must, even in so rough a meeting, have imbibed some of the culture of their foes. And in the mingling of all these influences which had touched him on all sides, it is certain that the Norman, who was always hospitable to new ideas, and held fast to all that came to him, either of an intellectual or a material kind, must have been very much improved and polished. So when young Prince Edward, son of Ethelred and Emma, and consequently descended on one side from Alfred the Great, and on the other from Rolf the Dane, was made king of England, after the death of Cnut and his sons, he took back to the English court the language and the manners in which he had been bred in the Norman court.

With this Edward, known as Edward the Confessor, the first Norman influence came to England, although it was not Edward who fixed and confirmed it there. It was a much greater and stronger man than Edward the Confessor, — no other than the great Duke of Normandy, whom we know best as William the Conqueror. William claimed that Edward had promised that his successor on the English throne should be the Norman duke ; and the story is also told that William had extorted an unwilling promise from Harold, King Edward's brother-in-law, that he would favor the Norman claim. As soon as Edward the Confessor died, however, Harold took the throne. But Duke William was on the alert to urge his claim. A man like a lion was this William of Normandy, — so strong and so brave that we can but admire him. In a very few months after Edward's death he had crossed the English Channel with his troops, beaten the army of Harold in the battle of Hastings, in which Harold was slain, and had made himself the crowned king of England, — the first of a long line of Norman kings. This Norman victory had an influence on literature which ranks as an event second in succession and importance only to the coming of Augustine and his monks with their parchments of the Scriptures.

As the knights of William the Conqueror spurred to

battle upon **the field of** Hastings, the **king's minstrel,**
Taillefer, who could fight all the better, doubtless, **because**
   1066   he could sing, made the English welkin ring with
the strains of **the** *Song of Roland*, which celebrated the deeds of Charlemagne's heroes against Arabian
foes. As the song rang gayly from the minstrel's lips, the
arrow of a foeman silenced him **forever. In** this musical
war-cry, so suddenly hushed in death, the new literary influence **first made itself heard in England.**

VII.

On Literature under the Normans, especially in the Reign of Henry II.; and the Legends of Arthur and his Knights of the Round Table.

NOTWITHSTANDING the pious labors **of** monks, beginning with the venerable Beda, there were few
books in England at the time of the Norman conquest, or
indeed for years after. When the Norman came to France
he brought with him little that could be called literature.
Romance, the spoken language of Normandy, was hardly a
written language in William's time. However, the fact that
a language is not a written language does not prevent the
making of songs in the vulgar tongue or the singing of
them by the people's minstrels. It was not long after the
coming of the Normans to England that all sorts of minstrels swarmed in France and Germany, — Trouveres, Troubadours, Jongleurs, Minnesingers, all singing like the lark,
until France, and especially the **South of** France, was like
a sky full of birds. Thus, **although** the Norman did not
bring many books when he came to England, he brought
an impetus to poetry, and the form in which to clothe it.
You will recognize that the spirit inherent in these descendants of the Northmen was akin to that which had
inspired the heroic lines **of** *Beowulf*, acted upon by the

refining forces it had met in France and Southern Europe.
But this spirit had now taken upon itself a new form.
The verses, without rhyme or rhythmic grace, in which the
Teutonic gleeman had sung the high deeds of his fathers,
were not heard among Norman singers. Poetry put itself
into melodious numbers, and the soft consonances of
rhyme took the place of the old-fashioned alliteration of
the earliest age of English poetry.

It is to the credit of the Norman kings that they were
always favorable to learning. William the Con- 1066
queror, although his reign was busy with the broils to
and intrigues which engaged a king struggling to 1087
keep his hold on a new kingdom, was never deaf to the
claim of letters. As soon as he was fairly at home in
England, he brought over the good Lanfranc, the Italian
scholar who had founded the famous school in Normandy,
and made him Archbishop of Canterbury. William's son,
Henry I., bore the surname of *Beauclerc*, " Fine Scholar ; "
and there were few princes of the Norman line in England who did not feel, or pretend to feel, an interest in
literature.

The history of England was still kept up in Latin. The
first great successor of Beda and Alfred in this field was
Ordericus Vitalis, who brought English history down to the
year 1141 ; following him came William of Malmesbury,
who told the story of the English from their landing in
Britain to the reign of King Stephen ; and then came
Henry of Huntingdon, who ended his work about the
time Henry II. came to the throne.

In the reign of Henry II. literature took a great
stride forward. There were many events that 1154
helped to this. The king himself was a patron to
of literary men, and his queen, Eleanor, had come 1189
from the very home and birthplace of the Troubadours,
and could herself make songs such as the singers of that
day sang to their gay lutes. There had been two crusades
to the Holy Sepulchre, and the united armies of Europe
had brought back from the East many refinements of taste

and many poetical ideas new to them. The system of chivalry, which did much to polish manners, was the ruling force in society; and it was this spirit that found expression in the lays of the Troubadour, and exalted the office of the singer till knights and princes were proud to be called verse-makers. With these influences to foster literature it is not surprising that a number of remarkable names should appear in England in this reign.

Among the first of these names is that of Geoffrey of Monmouth, who was not English, but Welsh, and belonged to the old British nation, so long since driven to Wales by the English advance into British territory. These Britons had imparted very little to their English conquerors, although, as I have told you previously, they had a literature of which they were justly proud.

The Welsh felt less bitterness against the Norman than his ancestors had felt against the English, and the tendency of Norman rule had been to break down the barriers which kept all knowledge of British history and poetry out of England, and thus to bring a fresh element into our literature. In 1147 this Geoffrey of Monmouth, who was a priest living under the patronage of the English court, wrote a history of his people which is very interesting indeed. Geoffrey says he was not the author of this book, but that it was a translation of the ancient Kymric tongue, which he, like all true Britons, could read and speak, and that it was one of the old books which the Welsh had carried over to Brittany when some of them fled there after the English invaded England. This book is very interesting to us, because in it we find the history of the famous King Arthur and his prophet Merlin, and an account of how the order of the Knights of the Round Table was founded.

The history begins by telling us that the race of Britons began with Brutus, a great-grandson of Æneas of Troy, who, after the manner of his famous grandsire, took his household gods and went to found a city in the island of Albion. After slaying a number of giants he found there,

the chief of whom was Gogmagog, Brutus built the city of
Troynovant (New Troy), which is now London, and began
the race of the Britons. From him in lineal order came
King Arthur, greatest and best of British kings.

There is nowadays a great deal of doubt about the
reality of King Arthur, and many regard him merely as a
myth of the old historians or the later poets. But although we may be sure that the story about Brutus, and,
indeed, most of the accounts of Arthur, are untrue, still
I do not see why there may not once have been a noble
king among the Britons called Arthur, who ruled wisely
and well, nor why some of the deeds told by Geoffrey
may not have been founded on fact. At any rate, Geoffrey
was for years believed in as an undoubted historian, and
from his time Arthur and Merlin and the Knights of the
Round Table have figured largely in literature, even to
the present day, when we find them in so many of the
modern poets.

Two other remarkable men of Henry II.'s time were
also Welsh by birth, — Walter Map and Gerald de Barri.
They were both priests, as were most literary men in these
early days; but Map was a shrewd, outspoken man, and a
clever writer, who did not let his office blind his judgment,
and he had a very sharp pen to use against the abuses of the
Church. Some of the songs, which are known as "songs
of Walter Map," are the first protests in England against
religious corruption, which we shall see wax strong in the
time of Wycliffe and the Reformers two hundred years
later. Map also wrote a sort of court journal, which gives
us little peeps into that old time, showing it as if the
people in it were still alive. But his great work in literature was his addition to the Romances of the Round Table,
which had now begun to be current in Europe and to draw
to them other romances, which Brittany, a country so rich
in fiction, was ready to add to the story of her favorite
King Arthur. The characters of Launcelot du Lake, Tristram and Isoud, Galahad, the Quest for the Holy Grail,
and many other incidents, which religion and chivalry had

interwoven with the original legends of Arthur and his knights, were spreading over Europe. It was natural that Walter Map, himself of Kymric race, should have found delight in the story of the British Arthur. He bound in one the scattered stories, bringing them together on English soil, and making them absolutely the property of English literature. Walter Map was preceded by two Trouveres, one of whom, Geoffrey Gaimar, put the History of Geoffrey of Monmouth into metre ; and the other, who was named Wace, also wrote the same history in verse, in a much better fashion, and presented it, when done, to Queen Eleanor. And from the time of these three, Map, Gaimar, and Wace, to that of Alfred Tennyson, the names of Arthur and his knights are familiar to all readers of English poetry. A literary contemporary of Map, Gerald de Barri (also known as Giraldus Cambrensis, or Gerald of Wales), seems to have been bright and witty, and although he wrote in Latin, used it in an easy, familiar style, like one who writes in his spoken language. He himself said : "Since words only give expression to what is in the mind, and man is endowed with the gift of speech only for the purpose of uttering his thoughts, what can be greater folly than to lock up and conceal things we wish to be clearly understood, in a tissue of unintelligible phrases and sentences? Is it not better, as Seneca says, to be dumb than to speak so as not to be understood?" But alas ! for us who would like to read Gerald in his native tongue, he, as well as all the other writers, except the Trouveres of whom I have just spoken, wrote in Latin, and the thirteenth century opens before we hear any great utterance in English speech after the time the Normans set foot in England.

VIII.

On the Struggles of the English Speech to hold its own against the Norman; of Old Ballads, especially the Robin Hood Ballads; the Old Geste of Robin Hood and Guy of Gisborne.

YOU may imagine how our sturdy English speech was struggling all this time to keep from being entirely driven out of the land by its fashionable rivals. The language of the Church and of letters was Latin; that of the court, the Troubadours and the Trouveres, was Norman-French. Yet the common people held stoutly to their mother-tongue. In those parts where the conquerors were most thickly settled it was often crowded to the wall; but in provinces more remote, where the Norman had not made his way, the English language was fairly spoken. It was not easy to uproot from the land the grand old speech brought to England by our forefathers. It was one of the grievances of the Englishman that his speech was neglected for the more fashionable Norman. You remember, if you have read "Ivanhoe," what Wamba the witless says to Gurth the swineherd as they are watching the swine.

"How call you those grunting beasts running about on their four legs?" demanded Wamba.

"Swine, Fool, swine," said the herd; "every fool knows that."

"And swine is good Saxon," said the jester. "But how call you the sow when she is flayed, and drawn and quartered, and hung up by the heels, like a traitor?"

"Pork," answered the swineherd.

"I am glad every fool knows that too," said Wamba; "and pork, I think, is good Norman-French. And so, when the brute lives, and is in charge of a Saxon slave, she goes by her Saxon name; but becomes a Norman, and is called pork, when she is carried to the castle hall to feast among the nobles. What dost thou think of this, Gurth, ha?"

4

"It is but too true doctrine, friend Wamba, however it got into thy fool's pate."

"Nay, I can tell you more," said Wamba, in the same tone: "there is old Alderman Ox continues to hold his Saxon epithet while he is under the charge of serfs and bondsmen such as thou, but becomes *Beef,* a fiery French gallant, when he arrives before the worshipful jaws that are destined to consume him. Mynheer Calf, too, becomes *Monsieur de Veau* in like manner: he is Saxon when he requires tendance, and takes a Norman name when he becomes matter of enjoyment."

Yet we must not be ungrateful to the Normans, for they brought into the language many words that are valuable, and many which we could hardly do without.

One way in which the speech of the people was preserved was by means of the old ballads, sung among them by native minstrels. These were true English songs, composed by untaught poets, many of whom, doubtless, were unable to write at all. To this class of old ballads belong those relating to Robin Hood, which were the literary offspring of the struggle between Norman and English. The strife for land-ownership, which drove the Englishman from field and dwelling-place, sometimes forced him into the forest and highway, where, outlawed from his own lands, he thought it only fair to take back what he could from his rich oppressor. Such an outlaw was Robin Hood, who, if we may believe anything that is told of him, was an Englishman of noble birth, living in the early thirteenth century. Upon his bold deeds, sympathized with by the English, the famous Robin Hood ballads were founded.

You can fancy how such a rude ballad, sung in their own spoken tongue, in the North of England, must have moved the people's hearts, and kept alive their love for their language and race. Most of these old ballads have been changed, no doubt, by being put into print; but some of them have kept the spirit of the time which produced them. Here is one of the oldest of these ballads, although we cannot be sure of the date of its composition. Probably

the earliest that has come down to us did not find its way
into manuscript before the fifteenth century. This is the
ballad of Robin Hood and Guy of Gisborne :—

> When shaws been sheen and swards full fayre,
>   And leaves both large and longe,
> Itts merrye walkyng in the fayre forreste
>   To heare the small birdes songe.
>
> The woodweele sang and wold not cease,
>   Sitting upon the spraye,
> Soe lowde he wakened Robin Hood
>   In the green wood where he lay.
>
> " Now, by my faye," sayd jollye Robin,
>   " A sweaven I had this night.
> I dreamt me of tow wighty yemen,
>   That fast with me can fight.
>
> " Methought they did me beate and binde,
>   And tooke my bowe me froe ;
> Iff I be Robin alive in this lande,
>   Ile be wroken me on them towe."
>
> " Sweavens are swift," sayd lyttle John,
>   " As the wind blowes over the hill ;
> For iff itt be never so loude this night,
>   To-morrow it may be still."
>
> " Buske yee, bowne yee, my merry men all,
>   And John shall goe with mee,
> For Ile goe seeke yond wighty yeomen,
>   In greenwood where they bee."
>
> Then they cast on theyr gownes of grene,
>   And tooke theyr bowes each one ;
> And they away to the greene forrest
>   A shooting forth are gone.
>
> Until they came to the merry greenwood,
>   Where they had gladdest to bee,
> There were they ware of a wighty yeoman,
>   That leaned against a tree.
>
> A sword and dagger he wore by his side,
>   Of manye a man the bane,
> And he was clad in his capull-hyde,
>   Topp, and taill, and mayne.

"Stand you still, master," quoth Little John,
  "Under this tree so grene,
And I will go to yond wight yeoman
  To know what he doth meane."

"Ah, John, by me thou settest noe store,
  And that I farley finde;
How often send I my men before,
  And tarry myselfe behinde?

"It is no cunning a knave to ken,
  And a man but heare him speake;
And were it not for bursting of my bowe,
  John, I thy head wold breake."

As often wordes they breeden bale,
  So they parted, Robin and John:
And John is gone to Barnesdale;
  The ways he knoweth eche one.

   .   .   .   .   .

Lett us leave talking of Little John,
  And thinke of Robin Hood,
How he is gone to the wight yeoman,
  Where under the leaves he stood.

"Good morrowe, good fellow," sayd Robin so fayre,
  "Good morrowe, good fellow," quo' he;
"Methinkes by this bowe thou beares in thy hand,
  A good archere thou sholdst bee."

"I am wilfulle of my waye," quo' the yeman,
  "And of my morning tyde."
"Ile lead thee through the wood," said Robin,
  "Good fellow, Ile be thy guide."

"I seeke an outlawe," the straunger sayd,
  "Men call him Robin Hood;
Rather Ild meet with that proud outlawe,
  Than fortye pound soe good."

"Now come with me, thou wighty yeman,
  And Robin thou soone shalt see.
But first, let us some pastime find,
  Under the greenwood tree.

"First let us some masterye make,
  Among the woods so even.
We may chance to meet with Robin Hood,
  Here at some unsett steven."

They cutt them down two summer shroggs,
   That both grew under a breere,
And sett them three score roode in twaine,
   To shoote the prickes yfere.

" Leade on, good fellowe," quoth Robin **Hood**,
   " Leade on, I do bidde thee."
"Nay, by my faith, good fellowe," hee sayd,
   " My leader thou shalt bee."

The first time Robin shot at the pricke
   He mist but an inch it fro.
The yeoman, he was an archer good,
   But **he** cold never do soe.

The second shoote had the wightye yeman,
   He shot **within** the garland ;
But Robin he **shotte** far better than **hee**,
   For **he** clave the pricke-wand.

" A blessing upon thy hart," he **sayd**,
   " Good fellowe, thy shooting is goode,
For, an thy hart be as good **as** thy hand,
   Thou wert better **than** Robin Hoode.

" Now tell me thy name, good fellowe," **sayd he**,
   Under the leaves of lyne.
" Nay, by my faith," quoth bold Robin,
   " Till thou have told me thine."

" I dwell by **dale** and downe," **quoth hee**,
   " And Robin to take Ime **sworne**;
And when I am called by my **right name**,
   I am Guy of good Gisborne."

"My dwelling **is in this** wood," sayes Robin.
   " By thee I set right **nought**.
I am Robin Hood of Barnesdale,
   Whom thou so long hast sought."

He that had neyther beene kyth nor kin
   Might have seen a full fayre fight,
To see how together these yeomen went,
   With blades both browne and bright.

To see how these yeomen together **they fought**,
   Two howres of a summer's day.
Yett neither Robin Hood nor Sir **Guy**
   Them fettled to flye away.

Robin was reachless on a roote,
    And stumbled at that tyde,
And Guy was quick and nimble withall,
    And hitt him upon the side.

"Ah! deere Ladye," sayd Robin Hood, "tho'
    That art both mother and may,
I think it was never man's destinye
    To dye before his day."

Robin thought on Our Ladye deere,
    And soone leapt up againe,
And strait he came, with a awkwarde stroke,
    And he Sir Guy hath slayne.

He took Sir Guy's head by the hayre
    And stuck it on his bowes end.
"Thou hast been a traytor all thy life,
    Which thing must have an end."

.   .   .

Robin did off his gown of greene,
    And on Sir Guy did throwe,
And he put on that capull-hyde
    That cladd him topp to toe.

"Thy bowes, thy arrowes, and little horn,
    Now with me I will beare,
And I will away to Barnesdale
    To see how my men doe fare."

IX.

How the English Language finally came to its own again, and what Books and Authors helped to keep it alive in the Twelfth and Thirteenth Centuries.

THE man to whom our thanks are due for the first great book written in English, after the death of the good King Alfred, is a priest named Layamon, who dwelt near his church at Earnley, on the banks of the Severn. He tells us in his quaint way that it became his chief thought "that he would of England tell the noble deeds, what the men were named, and whence they came, who English land first held." So he went on a journey to find three books

which were his inspiration. When he brought them home
he tells us how he took them, and turning over the leaves,
"*beheld them lovingly*, pen he took in fingers and wrote a
book-skin, the true words set together, and these three
books compressed into one."

Every one who loves books will feel his heart throb in
sympathy with this old student who thus lovingly handled
his newly acquired treasures, the three old books which
were the models for his own work. Layamon's book is
called *Brut*, and like Geoffrey of Monmouth's old history,
it takes up the line of British kings from Brutus; tells the
story of King Arthur and the Round Table; of King Lear
and his ungrateful daughters; and many other interesting
old stories, since used by poets. But the most interesting
fact to us about Layamon's *Brut* is that when the fashionable language of England was Norman-French, this book of
Layamon, in thirty-two thousand lines, had only fifty-two
Norman words; the rest was pure English.

Layamon's *Brut* appeared early in the thirteenth century.
Two other books, of about the same date, also helped to
keep alive the English language, although they did not
amount to much as literature. One of these, called the
Ormulum, was written by a pious brother of the Church,
named Ormin, who put Bible texts and passages of the
Church service into English verse, probably because the
common people could better keep the sacred lines in their
memories if they were written in rhythm and in their
spoken language. Another book of this period, written in
English, was the *Ancren Riwle*, or Rule for Anchoresses,
written by a bishop for three good ladies who, with their
domestics, had decided to lead the life of recluses. The
book sets forth minutely all rules for daily living, and the
contents include rules for the management of the five
senses, — seeing, hearing, smelling, etc., — as well as rules for
all domestic matters.

In the rules on *seeing*, the good bishop says : " Wherefore, my dear sisters, love your windows as little as possible.
See that they be small, the parlor or front windows nar-

rowest and smallest. See that your parlor windows be always fast on every side, and likewise well shut ; and mind your eyes there, lest your heart escape and go out, like David's, and your soul fall sick as soon as it is out." Reticence in speech is strongly praised, since the Virgin Mary was a silent woman, who spoke rarely. In respect to the sense of *smell*, patience in bad smells is urged. " In heaven," says the bishop, " they shall smell celestial odors who in this life have endured stench and rank smells of sweat from iron, or haircloth which they wore, or sweaty garments, or foul air in houses." All of which seems to modern ears like an encouragement to the good ladies to do without much washing, and to ignore the idea which has since gained ground that cleanliness is very near to godliness.

Although these books helped to preserve our English speech in ears that hated the Normans, yet it was not easy for writers of that time to accept the English as the language of literature. Those who wrote for posterity wanted a more stable language than that of a court which shifted from English to Norman and back again. Thus the great history writers of the thirteenth century, Roger of Wendover, and Matthew of Paris, wrote in Latin ; so did the greatest philosopher and scientist of his time, Roger Bacon, — a wonderful man, who has the credit of having invented gunpowder.

Near the close of the thirteenth century Robert of Gloucester wrote a rhyming history of England in his native tongue, in which he began with the British line of kings with Brut, and came down to Edward I. A little later than this Robert, came another Robert, Robert Mannyng of Brunne, who wrote a history in rhyme, and also a *Manual of Sins*, in which the seven deadly sins are moralized upon at length. He was a true patriot, and tells us he means to write in plain words, and that he " speaks no straunge Inglyss." He also writes with moral purpose, and tells his women readers not to paint their faces to make them fairer than they are by nature, and not to go about

with long trailing gowns, on whose tails the devil will
ride gayly.

Robert of Brunne wrote in the opening of the fourteenth
century, — a century which witnessed the final triumph of
English, and saw it made from thenceforth the rightful speech
of England. It was in the reign of Edward III. **1327–1377**
that this triumph came, although a century
earlier, Henry III., when he came to be king, had issued a
proclamation to the English in their own language. It was
indeed high time for English kings to adopt the language of
the land they lived in, for Normandy was no longer a possession of England ; it had been lost to the Crown by King
John Lackland, and had become altogether an alien land.
It was, therefore, good policy as well as good sense for the
kings of England to restore the neglected speech of their
country. But it was not until the language of France was
the speech of their enemies that the English king and people
united to crush it in England. When the stout yeomen
among whom King Edward III. and his brave son, the **1346**
Black Prince, fought at Cressy and Poitiers, had beaten
France in two great battles, both king and people willed
that the language of their foes should never more be the
language of England, and a royal decree declared that the
speech of the land should be henceforth English.

But before this, stronger powers than a king's edict had
been at work in literature. It was a fortunate day for language and for poetry when GEOFFREY CHAUCER was born.
He and a group of noble contemporaries had more power
to make the English language current than all the decrees
of a long line of kings. To them, and to the people, who
heard them gladly, we owe the great revival of the original
speech of our forefathers.

PART II.

FROM CHAUCER TO SPENSER.

1350 TO 1550.

X.

I THINK we have now an idea of the way in which literature began in England, and of its struggles to be heard
in the language native to the people, from the coming of
the English to the islands of Britain, down to the reign of
Edward III. In this reign appeared a group
of writers who firmly established the language in   1327 to 1377
literature. These men were GEOFFREY CHAUCER, JOHN
WYCLIFFE, JOHN GOWER, and WILLIAM LANGLAND. From
the time of these authors, written English took on such
form that you can read it to-day with little difficulty. Before
their time you would find even Robert of Brunne, who said
he wrote no strange English, rather hard to understand.

You have seen that since the coming of the first
Christian priests to England, literature owes its life to the
Church and to the labors of the Churchmen, who, from
the Venerable Beda onward, had devoted themselves to the
spread of learning and literature. There seem to have been
pure and pious men in these early days of the Church, who,
sincerely religious, devoted themselves to good works. But
during the years that followed the establishment of the
religion of Rome in England the Christian Church was
gradually growing corrupt. What taint there was in it of
corruption and hypocrisy had spread through the whole
body, and at the time we have now reached, many of the
religious teachers of the people had become so bad that the
good men among the priests, and the more intelligent part

of the people had their eyes open to the abuses practised by the clergy, and not frowned upon by the Church. And in the beginning of the fourteenth century the discontent felt on account of these abuses made itself heard through two powerful mouthpieces,— the poem of William Langland, and the preaching of John Wycliffe. Let me tell you first about William Langland's poem called the *Vision of Piers Ploughman*, which up to the end of the fourteenth century was the most popular poem — perhaps we might call it the first great popular poem — ever written in English.

William Langland was a priest, but one who loved goodness and hated hypocrisy, and his lines are full of satire against the falsehood and the vices of the religious teachers. The *Vision of Piers Ploughman* is a dream, or a succession of dreams, in the course of which the writer wakes up, goes about his business, then falls into another nap, and takes up the thread of his dream again. The poem is an allegory, which will remind you a little of *The Pilgrim's Progress*. At the opening of it the writer sees the world in his dream like a great Vanity Fair, in which mingle priests, merchants, soldiers, and husbandmen, each busy in his own way. Conscience, Pity, Reason, Law, and other abstract qualities are also represented as persons, and form some of the chief characters in the dream ; but as in most other allegories, if you leave the story only to follow the meaning that lies underneath, the brain will be bewildered and the interest lost. In the second sleep Piers Ploughman, a type of the poor and simple of the earth, to whom God reveals himself rather than to the rich and mighty, comes upon the scene. Ploughman was a happy name to catch the ear of the classes among whom it was meant this poem should be heard. Those who study *Piers Ploughman* will find in its lines the dawn-gleams of democracy, the recognition of certain rights belonging to the lowest man, which first found expression in poetry. Remember this, and the utterance of Langland will take on a fresh interest and a new life. The poem begins thus : —

About 1362 *(marginal note)*

" In a summer season,
When soft was the sun,
I put me into clothes,
As I a shepherd were;
In habit as a hermit,
Unholy of works,
Went wide in this world,
Wonders to hear,
And on a May morning,
On Malvern hills,
Me befell a wonder.
I was weary with wandering,
And went me to rest
Under a broad bank,
By a burn's side.
And as I lay, and leaned,
And looked in the waters,
I slumbered into a sleeping,
It swayed so merry [1]
Then gan I to dream
A marvellous dream
That I was in the wilderness,
Wist I never where.
As I beheld unto the east
On high to the sun,

I saw a tower on a hill
Wondrously built. . . .
A fair field of folk
Found I there between,
Of all manner of men,
The mean and the rich,
Working and wandering
As the world asketh.
Some put them to the plough,
Playing full seldom.
In setting and sowing
Working full hard.
In prayers and penance
Many took part
For love of our Lord,
Living full strict
In hopes to have after
Heavenly bliss. . . .
I found there friars,
All the four orders,
Preaching to the people
For profit to themselves;
Glosed the gospel
As it seemed good to them. " [2]

From these few lines you may get some idea of the style of the poem; but you cannot, from so brief an extract, form any idea of the influence it exercised against the corruption of priests and pardoners, who sold absolutions for sins which they committed themselves without caring to be absolved. And you can hardly imagine, even if you read it entire, what an interest this old poem was capable of exciting in its day.

The *Vision* was followed, in the opening of the fifteenth century, by *Piers Ploughman's Crede*, which was written by some unknown poet later than Langland, in imitation of his style. This is even more severe against the abuses of religion than the first poem, and its hero is still the poor

---

[1] *It swayed so merry*, — The waters flowed on with such a murmuring sound.

[2] I have given these extracts from *Piers Ploughman* in modern spelling, sometimes modernizing words, that they may be readily understood.

ploughman, who is able to teach truths to which his betters
are blind. He is introduced bending over the plough, in
ragged garments, with clouted shoes through which his toes
thrust themselves, slobbered with mud, driving lean and
hungry oxen. His wife walks beside him, with bare feet,
which track their way with blood, and in their work about
the field they sing a song " that sorrowful is to hear." Yet
from the lips of this poor ploughman come words of wisdom and consolation such as the rich and powerful might
gladly hear. In its teachings, and in the picture the poem
gives of the misery of the English peasant who tilled the
land, there was a spirit of reform and of philanthropy which
shows that the reformer was abroad in England at the opening of the fifteenth century.

In structure, the *Vision of Piers Ploughman* goes back
to the early form of English poetry. It is in short, un-
rhymed lines, words nearly all of one syllable, and in
the alliterative style of the *Beowulf.* Simple and direct in
diction, it was made to speak from the heart of the writer
to the common heart of the English people, and it deserved
to be, as it was, the most popular poem, up to that time,
ever written in English.

XI.

On Three Great Contemporaries of Chaucer, — John Wycliffe, John Mandeville, and John Gower.

ABOUT the time of the author of *Piers Ploughman*
came John Wycliffe, who stands as the first English
Reformer, and who ought to take a place beside Martin
Luther, the sturdy German Reformer of a later
time. Wycliffe, like Luther, was a monk, and like
him a sincere and pious man. His eyes were
early opened to the cheats practised by mendicant
friars, who went about begging from the people already

About
1324
to
1384

too heavily taxed for the Church, peddling the bones of some old saint, or some bits of wood which they pretended were pieces of the true cross, or other relics which they declared would insure the soul's salvation of the person who possessed them. Wycliffe preached boldly against all these abuses of religion, till the noble thought came to him to make a translation of the Bible for the common people, that, reading for themselves, they might understand the true meaning of the Scriptures and be freed from the impositions of unworthy priests. And thenceforward he made it his lifework, through persecution and abuse which followed him beyond the grave, to give the simple teachings of Jesus to the people. Shortly before his death he was summoned to the papal bar at Rome to answer for his heresies; but his bodily strength had failed, and he died before he could meet his accusers. Forty years after his death the Pope ordered that his bones should be dug up from the grave in which they had rested so many years, and should be burned and scattered abroad. This was done, and his ashes were cast into a stream which empties into the Avon. "Thus," says the old historian, Thomas Fuller, "this brook did convey his ashes into Avon; Avon into Severn; Severn into the narrow sea; and this to the wide ocean. And so the ashes of Wycliffe are the emblem of his doctrine, which is now dispersed the wide world over."

Wycliffe's translation of the Bible into simple, spoken English made the grand and poetic diction of the Scriptures common to all ears. It wrought almost as great an influence on language as the first introduction of Hebrew poetry had worked on literature. After opening up such a well of pure English, from which all who chose could drink freely, the language could not be again choked up and obscured by any foreign speech. The thirst of the people for the simple teachings of the gospels, so easily understood, that for so long a time had come to them mixed with all sorts of superstitions, can hardly be realized by us in this age of freedom. "A poor yeoman," says

5

John Foxe, the author of the *Book of Martyrs*, "has been known to give a load of hay for a few leaves of Paul or the gospels." Often the parchment was read till scarce a shred of it remained. You must fancy, since I have not time to tell you all about it, how the idea of liberty of thought and conscience among the people must have quickened the workings of that spirit which always breathes best in free air, — the true genius of English literature.

In the same age with *Piers Ploughman* came also John Mandeville, who wrote excellent English prose. His great work is an account of his travels in Palestine, and thence to India and China. No modern tourist can rival the charm of these oldest books of travels, such as were written by John Mandeville, by the Italian traveller Marco Polo, and by the early voyagers to our own country, who came two centuries after Mandeville. In those days the traveller saw and heard with the eyes and ears of a child, — he told all he saw, and believed all he heard. Sir John Mandeville has been accused of exaggeration because he told many incredible stories, — indeed, some now go so far as to deny his existence; but I think that he existed, and that he wrote nothing that he did not believe. We must remember that in his time fact seemed much stranger than fiction; the truest things he told were often received with greatest incredulity, while a story like the following was sure of full belief. He says, —

About 1300 to 1372

"Bethlehem is a little city, long and narrow and well-walled, and on each side enclosed with good ditches. . . . And toward the east end of the city is a very fair and handsome church with many towers, pinnacles, and corners strongly and curiously made. . . . And between the city and the church is the field *Floridus*, — that is to say, the field Flourished. For a fair maiden was blamed with wrong and slandered, and was condemned to be burned in that place; and as the fire began to burn about her, she made her prayers to our Lord, that as truly as she was not guilty, he would of his merciful grace help her and make it known to all men. And when she had thus said, she entered into the fire, and immediately the fire was extinguished, and the fagots that were burning become red rose-bushes, and **those that were not** kindled became white rose-bushes, full **of roses.** *And these were the first rose-trees and roses, both red and white,* **that ever** *any man* **saw.**"

This was considered by pious readers a **good,** sensible **story ; but when** Mandeville **began** to write **out his** ideas about the shape of the earth, men began to jeer at him, and **laugh at** his absurd notions. He gives at some length his ideas of geography and astronomy, derived from his extensive travel and observation, and finally says he believes this earth is round. " Nay, more," he says, " I tell you certainly **that** men may go all around the world, as well under as above, and might return **so again to their** own country if they had shipping and guides ; and always they would find men, land, and isles **as well as in our part** of the world. For they who are of **the antarctic are di-**rectly feet opposite of them who dwell under the polar **star, as well as we** and they **who** dwell under us are feet opposite **feet.**" As even in the time of Columbus, a **hundred and** fifty years later, the theory of the roundness **of the earth was** not generally received, I think this argues **very well for** Mandeville's understanding.

" Of Paradise," says the old traveller, simply, " I cannot speak properly, for I was not there. . . . The earthly paradise, as wise men say, is the highest place of the earth, and it is so high that it nearly touches the circle of the moon there as the moon makes her turn. And it is so high that **the flood of** Noah might not come to it. . . . And **this Paradise is** enclosed all about with a wall, **and men** know **not whereof** it is, for the wall is covered **all over with moss, as it seems,** and it seems not that the wall **is natural stone.** . . . **And** you shall understand that no man **that is** mortal may approach to that Paradise, for by land no man **may** go, for wild beasts that are in the deserts, and **for** the high mountains and great huge rocks that no **man may** pass by **for the dark** places that **are** there ; and by the **rivers** may no man go, for the water runs so roughly and so sharply, because it comes down so outrageously from the **high** places above that it runs in so great waves that no ship may **row or** sail against it. . . . Many lords have assayed with great will many times to **pass** by those rivers towards Paradise, with full great companies, but they might not speed in their voyage, and many died for weariness of rowing against the strong waves, and many of them became blind, and many deaf by the noise of the water, and some perished and were lost in the waves; so that no mortal man may approach that place without special grace of God; so that of that place I can tell you no more."

You will more fully understand how slightly English was esteemed as the language of literature when I tell you that Mandeville, according to his own account, first wrote his Travels in Latin, then translated them into French, and lastly put them into English, so as to be sure every man of his nation might be able to read them. The extracts I have given are in more modern English than he wrote; but his English is hardly more difficult that Chaucer's, and he is generally spoken of as the first prose writer in our language who can be read by a modern reader unacquainted with old English.

Last of the group before Chaucer comes John Gower, a very tiresome old poet whom nobody reads nowadays. **1320-1402** Chaucer gave him the title of "Moral Gower," which has stuck to him from that time to this. He wrote three books, one in Latin, one in French, and one in English. The English book has the Latin title of *Confessio Amantis* (the Confessions of a Lover). But although these Confessions are illustrated by a great many stories, many of which are interesting and have been used over again with much better effect by later poets, yet, on the whole, Gower is so dull that we will leave him for a much more interesting man, his friend and superior, Geoffrey Chaucer.

XII.

ON GEOFFREY CHAUCER, HIS LIFE AND POETRY.

GEOFFREY CHAUCER, the Father of English Poetry — what a proud title to wear for so Born 1328 many hundred years! — is a different sort of poet or 1340. from John Gower, whom I have just mentioned. Died 1400. The two men seem to have been good friends, however, and in the *Confessions of a Lover*, the goddess Venus tells the lover to —

> " Grete wel Chaucer when ye mete,
> As my disciple and my poete," —

which is a compliment that **Chaucer might well have re**-turned by his epithet of " **Moral Gower.**"

We do not know with certainty the date of Chaucer's **birth.** Some of his biographers think it is 1328 ; **others, 1340. The first date is** the one which has been the long-**est believed** to be the true one ; the last is that accepted by several modern scholars. For my part, I think the **exact** date really makes very little difference, so long as we **know** the great events amid which his life was surely passed, **the** great ideas which were **current in the age** during which he must have lived in full mental vigor, and the fact that this group of literary men of whom I have spoken were his **contemporaries. We know that** he died in 1400, and lived in the reigns of three kings, — Edward III., Richard II., and **Henry** IV.

We do not know much about the early part of his life. He was born in London, the son of a wine-dealer. One of **the first certain facts in** his life, after the uncertain date of his birth, is that he was a member of a noble family as one of the pages of the household, which, in those days, was a respectable, **indeed** an honorable, capacity. He was with the army of Edward III. when it went to invade France in

1359, and Chaucer was then made prisoner, and ransomed afterwards by the king. After this we hear of him frequently in the court records, — once as having a pitcher of wine sent him every day from the royal wine-cellars; another time as getting a pension from the Crown for services rendered; again as one of the ambassadors who went to France to arrange the marriage of Richard II.; and as concerned in other diplomatic missions. We know that his friend and patron was John of Gaunt, the Duke of Lancaster, called by Shakespeare "time-honored Lancaster," whose son became King Henry IV. Chaucer married a Lady Philippa, and it is claimed by several writers that John of Gaunt married a sister of this very lady. If this was so, Chaucer and his noble patron were brothers-in-law.

John of Gaunt was at one time the head of the Wycliffe party, and although he did not follow so far as Wycliffe led, he aided him in his earlier fight against papal power by his strong influence. It is probable that Chaucer also sympathized with Wycliffe, and that he took the generous side in religion and politics. I am sure I hope so, for I like to associate the "Father of English Poetry" with freedom of thought and speech, and to believe that he was as much of a man as a poet, or the better poet that he was a liberal, outspoken man. Almost at the close of his century, and near the end of his life, Chaucer took a house on the lands of Westminster Abbey, and sat down there to spend his latest days. When he died, he was buried in the Abbey, and you may there read his name on the stones of the wall in the "Poet's Corner," the first of that long line of great names which adorns that sacred spot in the grand old building.

Chaucer wrote many works, sometimes in prose, although most commonly in verse. Many of his earlier poems are little more than translations. The *Roman de la Rose*, which first made him known as a poet, was a translation from two French writers, although we may be sure Chaucer could not handle anything without leaving a good deal of himself in it. He never made any pretence of originality, and always shows himself a sincere man and without affectation in his work. Others of his principal poems are *The House of Fame*, *The Book of the Duchess*, *The Legend of Good Women*, *The Assembly of Fowls*, *Troilus and Cressida*. We have not time to look at these, but must come at once to his great work, *The Canterbury Tales*, the only one of his poems which is much read nowadays.

The Canterbury Tales is a collection of stories told by a party of men and women who meet at the Tabard Inn, which was situated in the High Street of Southwark, near London, to set out on a pilgrimage to the shrine of Saint Thomas à Becket in Canterbury cathedral, about fifty miles distant. They are a company taken from all ranks of life, and almost every condition is represented. Their number is nine-and-twenty, when they are joined by the poet and the host of the Tabard Inn.

In the Prologue, which forms the preface of the stories, nearly every person in the party is described in an easy and familiar style, as if Chaucer was introducing you in a manner to make you perfectly well acquainted with his character. Each figure drawn by his pen seems like a real person whom we see, rather than read about. The modern novelist, who prides himself on drawing life-like pictures of the men and women of this day, has never succeeded better than the old poet, who gives so perfect an idea of a group of every-day persons of the fourteenth century.

First of all comes the Knight, " who from the time he first began to riden out, he loved chivalry, truth, honor, freedom, and courtesy." He had been in many wars in the South and East, at the taking of Alexandria, at the siege of Grenada, and in wars against the heathen Turk. Yet, like other truly brave men, he is gentle and unassuming, " as meek of port as is a maid." " In truth," says Chaucer, " a very perfect, gentle knight." The next character, that of the Knight's son, the Squire, is a very different sort of person. He is a dashing young fellow, with curling hair and fair complexion ; a fine horseman, who can also dance gracefully,

write songs and sing them, "and play the flute like a lover."
Then comes Madame Eglantine, the prioress of a convent,
a sweet gentlewoman, who, although the bride of the Church,
wears as the motto on her brooch, "Love conquers all."
Here is her picture as Chaucer gives it : —

> "Ful wel she sang the service devine,
> Entuned in hire nose ful swetely ;
> And Frenche she spoke ful fayre and fetisly,
> After the schole of Stratford-atte-Bowe,
> For Frenche of Paris was to hire unknowe.
> At mete was she wel ytaughte withalle ;
> She let no morsel from hire lippes falle,
> Ne wette hire fingires in hire sauce depe.
> Wel coude she carie a morsel and wel kepe
> Thatte no droppe ne fell upon hire brest. . . .

> "But for to speken of hire conscience,
> She was so charitable and so pitous,
> She wolde weep if that she saw a mous
> Caughte in a trappe if it were ded or bledde.
> Of smale houndes hadde she that she fedde
> With rosted flesh and milk and wastel brede ;
> But sore wept she if on of hem were dede. . . .
> Hire nose was stretis ; hire eyes as grey as glas ;
> Hire mouth ful smale, and therto soft and red,
> But sickerly she had a fayre forehed. . . .

> "Full fetise was hire cloke, as I was ware.
> Of small corale aboute hire arm she bare
> A pair of bedes, gauded all with grene,
> And theron heng a broche of gold ful shene,
> On whiche was ywriten a crouned *A*,
> And after '*Amor vincit omnia.*'"

Can we not see Madame Eglantine as plainly as if she
stood before us in broad day, with her gray eyes, her little
soft red mouth, her fair forehead, and her dainty ways
when she sits at the table? The only other woman of the
party, except a nun attendant on the Prioress, who passes
without description, was the Wife of Bath, — a great contrast to the delicate Madame Eglantine : —

> "She was a worthy woman all hire live,
> Housbondes at the chirche doore had she had five."

And besides her matrimonial experiences, she had travelled much, having been in Jerusalem, Rome, Germany, and France. She had a fair face, though somewhat red and bold; her shoes were shining new, and her stockings of fine scarlet; she rode her ambling nag easily, and wore spurs like a man.

Next comes a Monk, in a fur-trimmed mantle, his hood fastened under his chin with a curious pin of gold, and his scarf tied in a love-knot. His companion is a merry Friar, who gives easy penance to his parishioners, and administers absolution "ful swetely."

> "Somwhat he lisped for his wantonnesse,
> To make his English swete upon his tonge."

The Clerk of Oxford, who follows, is lean, like his horse; his coat is threadbare; he might be twin-brother to the poor student of the present day. He would rather have a shelf full of books at his bed's head than rich clothes or any other pleasures. What a contrast to him is the Franklin, an English squire of the fourteenth century, with a beard white as a daisy, a full red face, and all the marks of a gourmand, —

> "Withouten bake mete never was his hous;
> Of fish and flesh, and that so plenteous,
> It snewed in his hous of mete and drinke."

Then come a quartet of mechanics, all dressed in the livery of their orders, each with well-filled purses, "and shaped to have been an alderman." The Miller, the Cook, the Doctor, the Lawyer, the Merchant, the poor Parson, and his brother, the Ploughman, — these last two, in our judgment, the only really pious persons in this company of religious pilgrims, — make up the party. Such is a little glimpse of that group who set out on a soft April day on that immortal pilgrimage to Canterbury.

XIII.

ON THE STORIES OF THE CANTERBURY PILGRIMS.

WHEN the Canterbury travellers first set out upon their journey, the jolly host of the Tabard proposes that they shall beguile the way by telling stories, each doing his share in turn. This is agreed upon, and it falls to the Knight to begin. He tells the story of Palamon and Arcite, two noble kinsmen who are sworn brothers in friendship till they both fall in love with the same lady, the fair Emelie, sister of Duke Theseus, who holds the two noblemen as his prisoners of war. I think you will find this, the Knight's Tale, the most interesting of all the stories. It is made gorgeous by the description of a tournament, — a description so vivid that we seem to see the waving of plumes, the glitter of armor, and the very dust that rises from the field of conflict when the knights spur towards each other with raised lances. Emelie, the heroine of this story, is one of the loveliest of all Chaucer's women. We see her first in a garden, where the birds are singing and the flowers blossoming under the shadow of the great stone tower where the knights who love her are shut up in prison. These are the lines in which Chaucer describes her : —

> " Till it felle ones in a morwe of May
> That Emelie, that fayrer was to sene
> Than is the lilie upon his stalke grene,
> And fresher than the May, with floures newe
> (For with the rose colour strof hire hewe,
> I n'ot which was finer of hem two).
> Er it was day, as she was wont to do,
> She was arisen, and al redy dight,
> For May woll have no slogardie a-night.
> The seson priketh every gentil herte,
> And maketh him out of his slepe to sterte. . . .
> Hire yelwe here was broided in a tresse,
> Behind hire back a yerde long, I gesse,
> And in the gardin as the sonne uprist
> She walketh up and doun wher as hire list,

> She gathereth floures, partie white and red,
> To make a sotile gerlond for hire hed,
> And as an angel hevenliche she song."

Meantime the two prisoners, **Palamon and** Arcite, enclosed in the great stone tower over the **garden, get their**
first sight of Emelie.

> " Bright was the sonne and clere that morwening,
> And Palamon, this woful prisoner,
> As was his wone, by leve of his gayler,
> Was risen, and romed in a chambre on high,
> In which **he all** the noble citee sigh,
> And eke the gardin, ful of branches grene.
> Ther as this freshe Emelie, the **shene,**
> **Was in hire walk, and romed up and down.**
> **This sorweful prisoner, this Palamon,**
> **Goth in his chambre,** roming to and fro,
> **And to** himself complaining of his woe. . . .
> **And so** befell, by aventure or eas,
> That through a window thikke of many a **barre**
> **Of yren** grete and square as any sparre,
> He cast his eyen upon Emelia,
> And therewithal he blent and cried, " A ! "
> **As** though he stungen were unto the herte.
> And with that crie Arcite anon upsterte,
> **And** saide, ' Cosin min, what eyleth thee ?
> **That art so** pale and dedly for to see ?
> **Why** criedst thou ? Who hath thee don offense ?
> For goddes love take all in patience
> Our prison, for it may none other be,
> Fortune hath yeven us this adversite.' . . .
> This Palamon answerde, and sayd again :
> ' This prison caused me not **for to crie,**
> But I was hurt **right now,** thrughout **min eye**
> Into min herte ; **that** woll my bane be,
> The fayrnesse **of a** lady that I see
> Yond in the gardin, roming to and fro,
> Is cause of all my crying and my wo.
> I n'ot whe'r she be woman or goddess.
> But Venus is it sothly, as I gesse.' . . .
> And with that word Arcita gan espie,
> Wher as this lady romed to and fro,
> And with that sight hire beautee hurt him so,
> That if that Palamon **were** wounded sore,
> Arcite is hurt as moche as he, or **more,**
> And with a sigh he saye pitously,
> ' The freshe beautee sleth me sodenly

Of her that rometh in the yonder place,
And but I have hire mercy and hire grace,
That I may seen hire at the leste way,
I n'am but ded, ther n'is no more to say.'
This Palamon, when he these wordes herd,
Dispitously he looked and answerd:
'Whether sayst thou this, in ernest or in play?'
'Nay,' said Arcite, 'in ernest, by my fay.' . . .
This Palamon gan knit his browes twey,
'It were,' quod he, 'to thee no gret honour
For to be false, ne for to be traytour
To me, that am thy cosin and thy brother,
Ysworn ful depe and eche of us to other. . . .
Thus art thou of my counseil out of doute,
And now thou woldest falsly ben aboute
To love my lady, whom I love and serve,
And ever shal til that man herte sterve.
Now, certes, false Arcite, thou shalt no so.
I loved hire firste, and tolde thee o my woe.' . . .
This Arcita full proudly spake again,
'Thou shalt,' quod he, 'be rather false than I.
And thou art false, I tell thee utterly,
For, par amour, I loved hire first or thou.
What wolt thou sayn? Thou wisted nat right now
Whether she were a woman or a goddesse.
Thin is affection of holiness,
And min is love as to a creature.
For which I tolde thee min aventure,
As to my cosin and my brother sworne;
I pose that thou lovedst hire beforn.
Wost thou not wel the old clerkes sawe,
That who shall give a lover any lawe? . . .
A man moste needes love maugre his hed,
He may not fleen though he shulde be ded. . . .
And therfore at the kinges court, my brother,
Eche man for himself, ther is non other.
Love if thee lust, for I love, and ay shal.
And soth, leve brother, this is al.' "

And on this throwing down of the gauntlet on the part of Arcite, the quarrel between the two kinsmen gets hotter and hotter, while in the garden below faire Emelie goes on picking her flowers, quite unconscious of all this pother over her head. I will not tell you all the story, because it is the one of all *The Canterbury Tales* which I should most strongly advise you to read.

The story of pious Custance is told by the Man of Law. It is of a beautiful princess of Rome who has wedded the Sultan of Syria, and on her nuptial eve is set adrift in an enchanted ship by her wicked mother-in-law. She floats over the ocean for many years till the vessel strands on the coast of Britain. Here she is succored by the governor of the port and his wife, Dame Hermegilde, till a false knight, who hates Custance because she has refused his love, slays Dame Hermegilde and accuses Custance of the murder. She is taken for trial before the king, and must die unless she can find a champion who will prove her innocence in a contest of arms with the accusing knight. The king, touched with pity at sight of Custance, asks if she has no champion. She falls on her knees and answers that she has no defender but God, and then, rising, looks piteously about her : —

> " Have ye not seen somtime a pale face
> Among a pres of him that hath ben lad
> Toward his deth, wher as he geteth no grace,
> And swiche a colour in his face hath had,
> Men mighten know him that was so bestad ?
> Amonges all the faces in that route
> So stant Custance, and loketh hire about."

Is it any wonder that at sight of that pale, innocent face the king is almost ready to get down from his throne and fight as her champion? He calls at once for a Breton book of the gospels, and as the knight swears on this that Custance is guilty, an unseen hand smites him, so that his neck is broken and his "eyes burst out of his face, in sight of everybody in that place." The British King Alla then marries pious Custance, so wonderfully protected, and in course of time, when the king is away on some foreign wars, a son is born to them. Custance falls a victim to the plots of her second mother-in-law, who manages to have her sent back on the wonderful ship again, where she miraculously floats about till her boy grows to manhood, when she is restored to her husband, and the tale ends happily. The picture of Custance when she is sent to the ship with her baby is in Chaucer's tenderest vein : —

> " Hire litel child lay weping in hire arm,
>   And kneling, pitously to him she said,
> ' Pees, litel sone, I wol do thee no harm.'
> With that hire couverchief of her hed she braid,
> And over his litel eyen she it laid,
> And in hire arme she lulleth it full fast,
> And into the heven hire eyen up she cast. . . .
> Therwith she loketh backward to the lond,
> And saide, ' Farewel, housbond rutheles ; '
> And up she rist, and walketh doun the strond.
> Toward the ship hire foloweth all the prees,
> And ever she praieth hire child to hold his pees ;
> And taketh hire leve, and with a holy entent,
> She blesseth hire, and into the ship she went."

Another of the most beautiful of all these stories, and the one which is, I think, most read, is the story of patient Griselda, told by the Oxford student. This tale, which Chaucer says he got from the Italian poet Petrarch, is of a meek woman who has married a man above her in rank, and is put to all sorts of cruel trials by her husband to prove her virtuous patience. She triumphs over all these tests, and is happy at last. We are so indignant at her treatment that we can hardly read the poem with patience ; and even Chaucer says, —

> " This story is said, not for that wives shuld
>   Folwe Grisilde, as in humilitee,
> For it were importable, tho they wold, —
>   But for that every wight in his degree
> Shulde be constant in adversitee
>   As was Grisilde ; therfore Petrark writeth
>   This storie, which with high stile he enditeth."

If you do not care to read all *The Canterbury Tales*, those I have mentioned are the three I would advise you to read first. A few of the stories are too coarse for modern taste, — those of the Miller, the Merchant, the Reeve, and one or two others. Chaucer, at the outset, declares he is not responsible for the moral of the stories, and only tells them as he heard them. I regret that he should have thought it worth while to tell all he heard. But it is easy enough for us to keep out of the way of the gross persons of the company, and most of the tales are pure enough for any time.

Chaucer's quaint old English deters many students now-adays from the attempt to read him. But a very little familiarity with him will make his language plain, with the occasional aid of a glossary to look up a word which has now become obsolete. And once mastered, the elder English of Chaucer is delightful, and close knowledge of it will help to revive many dear and homely words that are fast disappearing from our language, and aid to make clear the meanings of other words which we use without a full consciousness of their worth and richness. If we want to appreciate the beauty of our English tongue, we shall be greatly helped by an acquaintance with Chaucer, and shall learn what a debt we owe the Father of English poetry. And so we leave our good old poet reluctantly, as one with whom we should like to be better acquainted, to enter upon a century which is notable for two of the greatest events in the world's history. Let us see what these events are, and what influence they will be likely to work on literature.

XIV.

Telling of some of the Great Events of the Fifteenth Century, — of Caxton and his Printing-Press; and of the Romance of the Morte d'Arthur.

CHAUCER died in the opening year of the fifteenth century. With him literature seemed for a time to die also. The reign of the house of Lancaster brought in the hosts of bloody war; insurrections at home and battles abroad filled up the first half of the century; and when the house of York took the throne, there was little quiet in which to hear the voice of poet or scholar. Two names that closely follow that of Chaucer are all that we meet with of any consequence till the close of the century

1375–1461 The first is that of JOHN LYDGATE, a monkish schoolmaster who spent his leisure in writing poetry which we should pronounce very dull indeed, the

1370–1454 second is that of a lawyer, THOMAS OCCLEVE, who wrote verse duller even than Lydgate's. In the hundred years and more after Chaucer no such genius blazed out as we have seen in Wycliffe's prose and Chaucer's verse.

But although few new books were written, the old books grew more and more into demand, and in no previous century were handsomer copies made of the great masterpieces of literature than during this period. So great was the increase in the making of books that manuscript copying was no longer done wholly by monks, but became the work of men in every-day life. This change led naturally to the invention of printing; for as soon as book-making came to be a business of life, and not the pastime of scholars and priests, it passed into the hands of practical men, who would cast about to do the work more easily and rapidly than by the tedious way of handwriting. Wooden blocks as large as a book page were first made, which were soon superseded by single letters of movable type; and from that time books could be made quickly, although at first they were not beautiful books, like those made by the painstaking monks, with their many colored inks and slow, patient pens.

WILLIAM CAXTON, the first English printer, was a young

1412–1492 man when he went to live in Belgium, as apprentice to a London merchant. He stayed there till past middle life, and prospered in business. He was always of a book-loving turn, and in his spare time copied manuscripts for his own delight. It was thus natural that he should have become interested in the new art of printing which had begun in Germany, and flourished all about him; and when he was able to do so, he gladly dropped the

pen and took up the quicker mode of type-setting. In
1474 he came home to England with a printing-press of
his own, and began business in one of the buildings belonging to Westminster Abbey. Here, under the walls that had •
sheltered Chaucer when he finished *The Canterbury Tales,*
Caxton invited all who desired to come and buy his books
or give orders for printing. All sorts of people answered
this invitation; noble ladies and gentlemen of the realm
were ready and glad to lend him their precious manuscript
books to be copied by the printing-press, and his work
was honored as ought to be the work of a man who
adds faithfully to the knowledge and progress of the
world.

The list of the books which Caxton printed, shows good
taste on the part of our first printer and publisher. They
are from all sources, — a miscellaneous, but very interesting
library. The first book issued was a work on Chess, soon
followed by a translation of the story of Jason and the
Golden Fleece. He also published the first edition of
Chaucer's works, and the first edition of those of Gower and
John Lydgate. From his press came translations of Virgil's
Æneid, Ovid's *Metamorphoses,* and the *Consolation of
Boethius.* He printed the tales of Reynard the Fox so
famous even to this day; he gave to the English reader
the fables of Æsop, and also the *Book of Good Manners,*
and *The Craft to Know well how to Die.* Caxton deserves to be considered more than a mere craftsman in
book-making. Many of these works he translated himself, and by using, whenever he could, the simple spoken
English, he did good work in helping to form and make
stable our language.

' One of the most important books to our literature of
all the number issued from his press was the
Morte d'Arthur, — the old stories of Arthur and   **1485**
his Knights, which were translated by Sir Thomas Malory
from the French. In this book we have again the stories
which belong to the Arthurian romance, woven into one.
Here we see, more fully than ever before, the forms of King

6

Arthur, Merlin, Sir **Launcelot du Lake,** Sir Percivale, Sir Gawaine, Sir Tristram, and the peerless **and** perfect Galahad.   Here figure the beautiful Queen Guenever, Isoud the fair and Isoud **the** white-handed, Elaine the mother of Galahad, and Elaine the lily maid of Astolat; and many other knights and ladies who form part of this fascinating romance.

This *Morte d'Arthur,* **a** collection of the same stories, **added** to and enlarged, that had been made by Walter Map and his contemporaries, **is the** old book from which the **modern** poet Tennyson **has drawn** some of **the** beautiful stories which he tells in his *Idyls of the King.* The whole of Malory's book **is a prose** poem, so beautiful that I **am** going to quote for you one chapter, — that which tells of the **beautiful** Elaine **as** she floats down to Camelot **in her** funeral **barge.**

"So by fortune King Arthur and the Queen Guenever were speaking together at a window, and so as they looked into Thames they espied this black barget, and had marvel what it meant.   Then the King called Sir Kay, and showed it him. 'Sir,' said Sir Kay, 'wit you well, there is some new tidings.' 'Go thither,' said the King to Sir Kay, 'and take with you Sir Brandiles and Agravaine, and bring me ready word what is there.'   Then these three knights departed, and came to the barget, and went in; and there they found the fairest corpse lying in a rich bed, and a poor man sitting in the barget's end, and no word would he speak.   So these three knights returned unto the King again, and told him what they found.

"'That fair corpse will I see,' said the King.   And so then the King took the Queen by the hand and went thither.   Then he made the barget to be holden fast, and the King and the Queen entered, with certain knights with them.   And there he saw the fairest woman lie in a rich bed, covered unto her middle with many rich clothes, and all was of cloth of gold, and she lay as though she had smiled.   Then the Queen espied a letter in her right hand, and told it to the King.   Then the King took it, and said: 'Now I am sure this letter will tell what she was and why she is come hither.' . . .   And so when the King was come within his chamber he called many knights about him, and said he would wit openly what was written within that letter. Then the King brake it, and made a clerk to read it, and this was the intent of the letter : —

"*Most Noble Knight, Sir Launcelot: Now hath death made us two at debate for your love; I was your lover, that men called the fair Maiden of Astolat; therefore, unto all ladies I make my moan; yet pray for my soul, and bury me at the least, and offer ye my mass-penny. This is my last request. . . . Pray for my soul, Sir Launcelot, as thou art peerless.*

"This was all the substance of the letter. And when it was read, the King, the Queen, and all the knights wept for pity of the doleful complaints. Then was Sir Launcelot sent for. And when he was come, King Arthur made the letter to be read to him; when Sir Launcelot heard it, word by word, he said, 'My Lord Arthur, wit ye well, I am right heavy of the death of this fair damsel. God knoweth, I was never causer of her death by my willing, and that will I report me to her own brother. . . . I will not say nay, but she was both fair and good, and much was I beholden to her; but she loved me out of measure.' 'Ye might have showed her,' said the Queen, 'some bounty and gentleness that might have preserved her life.' 'Madam,' answered Launcelot, 'she would none other way be answered but that she would be my wife, or else my love; and of these two I would not grant her. . . . For, madam, I love not to be constrained to love, for love must arise out of the heart, and not by no constraint.' 'That is true,' said the King and many knights; 'Love is free in himself, and never will be bounden, for where he is bounden he loseth himself.' 'Then,' said the King to Sir Launcelot, ' it will be your worship that ye oversee that she be interred worshipfully.' 'Sir,' said Launcelot, 'that shall be done as I can best devise.' . . . And so upon the morn she was interred richly, and Sir Launcelot offered her mass-penny, and all at that time the knights of the Table Round that were there with Sir Launcelot offered.[1]

Malory's *Morte a'Arthur* was the last great book, and the most famous, that the fifteenth century produced. But although this century had given to the world so little literature, it had seen two great events which influenced the whole future of literature. Of one of these, the invention of printing, I have already spoken. The second was the discovery

---

[1] *Morte d'Arthur*, chap. xx., book xviii.

of the New World by Columbus, — an event so strange and full of mystery that it must have stimulated the imagination of the dullest and most commonplace man, and made for the time a place for poetry in the most matter-of-fact brain. Early in the sixteenth century, books of voyages to the New World began to appear in Italy and Germany, and the stories of men who had sailed in unknown seas, under skies glittering with new stars, excited the wonder of all who read them. English sailors who had voyaged with Sebastian Cabot to these new lands, brought back to home-ports tales rich in wonders. Thus the discovery of America was sure to work upon literature, although, in an age without tele-graphs or steam-engines or newspapers, the strongest forces must work more slowly than in our time, and the immediate results of such discoveries as those of printing and the New World were not seen in a day.

XV.

On Literature in the Reign of Henry VIII. ; More's Utopia ; Tyndale's Bible ; Skelton, the Court Poet ; the Sonnets of Surrey and Wyatt.

THE reign of Henry VIII. covers nearly the first half of the sixteenth century ; yet although the last half of this century is perhaps the most glorious of any period in our literature, its first years do not shine with the promise of that after-glory. There are a few great names, but not that crowd of rare spirits that make the age of Queen Elizabeth so resplendent. The great event of Henry's reign, however, — the separation of the Church of England from that of Rome, — did much to inspire the thought of the age which followed. Although Henry did not greatly care for the freedom of any man except himself, and meant to hold a tight rein over other men's actions and con-sciences, still he took a great stride towards freedom when he made the Church of England independent of that of Rome; and all advances towards freedom are sure to quicken the spirit of fine literature, which is the free expression of the highest thought of the best men of the age. Let me tell you briefly of the greatest men and the best work done in literature from the opening of the century to the time when the great Queen Elizabeth took her father's seat as an English sovereign.

The noblest and most memorable work of the age was done by WILLIAM TYNDALE, who undertook the translation of the Bible. His name deserves to be set high in the annals of English literature and language. Tyndale was only a poor tutor in the house of a nobleman in Gloucestershire, when one day as they sat at table, a religious discussion arose, in which a bigoted priest who was present said dogmatically, "Better be without God's laws than the Pope's." Tyndale took fire at this, and rising, grandly said : "In the name of God I *defy* the Pope and his laws ; and if God spares my life, I will cause the boy who drives the plough to know more of God's laws than either you or the Pope."

A few years later, in spite of persecution, he published his translation of the New Testament into English. **1525** I think that we may decide that this was the greatest literary work between the time of Chaucer and Spenser. The Bible, made accessible to the common people, was not only a religious book, but a fountain-head of literature. The daily speech of men and women was made rich by the introduction into it of the phraseology of the Scriptures rendered into the homely and eloquent English which Tyndale used ; and from that day to this, apt and fitting quotations from the Bible have been so imbedded in common speech that we use them often without **1536** out being aware of their source. Tyndale died in Holland at the stake, a martyr for the work he did, and the opinions he held.

Another noble gentleman, who also died for loyalty to his opinions, very near the time of Tyndale's martyrdom,

was Sir THOMAS MORE, one of the saintliest and most lovable characters in all this time. He did not follow the
1480–1535 king in his separation from the Church of Rome, but remained a stanch Catholic, and avowed his religious scruples against the divorce of the king from Queen Katharine, and the marriage with Anne Boleyn. He was executed on Tower Hill, dying with the serenity which became such a noble and true man. As he laid his head upon the block, he carefully put away his long full bread from under the axe, saying simply, "This should not be cut; it has never committed treason."

His great book, *Utopia,* was written in Latin, — a language which was still, and for a long time after, used by scholars in prose writings. Utopia was an imaginary land, a wonderful country whose society and laws were ideally perfect. A sailor, sunbrowned and strange as Coleridge's Ancient Mariner, who says he has been on voyages to the New World with the great discoverer Amerigo Vespucci, gives the account of this wonderful country and its romantic discovery. In this fabled Utopia, More could embody all his ideas of a perfect commonwealth, and so show by contrast the defects in laws and social conditions in England. And his ideas of religious charity and social reform are so generous and grand that this nineteenth century has not yet excelled them. But when he pictures an ideal city, and his highest conception of the material comforts of life, we shall find that we have to-day outstripped his best imaginings. For instance, he thus describes Amaurote, the chief city of the Utopians: —

"The city is compassed about with a high and thick stone wall full of turrets and bulwarks. A dry ditch, but deep and broad and overgrown with bushes, briers, and thorns, goeth about three sides or quarters of the city. To the fourth side the river itself serveth for a ditch. . . . The streets be *twenty feet broad.* On the back side of the houses, through the whole length of the street, lie large gardens. . . . The houses be curiously builded after a gorgeous and gallant sort, with three stories, one over another. The outsides of the walls be made of hard plaster, or else of brick, and the inner sides well strengthened with timber-work. . . . **They** keep the wind out **of** their windows with **glass, for it is there much used,** and **some** here also with fine linen cloth dipped **in oil** or amber, and that for two commodities, **for** by this means more light cometh in, and the wind is better kept out."

This picture of **the city** and its houses, while it may surpass in comfort those in More's day, does not excite any special envy in us , but when he speaks of justice among men, and religious tolerance, then he rises to heights as grand as we have attained. And at the close he makes a noble plea for laboring men, whose rights at that time had been little **heard of.**

"What justice **is this,**" he bursts out, "that a goldsmith, a usurer, or, to be **short, any** of those which do nothing **at** all, or else what **they do is such** as **is not necessary to** the **commonwealth, should have a pleasant and a wealthy living** either by idleness or by unnecessary business, **while in the mean** time poor laborers, carters, ironsmiths, carpenters, and plough- **laborers, by so** great and continual toil as drawing and bearing **beasts be** scant able to sustain, and again so necessary toil that **without it no** commonwealth **were** able to continue and endure **one year, should** yet get so hard and poor a living, and live so **wretched and** miserable **a life** that the state and condition of the laboring beasts may seem much better and wealthier. . . Is this not an unjust and unkind public weal which gives great fees and rewards to *gentlemen*, as they call them, **and to** gold- smiths and to such other which be either idle persons, or else only flatterers and devisers of **vain** pleasures, and of the con- trary part maketh no gentle **provision for** ploughmen, colliers, laborers, **carters**, ironsmiths, **and** carpenters? . . . Therefore, **when I** consider **and weigh in** my mind all these common- **wealths** which nowadays anywhere do flourish, so God help **me, I** can perceive nothing but a conspiracy of rich men, procuring their commodities under the name and title of the commonwealth."

These generous words from the pen **of a man** in high position, who might easily have been blind to the misery of those who were poorer and weaker than he, give Sir Thomas More a warm place in my liking, and the *Utopia* a high place among the books of the world.

JOHN SKELTON comes in as court poet of Henry·VIII., although I fancy him fitter for a bar-room than the court,

1460–1529 —a man of coarse manners and gross wit, although he had sprightliness and a good deal of humor. He had been tutor to Henry VIII. before Henry became king, and was high in favor at court. He was a clever rhymester, and wrote verses full of sparkling vivacity. Nobody before his time had shown how flexible the English language was, and how it could be twisted hither and thither in rhyme. But we should not now read Skelton's verses with much interest. This is partly because he was a writer of satire, and satire, however clever, is rarely interesting in any time but that in which it is written. One of his satires was a scorching attack upon the great Cardinal Wolsey, called *Why come ye not to Court?*

. The *Book of Philip Sparrow* is generally considered his most poetical work. It is a lament for a dead sparrow, which has so much ease and grace in rhyming that it has never lost its charm. But the most entertaining of his poems, to me, is *The Crown of Laurel.* In this the author goes to sleep under an oak, and in his dream hears an argument between the Goddess Pallas and the Queen of Fame as to whether Skelton shall have a place in the court of the latter. After a long discussion, all the great poets of the world are summoned to decide the matter. They come in stately train, led by Apollo. Among them, says the poem, —

> " I saw Gower, that first garnished our English rude;
> And Master Chaucer, that nobly enterprized
> How that our English might freshly be ennewed;
> The monk of Bury after them ensued,
> Dan John Lydgate : these English poets three,
> As I imagined, repaired to me."

The author is admitted into the House of Fame on an equality with these three great poets, and shortly after is called upon to praise a bevy of fair ladies, attendants of the Countess of Surrey. He praises these ladies in different

odes, dedicated to each by name. Some of these verses
are very pretty. He writes in this way to Lady Isabel
Pennell. He begins by comparing her to —

" The fragrant camomile,
　The ruddy rosary,
　The sovereign rosemary,
　The pretty strawberry,

The columbine, the nepte,
The gillyflower well set,
The proper violet."

And tells her : —

" Your color
Is like the daisy flower
After the April shower,

Star of the morrow gray,
The blossom of the spring,
The freshest flower of May."

Mistress Margaret Hussey is also addressed as —

" Merry Margaret,
　As midsummer flower,
　Gentle as falcon
　Or hawk of the tower,
　With solace and gladness,
　Much mirth and no madness,
　All good and no badness ;
　So joyously,
　So maidenly,
　So womanly

Her demeaning,
In everything
Far, far passing
That I can endite,
Or suffice to write,
Of merry Margaret
As midsummer flower,
Gentle as falcon
Or hawk of the tower. "

I know no other instance of a poet so cleverly exalting
himself as Skelton does in this poem of *The Crown of
Laurel.*

Two gallant and courtly figures come next in sight. They
are HENRY HOWARD, Earl of Surrey, and his friend, 1518-1547
SIR THOMAS WYATT. These gentlemen, familiar
with all the polite learning of their time, were 1503-1542
masters of verse-making. They introduced the form of
the Italian sonnet, and have the credit of having polished
and improved poetic expression, introducing, more than
it ever before had prevailed, the melody of the Southern
poetry into English verse. Wyatt wrote many songs and
sonnets. The titles to some of these are ludicrously sentimental. There is one "On my love that pricked her finger
with a needle ;" another, "On my love from whom he had
her gloves;" and still another, "The lover compareth his

heart to an overcharged gun." Could anything in poetry be more overstrained?

Poor SURREY was another of the victims of Henry VIII., and was beheaded on Tower Hill; while Wyatt, who died a little earlier than Surrey, narrowly escaped the same fate, and lay for a time in prison, in great danger from that dreadful axe in the Tower. Of these two poets, Surrey writes the better verses. A great many of them are dedicated to Geraldine, to whom he writes love-verses; although as this Geraldine was only thirteen years old, and probably could not understand what the poet meant by his protestations of devotion, there can be nothing very serious in the compliments he pays. Probably Surrey thought Geraldine was as pretty a name to figure in his verses as were the Lauras or Beatrices of the Italian poets whom he imitates. We will close this Talk by reading one of his songs to Geraldine : —

A PRAISE OF HIS LADY, WHEREIN HE REPROVETH THEM THAT COMPARE THEIR LADIES WITH HIS.

Give place, ye lovers, here before
   That spent your boasts and brags in vain;
My lady's beauty passeth more
   The best of yours, I dare well sayn,
Than doth the sun the candle light,
Or brightest day the darkest night.

And thereto hath a troth as just
   As had Penelope the fair,
For what she saith ye may it trust
   As it by writing sealed were;
And virtues hath she many moe
Than I with pen have skill to show.

I could rehearse, if that I would,
   The whole effect of Nature's plaint,
When she had lost the perfect mould
   The like to whom she could not paint;
With wringing hands how she did cry!
And what she said, I know it, I.

I know she swore with raging mind,
   Her kingdom only set apart;

There was no loss by law of kind
   That could have gone so near her heart ;
And this was chiefly all her pain,
She could not make the like again.

Since Nature thus gave her the praise
   To be the chiefest work she wrought,
In faith, methink some better ways
   On your behalf might well be sought
Than to compare, as ye have done,
To match the candle with the sun.

PART III.

FROM SPENSER AND SHAKESPEARE TO MILTON.

1550 TO 1608.

THE GOLDEN AGE OF ENGLISH POETRY.

INTRODUCTORY.

IN this third division of my Talks, I am going to tell you about the principal writers who appeared from the time Queen Elizabeth ascended the English throne, until the end of the reign of James I. There is no period of our literature which includes so many great names. Within the limits of a little more than half a century, Spenser, Shakspeare, Bacon, and Milton were born. And besides these four names that shine with such immortal lustre, are other names of poets, scholars, soldiers, discoverers, statesmen, and orators, who form a group unequalled before or since, in England's history.

Queen Elizabeth herself is a fitting central figure in this age. When she came to the throne, a young and beautiful woman, after the stormy struggles between Catholic and Protestant in her father's and sister's reigns, she seemed to bring peace and prosperity to the land. Her court and her people welcomed her as if she had been a creature almost divine. From the first this ideal sovereign inspired the poet's pen, and she appears in his verse as a being glorified by all that myth or legend or his own fancy can suggest.

Elizabeth had been educated by one of the most famous of schoolmasters, good Roger Ascham, who had trained her in Greek and Latin and other branches of learning. She could speak the principal court languages of Europe, and, better than that, could use her own language forcibly and well; she was well read in the current literature of her time; interested in the rising poets who sought her patronage; and, indeed, had tried her own fair hand at verse-making, and on occasion could turn a clever epigram in rhyme.

It was the tendency of Elizabeth's reign to bring in luxury of living and all kinds of elegancies in dress and manners. The queen was passionately fond of fine clothes and fine surroundings. She had in her wardrobe, for one item of dress alone, three thousand gowns, and her lords and ladies were not far behind her in extravagance. One gets in history some idea of the splendid dresses of her courtiers. One of Sir Walter Raleigh's portraits was painted in a white satin doublet richly embroidered, "with a great string of pearls round his neck, each big as a robin's egg," and a hat with a long feather, fastened by a great blazing ruby. Walter Scott, who writes the romance of history, but always keeps close to the fact, tells us of the Earl of Leicester's handsome clothes in his novel of *Kenilworth.*

The young Englishman when he left college was sent to France or Italy to finish his education and to polish and re-fine his manners, and he brought back with him all sorts of new fashions. The young travellers from England were noted for following all the extravagances then in vogue. Old John Lyly advises the young man, " Let not your minds be carried away with vain delights, as with travelling into far and strange countries, where you will see more wickedness than learn virtue and wit. Neither with costly attire of the new cut, the Dutch hat, the French hose, the Spanish rapier, and the Italian hilt." And Shakespeare hits off this weakness of the time in Portia's merry description of the English lord : " How oddly he is suited ! I think he bought his doublet in Italy, his round hose in France, his bonnet in Germany, and his behavior everywhere."

But the graduates from Oxford and Cambridge brought back from Italy more than fine clothes and polished man-ners, they brought the knowledge of a literature which worked a perceptible change on their own. Italian poetry, even in Chaucer's time, had exerted an influence over Eng-lish poetry ; later, Surrey and Wyatt, as we have just seen, had been disciples of the Italian school. But never was this influence so strongly marked as in this era we are now entering. A flood of romances, in prose and verse, from the rich fountain of Italian literature, poured into England. It seemed as if all the elements that could gratify the taste, stimulate the imagination, and enrich the fancy were brought all at once to bear upon the age **that** produced both Shakespeare and Spenser.

In an age so crowded with great writers, both in prose and poetry, it is hard to decide which we shall begin to **talk** about. But **in** my imagination the great figures of the time divide themselves into groups: Sir Philip Sidney and Sir Walter Raleigh, with one or two minor poets, form a circle about their grand central figure, Edmund Spenser; next to this group, apart **in** solitary greatness, stands Lord Bacon; then follows Shakespeare, towering like **a** Colossus above the crowd of dramatic poets that surround him; and last come the lyric poets, the singers whose gay music is heard all through the century from the **time** of Elizabeth to that **of** Charles II. So, beginning with Spenser and the figures that attend upon him, we will enter upon the Golden, **or, as it is generally** called, the Elizabethan, Age of English **poetry.**

XVI.

ON EDMUND SPENSER.

EDMUND SPENSER **is** the second great English poet in **the** line which begins with Geoffrey Chaucer. It **was almost two** hundred years after Chaucer **had** laid down his pen, when Spenser's great   1552-1598 **poem,** *The Fairy Queen*, was published. It is not every generation, not every century, even, that produces a great **poet.**

About the events of Spenser's early life there **is the** same vagueness and uncertainty that we find when we come to study the biographies of all our great poets. **Most** of the writers who undertake to tell us of the lives of Chaucer,

7

Spenser, or Shakespeare, make tiresome researches into family history, without much result. Evidently Genius is quite independent of genealogies, and the great poet does not, like the snail, carry his house on his back.

Spenser was born in London in 1552, or very near that date, and began his education at a London grammar-school. He went to Cambridge early, but left before his studies were completed, — forced to do so, some of his biographers think, by the poverty of his purse. From college he went to the North of England, and fell in love there with a beautiful Rosalinde (her last name no one has been able to find out with certainty), who seems to have been unable to love him in return; and to give vent to his disappointment, he wrote *The Shepherd's Calendar*, which first proved that he was a poet. Let us be grateful to the fair Rosalinde that she was indifferent to the poet, since we reap the benefit of her indifference.

The Shepherd's Calendar is dedicated to Sir Philip Sidney, who was one of Spenser's best friends and patrons. Sidney, Raleigh, and Spenser were very near each other in age, Sidney being about a year younger, and Raleigh less than a year older than the great poet. One of the finest things about these two men is that they were generous friends of Spenser; and there can be no better proof of Spenser's friendship for them than his dedication of *The Fairy Queen* to Walter Raleigh, and *Astrophel*, a lament which he wrote on Sidney's death.

When Spenser was about twenty-eight, he went to Ireland as secretary to the Lord-Lieutenant of Ireland, Lord Arthur Grey. There, after a time, a castle and some lands were given him, the share of a confiscated estate of a famous Irish rebel. In this castle — Kilcolman, on the banks of the river Mulla — he lived happily, working upon his greatest of poems, *The Fairy Queen*. He had been more fortunate in a second love than in the affair with Rosalinde, and was married to a lovely wife, to whom he wrote an *Epithalamion*, which is one of the grandest wedding hymns ever written. Here in his beautiful retirement, Sir Walter

Raleigh, then one of the officers in the English army in Ireland, paid him a visit. I fancy the two friends lying at ease on the green banks under the trees that bordered the Mulla, while Spenser read extracts from *The Fairy Queen*, and Raleigh praised it and answered with bits of verse of his own making. There, doubtless, they discussed poetry, politics, their common friends in London, and all the gossip of the time. It was not long after Raleigh's visit that Spenser published the first part of *The Fairy Queen*. He went to London, and Queen Elizabeth gave him a pension for his verses, which they richly deserved for the fine praises of her which the poem contains.

Spenser kept his home in Ireland for twelve years, although he was in England during that period for a year or two at a time. Towards the end of the year 1597 his affairs looked prosperous; the queen had recommended him to a good appointment, the first half of *The Fairy Queen* was published, and the last half begun, when a fresh rebellion broke out in Ireland. Spenser's house was burned, and he and his family were forced to fly. It is reported that his new-born infant was left in the castle in this hurried flight, and perished in the flames. He came to London overwhelmed by all these troubles, and died a few months later, broken-hearted and in poverty, and was laid in Westminster Abbey, near Chaucer.

Besides *The Shepherd's Calendar* and *The Fairy Queen*, Spenser wrote many other poems. The most beautiful among these shorter works is *Muiopotmos*, or the Tale of a Butterfly. This is like a picture, for brilliancy of color and description. If you want, with little study, to know Spenser's quality as a poet, read this poem, *Astrophel*, and a few extracts from *The Fairy Queen*, and you will get an excellent idea of him.

His poem of poems, *The Fairy Queen*, stands as one of the monuments of literature. There are few persons who have read it through, and their number is likely to grow less as the years go by. It is useless for any one to read poetry merely for the sake of saying he has read it, and

I certainly should advise no one to take up this poem unless he reads it purely for the enjoyment of it. To those who do enjoy it, there is no need to say anything in its praise. To those who would find the entire poem tedious, — and I think perhaps these will form the larger number, — I will briefly tell its plan, and give a few extracts as illustrations of the style.

In his dedication to Raleigh, Spenser himself gives his design. This was to write a poem in twelve books, each book representing some high virtue. Thus the Red-Cross Knight, in the first book, is Holiness; in the second book, Sir Guyon is Temperance; in the third book, Britomart, the heroine, illustrates Chastity; Cambell and Triamond are the heroes of the fourth book, the Legend of Friendship; Sir Artegall, in the fifth book, represents Justice; and Sir Calidore, in the sixth and last, is the embodiment of Courtesy. Spenser had planned to write twelve books, but finished only the first six, leaving a few fragments towards the last half of his work.

The stanza in which the poem is written has since his time been called *Spenserian*. It was the eight-line stanza used by the poets of Italy, to which a ninth line was added by Spenser, which gave it its name.

The poem is an allegory, and you will find in some editions of the work an explanation of the real events which are told in allegorical form, and the names of the real persons who are meant under the names of Arthur, Sir Guyon, Timeas, Amoret, Belphœbe, and the rest. For my part, I prefer to read Spenser for his poetry, and not for his allegory, and therefore I attempt no explanation of it here.

The first book of *The Fairy Queen* tells the story of Una, one of the most beautiful figures in all the poem. The picture of the gentle knight "pricking on the plain," while a gentle lady rides close beside him upon a lowly ass "more white than snow," is the very first picture that catches our eyes as we open the book. Soon after we see Una separated from her knight, who has been drawn away

from his true lady by an enchantress who assumes her
shape, and Una is described as in search of him : —

> " Yet she, most faithfull ladie, all this while,
> Forsaken, woefull, solitarie mayd,
> Far from all peoples' preace, as in exile,
> In wildernesse and wastfull deserts strayd
> To seeke her knight, who subtily betrayd,
> Through that late vision which th' enchaunter wrought,
> Had her abandoned ; she, of naught afrayd,
> Through woods and wastnes wide him daily sought,
> Yet wished tydinges none of him unto her brought.
>
> " One day, nigh wearie of the yrkesome way,
> From her unhastie beast she did alight,
> And on the grasse her dainty limbs did lay,
> In secrete shadow, far from all men's sight.
> From her fayre head her fillet she undight
> And layd her stole aside ; her angel's face,
> As the great eye of heaven, shyned bright,
> And made a sunshine in the shady place :
> Did never mortall eye behold such heavenly grace.
>
> " It fortuned, out of the thickest wood
> A ramping lyon rushed suddeinly,
> Hunting full greedy after salvage blood.
> Soone as the royall virgin he did spy,
> With gaping mouth at her ran greedily,
> To have at once devourd her tender corse ;
> But to the pray, when as he drew more ny,
> His bloody rage aswaged with remorse,
> And with the sight amazd, forgat his furious forse.
>
> " Instead thereof he kist her wearie feet,
> And lickt her lilly hands with fawning tong,
> As he her wronged innocence did weet.
> O, how can beautie maister the most strong,
> And simple truth subdue avenging wrong !
> Whose yielded pryde and proud submission,
> Still dreading death, when she had marked long,
> Her hart gan melt in great compassion,
> And drizling teares did shed for pure affection.
>
> . . . . . .
>
> " The lyon would not leave her desolate,
> But with her went along, as a strong gard
> Of her chast person, and a faythfull mate
> Of her sad troubles and misfortunes hard.

Still when she slept, he kept both watch and **ward**;
And when she waked, he wayted diligent,
With humble **service to her** will prepard.
From her fair eyes **he took** commandement,
And ever by her lookes conceived her intent."

The story **of** the fair Una ends happily, and we see her, at the **end** of the first book, united to her knight on a happy wedding day, when she lays her **sad** garments aside and appears in a gown —

" **All** lilly white, withoutten spot **or pride,**
That seemed like silke and silver woven neare,
But neither silke nor silver therein did appeare.

" The blazing brightnesse of her beautie's beame,
And glorious light of her sunshyny face
To tell, were as to strive against the streame :
My ragged rimes are all too rude and bace
Her heavenly lineaments for to enchase.
Ne wonder for her own dear-loved knight,
All were she daily **with** himselfe in place,
Did wonder much **at her celestial** sight ;
Oft had **he seene her faire, but** never so faire dight.

" **And ever, when his eie did her** behold,
His heart **did seeme to melt in** pleasures manifold."

XVII.

On Spenser's " Fairy Queen."

THE story of Florimel — a musical name **made out of** flowers and honey — is **another of the interesting** episodes in *The Fairy Queen.* She appears first in the **third book, a** beautiful **picture of** fright, fleeing on a white palfrey from **a monster who seeks to** devour her. She re-appears in many **cantos, in all sorts of** romantic adventures, until the fifth **book, when all her troubles are** ended amid **the** festivities **that attend her marriage to** the handsome Prince Marinell.

The women in Spenser's poem are a constant delight to the imagination. They live in his pages like creatures in some land of enchantment, and while they are not like real women in a real world, they are so natural to their surroundings that we cannot help believing in them as much as if they had actually existed.

The heroine of the third book is Britomart, a royal maid of Britain, who puts on a helmet and armor, and in disguise of a knight goes forth to seek her lover, Sir Artegall. In her course Britomart meets with all sorts of romantic adventures; yet Spenser has managed to preserve for his heroine all the sweet charm of womanliness, in spite of her Amazonian equipment.

Here are some stanzas which give an account of her battle with the scornful Marinell, afterwards the bridegroom of Florimel. The fourth canto of the third book begins with this description of the battle : —

> " Where is the antique glory now become
> That whylom wont in wemen to appeare?
> Where be the brave atchievements doen by some?
> Where be the batteilles, where the shield and speare,
> And all the conquests which them high did reare
> That matter made for famous poet's verse
> And boastful men so oft abasht to hear?
> Beene they all dead, and laide in doleful hearse,
> Or doen they onely sleepe, and shall againe reverse? . . .

> " Yet these, and all that els had puissaunce
> Cannot with noble Britomart compare,
> As well for glory of great valiaunce
> As for pure chastitee and vertue rare,
> That all her goodly deedes doe well declare
> Well worthie stock from which the branches sprong,
> That in late yeares so faire a blossome beare,
> As thee, O queene, the matter of my song,
> Whose lignage from this lady I derive along. . . .

> " But Britomart kept on her former course,
> Ne ever doft her arms. . . .
> So forth she rode, without repose or rest, . . .
> Till that to the sea coast at length she her addresst. . . .

" There she alighted from her light-foot beast,
And sitting down **upon** the rocky shore,
Badd her old squyre **unlace her** lofty creast
Tho having vewd **awhile the surges** hore
That 'gainst the craggy **cliffs did loudly** rore,
And in their raging surquedry disdayned
That the fast earth affronted **them so sore,**
And their devouring covetize restrayned ;
Thereat **she** sighed deepe, and after **thus** complayned :

" ' Huge sea of sorrow and tempestuous griefe
Wherein my feeble barke is **tossed** long,
Far from the hoped haven of **reliefe,**
Why doe thy cruel billowes beat so strong,
And **thy** moyst mountaines each on others throng,
Threatning to swallow up my fearefull lyfe ?
O, doe thy cruell wrath, and spightfull wrong
At **length** allay, and stint thy stormy strife,
Which in **thy** troubled bowels raignes and rageth ryfe. . . .

" ' **Thou God of winds, that raignest in the seas,**
That raignest also in the continent,
At last **blow up some gentle gale of ease,**
The **which may bring my ship, ere it be rent,**
Unto **the gladsome port of her intent !**
Then **when I shall myselfe in safety see,**
A table **for eternall moniment**
Of thy great grace and my great jeopardee,
Great Neptune, I avow to hallow unto thee.' . . .

" Thus as she her recomforted, she spyde
Where, far away, one all in armour bright,
With hasty gallop towards her did ryde.
Her dolour soone she ceast, and on her dight
Her helmet, to her courser mounting light ;
Her former sorrow into sudden wrath
(Both coosen passions of distroubled spright)
Converting, forth she **beates the** dusty path ;
Love and despight attonce her corage kindled hath.

" As when a **foggy mist hath overcast**
The face **of heven and the cleare ayre engrosste,**
The world in **darknes dwels ; till that at last**
The watry south **winde from the sea-borde coste**
Upblowing, **doth disperse the** vapour loste,
And poures itselfe forth **in a** stormy showre, —
So the fayre Britomarte, having discloste
Her clowdy care into a wrathfull stowre,
The mist of griefe dissolv'd did into vengeance powre.

" Eftsoones, her goodly shield addressing fayre,
    That mortall speare she in her hand did take,
    And unto battaill did herselfe prepayre.
    The knight, approaching, sternely her bespake :
    'Sir knight, that doest thy voyage rashly make
    By this forbidden way, in my despight,
    Ne doest by others' death ensample take,
    I rede thee now retyre whiles thou hast might,
Least afterward it be to late to take thy flight.'

" Y-thrild with deepe disdaine of his proud threat,
    She shortly thus : ' Fly they, that *need* to fly.
    Wordes fearen babes ; I mean not thee entreat
    To passe, but maugre thee will pass or dy.'
    Ne lenger stayd for th' other to reply,
    But with sharpe speare the rest made dearly knowne,
    Strongly the straunge knight ran, and sturdily
    Strooke her full on the breast, that made her downe
Decline her head, and touch her crouper with her crown.

" But she againe him in the shield did smite
    With so fierce furie and great puissaunce,
    That, through his three-square scuchin percing quite,
    And through his mayled hauberque, by mischaunce,
    The wicked steele through his left side did glaunce.
    Him so transfixed she before her bore
    Beyond his croupe, the length of all her launce ;
    Till sadly soucing on the sandy shore,
He tombled on an heape, and wallowd in his gore.

" Like as the sacred oxe, that carelesse stands
    With gilden hornes and flowry girlonds crownd,
    Proud of his dying honor and deare bandes,
    Whiles th' altars fume with frankincense arownd,
    All suddeinly with mortall stroke astownd
    Doth groveling fall, and with his streaming gore
    Distaines the pillours and the holy grownd,
    And the fair flowres that decked him afore, —
So fell proud Marinell upon the pretious shore."

The second book, which gives the adventures of Sir
Guyon, has some of the finest contrasts, from Spenser's
grandest style to his most beautiful and poetic. The visit
to Mammon's Cave is one of the strongest pieces of description, and the account of Guyon's entrance into the
gardens of the Bower of Acrasia is one of the most beautiful things in all the book. No other poet could describe

a garden as Spenser could. His description of the garden in the Fate of the **Butterfly** is as good as a painting of it, and the gardens of this Bower of Bliss are no less perfectly portrayed.

Sir Guyon **enters** these gardens through a gate framed of interlacing vines, whose luscious bunches of fruit seem to offer themselves to the hands of all who pass under it. Within this gate lies the bower of Acrasia, the mistress of the enchanted place. We will begin just where Guyon passes through the gateway : —

> " There the most daintie paradise on ground
> Itselfe doth offer to his sober eye,
> In which all pleasures plenteously abownd,
> And none does other's happinesse envye ;
> The painted flowres ; the trees upshooting hie ;
> The dales for shade ; the hilles for breathing space ;
> The trembling groves ; the christall running by ;
> And that which all faire workes doth most aggrace,
> The art which all that wrought, appeared in no place. . . .

> " And in the midst of all a fountaine stood. . . .

> " Infinit streames continually did well
> Out of this fountaine, sweete and faire to see,
> The which into an ample laver fell,
> And shortly grew to so great quantitee
> That like a litle lake it seemed to bee,
> Whose depth exceeded not three cubits hight.
> That through the waves one might the bottom see,
> All pav'd beneath with jaspar shining bright,
> That seemd the fountaine in that sea did sayle upright. . . .

> " Eftsoones they heard a most melodious sound,
> Of all that mote delight a daintie eare,
> Such as attonce might not on living ground,
> Save in this paradise, be heard elsewhere.
> Right hard it was for wight which did it heare
> To read what manner musicke that mote bee,
> For all that pleasing is to living eare
> Was there consorted in one harmoniee :
> Birdes, voices, instruments, windes, waters, all agree.

> " The joyous birdes, shrouded in chearefull shade,
> Their notes unto the voice attempred sweet ;
> The angelicall soft trembling voyces made
> To th' instruments, divine respondence meet ;

The silver-sounding instruments did meet
With the base murmur of the waters fall;
The waters fall with difference discreet,
Now soft, now loud, unto the wind did call:
The gentle warbling wind low answered to all. . . .

"The whiles some one did chaunt this lovely lay:
'Ah, see, whoso fayre thing dost fayne to see,
In springing flowre the image of thy day!
Ah, see the virgin rose, how sweetly shee
Doth first peepe foorth with bashful modestee;
That fairer seemes the lesse ye see her may!
Lo! see soon after, how more bold and free
Her bared bosome she doth broad display,
Lo! see soone after how she fades and falls away.'"

But it is not by such extracts as these that we can hope
to get any full idea of the riches of *The Fairy Queen*.
Only by reading for yourselves can you get any fair conception of the numberless figures that move on to the
stately music of Spenser's stanza. The lovely Amoret,
the spirited Belphœbe, the delicate Florimel, the learned
Canacee, the bold Satyrane, Braggadochio, whose name
tells his character, Sir Calidore, of exquisite courtesy, the
noble Sir Scudamour, the magnanimous Arthur, — these are
a few only of the graceful, chivalrous, and fascinating crea-
tions of our poet's unwearied fancy. Add to these the
elfin beings conjured by his magic pen, — the giants, dwarfs,
monsters; the sprites, composed of snow and wax, of fire
and dew. Then transport the mind to the scenery in
which he places his characters, — the fair green woods, the
sea grottoes, the noble castles, the subterranean caves, the
fairy gardens, — and you will just begin to fathom the in-
exhaustible depths of his fancy.

Spenser's poetry has always been a delight to young versifiers. Probably no other poet has ever inspired so many
men, great and little, to write verses. And that is quite
natural. He is so stimulating to the imagination, his verse
is such a store-house of fancy, that I can think of the
younger poets settling on it as the bees of Mount Hybla
on a flower-garden. None of our poets have so exuberant

an imagination, and of them all, Shakespeare's description fits Spenser best, — He is a creature of imagination all compact.

> " And as imagination bodies forth
> The forms of things unknown, the poet's pen
> Turns them to shapes, and gives to airy nothing
> A local habitation and a name."

XVIII.

On Sir Philip Sidney and the " Arcadia."

TO ALMOST every one who looks back in imagination upon the age of Queen Elizabeth, Sir Philip Sidney will appear one of the most interesting figures **1554–1586** among all those that graced her court. He was noble in birth, gifted in mind, handsome in person, a favorite courtier of the queen, a gallant soldier in the field, beloved by all who knew him, yet withal so modest, gentle, full of noble humanity, that he seems to have had all the virtues as well as all the graces of manhood. Nothing but good has ever been said of him, and one of the last acts of his life crowns gloriously all that goes before. He died of a wound which he got at Zutphen, where he was fighting in the cause of the Netherlands, in their wars with Spain. Just as he was to be taken from the field after he had received his death-wound, a bottle of water was brought him to drink. As he was about to put it to his lips he saw a wounded soldier carried by, who cast wistfully at the water his dying eyes. This Sir Philip seeing, gave the bottle to the poor man, saying simply, " Thy necessity is yet greater than mine." What fame of authorship could outshine the lustre of such a deed as this?

Yet although writing was not the pursuit of his life, he had great gifts as a writer. He died at thirty-two, and his brief day was full of other affairs than those of literature, which in him seems only the amusement of an idle hour.

If he had made it his first following, one can fancy he
might have risen to great heights.

His principal works are his sonnets from *Astrophel to
Stella*, in verse ; and the **Arcadia,** and *Defence of Poetry*,
in prose. The *Arcadia* is a romance inspired largely by the
ideas of love and chivalry which belong to the Middle
Ages. The plot is very simple. Sidney calls it " an idle
work, which, like the spider's web, will be thought fitter to
be swept away than worn to any other purpose." Two
young princes, in disguise, wander into the kingdom of
Arcadia, where King Basilius keeps his court, with his wife
Gynecia and his two daughters Pamela and Philoclea.
The two young strangers naturally fall in love with the two
princesses; and the various adventures of these princely
persons, with the stories of other heroes and heroines
woven into the narrative, and occasional passages in verse,
make up the *Arcadia.*

In spite of its faults — and it has sometimes even the fault
of dulness — it is rich in fine sentences, and lines that are
almost a poem by themselves. You can see the nobility
and the wisdom of Sidney's thoughts in such sentences as
meet the eye when one turns over the leaves at random :

" I am no herald to inquire of men's pedigrees ; it sufficeth me
if I know their virtues."

" They are never alone that are accompanied with noble
thoughts."

" Provision is the foundation of hospitality, and thrift the fuel
of magnificence."

" Oh, imperfect proportion of reason, which can too much fore-
see, and too little prevent ! "

" Condemning all men of evil because his mind had no eye to
espy goodness."

" There is no service like his that serves because he loves."

" What's mine, even to my soul, is yours ; but the secret of
my friend is not mine."

Of women he says, —

" Nature is no step-mother to that sex, how much soever some
men, sharp-witted only in evil speaking, have sought to disgrace
them."

The *Arcadia* contains many episodes, which, taken out from their context, would form complete and interesting stories by themselves. The best of these is the tale of Argalus and Parthenia, whose story appears at intervals throughout the book. These are two lovers, who after many haps and mishaps are united in wedlock. A beautiful passage describes them in their married estate as they are visited by a messenger who comes to summon Argalus to go to war in aid of the two princesses who have been taken prisoner by their foes : —

"The messenger made speed and found Argalus at a castle of his own, sitting in a parlor with his fair Parthenia, he reading in a book the stories of Hercules, she by him as to hear him read ; but while his eyes looked on the book, she looked on his eyes, and sometimes staying him with some pretty question, not so much to be resolved of the doubt, as to give him occasion to look upon her. A happy couple ! he joying in her, she joying in herself, but in herself, because she enjoyed him ; both increased their riches by giving to each other, each making one life double because they made a double life one ; where desire never wanted satisfaction, nor satisfaction ever bred satiety ; he ruling because she would obey, or rather because she would obey, she therein ruling.

"But when the messenger came in, with letters in his hand and haste in his countenance, though she knew not what to fear, yet she feared, because she knew not, but rose and went aside while he delivered his letters and message, and afar off she looked now at the messenger, and then at her husband, the same fear which made her loth to have cause of fear, yet making her seek cause to nourish her fear. And well she found there was some serious matter, for her husband's countenance figured some resolution between loathsomeness and necessity, and once his eye cast upon her, and finding hers upon him, he blushed, and she blushed because he blushed, then straight grew pale, because she knew not why he had blushed. But when he had read and heard, and despatched away the messenger, like a man in whom honor could not be rocked asleep by affection, with promise quickly to follow, he came to Parthenia ; and as sorry as might be for parting, and yet more sorry for her sorrow, he gave her the letter to read. She with fearful slowness took it, and with fearful quickness read it, and having read it, 'Ah, my Argalus,' said she, 'and have you made such haste to answer, **and are you so soon resolved to leave me?'**

" But he discoursing unto her how much **it imported his honor,** which, **since it** was dear to him, he knew **it** would **be dear unto** her, her reason, overclouded with sorrow, suffered her not presently to reply, but left the charge thereof to **tears** and sighs, which he, not able to bear, left her alone, and went to give order for his present departure.

" But by **that time he was armed and ready to** go, she had **recovered** a little strength of spirit again, and coming **out, and** seeing him armed, and wanting nothing for his departure but her farewell, she **ran** to him, took him by the arm, and kneeling down, without regard **who** either heard her speech or saw her demeanor: 'My Argalus, my Argalus,' said she, 'do not thus **forsake me.** Remember, alas ! remember that I have an interest in you which I will never yield shall be thus adventured. Your valor is already sufficiently known ; sufficiently have you already done for your country; enow, enow there are beside you to lose less worthy lives. Woe is me ! what shall **become of** me if you thus abandon me ? Then was it time **for you to fol-low** these adventures when you adventured nobody but yourself, **and were** nobody's but your own. But now, pardon me that **now or never I** claim mine own ; mine you are, and without **me** you can undertake no danger; and will you endanger Parthenia **?** Parthenia shall be in the battle of your fight, Parthenia **shall smart in** your pain, and your blood must be bled by Parthenia !'

" ' **Dear** Parthenia,' said he, 'this is the first time that ever **you** resisted my will ; I thank you for it, but persever not in it, and let not the tears of those most beloved eyes be a presage of that which you would not should happen. I shall live, doubt not ; for so great a blessing as you are, was not given unto me so soon to be deprived of it. Look for me, therefore, shortly, and victorious, and prepare a joyful welcome, and I will wish for no other triumph.' She answered not, but stood, as it were, thunder-stricken with amazement, for true love made obedience stand up against all other passions. But when he took her in his **arms, and** sought **to** print his heart on **her sweet lips, she** fell in a swound, so **as** he was fain to leave **her to her gentle-**women; and carried away by the tyranny of honor, though with many a back-cast look and hearty groan, went to the camp.''

The **story** follows Argalus to the field, where **he is killed in** combat with his enemy Amphialus, dying in the **arms of his** Parthenia, who arrives upon the field only to

receive his dying farewell, but not in time to save his life
by her entreaties to his foe. Soon after this, Parthenia,
dressing herself like a knight, in black armor, challenges
Amphialus, and from him receives her own death-wound.
Amphialus does not discover that it is Parthenia in disguise
with whom he is fighting, until he has fatally wounded her ;
and then he is overcome with grief and shame at what he
has done.

"Therefore [Amphialus], putting off his head-piece and
gauntlet, kneeling down unto her, and with tears testifying his
sorrow, he offered his, by himself accursed, hands to help her,
protesting his life and power to be ready to do her honor.
But Parthenia, who had inward messengers of the desired
death's approach, looking upon him, and straight turning away
her feeble sight as from a delightless object, drawing out her
words, which her breath, loath to depart from so sweet a body,
did faintly deliver : 'Sir,' said she, 'I pray you, if prayers
have place in enemies, to let my maids take my body un-
touched by you. . . . Argalus made no such bargain with you
that the hands that killed him should help me. I have of
them — and I not only pardon, but thank you for it — the
service which I desired. There rests nothing now, but that I
go live with him, since whose death I have done nothing but
die.' Then pausing, and a little fainting, and again coming to
herself, 'O sweet life, welcome !' said she. 'Now feel I the
bands untied of the cruel death which so long hath held me.
And, O life, O death, answer for me that my thoughts have,
not so much as in a dream, tasted any comfort since they were
deprived of Argalus. I come, my Argalus, I come. And, O
God, hide my faults in thy mercies, and grant, as I feel thou
dost grant, that in thy eternal love we may love each other
eternally.' . . . With that, casting up her hands and eyes to
the skies, the noble soul departed, one might well assure himself, to heaven, which left the body in so heavenly a demeanor."

Thus ends the story of Argalus and Parthenia, which is
only one of the many episodes of the *Arcadia*. Although
it is a little stilted for our modern taste, and many sentences are involved and over-full of words, there are touches
of nature and of feeling in it that will go straight to the
heart.

Close beside Sidney should come the name **of his biographer** and bosom **friend,** FULKE GREVILLE, LORD BROOKE,
who desired **to** have for his epitaph that he had been " Servant
to Queen Elizabeth, counsellor to King **James, and** friend
to Sir Philip **Sidney."** He was a courtier-poet, **who wrote**
plays and sonnets in verse, and a **life of his friend** Sidney in
prose, which is most to be valued **of** all his **works.**

It **is said that** Sidney intended the **princes in the**
Arcadia, Pyrocles and Musidorus, for himself and Lord
Brooke. The two gentlemen were very dear friends during
Sidney's short **life.** **Lord Brooke** long outlived his friend,
dying at an advanced **age.** One of the writers of the
time says of him **that of all** Queen Elizabeth's favorites
" he had the longest **lease and the smoothest** time without
rub," and that " he came **to court backed with a plentiful**
fortune, which, as he **was wont to say, was better held to-**
gether by a single life, wherein **he lived and died, a con-**
stant courtier of **the ladies."** He would **hardly have gained**
mention in the present **as a literary man if it were not for**
his **biography** of Sidney, which gives **him an honorable**
place **among** this group of worthies.

XIX.

LIKE Sir Philip Sidney, SIR WALTER RALEIGH **was a man**
of large gifts, and so versatile that what he
did in literature seems only the diversion of his   **1552–1618**
leisure hours. **Hardly less full** of beauty and charm **than**
Sidney, Raleigh **holds** our interest **to the end of** his long
life. Sidney died **in** early **manhood, but Raleigh** outlived
his generation. Spenser, Essex, **Shakespeare,** all were
dead, when, at sixty-six, he **laid his noble head** under the
axe of King James's headsman. **He was** not only a poet,

a scholar, and a man of scientific attainments, but also a clear-headed statesman, an adventurous sailor, a skilful military leader, and a polished orator.

Raleigh wrote the first part of a great *History of the World*. He never finished the work, and all there is of it is in one great, ponderous folio, which we should find dull reading. There is also a little volume of his poems collected, though it is disputed whether or not he wrote some of the best included in this handful. I like best of all his writings, or of any that have been ascribed to him, his private letters, which are written in vigorous English, in the style of a master of language. Here is an extract from one that he wrote to Robert Cecil, who had just lost his wife, a kinswoman of Raleigh. He begins, —

"There is no man sorry for death itself, but only for the time of death, every one knowing that it is a bond never forfeited to God. If, then, we know the same to be certain and inevitable, we ought to take the time of his arrival in as good part as the knowledge, and not to lament on the instant of every seeming adversity, which has been on the way to us from the beginning.

"It pertaineth to every man of a wise and worthy spirit to draw together into sufferance the unknown future to the known present. . . . It is true that you have lost a good and virtuous wife, and myself an honorable friend and kinswoman; but there was a time when she was unknown to you, for whom you then lamented not. She is now no more yours, nor of your acquaintance, but immortal, and not needing or knowing your love and sorrow. Therefore you do but grieve for that which now is as then it was, when not yours, only bettered, with this difference, that she hath past the wearisome journey of this dark world, and hath possession of her inheritance.

"I believe that sorrows are dangerous companions, converting bad into evil, and evil into worse. They are the treasures of weak hearts and foolish. . . . The mind of man is that part of God in us which, by so much as it is subject to any passion, by so much is it farther from him that gave it us. Sorrows draw not the dead to life, but the living to death."

Such noble and serene philosophy as this, Raleigh might not always be able to live up to, and, indeed, there were times when his own great troubles aroused in him passions of grief such as he argues against. But he lived a life **full of useful** activity, **and met death** bravely on **the scaffold.** Americans owe him remembrance because **he did more** than any other one man of his time to further the colonizing of America, — worked and planned for it till his fortunes failed. And when he was arrested **for treason** by King James, and imprisoned in the Tower, he still said, in a **spirit** of prophecy, — for American affairs never looked **more** hopeless, — " I shall yet live to see that an English **nation."**

When he **ascended the** scaffold, the little colony **at** Jamestown, Virginia, was eight years old, and the Puritans in Holland were just forming their plans for emigration to **the** New World. **As he closed his** eyes upon the world, is it just possible that Raleigh may have **seen,** in that one struggling offshoot from the parent State just fastened on the shores of Virginia, a dim foreshadowing **of** that great nation **of** English stock which in two centuries and **a half** should cover America from ocean to ocean?

The name of SAMUEL DANIEL has taken a place in **my** mind among the friends of Spenser, perhaps be- 1562–1619 **cause some** one has ventured a guess that the Rosalinde with whom Spenser fell in love when he wrote the *Shepherd's Calendar* was Rose Daniel, a sister of this poet. He was a musician's son, which has given his biographer reason to say that the poet inherited his father's talent and put it into his verse. He wrote such flowing, pure English that he was called " well-languaged Daniel," and some of his little songs are very graceful and musical. It is a pity that instead of writing lyrics, he should have taken a dry subject in history **for** the theme of his most **ambitious** poem. This was *The History of the Civil Wars,* in which he puts the Wars of the Roses into verse. It speaks **well** for his genius **that** he has managed **to infuse** a little breath of poetry into so prosaic a recital.

A subject even more prosaic than this of Daniel was used by another poet of this group. The *Pollyolbion,* written by MICHAEL DRAYTON, is nothing less than a geo-

graphical description of England, written in about thirty
thousand lines of twelve-syllabled verse. There is a great
deal that is interesting in the *Pollyolbion*, and in so much
verse there must be some poetry; but I am sure even
the genius of Spenser could not have made anything but a
dull poem out of such a dull theme, and, in consequence,
nobody ever reads the *Pollyolbion* nowadays.

XX.

On Francis Bacon, Baron Verulam, Viscount St. Albans.

FRANCIS BACON is the great philosopher, the most
profound thinker, of his age. His system of philosophy, which is called, from him, the Baconian system,
wrought a revolution in thought, and has had a great influence on human action from his time to ours. I shall not
attempt to explain his philosophy, because philosophy and
science do not come within the province of these Talks,
but will simply tell you that all his efforts were to make
philosophy of practical benefit to humanity, rather than to
keep men wandering in a vague region of inquiry upon points
that the mind never has been able to solve. He taught men
to reason from experience, to found their knowledge on
results gained by experience, applying it to works really
useful to mankind. Hitherto, the philosopher had been
a man occupied with abstract questions, carrying his head
aloft in the clouds; Bacon occupied himself with questions
that bore upon the comfort of human beings and the improvement of human conditions. As Macaulay has said,
in few words, "Bacon taught that philosophy was made for
man, not man for philosophy."

Francis Bacon was the youngest son of Sir Nicholas
Bacon, Lord Keeper of the Seal under Queen
Elizabeth. His uncle, Lord Burleigh, was Eng-
land's minister of finance for nearly half a century, and

1561–1626

Robert Cecil, Bacon's cousin, was one of the ablest and most powerful politicians of the later years of Queen Elizabeth and the first half of the reign of James I. Surrounded by kinsfolk so great, it might be fancied that Bacon's fortunes were assured ; but it seems to be the fact that the help he met from Burleigh or his other relatives of influence was small and grudgingly given, and it is certain that he owed his success to his own great ability.

That Bacon's was the greatest intellect of his age is hardly doubted ; but of the greatness and nobility of his character there are many doubts. The chief stain upon his name is that of ingratitude, which has never been wiped out. During his earlier life he had no friend more generous than the Earl of Essex, who befriended him when he most needed friendship. But when Essex was accused of treason, Bacon was chief counsel for the Crown, prosecuted the charge against the unhappy earl, proved it, and gained the sentence of death against his former friend and patron ; and finally, after the death of the earl, he wrote an account of his treason which still further blackened the character of the unfortunate Essex. Bacon's apologists plead that, as Queen's Counsel, it was his duty to his queen and his country to pursue this course ; but I think every generous spirit will condemn Bacon, and will rate higher the obligations of gratitude and friendship than those of political duty such as this.

Bacon rose rapidly in the reign of James I. He held his father's office of Lord Keeper, was then made Lord Chancellor, and finally was created Viscount St. Albans. Near the close of his life he was accused of corruption in his high office, was tried for this charge, made an abject confession, and was sentenced to be expelled from the House of Lords, to be heavily fined, and to be imprisoned in the Tower. His sentence was not carried out. The king released him from prison in two days, his fine was remitted, and he finally resumed his seat in the House of Peers ; but he never recovered from his disgrace, and it sullies to this day his character as a statesman.

His zeal for science caused his death. He was re-
volving in his mind a theory about the arrest of decay in
animals by means of cold; and when driving one severe
winter's day he alighted from his carriage and stuffed a dead
fowl with snow. He thus took the cold of which he died.
His will contains the following appeal to the judgment of
the future, and shows that he foresaw that his intellectual
greatness would overshadow the actions that marred the
nobleness of his life and character: "For my name and
memory, I leave it to men's charitable speeches, to foreign
nations, and to my own country after some time has passed
over."

Of all Bacon's writings, his Essays belong most to literature, and so most concern us. They were his first publication, and were at once widely read in his own country, and
translated into both French and Italian. Thirty years after
their first appearance, Bacon carefully revised them, added
to their number, and republished them, with a preface, in
which he says: "These, of all my works, have been most
current, — for that, as it seems, they come home to men's
businesse and bosomes." This is indeed the true secret
of the immortality of any man's written words, that they
should "come home to men's business and bosoms."

The Essays, which altogether make only one little volume, are brief dissertations on a great variety of subjects,
running through the gamut of human interests, as Death,
Adversity, Riches, Love, Friendship, Marriage, Gardens,
Building, and the Regimen of Health. These little papers
say more in brief space, and contain more practical wisdom,
than anything else I know, of their length, or even a good
many times their length, in the English language. I do not
know a better book to pick up and read two or three sentences to set one thinking wholesomely. It seems as if the
wisdom of a good many ages had been garnered here, ripe
and ready for the use of all future generations. I shall
quote one of the shorter essays entire, and then give extracts from two or three others. First, we will read this, on
Revenge : —

"Revenge is a kind of wild justice, which, the more man's nature runs to, the more ought law to weed it out. For, as to the first wrong, it doth but offend the law; but the revenge of that wrong putteth the law out of office. Certainly, in taking revenge, a man is but even with his enemy; but in passing it over, he is superior, for it is a prince's part to pardon. And Solomon, I am sure, saith: '*It is the glory of a man to pass by an offence.*' That which is past, is gone and irrevocable, and wise men have enough to do with things present and to come. Therefore, they do but trifle with themselves that labor in past matters. There is no man doth a wrong for the wrong's sake, but thereby to purchase himself profit, or pleasure, or honor, or the like. Therefore, why should I be angry with a man for loving himself better than me? And if any man should do wrong, merely out of ill nature, why? Yet it is but like the thorn or brier, which prick and scratch, because they can do no other. The most tolerable sort of revenge is for those wrongs which there is no law to remedy. But then let a man take heed the revenge be such as there is no law to punish, else a man's enemy is still beforehand, and it is two to one. Some, when they take revenge, are desirous the party should know whence it cometh. This is the more generous, for the delight seemeth to be, not so much in doing the hurt, as in making the party repent; but base and crafty cowards are like the arrow that flieth in the dark.

"Cosmos, Duke of Florence, had a desperate saying against perfidious or neglecting friends, as if those wrongs were unpardonable. 'You shall read,' he said, 'that we are commanded to forgive our enemies, but you never read that we are commanded to forgive our friends.' But yet the spirit of Job was in better tune. 'Shall we,' saith he, 'take good at God's hands, and not be content to take evil also?' And so of friends in a proportion.

"This is certain, that a man that studieth revenge keeps his own wounds green, which otherwise would heal and do well. Public revenges are for the most part fortunate, . . . but in private revenges it is not so. Nay, rather, vindictive persons live the life of witches, who, as they are mischievous, so end they unfortunate."

Here are a few sentences from his Essay of Death:

"Men fear Death as children fear to go in the dark. And as that natural fear in children is increased with tales, so is the other. . . .

" It is worthy the observing that there is no passion in the mind of man so weak but it mates and masters the fear of Death.   And therefore Death is no such terrible enemy when a man hath so many attendants about him that can win the combat of him.   Revenge triumphs over death ; Love slights it ; Honor aspireth to it ; Grief flieth to it ; Fear pre-occupateth it. . . .

" It is as natural to die as to be born, and to a little infant perhaps the one is as painful as the other.   He that dies in an earnest pursuit is like one that is wounded in hot blood, who for the time scarce feels the hurt.   And, therefore, a mind fixed and bent upon somewhat that is good, doth avert the dolors of death.   But above all, believe it, the sweetest canticle is *Nunc dimittis*, when a man has obtained worthy ends and expectations. "

These Essays have also many sentences which are a text for a whole sermon, as these : —

" A man that is young in years may be old in hours, if he have lost no time."

" Virtue is like a rich stone, — best plain set."

" They are happy men whose natures sort with their vocations."

And we will end these extracts from Bacon's Essays — which I hope will give you such a taste as shall make you desire to read them in full — with a sentence or two from his Essay on Studies, which every student should commit to memory : —

" Read not to contradict and confute, nor to believe and take for granted, nor to find talk and discourse, but to weigh and consider.   Some books are to be tasted, others to be swallowed, and some few to be chewed and digested. . . .

" Reading maketh a full man, conference a ready man, and writing an exact man.   And therefore, if a man write little, he had need have a great memory ; if he confer little, he had need have a present wit ; and if he read little, he had need have much cunning, to seem to know that he doth not.   Histories make men wise ; poets, witty ; the mathematics, subtle ; natural philosophy, deep ; moral, grave ; logic and rhetoric, able to contend.   Nay, there is no stand or impediment in the wit, but may be wrought out by fit studies." ·

I think after reading these extracts you will agree that there is much riches in small space in these Essays, and that this is a book which is to be " chewed and digested."

XXI.

On the English Drama and some of the Play-Writers
who came before Shakespeare.

ONE of the most wonderful things to note in this sixteenth century is the sudden growth of the English
drama.   Until after the middle of the century there are
few plays worth mentioning as literature.   All peoples have
some sort of drama early in their history, just as children
will act out in their plays that which they see done by
grown-up people, — the affairs of the household, the Church
service, the wedding, or the funeral.   The early English
drama was very like this sort of child's-play.   The drama
was usually under the direction of the Church, the plays being nearly all written by priests, and generally representing
some scene from the Old or New Testament.   These plays
(called miracle-plays, or mysteries) had such subjects as
the feast of Belshazzar, the raising of Lazarus, the expulsion
of Adam and Eve from Eden ; and it was not felt irreverent
to show the most sacred scenes and characters on the stage.
If you have heard or read any account of the Passion Play,
still represented in Germany, in which the trial and cruci-
fixion of Christ is dramatized, you will have some idea of
what these old plays were like.
One sometimes finds these early dramas very amusing.
For instance, in the play of *Noah's Flood,* Mrs. Noah is a
high-tempered scold, who refuses to go into the ark unless
all her neighbor-gossips are saved as well as herself, and
when carried into the ark by main force by her sons, she
boxes Noah's ears, in a towering rage, on entering.   The
play of *Lucifer's Fall* represents Lucifer as a stage villain

of the deepest dye ; and all sacred incidents are treated in the homeliest, most matter-of fact manner.   Up to the middle of the sixteenth century, the century in which Shakespeare was born, the literature of the drama was almost all of this crude sort.

I shall not weary you with a history of the early drama, or enumerate the old plays written before Shakespeare's time.   Let me tell you only that the first comedy that had **1551.** the form and spirit of English comedy was *Roister Doister,* written by an Eton schoolmaster, Nicholas Udall, and that the oldest tragedy was written by Thomas Sackville, and had for its subject *Ferrex and Porrex,* two British princes descended from the great Brutus.   Their story was told by Layamon, in the *Brut,* whence later poets took it.

Passing by most of the plays and play-writers who came before Shakespeare, I will touch briefly upon the four most remarkable men who preceded him in writing for the stage. These are George Peele, Robert Greene, John Lyly, and Christopher Marlowe.

GEORGE PEELE bore a bad reputation even in his time, **1552–1596?** which was not so fastidious as our own.   He seems to have been a ragged fellow, indifferent to fame or fortune, not caring whether he got his dinner by a song, a jest, or even beggary or fraud.   Yet he wrote plays in which there is a good deal of poetic merit, and he was a scholar of classical training, as his poetry shows.   *The Arraignment of Paris, The Old Wives' Tale, David and Bethsabe, The Battle of Alcazar,* are titles of his plays.

The Arraignment of Paris tells the classic story of the Judgment of Paris and the award of the golden apple. With the characteristic flattery of the age, Peele ends this drama by bringing in Diana to present the apple to Queen Elizabeth, who is judged to possess the beauty of Venus, the majesty of Juno, and the wisdom of Minerva, all combined in her own royal person.

Peele has a delicate, poetic touch, although he has less dramatic power than any of the four poets I have mentioned. His allusions to Nature are in the spirit of a true poet. He speaks of—

> "The primrose and the purple hyacinth,
> The dainty violet and the wholesome minth,
> The double daisy, and the cowslip, queen
> Of summer flowers, do overpeer the green,
> And round about the valley as ye pass,
> Ye may ne see, for peeping flowers, the grass."

We can hardly believe that the man who was familiar with such blossoms could be a frequenter of miserable taverns and a low fellow given to coarse jests and rude buffoonery.

ROBERT GREENE'S life is not more pleasant to read of than that of George Peele, his friend and associ- **1560-1592** ate. Greene was a man of education, and says he had a degree from both Oxford and Cambridge. He travelled on the Continent, and wasted his time in bad company, until finally he lost his health and his credit with his friends. "Then," he says, "I became an author of plays and of penny-a-line pamphlets, so that I soon grew famous in that quality, that who for that trade known so ordinary about London as Robin Greene."

His death was caused by a supper in which he ate and drank too much of pickled herring and Rhenish wine. He died in a wretched lodging, where the wife of a poor shoemaker tended him in his last moments, and after death crowned him, at his request, with the poet's garland of bay-leaves. Can you imagine anything more grim than the dead poet in his miserable garret, crowned with the green wreath of bays?

Greene wrote a very large number of novels, poems, plays, and a great many pamphlets or shorter works, which, in that day, were called prose tracts. Of these prose tracts, the two most notable are *The Triumph of Time*—a very pretty story, and well told, used by Shakespeare for the plot of *The Winter's Tale*—and *The Groat's Worth of Wit, bought with a Million of Repentance,* written in his last illness, in which he recounts the chief facts of his life.

and gives vent to his penitence for his bad and useless
career.   This last tract has been much talked about, because there is an ill-natured allusion in it to Shakespeare,
which makes it seem as if Greene and his companions were
rather jealous of Shakespeare's success as a play-writer, and
accused him of using some of their works as the foundation
for his more popular plays.

Greene wrote five plays known to be his.   He may have
written a good many more which have not come down to
us.   The best of his plays, I think, is *The Honorable
History of Friar Bacon and Friar Bungay*.   The plot of
this is varied ; one part of it turns on the loves of Prince
Edward and his friend Ned Lacy, Earl of Lincoln, for
Margaret, a gamekeeper's fair daughter ; the other part of
the plot relates to the great friar, Bacon, the most learned
Englishman of the thirteenth century, of whom many wonderful fables were told in English legend and ballad.

Bacon and Bungay have made a brass head, which, it
has been predicted, will speak, and tell them how to make
a wall to surround England, and render her proof against
all foes.   When the head is done, the friar, worn out with
sleepless work, sets his servant, Miles, to watch it while he
gets a little sleep.   Here is the scene in which Miles is
set to watch : —

[*Enter Friar Bacon, with a lighted lamp* **and a** *book in his hand,
Miles following him, armed in a ridiculous manner, from head to foot.*]

Bacon (*drawing the curtains and revealing the brazen head*).   Miles,
where are you?

Miles.   Here, sir.

Bacon.   How chance you tarry so long?

Miles.   Think you that the watching of the brazen head craves no
furniture?   I warrant you, sir, I have so armed myself that if all your
devils come, I will not fear them an inch.

Bacon.   Miles, thou know'st that I have dived into hell,
         And sought the darkest palaces of the fiends;
         That with my magic spells great Belcephon
         Hath left his lodge and kneeled at my cell;
         The rafters of the earth rent from the poles,
         And three-formed Luna hid her silver looks,
         Trembling upon her concave continent,
         When Bacon read upon his magic book.

With seven years tossing necromantic charms,
Poring upon dark Hecate's principles,
I have framed out a monstrous head of brass,
That, by the enchanting forces of the devil,
Shall tell out strange and uncouth aphorisms,
And girt fair England with a wall of brass.
Bungay and I have watched these threescore days,
And now our vital spirits crave some rest. . . .
Now, Miles, in thee rests Friar Bacon's weal;
The honor and renown of all his life
Hangs in the watching of this brazen head. . .
This night thou watch, for ere the morning star
Sends out his glorious glister in the north,
The head will speak; then, Miles, upon thy life,
Wake me, for then, by magic art, I 'll work
To end my seven years' task with excellence. . . .
Draw close the curtains, Miles; now, for thy life,
Be watchful and —   *[He falls asleep.*

Miles. So! I thought you would talk yourself asleep anon, and 't is no marvel, for Bungay on the days, and he on the nights, have watched just these ten and fifty days. Now this is the night, and 't is my task and no more. Heaven bless me! what a goodly head it is, and a nose! You talk of *nos autem glorificare,* but *here* 's a nose that I warrant may be called *nos autem populare,* — for the people of the parish. Well, I am furnished with weapons; now, sir, I will set me down by a post, and make it as good as a watchman to wake me if I chance to slumber. . . . *[A great noise of thunder heard.]* Up, Miles, to your task; here 's some of your master's hobgoblins abroad.

[Thunder — The head speaks.]

Head. Time is.
Miles. Time *is.* Why, Master Brazen-head, have you such a capital nose and answer you with syllables, "Time is"? Is this all my master's cunning to spend seven years study about time is? Well, sir, it may be we shall have better some orations of it anon. I 'll watch you as narrowly as ever you were watched.   . .

[Thunder and lightning.]

The Head. Time was.
Miles. Well, Friar Bacon, you have spent your seven years' study well, that can make your head speak but two words at once, "Time was." Yea, marry, time was when my master was a wise man, but that was before he began to make the brazen head. . . . What! a fresh noise! Take thy pistols in hand, Miles.

[Thunder again.]

The Head. Time is past.
[Flash of lightning, in which a hand appears with hammer that breaks the head.]

Miles (in affright). Master! master! Up! your head speaks!
There's such a thunder and lightning that I warrant all Oxford is up
in arms. Out of your bed; the latter day is come.

Bacon (arousing). Miles, I come. Oh, passing warily watched!
Bacon will make thee next himself in love. When spake the head?

Miles. When spake the head? Did you not say that it should tell
strange principles of philosophy? Why, sir, it speaks but two words
at a time.

· *Bacon.* Why, villain, hath it spoken oft?

Miles. Oft? Ay, marry hath it, — thrice; but in all these three
times it hath uttered only seven words.

Bacon. As how?

Miles. Marry, sir, the first time he said, "Time is," as if Fabius
Commentator should have pronounced a sentence; then he said,
"Time was;" and the third time, with thunder and lightning, as in
great choler, he said, "Time is past."

Bacon. 'T is past, indeed!
　　　Ay, villain, time is past!
　　　My life, my fame, my glory, — all are past!
　　　Bacon, the turrets of thy hope are ruined down,
　　　Thy seven years' study lieth in the dust,
　　　Thy brazen head lies broken, through a slave
　　　That watched and would not when the head did will.

There is a near approach to the brightness and wit of
later English comedy in Greene; and although there is a
great deal of rubbish in his writings, there is also much
poetry, and much ingenuity in the construction of his
plots. I have always felt a sympathy with his fate since
I read this sentence in some old biography: "It is
reported that he was *the first English poet who ever wrote
for bread.*"

We could not pass JOHN LYLY by without mention. He
seems to have been more respectable in manners
1553–1601 and social position than most of this group of
play-writers, and he wrote one book, fashionable beyond all
others in its day, which gave a new word to the language.
This is the romance of *Euphues*, from which the word
euphuism is derived. One hardly knows how to define
euphuism. The dictionary says it is "a fastidious delicacy
of language;" but that does not fully express it. It was
a style of speaking and writing full of stilted and affected
phrases, redundant in comparisons, crowded with foreign

and classical allusions, — a simple meaning wrapped up in a mass of words. We wonder that it could have been popular with people of sturdy English common-sense at any time. Yet in the court of Elizabeth euphuism was so fashionable that all the lords and ladies talked in this affected way, and one of the historians says : " That beauty in court which could not parley euphuism was as little regarded as she which now there speaks not French."

Yet, in spite of its absurdities, Lyly's book has merit, and does not deserve the abuse that has been thrown upon it by critics who seem to believe it as absurd as the speech of those who imitated it. It is full of good sense, although sometimes expressed in such a roundabout manner ; and better advice than he gives for the rearing and education of youth has rarely been written. And the book is full of noble sentences, like these : —

" It is not descent of birth that maketh gentlemen,—not great *manors*, but good manners, that express the image of dignity. There is copper coin of the same stamp that gold is, yet is it not current."

" The wise man liveth as well in a far country as in his own home. It is not the nature of the place, but the disposition of the person, that maketh life pleasant."

" The greatest harm you can do to the envious is to do well."

" If you will be cherished when you be old, be courteous when you be young."

These sentences, gleaned at random from *Euphues*, show how much there is fine in it ; and when I hear it spoken of as a book " which did incalculable mischief by vitiating the taste and corrupting the language," I feel like saying, in the words of a modern writer, Charles Kingsley, " Have these critics ever read it ? If they have, I pity them if they have not found it, in spite of occasional tediousness and pedantry, as brave, righteous, and pious a book as a man need look into."

Euphues must be classed among works of fiction, although it hardly meets any of our ideas of a novel. The chief character in the book is Euphues, a young gentleman of

Athens, who writes long letters and keeps up interminable conversations with the other characters, but chiefly with the heroine, Lucilla, with whom he is in love. By and by Lucilla jilts him, which gives him an opportunity to inveigh in the following style against women, in one of his letters to his friend Philautus : —

" It is a world to see how commonly we are blinded with the collusions of women, and more enticed by their ornaments being artificial than their proportions being natural. I loathe almost to think on their ointments and apothecary drugs, the sleeking of their faces and all their slibber sauces, which bring queasiness to the stomach, and disquiet to the mind.

" Take from them their periwigs, their paintings, their jewels, their rolls, their bolsterings, and thou shalt soon perceive a woman is the least part of herself. When they once be robbed of their robes, then will they appear so odious, so ugly, so monstrous that thou wilt rather think them serpents than saints, and so like hags that thou wilt fear rather to be enchanted than enamoured. Look in their closets, and there shalt thou find an apothecary's shop of sweet confections, a surgeon's box of sundry salves, a pedlar's pack of new fangles. Besides all this, their shadows, their spots, their lawns, their ruffs, their rings. If every one of these things severally be not of force to move thee, yet all of them jointly should mortify thee. . . . And yet, Philautus, I would not that all women should take pepper in the nose, in that I have disclosed the legerdemains of a few, for well I know none wince except she be galled, neither any be offended unless she be guilty."

Although *Euphues* is the most famous of Lyly's works, yet he was noted in his time as a writer of plays. Several of these had appeared before Shakespeare began to be known as a dramatist. The best of his plays is *Campaspe*. Its principal characters are Alexander of Macedon and the painter Apelles. Alexander is in love with a beautiful young girl, Campaspe, whom he has taken captive in war, and employs Apelles to paint her portrait. The artist also loves Campaspe, and when the monarch discovers this, he hesitates for a moment between jealousy and generosity, but at last resigns her to Apelles. It is a very pretty plot, although simple and without strong dramatic interest. It

is written, **not in blank verse,** but in prose, in sentences
that remind **one** of *Euphues ;* but Lyly proved that **he was**
a poet by the beautiful lyrics found in his **plays. One of**
the most perfect of **these is** the song of *Cupid and Campaspe,* **sung by the** painter Apelles as **he works at his easel**
on the portrait of Campaspe : —

> " Cupid and my Campaspe played
> **At** cards for kisses : Cupid paid.
> He stakes his quiver, bow, and arrows,
> His mother's doves and team of sparrows :
> Loses them, too. Then down he throws
> The coral of his lip, the rose
> Growing on 's cheek (but none knows how),
> With these **the** crystal **of** his brow,
> And then **the dimple of his chin :**
> All these **did my Campaspe win.**
> At last he set **her both his** eyes :
> She won, and Cupid blind did rise.
> O Love, has she done this to thee ?
> What shall, **alas!** become of me ? "

XXII.

ON CHRISTOPHER MARLOWE, THE GREAT PREDECESSOR OF SHAKESPEARE.

THE greatest of **all the** dramatic poets who wrote before Shakespeare was CHRISTOPHER MARLOWE, whom
his friends familiarly called "Kit." **He was a**
boon companion of Greene and Peele, a little **1564–1593**
younger than either, — born, indeed, in the very year with
our great Shakespeare. But he began to write much earlier, and when he died, only three or four of Shakespeare's
works had appeared.

As soon as Marlowe left college he went to London **and**
began to write for the theatre ; very likely he acted too, as
most of the play-writers did when they failed **to** earn a live-
lihood by the pen alone. He must have begun to write very

young, for he was the author of at least six plays, and took part, probably, in the writing of several others; yet he was only twenty-nine when his life came to a disreputable and tragic end.   A quarrel arose between himself and a boon companion named Francis Archer in a tavern which they frequented, and as Marlowe angrily drew his dagger, Archer seized his hand and stabbed him in the head, so that, according to an old rhyme which tells the story, —

> " He groaned, and word spake never more,
>   Pierced through both eye and brain."

Marlowe has a bad reputation, although whether it was entirely deserved it would be difficult now to tell.   The Puritans had begun in his time to wage a fierce war against the stage and all dramatic writings, and they lost no opportunity to hold up to horror all persons who were concerned in plays or play-writing.   The manner of Marlowe's death added to the bad odor in which he was held by his enemies, but we must remember that this was an age in which tavern quarrels and street broils were not infrequent, and better men than Marlowe were quick to draw daggers, and to use them.   Although he was no better, he may have been no worse than many other men whose names have not been so roughly handled.   However this may be, a strong moral was drawn from Marlowe's death by the opposers of the drama, and a ballad on the subject, called *The Atheist's Tragedy*, in which Marlowe is called *Wormall*, ends with this stanza : —

> "Take warning, ye that plays do make,
>   And ye that them do act ;
> Desist in time, for Wormall's sake,
>   And think upon this fact."

The first play by Marlowe of which we have any knowledge is the first part of *Tamburlaine the Great*.   It is claimed by the most careful students that this is the first play in which blank verse was used in a public theatre. Before this, the plays had been either in prose or rhyme, blank verse having been used only in private performances at court, or before college **societies**. You will be interested, **therefore,** to read a little of **this** verse, which is thus **claimed** **to be the** beginning of English dramatic poetry.

Tamburlaine, the hero of the play, is a shepherd **who has** taken up arms with design to become king **of Persia. He** **is,** like **all** Marlowe's heroes, a man of boundless **ambition** and courage. These lines which I quote are from his speech **to** Theridamas, one of the captains of **the** king of Persia, who **has been** sent to take Tamburlaine prisoner. The great warrior thus persuades the envoy of the **king to** desert his master **and** follow the fortunes of the great Tamburlaine : —

> *Tamburlaine.* In thee, thou valiant man of Persia,
> I see the folly of thy emperor.
> Art thou but captain of a thousand horse,
> That by characters graven in thy brows,
> And by thy martial face and stout aspect,
> Deserves to have the leading of a host?
> Forsake thy king, and do but join with me,
> And we will triumph over all the world.
> I hold the Fates bound fast in iron chains,
> And with my hand turn **Fortune's** wheel about;
> And sooner shall the **sun fall** from his sphere,
> Than Tamburlaine be slain or overcome.
> **Draw** forth thy sword, thou mighty man-at-arms,
> Intending but to raze my charmed skin,
> And Jove himself will stretch his hand from heaven
> **To ward** the blow and shield me safe from harm.
>   .   .   .   .   .
> If thou wilt stay with me, **renowned** man,
> And lead thy thousand **horse, with** my conduct,
> Besides thy share of this Egyptian prize,
> Those thousand horse shall sweat with martial spoil
> Of conquered kingdoms and of cities sacked;
> Both we will walk upon the lofty cliffs,
> And Christian merchants, that with Russian stems
> Plough up huge furrows in the Caspian Sea,
> Shall rail to us as lords of all the lake;
> Both we will reign as consuls of the earth,
> And mighty kings shall be our senators.
> Jove sometimes masked in a shepherd's weed,
> And by those steps that he has scaled **the heavens,**
> May we become immortal like the gods.
> Join with me now in this my mean estate

> (I call it mean, because, being yet obscure,
> The nations far removed admire me not),
> And when my name and honor shall be spread
> As far as Boreas claps his brazen wings,
> Or fair Boötes sends his cheerful light,
> Then thou shalt be competitor with me,
> And sit with Tamburlaine in all his majesty.

This speech is in a lofty spirit of boasting, but it showed the power of what Ben Jonson called " Marlowe's mighty line."

Of all Marlowe's plays, none has been so famous as *Faustus,* which has the same plot that the great German poet, Goethe, used afterwards. There is great power in Marlowe's play, although in parts it is very weak and puerile. Faust sells his soul to Mephistopheles on condition that for twenty-four years Mephistopheles shall be his servant and do his will. The finest passage in *Faustus* is the close of the play, in which he awaits the fiends who are to bear away his soul to eternal torment. As the clock slowly strikes eleven, Faust is left in his chamber alone. Faust speaks : —

> Ah, Faustus,
> Now hast thou but one bare hour to live,
> And then thou must be damned perpetually!
> Stand still, you ever-moving spheres of heaven,
> That time may cease, and midnight never come!
> Fair Nature's eye, rise, rise again, and make
> Perpetual day; or let this hour be but
> A year, a month, a week, a natural day,
> That Faustus may repent, and save his soul.
>
>   .   .   .   .   .   .
>
> [*The clock strikes the half-hour.*]
>
> Ah! half the hour is past; 't will all be past anon.
> O God!
> If thou wilt not have mercy on my soul,
> Impose some end to my incessant pain;
> Let Faustus live in hell a thousand years,
> A hundred thousand, and at last be saved!
> Oh, no end is limited to damned souls!
> Why wert thou not a creature wanting soul?
> Oh, why is this immortal that thou hast?
>   . . . All beasts are happy,

For when they die,
Their souls are soon dissolved in elements;
But mine must live, still to be plagued in hell.
        [*Clock strikes twelve.*]
It strikes! it strikes! now, body, turn to air,
Or Lucifer will bear thee quick to hell!
        [*Storm of thunder and lightning.*]
Oh, soul, be changed to little water drops,
And fall into the ocean, ne'er be found!
[*At this the devils enter and bear off Faustus.*]

The hero of another of Marlowe's plays, *The Jew of Malta*, is frequently compared with Shakespeare's Shylock, although there is really very little likeness between the characters in the two plays. Barabas, the Jew of Malta, is, like Shylock, a man of intellect and power. He says of himself, "Barabas is born to better chance, and framed of finer mould than common men." But he does not excite our sympathy as Shylock does. His cruelty is overdrawn, his malignity becomes vulgar, and the heaped-up horrors of the play become at last ridiculous. But although the play is unequal, there are strong passages in it. When the governor of Malta has taken from the Jews half their property to fill the treasury of the city, and has ordered that Barabas be stripped of half his wealth, the old Israelite thus hurls curses after him : —

The plagues of Egypt and the curse of Heaven,
Earth's barrenness, and all men's hatred,
Inflict upon them, thou great *Primus Motor*,
And here, upon my knees striking the earth,
I ban their souls to everlasting pains
And extreme tortures of the fiery deep,
That thus have dealt with me in my distress. . . .
    1st Jew. Yet, Brother Barabas, remember Job.
    Barabas. What tell you me of Job? I wot his wealth
Was written thus : he had seven thousand sheep,
Three thousand camels, and two hundred yoke
Of laboring oxen; but for every one of these,
Had they been valued at indifferent rate,
I had at home, and in mine argosy .
As much as would have bought his beasts and him,
And yet have kept enough to live upon. . . .
    2d Jew. Good Barabas, be patient.

Barabas. Ay, I pray you leave me in my patience.
You, that were ne'er possessed of wealth, are pleased with want;
But give him liberty at least to mourn,
That in a field, amidst his enemies,
Doth see his soldiers slain, himself disarmed,
And knows no means for his recovery.

There is, I am sure, great power in the passages I have quoted, and when we remember they were written by a man so young, when the English drama existed only in very crude forms, and without passion or dramatic interest, we must admire a genius of such originality, which blazed so highly and went out so suddenly.

Besides these which I have mentioned, Marlowe wrote the *Tragedy of Edward II.*, which has reminded some readers of Shakespeare's *Richard II.*, principally because the fate of these two kings has so much resemblance. There are also two other plays, of *Lust's Dominion* and the *Massacre at Paris*, which are doubtfully ascribed to him, both of which are very much in his style. In nearly all these plays his heroes, like Barabas and Tamburlaine, are men of great thirst for power and of unbridled ambition. Perhaps Marlowe painted in them the passions that ruled in his own breast; perhaps, too, like Faust, he was consumed with insatiate desire for dominion over the whole realm of knowledge. In spite of his faults, none of the dramatists before Shakespeare approach him in genius, and I leave him regretfully, wishing we might dwell longer on his merits.

There are several other names, well noted in their time, which meet us on the threshold of the Shakespearean age. THOMAS KYD was one of the popular play-writers in London when Shakespeare first began to try his hand at authorship, and Kyd's *Spanish Tragedy* then delighted the theatre-goers. THOMAS NASH, also a play-writer, and a friend of Marlowe and Greene, had produced his play of *Will Summer's Last Will and Testament*, in a barn on the outskirts of London, when the players were driven outside the city by the raging of the plague. In this play is a most musical little spring-song, which will give you **an idea of Nash's** quality as **a poet :** —

> " Spring, the sweet spring, is the year's pleasant king ;
>   Then blooms each thing, then maids dance in ring,
>   Cold doth not sting, the pretty birds do sing
>   Cuckoo, jug, jug, pu-we, to-witta-woo !

> " The palm and May make country houses gay,
>   Lambs frisk and play, the shepherds pipe all day,
>   And hear we aye birds tune this merry lay,
>   Cuckoo, jug, jug, pu-we, to-witta-woo !

> **" The fields breathe sweet, the** daisies kiss our feet,
>   **Young lovers meet, old wives** a sunning sit ;
>   **In every street these tunes** our ears do greet,
>   **Cuckoo, jug, jug,** pu-we, to-witta-woo ! "

Another poet, THOMAS LODGE, wrote several **plays, a** number of them in conjunction with other play- Birth unwriters. His best work, for **us,** is **a beautiful** known. story called *Rosalynd, or, Euphues' Golden* Died **1625.** *Legacy,* a really golden bequest, because Shakespeare used it for the plot of that most beautiful play, *As You Like It.* Lodge early gave up writing stories and dramas, and afterwards became **a** physician. He wrote a treatise **on the** plague which raged in London, but he could **not** have found its cure, for he died of the disease shortly afterwards.

I have thus briefly touched upon **the** chief names among the dramatists who heralded Shakespeare, the poets who were at work for the stage when he first came to London. They were nearly all men of fiery imagination, using language with a freedom and unconventionality which no modern poet could venture upon, and which would not, to-day, **be** tolerated. These men set the fashion for later poets, **and** helped establish the rules laid down by our grammarians and dictionary-makers ; nowadays words have each **their** rank and place in language, and whoever dares misuse **one** is arraigned by a host of verbal critics.

The most fortunate **thing** in the beginning **of** the English drama is that these early writers were not afraid to be original. They adhered to no models, and did not follow the rules of the elder literature of Greece and of Rome. True, they were men of classical learning, and their verses are stuffed full of classical allusions which show this. Greene's milkmaids and farmers talk of Apollo and Diana, and other gods and goddesses, as if they were fellow-servants, and the names of ancient myth and history constantly appear in Marlowe and Peele. Yet, in spite of this, they kept dramatic poetry free from bonds. They gave it a living reality, and put into it human passion. In a word, they made a *national* drama.

The English drama owes its best part to that sturdy Teutonic spirit, underlying all that is best in our literature, which resented too much innovation on its native quality, and would speak out for itself, in spite of fashions of speech regarded as more exact or more comely. These earlier dramatists were fit precursors of Shakespeare, who, great as he was, owed much to the fact that such men preceded him.

XXIII.

On William Shakespeare, his Life, Character, and Works.

WILLIAM SHAKESPEARE is the greatest name in English poetry, and ranks among the greatest of the world. The Greek Homer, the Italian Dante, the English Shakespeare, are three grand figures that stand out pre-eminent in the history of the world's literature for three thousand years.

1564–1616

Of the man Shakespeare very few facts are known ; but this concerns us less, because it is with the poet, and not with the man, that we have to deal. He was born at Stratford-upon-Avon, in Warwickshire, of a respectable family, his father a well-to-do townsman who held several offices. He went to the grammar-school in his native town probably till he was about fourteen. Then some of his biographers think he may have been a lawyer's clerk, as that would explain the close knowledge of law terms that he shows in his plays; others argue that he taught school; others still, that he was an apprentice to a butcher. Whether he followed any or all of these callings, is not certain; the only fact of which we are certain, between the time of his leaving school and going to London, is that at eighteen he married Anne Hathaway, who lived in the village of Shottery, a mile or two from Stratford, and that after the birth of three children, and when he was about twenty-three years old, he went to London to seek his fortune.

There is an old story that he went deer-poaching at Charlecote, the estate of Sir Thomas Lucy, a few miles from Stratford, and that his arrest and trial for this trespass were the direct cause of his leaving his native town. But this story has been doubted; and so has another tradition that when he reached London he first gained a scanty living by holding horses outside the theatre for gentlemen who came to see the play. Whether either of these stories is true makes very little difference in this history. It is certain that he was not long in London before he was employed in a company of players in some capacity. He was an actor as well as a play-writer; we do not know which calling he took up first. It seems to me probable that his first plays were written in collaboration with other play-wrights, or that he first revised and adapted other men's works to meet the demands of stage action. In such kind of attempts he could prove his ability before producing any drama entirely original. In any case, his rise was rapid. He had not been in London five years before he began to be known as a writer and to be heard of in the company of the best wits of the time; in ten years he was able to buy one of the finest estates in his native town; three or four years later, he bought more lands, gardens, and orchards in Stratford; and finally, in the year 1616, when he was fifty-two years old, a prosperous man, in the full vigor of life, he died suddenly of a fever, and was buried in the little church in his native town. This bald outline of a life is all we have of our greatest poet.

There has been much question and debate about the amount of Shakespeare's learning, and although there are some ingenious arguments to prove him a scholar, it seems evident that his opportunities for scholastic education were not equal to those of most literary men of his time. He was fourteen when he left the town grammar-school, and he never entered college. But we may be sure he did not miss any of his opportunities. I fancy him an eager reader of all the books he could lay hands on. The popular ballads, the old chronicles, the tales translated from Latin, French, and Italian, which were printed in small, paper-covered pamphlets, and called chap-books, — all these would furnish food for his devouring imagination. He had also, I can easily fancy, an eager ear, which was no less a source of culture than the eye. No speech of the clever people he met in London fell unheeded when Shakespeare was by. In the circle into which he came, conversations on poetry and philosophy, on the new theories in science and medicine, on all the great events of the time, must have been constantly going on about him. He must have heard the new philosophy of Bacon discussed by the most thoughtful men of the day; he could hear the cases of law argued by the most astute lawyers; the literature of Greece and that of Rome were quoted from and discussed by the scholars from the university, who, like himself, were getting their bread by writing for the stage; the brilliant actions of Queen Elizabeth's soldiers and sailors were the theme of discourse at every tavern; the romantic voyages of English ships in the attempts at the settlement of this untried continent, were recounted by men who took part in them. Never was any age richer in ideas than the age of Shakespeare; the very air swarmed with them, and all that he heard he gathered up into the vast storehouse of his brain and reproduced in lines that have since made the world wonder at the boundless depths, the prophetic heights, of his knowledge. This was *genius*, that could make even a commonplace suggestion that had fallen from the lips of some of his associates wear in his verse an air of prophecy. One of the most potent qualities of all the great poets of the world is this power of absorbing all that touches them, of appropriating from every channel all that can feed and enrich them ; and this quality evidently was Shakespeare's in an unusual degree.

When he died, in 1616, his plays had never been collected in a volume, and, indeed, many of them had never been printed at all. This has been a matter of wonder among many critics, and from this some have argued that Shakespeare was quite indifferent to his own fame. I do not believe this theory to be true. If we can judge anything of his personal feeling from his Sonnets, where he seems to have revealed *himself* as he never does in his plays, his genius had that consciousness of its own power which great genius almost always possesses. Again and again he claims the immortality of his lines, as when he says : —

> " Not marble, nor the gilded monuments
>   Of princes, shall outlive this powerful rhyme ;
> But you shall shine more bright in these contents,
>   Than unswept stone besmeared with sluttish time."
>
> SONNET LV.

> " Or I shall live your epitaph to make,
>   Or you survive, when I in earth am rotten ;
> From *hence* your memory death cannot take,
>   Although in me each part will be forgotten.
> Your name from *hence* immortal life shall have,
>   Though I, once gone, to all the world must die :
> The earth can yield me but a common grave,
>   When you entombed in men's eyes shall lie.
> *Your monument shall be my gentle verse,*
>   *Which eyes not yet created shall o'er-read,*
> *And tongues to be, your being shall rehearse,*
>   *When all the breathers of this world are dead ;*
> *You still shall live — such virtue hath my pen —*
>   *Where breath most breathes, even in the mouths of men."*
>
> SONNET LXXXI.

In many like instances in his Sonnets does he show that he did not esteem himself too lightly.

It seems very reasonable to believe, therefore, that the latest work of his life, when he had gained fortune and leisure, would have been to revise and edit all his works. Up to the time of his death it would have been unbusiness-like and unprofitable to interrupt his work for the theatre (a theatre in which he held a pecuniary interest) in order to print his plays, and so destroy in a measure their acting value. Shakespeare, by all the arguments we can draw from his life, was a thrifty, business-like man, interested in the accumulation of property and the building up of a name and an estate in his native Stratford. It would have been both foolish and improvident to cut off so suddenly a good income. But when he settled down at home in Stratford, he was still in the vigor and prime of life, with leisure before him to revise and rewrite all his plays in his own careful and painstaking way, and so put them into the shape in which he would have given them to the future. I cannot doubt he meant to do this, when that churl, Death, came in, and stopped his intent; and so we lost one of the best legacies the past could have made us, —the plays of Shakespeare edited by himself.

Seven years after Shakespeare's death, John Heminge and Henry Condell, two of his fellow-actors, who had known him well during his career as player and drama-tist, published the first edition of his works in a volume containing thirty-six plays. This is known as the Folio of 1623, and is the most valuable for students of Shake-speare. Previously eighteen of these plays had been printed separately in smaller books, called Quartos. As the popu-lar plays were withheld from publication while they were performed on the stage, many of the dramas were taken down in a kind of short-hand at the theatre and printed by some publisher, who would get them by foul means if he could not by fair payment. Such copies must necessarily be full of mistakes, and as the actors, and especially the clowns, often spoke much more than was set down for them, there were often gross interpolations in these unauthorized editions. Some of these Quartos had been more than once printed, and of the thirty-six plays eighteen had appeared in this way. Heminge and Condell, therefore, had for the basis of their work the best of these Quartos, such stage copies of the plays as they could get, and that intimate knowledge of the dramas, in which, as members of the company that first produced them, they must often have performed different parts. But even with their best care, these first editors of Shakespeare, to whom we all owe a debt of gratitude, could not avoid some mistakes in a work so full of difficulties.

To these thirty-six plays *Pericles* was afterwards added, making thirty-seven, — the number now usually included in the collection of his works. But besides these thirty-seven, there are a number of others which have been claimed as Shakespeare's. There are three old plays still in existence which were printed in quarto, with Shakespeare's name on the title-page, and there are several others, with the initials W. Sh., or W. S., which Heminge and Condell did not put in their edition. Probably these plays are not Shakespeare's, but were printed with his name by some publisher who knew Shakespeare's popularity as a writer would be likely to sell any play that bore his name, or even his initials, on the title-page.

It was also a common custom, at this time, for writers for the stage to unite together to produce a play. There are some plays which have as many as five writers concerned in them, and two and three is a very common number in this joint authorship. *The Two Noble Kinsmen*, a play afterwards included among Beaumont and Fletcher's works, bore the name of Fletcher and Shakespeare as authors when first published in quarto ; and the play of *Henry VIII.*, in Shakespeare's works, is by many critics believed to be the joint production of Shakespeare and Fletcher again. Thus you will see that it is quite probable that some plays may have been put among Shakespeare's of which he was only the writer in part, and that others may have been left out in which Shakespeare may have had some share with other writers. Some of the thirty-seven plays which we now call Shakespeare's are thus under dispute.

First in doubtfulness comes *Titus Andronicus,* of which I shall say, for my own part, I do not think he wrote any portion of it.[1] It is also believed by many scholars that few entire scenes in *Pericles* are by Shakespeare, and that *Timon of Athens* was a sketch of a play from his hands filled out by other dramatists.

The *Taming of the Shrew* is certainly founded on an older play of the same title, which it follows in incident. As to the three parts of *Henry VI.,* they are mostly all under dispute, some critics believing that Shakespeare did not write the first part, and that the second and third parts are alterations of two old plays which still exist in evidence ; while others claim that he wrote all three, and that the older plays are his own earlier version of the plays, which he afterwards finished and revised more carefully. There has been a great deal written on both sides on all these plays, and most of the disputed points must forever remain undecided, or only a matter of individual opinion, and many lines which lie within the covers of his plays will be read a little doubtfully.

With regard to the sources for the plots of the plays, our knowledge is clearer. We know whence most have been derived, and from this evidence it would seem that Shakespeare rarely invented his plots. He took them wherever he found them, — in old poems, stories, translations from French or Italian ; in the old Roman or current English history, — wherever he could find a dramatic incident. In Holinshed's Chronicle History may be found many

---

[1] I have for a long time believed that *Titus Andronicus* was written by the same poet who wrote *Lust's Dominion,* a play sometimes ascribed to Marlowe. The hero of both plays is a Moor, and there is a general resemblance, while some lines are strikingly alike, as, for instance : —

> And do not now with quarrels shake the state,
> Which is already too much ruinate.
> > *Lust's Dominion.*

> Then afterwards to order well the state,
> That like events may ne'er it ruinate.
> > *Titus Andronicus.*

a hint. There he read of the troubled reign of Duncan of Scotland, his murder by Macbeth, the appearance of the three witches, and the fight between Macduff and Macbeth. In Plutarch's Lives he read of great Cæsar's assassination, the conspiracy and death of Brutus, as well as the loves of Antony and Cleopatra. In some charming novels by Greene and by Thomas Lodge he got the plots for *Winter's Tale* and *As You Like It.* Thus the eye of the dramatist was quick to see in all places whatever would serve his purpose. The inventive power of the novelist either he did not have, or did not care to use. I sometimes fancy that the lack of this power stimulated the power of the dramatist, — that he could better work the men and women of his imagination, when, like the men and women of the real world, they were controlled by a destiny which he had not shaped for them.

From this slight glance I have given you of his methods, you will see that Shakespeare was a busy, hard-working man, absorbed and interested in affairs which filled his life for over twenty years. While so many of the other poets, like Greene, Peele, and Marlowe, lived and died in drunkenness and misery, Shakespeare was a prosperous shareholder in the theatre where he was also an actor. While busy with his own work for the stage, he was interested in revising and criticising the works of other men ; and all this time he was building up a good name and estate in his native town, which was very likely the main purpose of his life. The greatest poet of his age, he was also a practical man, with a breadth of intellect which could include the details of the petty affairs of life.

In studying Shakespeare, go first of all to his works, and not to critics. To know thoroughly Shakespeare's plays with appreciative knowledge would be of itself a liberal education. Even if you should read thoroughly only four such plays as *Hamlet, The Merchant of Venice, Julius Cæsar,* and *As You Like It,* you would have in your mind a treasure which would be priceless.

XXIV.

EXTRACTS FROM SHAKESPEARE'S PLAYS, — "RICHARD II.;"
"HAMLET;" "THE TEMPEST."

IN illustration of Shakespeare's poetry, I am going to
give extracts from plays written at different periods.
First, from *Richard II.*, which was written in the earlier
period of his career; then from *Hamlet*, which was probably produced in the middle of his life as author; and,
finally, from *The Tempest*, which is one of the latest, if not
the very latest, of his productions. The scene from *Richard
II.* is that in which John of Gaunt, the uncle of the king,
lying at point of death, calls for Richard, that he may warn
him of his misgovernment, which is bringing so many
troubles on the realm.

As the scene opens, Gaunt lies on a couch, his brother,
the Duke of York, standing near : —

> *Gaunt.*   Will the king come, that I may breathe my last
> In wholesome counsel to his unstaid youth?
> *York.*   Vex not yourself, nor strive not with your breath ;
> For all in vain comes counsel to his ear.
> *Gaunt.*   Oh, but they say the tongues of dying men
> Enforce attention like deep harmony :
> Where words are scarce, they are seldom spent in vain,
> For they breathe truth that breathe their words in pain.
> He that no more must say is listened more
> Than they whom youth and ease have taught to glose ;
> More are men's ends marked than their lives before :
> The setting sun, and music at the close,
> As the last taste of sweets, is sweetest last,
> Writ in remembrance, more than things long past :
> Though Richard my life's counsel would not hear,
> My death's sad tale may yet undeaf his ear.
>
> .   .   .   .
>
> Methinks I am a prophet new inspired,
> And thus, expiring, do foretell of him :
> His fierce, rash blaze of riot cannot last,
> For violent fires soon burn out themselves ;
> Small showers last long, but sudden storms are short ;

He tires betimes that spurs too fast betimes;
With eager feeding food doth choke the feeder.
Light vanity, insatiate cormorant,
Consuming means, soon preys upon itself.
This royal throne of kings, this scepter'd isle,
This earth of majesty, this seat of Mars,
This other Eden, demi-paradise,
This fortress built by Nature for herself
Against infection and the hand of war,
This happy breed of men, this little world,
This precious stone set in the silver sea,
Which serves it in the office of a wall
Or as a moat defensive to a house,
Against the envy of less happier lands,
This blessed plot, this earth, this realm, this England,

This land of such dear souls, this dear, dear land, —
Dear for her reputation through the world, —
Is now leased out (I die pronouncing it)
Like to a tenement or pelting farm:
England, bound in with the triumphant sea,
Whose rocky shore beats back the envious siege
Of watery Neptune, is now bound in with shame,
With inky blots and rotten parchment bonds:
That England, that was wont to conquer others,
Hath made a shameful conquest of itself.

This, as I have said before, is from one of Shakespeare's earlier plays. You will notice, in studying his works, that when Shakespeare was younger he very often used rhymed couplets, as in this extract, instead of blank verse. As he grew older he used rhyme less and less. In *Hamlet* and *As You Like It*, which he wrote about the middle of his life, there are few rhymes, except occasionally a couplet at the close of a scene; in *The Tempest* and *The Winter's Tale*, which are among his latest plays, he almost altogether discarded rhymes.

Hamlet is one of Shakespeare's grandest plays, — probably no other is so much acted, read, and studied as this one. It is difficult to select from a play which is so perfect as a whole; but as an example of Shakespeare's wonderful humor, which could touch at the same time both tears and laughter, I have selected the scene in which two gravediggers are making a grave for Ophelia, who has gone mad, and in her madness was drowned. **The two** grave-diggers **enter the** churchyard, spades **in hand;** the first **is a jolly old man who has been so long at his business that it is pure custom with** him **; the second is younger, but less active in wit than his companion. The old man** begins thus : —

1st Clown. **Is she to be buried in** Christian burial that wilfully **seeks** her own salvation ?

2d Clown. I tell thee she **is: and therefore** make her grave straight : **the crowner hath sat on her, and finds it Christian** burial.

1st Clown. **How can that be, unless she drowned** herself in her own defence ?

2d Clown. Why, 't is found so.

1st Clown. **It** must be *se offendendo ,* **it** cannot be else. For here **lies the point : If I drown** myself wittingly, it argues an act : and an **act hath** three branches ; **it is,** to act, to **do,** and to perform : argal, she **drowned** herself wittingly.

2d Clown. Nay, but **hear** you, goodman delver —

1st Clown. **Give me leave.** Here lies the water ; good : **here** stands **the man; good : if the man go to** this **water, and** drown himself, it is, will he, **nill he, he goes, — mark** you that **; but if the** water **come to him and drown him, he drowns not himself:** argal, he that is not guilty **of his own death shortens not his own life.**

2d Clown. But is this law ?

1st Clown. **Ay, marry, is 't; crowner's quest law.**

2d Clown. **Will you ha' the truth on 't ?** If **this had** not been **a gentlewoman, she should have been buried out of** Christian **burial.**

1st Clown. **Why,** there thou say'st : and the more pity that great **folk** should have countenance in this world to drown or hang themselves, more than their even Christian. Come, my spade. There is **no** ancient gentlemen but gardeners, ditchers, and grave-makers : they **hold up** Adam's profession.

2d Clown. Was he a gentleman ?

1st Clown. He was the first **that** ever bore arms.

2d Clown. **Why, he had none.**

1st Clown. What, art a heathen ? How dost thou understand the Scripture ? **The Scripture** says Adam **digged:** could he dig without arms ? I 'll put **another** question to **thee ; if** thou answerest me not to the purpose, **confess** thyself —

2d Clown. **Go to.**

1st Clown. **What is he that** builds stronger than either the mason, **the shipwright, or the carpenter ?**

2d Clown. The gallows-maker, for that frame outlives a thousand tenants.

1st Clown. I like thy wit well, in good faith : the gallows does **well;** but *how* does it well ? It does well to those that do ill : now thou dost ill to say the gallows is built stronger than the church : argal, the gallows may do well to thee. To 't again, come.

2d Clown. Who builds stronger than a mason, a shipwright, or a carpenter ?

1st Clown. Ay, tell me that, and unyoke.

2d Clown. Marry, now I can tell.

1st Clown. To 't.

2d Clown. Mass, I cannot tell.

[*Enter Hamlet, the Prince off Denmark, and his friend Horatio, at a distance.*]

1st Clown. Cudgel thy brains no more about it, for your dull ass will not mend his pace with beating; and when you are asked this question next, say a *grave-maker.* The houses that he makes last till doomsday. Go, get thee to Yaughan; fetch me a stoup of liquor.

[*2d Clown exit.*

1st Clown [*digs and sings*] —

> In youth, when I did love, did love,
> Methought 't was very sweet
> To contract, O, the time, for, ah, my behove,
> O, methought, there was nothing meet.

Hamlet. Has this fellow no feeling of his business, that he sings at grave-making ?

Horatio. Custom hath made it in him a property of easiness.

Hamlet. 'T is e'en so : the hand of little employment hath the daintier sense.

1st Clown [*sings*] : —

> But age, with his stealing steps,
> Hath claw'd me in his clutch,
> And hath shipped me intil the land,
> As if I had never been such. [*Throws up a skull.*

Hamlet. That skull had a tongue in it, and could sing once : how the knave jowls it to the ground, as if it were Cain's jawbone, that did the first murder ! It might be the pate of a politician, which this ass now overreaches ; one that would circumvent God, might it not ?

Horatio. It might, my lord.

Hamlet. Or of a courtier ; which could say, "Good morrow, sweet lord ! How dost thou, good lord ?" This might be my lord such-a-one, that praised my lord such-a-one's horse, when he meant to beg it ; might it not ?

Horatio. Ay, my lord.

Hamlet. Why, e'en so ; and now my Lady Worms ; chapless, and knocked about the mazzard with a sexton's spade : here 's fine revolution, if we had the trick to see 't. Did these bones cost no more the breeding, but to play at loggats with 'em ? Mine ache to think on't. . . . [*Clown throws up another skull.*

Hamlet. There 's another ! Why might not that be the skull of a lawyer ? Where be his quiddets now, his quillets, his cases, his tenures, and his tricks ? Why does he suffer this rude knave now to

knock him about the sconce with a dirty shovel, and will not tell him
of his action of battery? Hum! This fellow might be in 's time a
great-buyer of land, with his statutes, his recognizances, his fines, his
double vouchers, his recoveries: is this the fine of his fines, and the
recovery of his recoveries, to have his fine pate full of fine dirt? Will
his vouchers vouch him no more of his purchases, and double ones
too, than the length and breadth of a pair of indentures? The very
conveyances of his lands will hardly lie in this box; and must the
inheritor himself have no more? . . . I will speak to this fellow.
[*To the Clown.*] Whose grave 's this, sir?

1st Clown. Mine, sir. . . .

Hamlet. I think it be thine indeed; for thou liest in 't.

1st Clown. You lie out on 't, sir, and therefore it is not yours:
for my part, I do not lie in 't, and yet it is mine. . . .

Hamlet. What man dost thou dig it for?

1st Clown. For no man, sir.

Hamlet. What woman, then?

1st Clown. For none, neither.

Hamlet. Who is to be buried in 't?

1st Clown. One that was a woman, sir; but, rest her soul, she 's
dead.

Hamlet. How absolute the knave is! We must speak by the
card, or equivocation will undo us. By the Lord, Horatio, these
three years I have taken note of it; the age is grown so picked that
the toe of the peasant comes so near the heel of the courtier, he galls
his kibe. . . .

1st Clown [*picking up a skull*]. Here's a skull now; this skull
has lain in the earth three and twenty years.

Hamlet. Whose was it? . . .

1st Clown. A pestilence on him for a mad rogue! 'a poured a
flagon of Rhenish on my head once. This same skull, sir, was Yorick's
skull, the king's jester.

Hamlet. This!

1st Clown. E'en that.

Hamlet. Let me see. [*Takes the skull.*] Alas, poor Yorick!
I knew him, Horatio: a fellow of infinite jest, of most excellent
fancy: he hath borne me on his back a thousand times; and now,
how abhorred in my imagination it is! my gorge rises at it. Here
hung those lips that I have kissed I know not how oft. Where be
your gibes now? your gambols? your songs? your flashes of merri-
ment, that were wont to set the table on a roar? Not one now, to
mock your own jeering? Quite chop-fallen? Now get you to my
lady's chamber, and tell her, let her paint an inch thick, to this favor
she must come; make her laugh at that.

One needs to read over this scene many times to see how
much there is in it, — to detect all the wit, humor, pathos,
and profound moralizing.

The *Tempest* is one of Shakespeare's very latest works. It is a play of magic and fairy, more so than any other, except *A Midsummer Night's Dream.* Prospero, the Duke of Milan, who has been banished to a distant island in the seas, has there pursued the study of magic, and has for his assistant a sprite of the air, the tricksy Ariel. By the aid of Ariel, Prospero has raised a violent storm, in which he has drawn the fleet of the king of Naples into an inlet of the isle. Among the attendants of the king, on board his ship, is the unworthy brother of Prospero, who usurped his dukedom and sent him adrift on the ocean with his daughter to find a home on this lonely island. By his magic, Prospero succeeds in getting back his dukedom; and the plays ends with a marriage between his daughter and the son of the king of Naples. This is a bald outline of the beautiful story, which is more interesting to us because Shakespeare wrote it just after reading an account of a strange shipwreck, on one of the Bermuda Isles, of an English vessel which was bound for the colony of Virginia; so that it is in that way connected with our country.

The scene which I quote is that in which Prospero, after raising the tempest, tells his daughter the story of their banishment from Milan. The scene is before the cell of Prospero. He enters with his daughter Miranda :—

Miranda. If by your art, my dearest father, you have
Put the wild waters in this roar, allay them.
The sky, it seems, would pour down stinking pitch,
But that the sea, mounting to the welkin's cheek,
Dashes the fire out. Oh, I have suffered
With those that I saw suffer : a brave vessel,
Which had, no doubt, some noble creature in her,
Dashed all to pieces. Oh, the cry did knock
Against my very heart. Poor souls, they perished.
Had I been any god of power, I would
Have sunk the sea within the earth, or e'er
It should the good ship so have swallowed and
The fraughting souls within her.
  Prospero.   Be collected :
No more amazement : tell your piteous heart
There 's no harm done.
  Mira.   Oh, woe the day !
  Pros.   No harm.

I have done nothing but in care of thee,
Of thee, my dear one, thee, my daughter, who
Art ignorant of what thou art, nought knowing
Of whence I am, nor that I am more better
Than Prospero, master of a full poor cell,
And thy no greater father.
   Mira.   More to know
Did never meddle with my thoughts.
   Pros.   'T is time
I should inform thee farther. Lend thy hand,
And pluck my magic garment from me. So :
Lie there, my art. Wipe thou thine eyes ; have comfort.
                        [He lays down his mantle.
The direful spectacle of the wreck, which touched
The very virtue of compassion in thee,
I have with such provision in mine art
So safely ordered that there is no soul —
No, not so much perdition as an hair,
Betid to any creature in the vessel
Which thou heard'st cry, which thou saw'st sink. Sit down,
For now thou must know farther.
   Mira.   You have often
Begun to tell me what I am, but stopped
And left me to a bootless inquisition,
Concluding " Stay, not yet."
   Pros.   The hour 's now come :
The very minute bids thee ope thine ear ;
Obey, and be attentive. Canst thou remember
A time before we came unto this cell ?
I do not think thou canst, for then thou wast not
Out three years old.
   Mira.   Certainly, sir, I can.
   Pros. By what ? by any other house or person ?
Of any thing the image tell me that
Hath kept with thy remembrance.
   Mira.   'T is far off,
And rather like a dream than an assurance
That my remembrance warrants. Had I not
Four or five women once that tended me ?
   Pros. Thou hadst, and more, Miranda. But how is it
That this lives in thy mind ? What seest thou else
In the dark backward and abysm of time ?
If thou remember'st aught ere thou camest here,
How thou camest here thou mayst.
   Mira.   But that I do not.
   Pros. Twelve year since, Miranda, twelve year since,
Thy father was the Duke of Milan and
A prince of power . . .

Mira.   Oh, the heavens !
What foul play had we, that we came from thence ?
Or blessed was 't we did ?
   Pros.   Both, both, my girl :
By foul play, as thou say'st, were we heaved thence,
But blessedly holp hither.
   Mira.   Oh, my heart **bleeds**
To **think o' the** teen that I have turned you to,
Which is from my remembrance ! Please you, farther.
   Pros. My brother and thy uncle, called Antonio —
I pray thee, mark me — that a brother should
Be so perfidious ! — he whom next thyself
Of all the world I loved and to him put
The manage of my state ; as at that time
Through all the signories it was the first
And Prospero the prime duke, being so reputed
In dignity, and for the **liberal** arts
Without a parallel ; those being **all my study,**
The government I cast upon my brother
And to my state grew stranger, being transported
And rapt in secret studies. Thy false uncle —
Dost thou attend me ? . . .
   Mira. Oh, good sir, **I do.**
   Pros.   I pray thee mark me.
I, thus neglecting worldly ends, all dedicated
To closeness and the bettering of my mind
With that which, but by being so retired,
O'er-prized all popular rate, in my false brother
Awaked **an** evil nature ; and my trust,
Like a good parent, did beget of him
A falsehood in its contrary as great
As my trust was ; which had indeed **no limit,**
A confidence sans bound. He being thus lorded,
Not only with what my revenue yielded,
But what my power might else exact, **like one**
Who having into truth, by telling of it,
Made such a sinner of his memory
To credit his own lie, he did believe
He was indeed the duke. . . . **Hence** his ambition growing —
Dost thou hear ?
   Mira.   Your tale, sir, would cure deafness.
   Pros. To have no screen between this part he played
And him he played it for, he needs will be
Absolute Milan. Me, poor man, my library
Was dukedom large enough : of temporal royalties
He **thinks** me now incapable ; confederates —
So dry he was for sway — with the king of Naples
To give him annual tribute, do him homage,

Subject his coronet to his crown, and bend
The dukedom yet unbowed — alas, poor Milan! —
To most ignoble stooping.
   Mira.   Oh, the heavens! . . .
   Pros.   Now the condition.
This king of Naples, being an enemy
To me inveterate, hearkens my brother's suit,
Which was, that he, in lieu o' the premises
Of homage and I know not how much tribute,
Should presently extirpate me and mine
Out of the dukedom, and confer fair Milan,
With all the honors, on my brother.   Whereon,
A treacherous army levied, one midnight
Fated to the purpose did Antonio open
The gates of Milan, and i' the dead of darkness,
The ministers for the purpose hurried thence
Me and thy crying self.
   Mira.   Alack, for pity!
I, not remembering how I cried out then,
Will cry it o'er again : it is a hint
That wrings mine eyes to 't. . . .
              . . . Wherefore did they not
That hour destroy us ?
   Pros.   Well demanded, wench :
My tale provokes that question.   Dear, they durst not,
So dear the love my people bore me, nor set
A mark so bloody on the business, but
With colors fairer painted their foul ends.
In few, they hurried us aboard a bark,
Bore us some leagues to sea; where they prepared
A rotten carcass of a boat, not rigged,
Nor tackle, sail, nor mast ; the very rats
Instinctively have quit it : there they hoist us,
To cry to the sea that roared to us, to sigh
To the winds whose pity, sighing back again,
Did us but loving wrong.
   Mira.   Alack, what trouble
Was I then to you !
   Pros.   Oh! a cherubin
Thou wast, that did preserve me!   Thou didst smile,
Infused with a fortitude from heaven,
When I have decked the sea with drops full salt,
Under my burden groaned ; which raised in me
An undergoing stomach to bear up
Against what should ensue.

XXV.

ON THE DRAMATIC POETS WHO LIVED IN SHAKESPEARE'S TIME: BEN JONSON; BEAUMONT AND FLETCHER.

THERE was no branch of English literature which grew so suddenly and blossomed so richly as dramatic poetry. The names that appear as writers for the stage between the dates of Shakespeare's birth and death are almost legion. I do not think it would be worth my pains to tell you, or yours to remember, the names even of half these writers. They had merits, and won some success in their day; but we should hardly be better or wiser for knowing more than a small share of these works. I will only mention the names of some **of the greatest** writers and their most noted dramas, and **give here and** there an illustration of the quality of their **poetry.**

BEN JONSON is generally placed next Shakespeare in the history of the drama. " Rare Ben Jonson " he is 1573-1637 called **in** his epitaph in Westminster Abbey. I do not think he should rank next Shakespeare **as a poet, and I** think his plays neither so poetical nor so powerful as those of some others of his fellows. They were very well adapted to the time for which they were written, although the wit, which may have been relished in that day, seems to me heavy and dull. The characters in his comedies are distinct and individual, although more like caricatures than real types. He is learned and painstaking in his tragedy, but he never moves me by any touch of sympathy or human interest in his characters or their actions, and I **do not** believe his plays are now interesting, or will ever again interest any one, except the scholar who makes **the** study of literature his special pursuit.

I think, therefore, that the position Jonson gained in his own time, and the reputation he has held ever since, he gained **more** by certain mental powers he possessed than by the **pre-eminence of his** poetry. He was a man who, by force of character and a power of criticism, exerted a strong influence on his age. We shall see in several later periods in literature certain men who, impressing them-selves and their opinions vividly upon their fellows, get great supremacy over them. Ben Jonson was something such a power in his age as two centuries later Samuel John-son was in his. It takes a great man to gain such a posi-tion, and therefore I do not underrate rare old Ben when I say that he owes as much to this power as to his ability as a poet. Certainly he had good taste and good judg-ment. He did much towards establishing rules for criti-cism and language. Among his others works, he is the author of an English grammar, which is now a curiosity among text-books.

Ben had known hard fortune when he came to London and began to write for the stage. He was first an actor, like almost all the other play-writers, but does not seem to have been brilliantly successful in this calling. One of his fellows says that " he left bricklaying and took to play-act-ing," as if he meant to hint that neither trade had gained by Jonson's change. There is an old story to the effect that Jonson sent his first comedy to the theatre in which Shakespeare was already a prosperous and influential mem-ber. The comedy had been rejected, and the poor author was going away in discouragement, when Shakespeare asked to look at it, saw its merit, and through his means it was performed. This play was *Every Man in His Humor*, one of the best of Jonson's comedies.[1]

Jonson and Shakespeare seem to have been good friends, and it was Jonson who wrote that fine elegy on Shakespeare which predicts that " he was not for a day, but for all time." Jonson was a man of much more learning than Shakespeare, and seems to have been rather vain of his attainments. He says that " Shakespeare had little Latin

[1] This story has been contradicted as improbable, but it is to be noted that any story which sheds a gleam of light on the dull annals of the past is sure to be contradicted, whether it be probable or not, by some dry-as-dust critic.

and less Greek," in a way that intimates how inferior Shakespeare was in that respect to himself. And there is another story — which I tell with proper fear that it may not be true — that Shakespeare was once asked to be sponsor to an infant; and when some one asked him what he would give his godchild, answered: "I will give him a dozen *Latin*[1] spoons, and Ben shall translate them." Whether this story be true or not, there was, no doubt, many a sharp passage of wit between Jonson and Shakespeare. They were both members of a club, said to have been founded by Raleigh, which used to meet at the Mermaid Tavern, in London, where wit sparkled like fireworks. If the walls of the old tavern could only have reported what had been said within them, what a feast of good things we might have had! But this was before the age of newspapers, and the club at the Mermaid had no reporter to take down their witty speeches.

To return to Jonson's plays. His tragedies of *Catiline* and *Sejanus* have plots drawn from classic sources. His best comedies are *Volpone, The Silent Woman,* and *Every Man in His Humor.* To give you an idea of his plots, which in most cases seem (unlike Shakespeare's) to be original in construction, let me tell you the story of *The Silent Woman.*

The hero, a young gentleman, has an eccentric uncle who cannot bear the slightest noise, and has shut himself up from everything which can molest him or break his quiet. He quarrels with his nephew, who expects to be his heir, and resolves to disinherit him and marry. The Silent Woman is accordingly introduced to him, — a woman warranted to speak very seldom, and then hardly above a whisper. He is charmed with her, and hurries on the wedding; but as soon as the knot is tied, the Silent Woman turns into a fluent talker and a termagant. Hosts of friends come in to visit her, a band of instruments enters, playing loudly, and the old man is on the point of going mad, when his scapegrace nephew comes to his relief.

---

[1] "Latten" was a cheap metal, of which spoons were made.

He offers to show his **uncle a way of release from the** marriage if he will sign an agreement by which his fortune after death, and an annuity **during** his life, are **secured to** the nephew. **The poor old man** gladly **assents, and the** fact is disclosed that the Silent Woman is a boy who has been trained to play this trick, that the marriage is no marriage, **and thus the** play ends. No doubt this was very amusing when it **was** first performed, but it has lost its flavor of wit **for our day, and there are few lines** in it worth preserving **as literature.**

Jonson wrote a large number of plays, both comedies and tragedies. He also wrote a number of masques, for representation in the court, when he was made poet-laureate to James I.; and in these is some of his best poetry. These masques were generally written for some special occasion of festivity, — royal birthdays or marriages, or court celebrations. They were also sometimes performed in the open air in the course of the journey of a sovereign, or at his reception at some noble house. You will get a very good idea of a masque **if** you **read,** in Scott's novel of *Kenilworth,* the account of Elizabeth's visit to the Earl of Leicester and of the masque performed there.

Although Jonson, in my opinion, does not show a very **fine** imagination in his most famous dramas, he is a very musical lyric poet. This is shown in the songs which we **find in his** plays and in the masques, as well as among his short poems. I presume you have heard this song of **his,** beginning, —

> " Drink to me only with thine eyes,
> And I will pledge with mine,"

which is one of the most beautiful of the early songs. **Here** is another **song** from one of his masques :—

To Charis.

> Do but look on her eyes, they do light
> All that Love's world compriseth.
> Do but **look** on her hair, **it** is bright
> As Love's star when it riseth.

Do but mark her forehead, smoother
Than words that sooth her ;
And from her arched brows such a grace
Sheds itself through the face.

Have you seen but a bright lily grow
   Before rude hands have touched it ?
Have you marked but the fall of the snow
   Before the soil hath smutched it ?
Have you felt the wool of the beaver,
Or swan's down ever ?
Or have smelt of the bud of the brier,
Or the nard in the fire ?
Or have tasted the bag of the bee ?
Oh, so white ! Oh, so soft! Oh, so sweet is she.

It is singular that a man who could write so graceful a
lyric should not have put more such poetry into his dramatic writings.

One of the most interesting facts of Jonson's life to us
is a visit he made to the Scottish poet Drummond, in one
of the last years of the sixteenth century. In this visit he
told many anecdotes, and seems to have expressed his
opinions freely on his contemporaries, their characters and
their writings. Drummond, like a thrifty Scotchman who
let nothing go to waste, kept notes of the visit, and they
are printed, so that we all can read this precious gossip.
At the end of the notes Drummond gives his opinion of
Jonson in these words, with which we will take leave of
him : —

" Ben Jonson was a great lover and praiser of himself, a
contemner and scorner of others, given rather to lose a friend
than a jest ; jealous of every word and action of those about
him, especially when in drink, which is one of the elements in
which he lived ; a dissembler of the parts that reign in him ; a
bragger of some good that he wanted ; thinketh nothing well
done but what he or some of his friends have done. He is
passionately kind and angry, careless either to gain or keep ;
vindictive, but he be well answered at himself ; interprets best
sayings and deeds of others often at the worst. He was for any
religion, being versed in both ; oppressed with fancy that hath
o'ermastered his reason (a general disease in many poets) ; his

inventions are smooth and easy, but, above all, he excelleth in a translation."

I have told you previously how common it was for two or more authors to unite together in writing works for the theatre. There is hardly a play-writer of the age who is not known to have thus collaborated ; but there are no two

1586-1615-16   names so closely linked in authorship as those of FRANCIS BEAUMONT and JOHN FLETCHER.

1576-1625   They are always spoken of as a pair of poets, and their works have always been printed under their joint names.

The fact that Beaumont and Fletcher were brothers in heart, as well as brother workers, is one fact that makes them interesting to us, and has helped, no doubt, to bind them so closely together in fame. They were the dearest of friends, lived in one house, shared one apartment, and, it is said, wore each other's clothes. Beaumont, who was ten years younger than Fletcher, died almost ten years before his friend. It is thought that an overtasked brain was the cause of his death. Fletcher lived till 1625, the year the plague visited London. He was intending to leave the city, and only waited for a suit of clothes to be sent home by his tailor, when the plague seized him and he died.

There are fifty-two plays in the volumes printed under the joint names of Beaumont and Fletcher ; but as Fletcher outlived Beaumont ten years, many of these plays were written after Beaumont's death. Some were entirely Fletcher's work, and others were written with other play-writers of the time, Massinger, Middleton, Rowley, and others. His most notable co-worker was Shakespeare, with whom he wrote *The Two Noble Kinsmen,* and whom he aided also, it is said, in *Henry VIII.*[1] A recent scholar gives the authorship of the plays thus : —

[1] There is a difference of opinion among critics as to whether Fletcher had any share in *Henry VIII.* I think, however, that any one who studies Shakespeare and Fletcher's style, and has a fine ear for metres, will decide that Fletcher had a share in the play.

It is not easy to decide just how the poets shared their work in these literary partnerships, whether a plot was decided upon, and each took certain scenes as his share, or if each took certain characters in a scene, and wrote their speeches. Beaumont and Fletcher certainly wrote together with great harmony, and their styles very closely blended. Some critic says that " Beaumont excelled in that judgment requisite for forming plots, and Fletcher in the fancy and vivacity which characterize the poet."

There is a story told of their being once at a tavern, consulting together over a bottle of wine, when Fletcher was heard to whisper mysteriously, " I will kill the king." The horrified waiter would have had them arrested for conspiracy if it had not been clearly proved that the two poets were only concocting the plot of a new play.

You can easily imagine that the fifty-two plays which pass under the title of Beaumont and Fletcher's works must be very unequal in merit, since so many different poets had a share in them. The best among them certainly are those written jointly by these two authors.

The comedies written by Fletcher alone are very brilliant, the dialogue is natural and sprightly, — a model for later comedy style ; but among the serious plays, those in which both these poets took part have the highest flights of poetry and strongest dramatic interest. Some of the best are *Philaster, Valentinian, The Maid's Tragedy*, and *Thierry and Theodoret.* Of all their plays I like best *Philaster, or Love Lies Bleeding ;* and from this I have made some extracts for you to read.

The plot is of a Prince Philaster, the rightful heir to the crown of Sicily, which crown has been usurped by the reigning king, who desires to leave the succession to his

daughter Arethusa. **Philaster** lives at liberty in **Sicily** so
much beloved **by the people that the** king **dares not im-**
prison **or** make **away with him, although** he is plotting by
the marriage of Arethusa with a Spanish **prince to bring in**
foreign **aid to strengthen his power. But Arethusa** loves
Philaster and **is beloved by him, so that** in **the** end all
difficulties are solved by their **marriage.** Philaster **is** also
loved by Euphrasia, daughter **of one of** the lords of **Sicily,**
who has taken the disguise **of a page** (Bellario) **to** follow
Philaster, who guesses **neither** the secret of her love nor
her birth.

Philaster thus describes this **page,** Bellario, **to** Arethusa :

> " **I** have a boy
> Sent by the gods, I hope, to this intent,
> Not yet seen in the court.   Hunting the buck,
> I found him sitting by a fountain's side,
> Of which he borrowed some to quench **his thirst,**
> And paid the nymph **again** as much **in tears.**
> A garland lay him by, made **by** himself
> Of many several flowers **bred in the** vale,
> Stuck in that mystic **order that** the rareness
> **Delighted me.**   But ever when he turned
> **His tender eyes upon 'em,** he would weep
> As if **he meant to make 'em** grow **again.**
> Seeing such pretty helpless innocence
> Dwell in his face, I asked him **all his story.**
> He told **me that his parents gentle died,**
> Leaving him to the mercy **of the fields,**
> Which gave him roots, and **of the** crystal springs,
> **Which** did not stop their courses, and the sun,
> **Which still,** he thanked him, yielded him his light.
> **Then took** he up his garland, **and did** show
> What every flower, as country people hold,
> Did signify ; and how **all,** ordered thus,
> Expressed **his grief.   And, to my thoughts, did** read
> The prettiest lecture of his **country art**
> That could be **wished ;** so that methought I could
> Have studied it.   I gladly entertained him,
> Who was glad **to follow, and have got**
> The trustiest, **loving'st, and the gentlest boy**
> That ever master **kept.   Him will I send**
> To wait on you, and bear our hidden love."

The following speech is made by Euphrasia when her disguise has been discovered by Philaster and the court ; and

the former demands of her why she has thus concealed her
sex. She answers, —

> "My father oft would speak
> Your worth and virtues ; and as I did grow
> More and more apprehensive, I did thirst
> To see the man so praised. But yet all this
> Was but a maiden longing, to be lost
> As soon as found ; till sitting in my window,
> Printing my thoughts in lawn, I saw a god,
> I thought (but it was you), enter our gates.
> My blood flew out, and back again as fast
> As I had puffed it forth and sucked it in
> Like breath. Then was I called away in haste
> To entertain you. Never was a man,
> Heaved from a sheepcote to a sceptre, raised
> So high in thoughts as I. You left a kiss
> Upon those lips then which I mean to keep
> From you forever. I did hear you talk
> Far above singing ! After you were gone,
> I grew acquainted with my heart, and searched
> What stirred it so. Alas ! I found it love ;
> Yet could I but have lived
> In presence of you, I had had my end.
> For this I did delude my noble father
> With a feigned pilgrimage, and dressed myself
> In habit of a boy ; and for I knew
> My birth no match for you, I was past hope
> Of having you ; and understanding well
> That when I made discovery of my sex
> I could not stay with you, I made a vow,
> By all the most religious things a maid
> Could call together, never to be known,
> While there was hope to hide me from men's eyes,
> For other than I seemed, that I might ever
> Abide with you. Then sat I by the fount
> Where first you took me up."

Like all the rest of these poets, Fletcher wrote very
pretty songs, which occur in a number of his plays. Here
is one, which is in the same strain as Milton's *Penseroso*,
in which he praises the charm of Melancholy : —

> "Hence all you vain delights,
>   As short as are the nights
>   Wherein you spend your folly !

There 's nought in this life sweet,
If men were wise to see 't,
   But only melancholy,
   Oh, sweetest melancholy.

" Welcome, folded arms and fixed eyes,
  A sigh that piercing mortifies,
  A look that 's fastened to the ground,
  A tongue chained up without a sound!
  Fountain-heads and pathless groves,
  Places that pale passion loves !
  Moonlight walks, where all the fowls
  Are warmly housed, save bats and owls !
  A midnight bell, a parting groan !—
  These are the sounds we feed upon ;
  Then stretch our bones in a still gloomy valley, —
  Nothing 's so dainty sweet as lovely melancholy."

XXVI.

On George Chapman, John Webster, John Marston, and other Dramatists.

A GROUP of lesser names follows on Jonson and Beaumont and Fletcher. One of the oldest among **1557–1634** them is George Chapman, the first translator of Homer into English verse. This is his really great title to fame, although he wrote many plays, and was much esteemed as an original poet. He was born seven years before Shakespeare, and lived to be almost eighty. A writer who knew him in his latest days says : " He was much resorted to latterly by young persons of parts, as a sort of poetical chronicle, but was very choice whom he admitted to him, and preserved in his own person the dignity of poetry, which he compared to a flower of the sun, that disdains to open its petals to the light of a smoky candle." This is to my mind a delightful picture of one of the patriarchs of the noble age of Elizabethan literature holding court to receive the generation who were so unfortunate as to be born later.

John Marston and **John** Webster were both poets of a higher order than **Chapman.** WEBSTER wrote two plays, *Vittoria Corombona* and *The Duch-* **1582?–1652** *ess of Malfi*, which I think more powerful and more dramatically effective in the elements **of horror** and pathos they possess, than anything produced by **these** dramatic poets, always excepting Shakespeare. Webster also wrote a tragedy on the moving story of the Roman maiden Virginia; and I will quote you, as an example of his pathetic style, the speech of Virginius in which he bids farewell to his daughter **before he** sacrifices her : —

Virginius [embracing **Virginia**].
    Farewell, **my sweet Virginia ; never, never**
    Shall I taste fruit of the most blessed hope
    I had in thee. Let me forget the thought
    Of thy most pretty infancy, when **first**
    Returning from the wars, I took delight
    To rock thee in my target; when my girl
    Would kiss her father in his burganet
    Of glittering steel, hung 'bout his armed neck,
    And, viewing the bright metal, smile to see
    Another fair Virginia smile on thee; . . .
    And when my wounds have smarted, I have sung
    With an unskilful, yet a willing voice,
    To bring my girl asleep.

MARSTON is celebrated **for** his grim and satirical humor, which he shows forcibly in *The Malcontent*, the **1575–1624** most noted, **or best known, of all** his dramas; but the same spirit appears in **all** he wrote. Like Shakespeare's Fool, he " rails on Lady Fortune in good set terms." One **of** the characters in his play of *What You Will* says " **Fortune is blind ;** " on which the hero cries fiercely, —

        " You lie, you **lie!**
    None but a madman would deem **Fortune** blind.
    How can she see to wound desert so nice,
    Just in the speeding place? to girt lewd brows
    With honor's wreath? Ha! Fortune blind? Away!
    How can she, blinded, then so rightly see
    To starve rich worth and glut iniquity?"

And another speech from the same character : —

> " Love ! hang love !
> It is the abject outcast of the world.
> Hate all things ; hate the world, — thyself, all men ;
> Hate knowledge ; strive not to be overwise, —
> It drew destruction into Paradise ;
> Hate honor, virtue, — they are baits
> That entice men's hopes to sadder fates ;
> Hate beauty, — every ballad-monger
> Can cry his idle, foppish humor ;
> Hate riches, — wealth 's a flattering Jack,
> Adores to the face, mews 'hind thy back,
> He that is poor is firmly sped,
> He never shall be flattered ;
> Love only hate ; affect no higher
> Than praise of heaven, wine, a fire,
> Luck of thy days in silent breath,—
> When that 's snuffed out, come Seignor Death ! "

Whether this was Marston's native humor, and the one in
which he lived, I do not know, but it is certainly not a very
agreeable one to contemplate.

In contrast to him is the sunny-tempered THOMAS
DEKKER, who was a prolific writer of dramas and
1575–1641 of prose tracts. His plays have not much dramatic interest, although some of the characters are wonderfully life-like and vivid, and there is a serene and noble
philosophy in his lines that puts to shame the cynicism
that inspires so much of Marston's pen. Here is a
specimen : —

> " Why should we grieve at want ? Say the world made thee
> Her minion, that thy head lay in her lap,
> And that she danced thee upon her wanton knee ?
> She could but give thee a whole world, — that 's all,
> And that all 's nothing ; the world's greatest part
> Cannot fill up one corner of thy heart.
>
> Were twenty kingdoms thine, thou 'dst live in care,
> Thou could'st not sleep the better, nor live longer,
> Nor merrier be, nor healthfuller, nor stronger.
> If, then, thou wantest, make that want thy pleasure ;
> No man wants all things, nor has all in measure."

In the same spirit as this is a beautiful song, which I find in an old play of which Dekker was joint author with two other of the dramatists; and the song was without doubt written by Dekker: —

"Art thou poor, yet hast thou golden slumbers?
        Oh, sweet content!
Art thou rich, yet is thy mind perplexed?
        Oh, punishment!
Dost thou laugh to see how fools are vexed,
To add to golden numbers golden numbers?
        Oh, sweet content!

    "Oh, sweet, oh, sweet content!
Work apace, apace, apace;
Honest Labor wears a bonny face!

"Canst drink the waters of the crispèd spring?
        Oh, sweet content!
Swim'st thou in wealth, yet sink'st in thine own tears?
        Oh, punishment!
Then he that patiently want's burden bears,
No burden bears, but is a king, a king.
        Oh, sweet, oh, sweet content!"

In one of Dekker's plays there is an old man, Orlando Friscobaldo, who has always been a great favorite of mine. I think there is no character in any of these old plays whose wise and witty sayings come so near my heart as these of old Orlando. Here is a scene in which he meets Hippolito, the hero of the play: —

Orlando My noble lord! the Lord Hippolito! the duke's son! his brave daughter's brave husband! How does your honored lordship? Does your nobility remember so poor a gentleman as Signor Orlando Friscobaldo,— old mad Orlando?

Hip. Oh, sir, our friends, they ought to be unto us as our jewels,— as dearly valued, being locked up and unseen, as when we wear them in our hands. I see, Friscobaldo, age hath not command of your blood; for all Time's sickle has gone over you, you are Orlando still.

Orl. Why, my lord, are not the fields mown and cut down, and stripped bare, and yet wear they not pied coats again? Though my head be like a leek, white, may not my heart be like the blade, green?

Hip. Scarce can I read the stories in your brow which age has writ there; you look youthful still.

Orl. I eat snakes, my lord; I eat snakes My heart shall never have a wrinkle in it so long as I can cry "Hem!" with a clear voice.

Hip. You are the happier man, sir!

Orl. Happy man? I'll give you, my lord, the true picture of a happy man; I was turning leaves over this morning, and found it. An excellent Italian painter drew it; if I have it in the right colors, I'll bestow it on your lordship.

Hip. I stay for it.

Orl.   He for whom poor men's curses dig no grave;
He that is neither lord's nor lawyer's slave;
He that makes *this* his sea, and that his shore;
He that in 's coffin 's richer than before;
He that counts youth his sword, and age his staff;
He whose right hand carves his own epitaph;
He that upon his death-bed is a swan,
And dead, no crow, — he is a happy man.

Hip. It 's very well; I thank you for this picture.

Orl. After this picture, my lord, do I strive to have my face drawn, for I am not covetous, am not in debt, sit neither at the duke's side, nor lie at his feet. . . . I sowed leaves in my youth, and I reap now books in my age. I fill this hand, and empty this; and when the bell shall toll for me, if I prove a swan and go singing to my nest, why so! . . . May not old Friscobaldo be merry now, ha?

Hip. You may; would I were partner in your mirth!

Orl. I have a little, — have all things; I have nothing. I have no wife, I have no child, have no chick; and why should I not be in my jocundare?

Hip. Is your wife, then, departed?

Orl. She 's an old dweller in those high countries (*pointing to heaven*), yet not from me; here, she 's here (*touching his heart*) a good couple are seldom parted.

Hip. You had a daughter too, sir, had you not?

Orl. Oh, my lord, this old tree had one branch, and but one branch growing out of it. It was young, it was fair, it was straight; I pruned it daily, drest it carefully, kept it from the wind, helped it to the sun; yet, for all my skill in planting, it grew crooked; I hewed it down, what 's become of it I neither know nor care.

Hip. Then I can tell you what 's become of it. The branch is withered.

Orl. So 't was long ago.

Hip. Her name, I think, was Bellafront. She 's dead.

Orl. Ha! dead?

Hip. Yes; what was left of her not worth the keeping, even in my sight, was thrown into a grave.

Orl. Dead! My last and best peace go with her! I see Death 's a good trencherman; he can eat coarse meat as well as the dantiest. Is she dead?

Hip. She 's turned to earth.

Orl. Would she were turned to heaven! Umph! is she dead? I am glad the world has lost one of his idols. In her grave sleep all my shame and her own; and all my sorrows and all her sins.

Hip. I'm glad you are wax, not marble; you are made
Of man's best temper, — there are now good hopes
That all these heaps of ice about your heart,
By which a father's love was frozen up,
Are thaw'd in these sweet showers fetched from your eyes.
We are ne'er like angels till our passions die.
She is not dead, but lives under worse fate;
I think she's poor, and more to clip her wings,
Her husband at this hour lies in jail
For killing of a man. To save his blood
Join all your force with mine; mine shall be shown ·
The getting of his life preserves your own.

Orl. In my daughter, you will say. Does she live, then? I am sorry I wasted tears upon a wanton. But the best is I have a handkerchief to drink them up; soap can wash them all out again. Is she poor?

Hip. Trust me, I think she is. . . . When did you see her?

Orl. Not seventeen summers.

Hip. Is your hate so old?

Orl. Older. It has a white head, and shall never die till she be buried; her wrongs shall be my bedfellow. . . .

Hip. Nay, but Friscobaldo —

Orl. I detest her; I defy both; she's not mine, she's —

    .   .   .   .

Hip. Fare you well, for I'll trouble you no more. [*Exit Hippolito.*

Orl. [*Looking after him.*] And fare you well, sir; go thy ways; we have few lords of thy making. 'Las, my girl, art thou poor? Poverty dwells next door to despair, — there's but a wall between them. Despair is one of hell's catchpoles; and lest that devil arrest her, I'll to her. Yet she shall not know me: she shall drink of my wealth as beggars do of running water, freely, yet never know from what fountain's head it flows. Shall a silly bird pick her own breast to nourish her young ones, and can a father see his child starve? That were hard. The pelican does it, and shall not I?

I think I have quoted enough to show you that Dekker's "heart had no wrinkles in it," if his poetry was prompted by his disposition.

MASSINGER and FORD are near the end of the list of the great poets of this era. They each wrote a num- 1584–1640
ber of dramas, and one of Massinger's, *A New
Way to Pay Old Debts*, still is an acting play, 1586–1636
— partly because the principal character, Sir Giles Overreach, has so much power that the part is a favorite with actors. But I think we should be little interested to read the plays

of these authors, or those of JAMES SHIRLEY, who ranks
among the last of this line of dramatic writers.
1596–1666
He was born in Elizabeth's reign, and lived till
that of Charles II.   He wrote many plays, in one of which
occurs a song which was a favorite with the Merry Monarch;
and with this song, by which we may remember Shirley,
I will close this long Talk on our dramatists: —

> "The glories of our blood and state
> Are shadows, not substantial things;
> There is no armor against fate;
> Death lays his icy hand on kings;
> Sceptre and crown
> Must tumble down,
> And in the dust be equal made
> With the poor crooked scythe and spade.
>
> "Some men with swords may reap the field,
> And plant fresh laurels where they kill;
> But their strong nerves at last must yield, —
> They tame but one another still;
> Early or late
> They stoop to fate,
> And must give up their murmuring breath
> When they, pale captives, creep to death.
>
> "The garlands wither on your brow;
> Then boast no more your mighty deeds;
> Upon death's purple altar now
> See where the victor-victim bleeds.
> Your hearts must come
> To the cold tomb:
> Only the actions of the just
> Smell sweet and blossom in the dust."

XXVII.

ON THE SINGERS OF THE GOLDEN AGE OF POETRY, — DONNE, WOTTON, WITHER, HERBERT, AND HERRICK.

IN speaking of the dramatic poets, we have noted how many of the play-writers wrote beautiful little lyrics, which we find occurring in their plays, as the Spring song of Thomas Nash (page 135), or the Labor song of Thomas Dekker, which we have read (page 165). If you have ever opened a volume of Shakespeare's plays, I think you could not fail to be caught by the beauty of the lyrics scattered through the book, — as Ariel's melodious lay in the *Tempest:*

> " Come unto these yellow sands,
>   And then take hands,
> Court'sied when you have, and kiss'd
>   The wild waves whist."

Or the spirited serenade from *Cymbeline,* —

> " Hark, hark! the lark at heaven's gate sings,
>   And Phœbus 'gins arise,
> His steeds to water at those springs
>   On chaliced flowers that lies ;
> And winking Mary-buds begin
>   To ope their golden eyes :
> With everything that pretty bin,
>   My lady sweet, arise ;
>   Arise, arise ! "

Ben Jonson, Beaumont and Fletcher, Webster, Marston, and dramatists of lesser rank all studded their plays with songs, some of them so musical and so fanciful that they are often like jewels shining out in a heap of rubbish ; for many of these plays are only the rubbish of literature, redeemed by an occasional fine line, or by one of these beautiful lyrics.

There are also many poets not dramatic, but purely lyric, who sang like larks in this sky. I could count you a score or two through the period covered by the reigns of

Elizabeth, James, and Charles I. The mention of half a score must content us, and I propose to group together in this Talk the principal lyric poets from the time of Spenser to that of Milton.

JOHN DONNE comes first on my list. Early in life he was

1573-1631 secretary to an earl, and while in this position he fell in love with the earl's niece and married her clandestinely, which so offended the lady's family, and especially her father, that he had the poet turned out from office and actually imprisoned him in the Tower. He was released, however, and won enough renown later to make his stupid old father-in-law ashamed of himself; for Donne became one of the most distinguished preachers of his time, and was made finally the Dean of St. Paul's Cathedral. His marriage turned out very happily. His wife seems to have been romantically devoted to him, and once when he was to go on a journey, she formed the design of going with him in the disguise of his page, but was discovered before she could carry out her plan. She died before Donne reached the height of his success, and he grieved for her all his life after.

Donne has been put at the head of the "metaphysical poets," who gained that title from Dr. Johnson, because, as he says, they "were men of learning, and to show their learning was their sole endeavor;" so that, instead of writing poetry, they wrote only verses, and often "such verses as stood the test of the finger better than the ear." Johnson's criticism is only occasionally true of the best of these poets, though these best sometimes deserve the worst that he says of them.

For instance, in one poem Donne compares his heart to a mirror shattered into pieces by love, and goes on to prove that as the pieces of broken glass show a hundred lesser faces, "so his broken heart could feel lesser passions, but never one great love like that his lady inspired." In another poem, entitled an *Ode to a Flea* which has bitten both himself and his beloved, he talks about their blood being wedded in the black temple of the "insect's body"!

If this is metaphysical poetry, the less we have of it the better. But Donne was not always so absurd. Here is something in a better vein, — a quaint good-by song on going away for a short absence. We will fancy he wrote it to console Mrs. Donne when he went on the journey from which she was prevented from accompanying him as a page:

> "Sweetest love, I do not go
>   For weariness of thee,
> Nor in hope the world can show
>   A fitter love for me,
>   But since that I
> Must die at last, 't is best
> Thus to use myself in jest
>   By feigned death to die.
>
> "Yesternight the sun went hence,
>   And yet is here to-day;
> He hath no desire nor sense,
>   Nor half so short a way.
>   Then fear not me,
> But believe that I shall make
> Hastier journeys, since I take
>   More wings and spurs than he.
>
> .   .   .   .   .
>
> "Let not thy divining heart
>   Forethink me any ill;
> Destiny may take thy part,
>   And may thy fears fulfil
>   But think that we
> Are but laid aside to sleep;
> They who one another keep
>   Alive, ne'er parted be."

Near Donne in point of time is Wotton, a statesman of the time of James I. For the following familiar song, alone, he deserves to be remembered: — 1568–1639

> "How happy is he born and taught
>   That serveth not another's will, —
> Whose armor is his honest thought,
>   And simple truth his utmost skill!
>
> "Whose passions not his masters are,
>   Whose soul is still prepared for death, —
> Untied unto the world by care
>   Of public fame or private breath.

.   .   .   .   .

> " Who hath his life from rumors freed,
>   Whose conscience is his strong retreat ;
>   Whose state can neither flatterers feed
>   Nor ruin make oppressors great.
>
> .   .   .   .   .
>
> " This man is freed from servile bands
>   Of hope to rise, or fear to fall, —
>   Lord of himself, though not of lands ;
>   And, having nothing, yet hath all."

GEORGE WITHER was a most voluminous writer of prose as well as poetry. He took the Puritan side in the political troubles which came in the reign of Charles I., and wrote satires in verse and tracts in prose on the part of the Roundheads. His zeal got him two or three times imprisoned, and once he was in close danger of losing his life. At this time Sir John Denham, a Royalist, who was also a poet, interceded for Wither, saying that he wanted him spared, that there might be in England one poet accounted worse than he (Denham). This witty intercession of his brother poet probably saved Wither's life.

1588–1667

His published works number almost one hundred. Among so much prose and verse, satires, hymns, love-songs, etc., there must be some worthless stuff. Yet Wither wrote lyrics which place him among the very best of the singers. I have chosen his rhymes on *Christmas* because they have so spirited a ring, and give such a vivid picture of a jovial English Christmastide : —

> " Lo, now is come our joyful'st feast,
>   Let every man be jolly ;
>   Each room with ivy leaves is drest,
>   And every post with holly.
>   Though some churls at our mirth repine,
>   Around your foreheads garlands twine,
>   Drown sorrow in a cup of wine,
>   And let us all be merry.
>
> " Now all our neighbors' chimneys smoke,
>   And Christmas blocks are burning ;
>   Their ovens they with baked meats choke,
>   And all their spits are turning.

Without the door let sorrow lie,
And if for cold it hap to die,
We 'll bury 't in a Christmas pie,
And evermore be merry.

" Now every lad is wondrous trim,
And no man minds his labor ;
Our lasses have provided them
A bagpipe and a tabor ;
Young men and maids, and girls and boys
Give life to another's joys,
And you anon shall by their noise
Perceive that they are merry.

" Rank misers now do sparing shun,
Their hall of music soundeth ;
And dogs thence with whole shoulders run,
So all things there aboundeth.
The country folk themselves advance
With crowdy-muttons out of France,
And Jack shall pipe, and Gill shall dance,
And all the town be merry.

"Ned Swash hath fetcht his bands from pawn,
And all his best apparel ;
Brisk Nell hath bought a ruff of lawn
With droppings of the barrel.
And those that hardly all the year
Have bread to eat, or rags to wear,
Will have both clothes and dainty fare,
And all the day be merry.

" Now poor men to the justices
With capons make their errants,
And if they hap to fail in these
They plague them with their warrants.
But now they feed them with good cheer,
And what they want they take in beer,
For Christmas comes but once a year,
And then they shall be merry.

.   .   .

" The client now his suit forbears,
The prisoner's heart is eased ;
The debtor drinks away his cares,
And for the time is pleased ;
Though others' purses be more fat,
Why should we pine or grieve at that ?
Hang sorrow ! Care will kill a cat ;
And therefore let 's be merry.

"Hark! how the wags abroad do call
  Each other forth to rambling;
Anon you 'll see them in the hall
  For nuts and apples scrambling.
Hark! how the roofs with laughter sound,
Anon they 'll think the house goes round,
For they the cellar's depth have found,
  And there they will be merry.

  .   .   .   .   .

"Then wherefore in these merry days
  Should we, I pray, be duller?
No, let us sing some roundelays
  To make our mirth the fuller;
And while we, thus inspired, sing,
Let all the streets with echoes ring,
Woods and hills and everything
  Bear witness, we are merry."

Robert Herrick and George Herbert, who flourished in the reigns of James I. and Charles I., were clergymen as well as poets, but, as clergymen and poets, both were of a very different order. HERBERT was a saintly character, and his poetry is nearly all devotional, breathing a spirit of real piety. He lived in a sort of hallowed retirement, always in rather delicate health, tended by a loving and beloved wife, and dying in the odor of sanctity. He was a friend of Donne, and writes in the same style of fantastic imagery, although he never wrote any verses in so light a humor as Donne. Nearly all his songs were religious. Here is a stanza or two in his characteristic vein: —

1593-1632

"I made a posy while the day ran by;
  Here will I smell my remnant out, and tie
    My life within this band;
But time did beckon to the flowers, and they
By noon most cunningly did steal away,
  And withered in my hand.

  .   .   .   .   .

"Farewell, dear flowers, sweetly your time ye spent;
  Fit, while ye lived, for smell or ornament,
    And after death, for cures.
I follow straight, without complaints or grief,
Since, if my scent be good, I care not if
    It be as short as yours."

The following hymn of his, with which I have **no doubt**
you are familiar, **is, I think,** the best **thing he ever wrote;**
and yet, in the last verse, in which **he compares the soul**
to seasoned timber, you can see the **fantastic sort of con-**
ceits which marred the poetry of **all this style** of writers,
and gained them the epithet " metaphysical " : —

> "**Sweet** day, so cool, so calm, so bright,
> The bridal of the earth and sky ;
> The dews shall weep thy fall to-night,
>   For thou must die.
>
> "**Sweet rose, whose hue,** angry and brave,
> **Bids** the rash gazer wipe his eye,
> **Thy root is** ever in its **grave,**
>   **And thou must die.**
>
> "**Sweet spring, full of sweet days and roses,**
> **A box where sweets compacted lie,**
> My music shows ye have your closes,
>   And all must die.
>
> " Only a sweet and virtuous soul,
>   Like seasoned timber, never gives,
> But though the whole world turn to coal,
>   Then chiefly lives."

HERRICK, **as I** have intimated, was very different from
Herbert. The latter wrote only pious **verses.** 1591–1662
Herrick **was a** lively rhymester, making **love-**
songs, drinking-songs, epigrams, and couplets on all worldly
subjects. Herbert loved quiet and retirement, and could
hardly be induced to come out into the world. Herrick
sought society and convivial company, and railed at the
country. Yet, of the two, Robert Herrick is the more
musical poet, although he wrote much that would better
never have been written. And although he professed **to**
hate **the** country, and when he had a vicarage in **Devon-**
shire frankly vented his dislike in these lines, —

> " More discontent I never had,
>   Since I was born, than here,
> Where I have been, and still am, sad,
>   In this dull Devonshire " —

yet, as he himself says, his best verses are inspired by brooks, birds, and blossoms, and no poet of the age wrote so beautifully of Nature as Herrick. I think this ode to *Primroses Filled with Morning Dew* is one of the most beautiful lyrics of his age, perhaps of any age of our poetry : —

" Why do ye weep, sweet babes !   Can tears
      Speak grief in you,
      Who were but born
   Just as the modest morn
   Teemed her refreshing dew ?
Alas ! you have not known that shower
      That mars a flower,
      Nor felt th' unkind
   Breath of a blasting wind,
   Nor are ye worn with years,
      Or warped as we,
   Who think it strange to see
Such pretty flowers (like to orphans young),
Speaking by tears before ye have a tongue.

" Speak, whimp'ring younglings, and make known
      The reason why
      Ye droop and weep.
   Is it for want of sleep,
   Or childish lullaby ?
Or that ye have not seen yet
      The violet ?
   Or brought a kiss
From that sweetheart to this ?

" No, no; this sorrow shown
      By your tears shed
   Would have this lecture read,
That things of greatest, so of meanest worth,
Conceived with grief are, and with tears brought forth."

Herrick was driven from his parish during the civil war, and went to London, where he lived for some time very poor. Here he and Ben Jonson were great friends, and used to sup together at a tavern, where they held what Herrick calls " lyric feasts." But London never inspired such verses as did the country sights, — the daffodils, violets, and May-days of which he wrote so feelingly. After a time he went back to his vicarage and wrote more

sober verses.   In one of these he prays devoutly for pardon
for some of his unhallowed rhymes : —

> " Forgive me, God, and blot each line
> Out of my book that is not thine."

But as Heaven is not likely to do for any one that which
he could easily do for himself, the lines remain unblotted to
this day.

XXVIII.

The Singers of the Golden Age of Poetry, — Carew, Suckling, Lovelace, Waller.

CAREW, Suckling, and Lovelace have the air of courtiers,
and were all men of the world.   Thomas Carew held
an office in the court of Charles I., and was a witty
and accomplished gentleman, whose sonnets for   **1589–1639**
ten or fifteen years before the Puritans came into power
were the most popular verses of their time.   They were
set to music, and the ladies sang them to their harpsichords.
As you can fancy, they were love-songs that Carew wrote.
Indeed, have not nearly all the lyric poets of the world
sung either to Love or Death?   Their verses are set to a
tender air or a sad one.   Carew writes thus of his love
when spring approaches : —

> " Now that the winter's gone, the earth hath lost
> Her snow-white robes, and now no more the frost
> Candies the grass, or casts an icy cream
> Upon the silver lake or crystal stream ;
> But the warm sun thaws the benumbed earth
> And makes it tender, gives a second birth
> To the dead swallow, wakes in hollow tree
> The drowsy cuckoo and the humble-bee.

> " Now do a choir of chirping minstrels bring
> In triumph to the world the youthful spring ;
> The valleys, hills, and woods, in rich array,
> Welcome the coming of the longed-for May.
> Now all things smile, only my love doth lower,
> Nor hath the scalding noon-day sun the power

12

> To melt that marble ice, which still doth hold
> Her heart congealed, and makes her pity cold.

> . . . " All things keep
> Time with the season, only she doth carry
> June in her eyes, in her heart January."

It will be noticed that the extravagance of poets in their love-songs increases. The fashion which Surrey and Wyatt brought in of addressing the lady of their verses as if she were more a goddess than a mortal was carried to a ridiculous pitch. Carew is one of the poets who helped to this exaggerated style. The following verses, in which he writes to his lady that she has usurped the office of the sun, and can make darkness and light at her pleasure, was a common fiction in the verse of these poets of the seventeenth century : —

> " If when the sun at noon displays
>   His brighter rays,
>   Thou but appear,
> He, then, all pale with shame and fear,
>   Quencheth his light ;
> Hides his dark brow, flies from thy sight,
>   And grows more dim,
> Compared to thee, than stars to him.
> If thou but show thy face again
> When darkness doth at midnight reign,
> The darkness flies, and light is hurled
> Round about the silent world
> So, as alike thou drivest away
> Both light and darkness, night and day."

SIR JOHN SUCKLING, a charming and graceful writer, although he had ample gifts, seems to have prized **1609-1641** very lightly his gifts as poet. In one of his witty rhymes called a *Session of Poets*, Apollo has assembled them all to see who shall be crowned with the wreath of laurel. Suckling describes in his sprightly style all the different aspirants for the honor, as they were noted by Apollo, till he touches himself thus : —

> " Suckling next was called, but did not appear ;
> And straight one whispered Apollo i' the ear,
> That, of all men living, he cared not for 't ;
> He loved not the Muses so well as his sport."

Suckling's verses are true verses of society, gay, not over-earnest, and with an occasional ring of cynicism in their lines. The best and most noted of all his poems is *The Ballad on a Wedding*, in which his description of the bride will always be fresh and new. Here are a few stanzas from it : —

> "The maid — and thereby hangs a tale,
> For such a maid no Whitsun-ale
>   Could ever yet produce ;
> No grape that 's kindly ripe could be
> So round, so plump, so soft as she,
>   Nor half so full of juice.
>
> " Her finger was so small, the ring
> Would not stay on, which they did bring,
>   It was too wide a peck ;
> And, to say truth (for out it must),
> It looked like the great collar (just)
>   About our young colt's neck.
>
> " Her feet beneath her petticoat,
> Like little mice, stole in and out
>   As if they feared the light.
> But oh, she dances such a way,
> No sun upon an Easter day
>   Is half so fine a sight.
>
> " Her cheeks so rare a white was on,
> No daisy makes comparison ;
>   Who sees them is undone.
> For streaks of red were mingled there
> Such as are on a Catherine pear, —
>   The side that 's next the sun.
>
> " Her lips were red, and one was thin
> Compared to that was next her chin, —
>   Some bee had stung it newly ;
> But, Dick, her eyes so guard her face,
> I durst no more upon them gaze
>   Than on the sun in July.
>
> " Her mouth 's so small, when she doth speak
> Thou 'dst swear her teeth her words did break,
>   That they might passage get ;
> But so she handled still the matter
> They came as good as ours, or better,
>   And are not spent a whit."

Suckling was an ardent loyalist, and when the civil war began, embarked in it with all his heart and with characteristic extravagance. He equipped a company of one hundred horse in such gorgeous array that they were said to have cost him twelve thousand pounds. Then he led his dandy troops on an expedition which achieved nothing, and was ridiculed by the Puritans in a witty lampoon. One of his biographers says that Sir John took all this, and the defeat of the royal party, so sorely to heart that he went to the Continent, and ended his life by a dose of poison.

RICHARD LOVELACE, with his romantic name, was another gallant poet of the court of Charles I., and loyal to the king through all misfortunes. He was a soldier in the civil war, was twice imprisoned by the Puritans, and at last set free, ruined in fortune and broken in health. The verses he wrote to Lady Lucy Sacheverel, whom he calls Lucasta in his verses, are in the noblest vein : —

1618–1658

> " Tell me not, sweet, I am unkind,
>   That from the nunnery
> Of thy chaste breast and quiet mind
>   To war and arms I flee.
>
> " True, a new mistress now I chase, —
>   The first foe in the field, —
> And with a stronger faith embrace
>   A sword, a horse, a shield.
>
> " Yet this inconstancy is such
>   As you, too, shall adore ;
> I could not love thee, dear, so much,
>   Loved I not honor more."

Our hearts must ache to think of the sad end of this gallant courtier who could write verses so brave and tender. There is another beautiful song, *To Althea*, written in prison, in which he says, —

> " Stone walls do not a prison make,
>   Nor iron bars a cage ;
> Minds innocent and quiet take
>   That for a hermitage.

> "If I have freedom in my love,
>   And in my soul am free,
> Angels alone, that soar above,
>   Enjoy such liberty."

It is said he really wrote these lines in prison, and that the lady of his love, believing he had died of his wounds received before he was imprisoned, married another, perhaps while he was writing these very verses to her; and when he was at last set free, a ruined man, he found the woman of his dreams a happy wife. He died soon after of a slow consumption, and in his last days was often seen, his handsome face pale and wan, his once elegant person clad in ragged habiliments, going down the dirty London alley where he had his lodgings, and where at the last he died a sad and lonely death. Poor fellow!

EDMUND WALLER is the last of this group of singers, as sparkling, musical, and full of gayety as the best. **1605–1687** He also was a courtier of Charles I., but changed his colors easily, and when Cromwell was Lord Protector, became his adherent, and wrote a panegyric on him after death, which is a grand tribute. But as soon as Charles II. came to the throne, Waller had a poem of congratulation to offer him. When Charles, who was as shrewd as he was unprincipled and good-natured, said that the poem on Cromwell was better than that the poet offered him, Waller answered, with ready wit, "Poets succeed better in fiction than in truth, your Majesty."

The name Waller celebrated was that of a lady he called Sacharissa,— a name ever since famous in verse. Generally, his verses are light as air; but there is one song which has a touch of sadness, as if written in a minor key: —

> "Go, lovely rose,
> Tell her that wastes her time and me
>   That now she knows
> When I resemble her to thee
> How sweet and fair she seems to be.
>
> "Tell her that's young,
> And shuns to have her graces spied,
>   That hadst thou sprung

In deserts where no men abide,
Thou must have uncommended died.

"Small is the worth
Of beauty from the light retired;
  Bid her come forth,
Suffer herself to be desired,
And not blush so to be admired.

"Then die! that she
The common fate of all things rare
  May read in thee,
How small a part of time they share
That are so wondrous sweet and fair."

Of all Waller's songs I like this best, because it sounds most in earnest; for, after all, these early song-writers do not impress us as being very much in earnest in the tributes they pay to their Julias and Chloes and Sacharissas. Is it a charm or a defect of these dainty love-verses that they do not sound as if they came out of the depths of the heart? It may be a part of their charm that they make no large demands on our feeling. Thus, to go back to the elder poets and to read their lays is as restful as listening to that music that asks of the listener neither thought nor tears. They make no pretence of intensity or earnestness; they are as frank as was Waller when his Sacharissa, grown an old woman, asked, "When will you ever sing such songs about me again?" and he answered, "When you are again young and beautiful." So these poets sang to youth, to beauty, the bright eye and the red lip, the bloom on the peach, the unwithered rose. The soul behind all these they did not celebrate, except in rare verses, which are a solitary burst of music. Hence they carol like birds in the sky, clear, fresh, and full of joyousness, like the lark, "that singing still doth soar, and soaring ever singeth."

PART IV.

THE CIVIL WAR AND THE RESTORATION.

MILTON TO DRYDEN.

1608 TO 1700.

INTRODUCTORY.

BEFORE going further with the history of the literature and literary men of the seventeenth century, I wish to touch upon a political struggle which came to an issue in the reign of Charles I., — the contest between the Puritans and the Royalists.

The Puritans, who were a small body in Elizabeth's reign, had been constantly growing stronger. They were the party of extreme Protestants, who, not satisfied with the separation of the English Church from the Church of Rome, wanted many other reforms. They clamored for a change in manners, in politics, and in the church. Their leaders believed in plain meeting-houses and simple forms of worship, and opposed the ceremonies retained in the English Church, because they reminded them of the Church of Rome, which was so odious to them. In politics, their ideas were as revolutionary as their ideas in religion. The greater part of them belonged to the people of the middle class, who had done more than any other for the prosperity of England, but had not shared the privileges of the nobles, and began to feel they were shut out from many rights which they ought to claim. There were among them a strong spirit of revolt and many republican ideas. In the time of James I. a good deal had been said in the court circles and among the nobility about the "divine right of kings," which was especially hateful to the Puritans, who believed that the only power not to be questioned was the power of God, and denied divine right to either pope or kings. True, not all the nobles held these extreme ideas of monarchy. Walter Raleigh opposed them, and in some of his latest letters, written to the young Prince Henry, the eldest son of James I., while he was in the Tower, he urged him not to accept the extreme ideas of a monarch's power over his people. "Preserve to your future subjects," Raleigh writes in one of these letters, "the *divine right* of being free agents, and to your own royal house the divine right of being their benefactors." But king and court were not so wise as was Raleigh, and, unfortunately, the young Prince Henry, who listened to and admired his counsels, died, and left the throne to the prince's narrow-minded brother, Charles I. If he had lived, we should probably have had a different chapter in English history, in which Oliver Cromwell would have been left out.

In manners and modes of living, also, the Puritans favored a reform. They were inclined to wear clothes of plain cut and sober colors; they cropped their hair and shaved their faces, and so got the name of *Roundheads* from their opponents. Their speech was serious and full of Bible quotations, and it was claimed that their constant psalm-singing had given their voices a nasal twang. They took up for their guidance many of the laws of the Hebrews under Moses, and gave their children Hebrew names taken from the Old Testament. They were austere in conduct, discouraged games and amusements, and were especially hostile to the theatre. You can imagine, without my telling you, what an influence all these ideas would have on literature.

The Royalists, who were also called *Cavaliers*, were in broadest contrast to the Puritans. The Cavalier loved mirth and revelry. He kept merry Christmas each year, and went to see a play when in London. He wore bright-colored silks and velvets, and his hair and beard were long and flowing. He had not been so long weaned from the Church of Rome that he could feel as if he were in church when he sat on a bench inside the four bare walls of a Puritan "meeting-house," and heard a preacher without a robe. He wanted cathedral and altar, fine singing in his choir, and the imposing ceremonies of worship. Above all, like every "true-born Englishman," he loved his sovereign, whether

he or she happened **at the time** to be English like Elizabeth, or Scotch like **James I., or** German **as a century
later was George of Brunswick.**

The Puritans **as well as the Cavaliers were** loyal **Englishmen, and** if Charles I. had been a wise, far-seeing **ruler, he**
might have guided his kingdom through the storm without
shipwreck. Instead of this, he was bigoted, narrow-minded,
and blind to the best interests of his people. He had an
absurd idea of the divine right of kings, and by his per-
sistence in unjust authority he lost his cause, when a little
yielding would have gained it. At length he so alienated
the Puritan party that they broke out in open rebellion.
Their leader was Oliver Cromwell, a man of great power,
ambition, and military ability. Under his leadership the
Puritans were so **successful that they carried everything be-**
fore them, and, seizing the king, **they tried him for**
treason against the liberties of the people, beheaded **1649**
him, **and** took the government into their own hands.

From the time the rebellion began, until his death in
1658, Oliver Cromwell **was** really the ruler **of** England.
He was not called so, however, till five years before **his**
death, when he received the title of Lord **Protector. He
ruled** England severely, like the autocrat he was, but with
ability **and** wisdom. When he died, an attempt was made
to create his son Richard Lord Protector after him ; but by
this time the English people, who loved the royal line in
spite of its faults, would have no more of Cromwellian rule.
They had yearned after the son **of** their dead king, who
had been since youth exiled from his country, and bringing
home this hereditary prince, they made him King Charles II.
This restoring of the prince to **his** father's throne
is **a** notable point in English history, and is known **1660**
as the *Restoration.*

Never did any English sovereign **have a nobler oppor-**
tunity to make himself immortal in history and **blessed in**
the memories **of** his **people than Charles II. He was
welcomed** to the throne with **such joy as** the cool-blooded
English rarely show. If there had been in him one spark

of kingliness or of true manliness, he might have been a great monarch. He could easily, by his influence, have ennobled politics, have made manners pure without making them too severe, have elevated literature, and have kept religion on a high level, free from the gloom and hardness of Puritanism on the one side, and the empty hollowness of forms on the other. All this Charles by his own example, if he had been a noble gentleman, might have done. But he was an unprincipled, dishonorable man. He brought with him a crowd of courtiers, many of whom had been in France, and who had brought back all the vices they found there to graft them on those of England. Literature, especially the drama, reflected all these vices. Never was the stage so degraded as in the reign of Charles. Women went in masks to the theatre, ashamed to show their faces there ; and men of rare wit and great brilliancy devoted all their talents to the production of a poetry so full of coarseness that it is now, happily, almost unread and unknown.

As would be natural, nearly all the literary men and poets, from the beginning of the civil war, were on the side of the king, and many of them shed their blood for his sake. From the earliest times that the minstrel first sounded his harp in the banquet halls of his chief, the poet has generally been under the king's patronage. Most of the singers of whom I have already spoken were Royalists, — Lovelace, Suckling, Herrick, and the rest. Waller was a turncoat, and could write odes either for Cromwell or Charles II., as occasion offered ; and Wither is almost the only man among them who was a Puritan and suffered in the cause. There was, however, one poet, so great that he overtopped all others, and made amends for the loss of all the rest, whose heart and brain were enlisted in the Puritan cause. This was JOHN MILTON, the great English epic poet, — the great poet immediately following Shakespeare ; and it is with him that I begin my account of the writers of this period.

XXIX.

ON JOHN MILTON.

EIGHT years before the death of Shakespeare, John
Milton was born. His father's house was
in Bread Street, London, where the clanging of
Bow Bells must have been one of the first sounds in his
baby ears. Close by, in the same street, was the Mermaid
tavern ; and when a toddling child, Milton may have seen
the figures of Shakespeare, Beaumont and Fletcher, Ben
Jonson, or any of the notable members of that club at the
Mermaid, as they passed the door of his father's house on
their way to the famous old inn.

1608-1674

Milton stands alone in my imagination, a grand and
solitary figure in English literature. We do not see him as
we see Shakespeare, surrounded by a group of poets of his
own kind, even though far below him in genius, or, like
Shakespeare again, followed by a host of imitators. He
stands apart, dignified, sublime, the great epic poet of our
language.

Somebody says, in a description of Milton's father, that
he " was a good musician and a bad poet." That the elder
Milton had an excellent talent for music is proved by some
of his compositions which still remain, and he loved the
art so much that his son was trained in the knowledge of
it from babyhood. Perhaps this early culture attuned Milton's ear to catch that grand movement and harmony which
are the charm and power of his poetry.

He was a precocious boy, delicate and scholarly, and so
beautiful, with his fair skin, curling light hair, and brown
eyes, that his fellow-students in college nicknamed him the
" Lady." He wrote verses at seventeen, studied till midnight when a mere child, and in college says of himself :
"There for seven years I studied the learning and arts
wont to be taught, far from all vice and approved by all

good men." At twenty-four he left college, and spent four or five years in writing and study. During this time he wrote his two plays, *Comus* and *Arcades*, his lyrics, *L'Allegro* and *Il Penseroso*, together with the *Lament for Lycidas*, and some sonnets. After this he went to France and Italy. Here he spent a happy season, going to literary parties in Rome, where he met the poets and scholars of the time, and making some lifelong friends in these journeyings. But the strife between the court and the Puritans had broken out fiercely. England had begun to be in a turmoil, and Milton was too anxious about his country to stay away in content; so he returned, and, taking a house in St. Bride's Churchyard, began as a schoolmaster, teaching his two nephews and some other pupils their Greek, Latin, and mathematics, and writing meanwhile vigorous tracts in favor of the revolutionary sentiments every day growing stronger. No more verse like *L'Allegro*, no masques like *Comus*, were again to come from his pen.

When Cromwell became Lord Protector of England, Milton was made his Latin secretary, and was in close commerce with the heads of the Puritan party, writing in favor of political liberty and the liberty of the Press. During this time he undertook an answer to the theory of the divine right of kings, which, since the beheading of Charles I., had been strongly proclaimed in Europe. His physicians, who saw symptoms of coming blindness, begged him not to begin this work; but he would not be moved from what he thought was duty, and continued until he became totally blind.

After Cromwell's death, and Charles II. had been restored to the throne of his father, Milton, whose life was for a time in danger, settled down in the leisure of old age and blindness, with the design of writing a great poem, — a design which, no doubt, had been in his thoughts while affairs of state had held him busy. For twenty years he had written no poetry. Now he resolved that he would take something worthy of him, — a heroic subject with heroic treatment. He would write no more light verses, as in his earlier poems; no rhymes, which he now called " the jingling sound of like' endings, . . . the invention of a barbarous age to set off wretched matter and lame metre."

He first thought of taking the British King Arthur for the hero of his work; but finally chose a supernatural subject, — the revolt of Satan in Heaven, and the expulsion of Adam and Eve from Paradise, which, in an earlier age, had been the theme of Cædmon's untaught pen. *Paradise Regained* followed *Paradise Lost,* and these epics, with the tragedy of *Samson Agonistes,* whose hero was the mighty Hebrew smitten with blindness, were the work of Milton's latest days.

You will notice that Milton's writings are in three distinct groups, — his early poems, written in the lyric style; his prose works, composed in the middle period of his life; and his later poems, written in the epic style, — with the exception of *Samson Agonistes,* which is a drama, — and only in blank verse.

I fancy that Milton, in his later days, when he wrote *Paradise Lost,* did not have a great admiration for his early poems. Yet they are so musical and so graceful that I am very glad he did not hold his severe opinions about rhyme when, in early manhood, he wrote these fanciful verses, with their "jingling sound of like endings."

The lightest of all his pieces are *L'Allegro* and *Il Penseroso,* the first an ode to Mirth, and the last an ode to Melancholy. In the first, after bidding " loathed Melancholy" begone, he continues with this gay invocation:

" Haste thee, Nymph, and bring with thee
Jest and youthful Jollity,
Quips and cranks and wanton wiles,
Nods and becks and wreathed smiles
Such as hang on Hebe's cheek,
And love to live in dimple sleek;
Sport that wrinkled Care derides,
And Laughter, holding both his sides.
Come, and trip it as ye go,
On the light fantastic toe;
And in thy right hand lead with thee
The mountain nymph, sweet Liberty;

And if I give thee honor due,
Mirth, admit me of thy crew,
To live with her, and live with thee,
In unreproved pleasures free."

Then the poet goes on to paint the delights of a day in the country.   At early morn he awakes —

" To hear the lark begin her flight,
And singing startle the dull night,
From his watch-tower in the skies,
Till the dappled dawn doth rise ;
Then to come in spite of sorrow,
And at my window bid good-morrow,
Through the sweet-brier, or the vine,
Or the twisted eglantine ;
While the cock, with lively din,
Scatters the rear of darkness thin,
And to the stack, or the barn-door,
Stoutly struts his dames before .
Oft listening how the hounds and horn
Cheerly rouse the slumbering Morn,
From the side of some hoar hill,
Through the high wood echoing shrill.
Sometime walking not unseen
By hedge-row elms, on hillocks green,
Right against the eastern gate,
Where the great Sun begins his state,
Robed in flames, and amber light,
The clouds in thousand liveries dight.
While the ploughman, near at hand,
Whistles o'er the furrowed land,
And the milkmaid singeth blithe,
And the mower whets his scythe,
And every shepherd tells his tale
Under the hawthorn in the dale.
Straight mine eye hath caught new pleasures,
Whilst the landscape round it measures ;
Russet lawns, and fallows gray,
Where the nibbling flocks do stray,
Mountains, on whose barren breast
The laboring clouds do often rest ;
Meadows trim, with daisies pied,
Shallow brooks, and rivers wide.
Towers and battlements it sees,
Bosomed high in tufted trees,
Where perhaps some beauty lies,
The Cynosure of neighboring eyes.

.   .   .   .   .   .

> Sometimes with secure delight
> The upland hamlets will invite ;
> When the merry bells ring round,
> And the jocund rebecks sound
> To many a youth and many a maid,
> Dancing in the checkered shade ;
> And young and old come forth to play
> On a sunshine holiday,
> Till the livelong daylight fail."

So the day passes in innocent sport till sunset, when the country folk gather to take their spicy nut-brown ale, and tell stories of fairies and of the good little house-goblins who do the housework when the maids are asleep, contented if a bowl of cream be set out for them to drink when work is over. Their stories done, the country people creep to bed, while the poet goes towards the city and its pleasures : —

> " . . . The busy hum of men,
> Where throngs of knights and barons bold,
> In weeds of peace high triumphs hold,
> With store of ladies, whose bright eyes
> Rain influence, and judge the prize
> Of wit or arms, while both contend
> To win her grace whom all commend.
> There let Hymen oft appear,
> In saffron robe, with taper clear,
> And pomp and feast and revelry,
> With mask and antique pageantry ,
> Such sights as youthful poets dream
> On summer eves by haunted stream.
> Then to the well-trod stage anon,
> If Jonson's learned sock be on,
> Or sweetest Shakespeare, Fancy's child,
> Warble his native wood-notes wild."

Thus the day of pleasure ends in a gush of soft music, when the poet sinks to rest, lapped in " Lydian airs —

> " Married to immortal verse,
> Such as the meeting soul may pierce
> In notes with many a winding bout
> Of linked sweetness long drawn out ;
> With wanton heed, and giddy cunning,
> The melting voice through mazes running ;

> Untwisting all the chains that tie
> The hidden soul of harmony.
>
> .   .   .   .   .
>
> These delights, if thou canst give,
> Mirth, with thee I mean to live."

The companion to *L'Allegro* was *Il Penseroso*, in which he sings the praise of sadness as he has sung that of mirth. But Milton's melancholy, like his mirth, is temperate and not passionate.   He addresses a —

> " Goddess sage and holy,
>   Hail ! divinest Melancholy,
>   Whose saintly visage is too bright
>   To hit the sense of human sight ;
>   And therefore, to our weaker view,
>   O'erlaid with black, staid Wisdom's hue.
>
>   .   .   .   .   .
>
>   Come, pensive Nun, devout and pure,
>   Sober, steadfast, and demure,
>   All in a robe of darkest grain,
>   Flowing with majestic train,
>   And sable stole of cyprus lawn,
>   Over thy decent shoulders drawn.
>   Come, but keep thy wonted state,
>   With even step and musing gait,
>   And looks commercing with the skies,
>   Thy rapt soul sitting in thine eyes :
>   There held in holy passion still,
>   Forget thyself to marble, till
>   With a sad leaden downward cast,
>   Thou fix them on the earth as fast."

In contrast to Mirth, whose course was begun in the joyous day by the singing of the lark, Melancholy is of the evening, and her bird is the sad nightingale, who sings in dusky twilight.   The poet paints himself wandering over the smooth-shaven green, watching the moon, half hid by fleecy clouds ; or later, going to his study, —

> " Where glowing embers through the room
>   Teach light to counterfeit a gloom ; "

till finally, in his lonely tower, he lights his midnight lamp and watches out the night with his books.   Plato, Homer, the great tragic poets, and our own Chaucer, all speak to

him from their pages in "Sage and solemn tunes, . . .
where more is meant than meets the ear," till morning
dawns again.

> "Thus, Night, oft see me in thy pale career,
> Till civil-suited Morn appear ;
> Not tricked and frounced, as she was wont
> With the Attic boy to hunt,
> But kerchiefed in a comely cloud,
> While rocking winds are piping loud :
> Or ushered with a shower still,
> When the gust hath blown his fill,
> Ending on the rustling leaves
> With minute drops from off the eaves.
> And when the sun begins to fling
> His flaring beams, me, Goddess, bring
> To arched walks of twilight groves
> And shadows brown that Sylvan loves,
> Of pine or monumental oak,
> Where the rude axe, with heaved stroke,
> Was never heard the nymphs to daunt,
> Or fright them from their hallowed haunt.
> There in close covert by some brook,
> Where no profaner eye may look,
> Hide me from day's garish eye ;
> While the bee with honeyed thigh,
> That at her flowery work doth sing,
> And the waters murmuring
> With such consort as they keep,
> Entice the dewy-feathered Sleep ;
> And let some strange mysterious dream
> Wave at his wings in airy stream
> Of lively portraiture displayed,
> Softly on my eyelids laid.
> And as I wake, sweet music breathe
> Above, about, or underneath,
> Sent by some spirit to mortals good,
> Or th' unseen Genius of the wood.
> But let my due feet never fail
> To walk the studious cloister's pale,
> And love the high embowed roof,
> With antique pillars massy proof,
> And storied windows richly dight,
> Casting a dim religious light.
> There let the pealing organ blow
> To the full-voiced choir below,
> In service high, and anthems clear,
> As may with sweetness through mine ear,

Dissolve me into ecstasies,
And bring all Heaven before mine eyes.
　　And may at last my weary age
Find out the peaceful hermitage —
The hairy gown and mossy cell,
Where I may sit, and rightly spell
Of every star that Heaven doth show,
And every herb that sips the dew ;
Till old experience do attain
To something like prophetic strain.
　　These pleasures, Melancholy, give,
And I with thee will choose to live."

XXX.

Milton's "Comus," "Paradise Lost," and "Samson Agonistes."

I HAVE before told you something about the *masques*, — a kind of dramatic entertainment fashionable all through the reign of Elizabeth to the time of Charles I. These masques were frequently performed at court in the palace of the sovereign, and were often a part of the Christmas entertainment in the houses of the nobility. At that time no women ever performed in the plays in any public theatre, but in these masques, or private entertainments, the ladies, as well as the gentlemen, took part. It was therefore quite the fashion to write a masque, and the best writers of the time were proud to try their hand at it. The great Lord Bacon wrote masques, in the time of Elizabeth and James I., and the principal dramatic poets, except Shakespeare, have one or more among their works. We shall not be surprised, therefore, to learn that Milton wrote two masques, — the *Comus* and *Arcades*. The last of these, which is only a fragment, was played before the Countess of Derby, at Hatfield, by some of her family, and *Comus* was given at Ludlow Castle, the country house of the Earl of Bridgewater. The chief characters in *Comus*, a young maiden and her brothers, were played by the Lady Alice Egerton, daughter of the earl, and his sons, Lord Brackly and Sir Thomas Egerton. The story is of a lady who, in coming through the forest, is separated from her two brothers, her companions. The wood is haunted by Comus, a spirit of unwholesome mirth, who, with a crew of monsters in the forms of men with the heads of beasts, is holding wild revels there. Comus, disguised as a shepherd, under pretence of leading the lady to her brothers, beguiles her to his palace, where he tries to bring her under his enchantments; but as she is too pure and good to be harmed by his spells, he leaves her, after succeeding in fixing her to a chair in the banquet-room, which holds her fast so that she cannot move from it. Here she is found by her brothers, led by her guardian spirit, and with the aid of the river-nymph Sabrina she is rescued and brought to her father's castle.

This is the plot of *Comus*, which Milton is said to have founded on the fact that the Lady Alice had recently missed her way in some woodland excursion, and thus caused some alarm to her friends. It is a very simple plot, but. Milton has woven in it a most exquisite play. It is too perfect a whole to quote in passages, and must be read entire ; but no one who wishes to know Milton as a poet in youth should fail to read the *Comus*.

It is as a poet that we consider Milton, and so we must pass by his prose works, many of which were written in Latin ; but, in passing, I must tell you that his plea for the liberty of the Press (a prose tract which bears the hard title of *Areopagitica*) is the one of all his prose works best worth your reading. Milton's pen and influence were generally used for freedom, — freedom of speech, freedom of thought, freedom of belief; and although there are occasions on which he was not so generous as we who live in the present might wish he had been, yet he was so far ahead of his time in his thought that we must admire him as a grand mouthpiece of Liberty.

There is something that touches the heart in the picture we have of him in the last of life, when he sat down, blind and poor, to write *Paradise Lost.* I am sorry that very few people nowadays read *Paradise Lost,* and I fear as time goes on that it will be even less read. Unfortunately, the poem in its subject and its characters does not come within the scope of human interest, and the greatest poet in the world would find it difficult to keep the attention of his readers if he did not write about things that excite the sympathy or touch the emotions. Notwithstanding the grand style and organ-like melody of *Paradise Lost,* a great many who attempt to read it put it away as tiresome. Yet any one who has an ear for a grand poetic measure, so superb in harmony that it has never been equalled in English verse from Chaucer to this day, must be charmed by Milton's mighty line. It seems to me that the poet's early musical training shows in his style. It is after the manner of a grand instrument; your ear would be held captive if you did not heed the sense, and from beginning to end, wherever his theme leads him, he preserves the same unbroken harmony.

That Milton was able to touch the heart of his reader, and that if he had chosen a subject within the sphere of natural human sympathy he could have held the interest, is proved by the fact that when he claims our sympathy, he does it with great power. We shall feel this in Book Third of *Paradise Lost,* which begins by an all-hail to Light, " Offspring of Heaven first-born," where he goes on with touching sadness, —

> " But thou
> Revisit'st not these eyes, that roll in vain
> To find thy piercing ray, and find no dawn;
> So thick a drop serene hath quenched their orbs,
> Or dim suffusion veiled. Yet not the more
> Cease I to wander, where the Muses haunt
> Clear spring, or shady grove, or sunny hill,
> Smit with the love of sacred song; but chief
> Thee, Sion, and the flowery brooks beneath,
> That wash thy hallowed feet, and warbling flow,
> Nightly I visit. . . .
> Then feed on thoughts, that voluntary move
> Harmonious numbers; as the wakeful bird
> Sings darkling and in shadiest covert hid,
> Tunes her nocturnal note. Thus with the year
> Seasons return; but not to me returns

Day, or the sweet approach of even or morn,
Or sight of vernal bloom, or summer's rose,
Or flocks, or herds, or human face divine ;
But cloud instead, and ever-during dark
Surrounds me, from the cheerful ways of men
Cut off, and for the book of knowledge fair
Presented with a universal blank
Of nature's works, to me expunged and rased,
And wisdom at one entrance quite shut out.
So much the rather thou, Celestial Light,
Shine inward, and the mind through all her powers
Irradiate, there plant eyes, all mists from thence
Purge and disperse, that I may see and tell
Of things invisible to mortal sight."

In his tragedy of *Samson,* Milton also touches on the same subject in a strain of patient and majestic sorrow. It seems as if the figure of the blind Samson was akin to Milton, and that he chose him for his hero because he felt the resemblance. Thus Samson soliloquizes as he sits in Gaza, —

"But, peace, I must not quarrel with the will
Of highest dispensation, which herein
Haply had ends above my reach to know;
Suffices that to me strength is my bane,
And proves the source of all my miseries,
So many and so huge, that each apart
Would ask a life to wail ; but chief of all,
O loss of sight, of thee I most complain!
Blind among enemies, oh, worse than chains,
Dungeon, or beggary, or decrepit age !
Light, the prime work of God, to me is extinct,
And all her various objects of delight
Annulled, which might in part my grief have eased.
Inferior to the vilest now become
Of man or worm ; the vilest here excel me ;
They creep, yet see; I, dark, in light exposed
To daily fraud, contempt, abuse, and wrong,
Within doors, or without, still as a fool
In power of others, never in my own ;
Scarce half I seem to live, dead more than half.
Oh, dark, dark, dark, amid the blaze of noon
Irrevocably dark, total eclipse,
Without all hope of day !
O first created Beam, and thou great Word,
Let there be light, and light was over all,

Why am I thus bereaved thy prime decree?
The sun to me is dark
And silent as the moon
When she deserts the night,
Hid in her vacant interlunar cave.
Since light so necessary is to life,
And almost life itself, if it be true
That light is in the soul,
She all in every part, why was the sight
To such a tender ball as th' eye confined,
So obvious, and so easy to be quenched,
And not as feeling through all parts diffused,
That she might look at will through every pore?
Then had I not been thus exiled from light,
As in the land of darkness, yet in light.
To live a life half dead, a living death,
And buried ; but, oh, yet more miserable,
Myself my sepulchre, a moving grave,
Buried, yet not exempt
By privilege of death and burial
From most of other evils, pains, and wrongs,
But made hereby obnoxious more
To all the miseries of life, —
Life in captivity
Among inhuman foes."

Milton's later poetry must be read in grand passages like these, to be appreciated. There are few young readers who will read *Paradise Lost* entire, and they will be likely to enjoy his youthful poems most. Indeed, we are not apt to be pleased with epic poetry in youth. The incidents of the dramatic poem or the music of the lyric then please us best; and until life is mature we can rarely see fully the greatness of Homer or Milton, and set them in their place among the poets of the world.

But if we did not care for Milton's poetry, we should admire him as a man. He wrote his great poems in an age when literature reflected the license that followed in natural reaction from the severe rule of the Puritans. Never was literature so degraded as in that age, when the reigning poets, from the laureate down, put common decency to the blush, cried out upon everything sacred, and believed neither in honor nor virtue among men or women. Amid all these Milton shone like a star, living the life of an ascetic, and by the practice of a noble temperance preparing himself to compose his grand epic. Thus he stands apart from and above his contemporaries, a noble, self-centred man, who in an age of license sang only to the highest ideals and in praise of the loftiest virtue.

> " Love Virtue ; she alone is free :
> She can teach ye how to climb
> Higher than the sphery chime ;
> Or if Virtue feeble were,
> Heaven itself would stoop to her."

XXXI.

On Milton's Contemporaries, —Marvell, Cowley, and Butler.

MILTON was the great poet of his century ; there is no other man of the time worthy to rank beside him, either among Puritans or Cavaliers. His place in literature is all the more distinctive because he was a Puritan, and nearly all the other poets of the time were Royalists, devoted to the king's cause. There is one other writer who was in sympathy with Milton, who deserves to be mentioned near him. This is Andrew Marvell, who, although a Puritan, was a moderate man, and knew how to find the middle path, in which tolerance and common-sense usually walk together.

Marvell lived in Lincolnshire, a county which was famous for Puritans, and sent so many emigrants to America in the early settlement of New England. 1620–1678 After Charles II. was restored to the throne, Marvell was sent to represent his native town in Parliament, and held the seat in firm opposition to the vices of the rulers. He was a man so wise and witty that the king could not help admiring him, and once sent a lord of the treasury to see if he could not be won over to the royal side. Marvell

received his guest hospitably, but gave him mutton for dinner on three successive days; and when the courtier at
last offered him place and money to change his politics,
the stanch old Roundhead told him plainly that since he
could dine contentedly every day on a shoulder of mutton,
the king could offer him no inducement to change his
colors.

Marvell's writings are principally political satires, witty
in his time, but not interesting now.   He has, however, a
few poems that from their sentiment have been able to
outlive his age, and I select one of the shortest.   It is on
Eyes and Tears, and is, as you will notice, in the style of
the metaphysical poets, with its talk about " watery lines
and plummets," and the sun " distilling the world with
chemic ray."   In spite of this, there are some pretty
thoughts in the verses, and the last dozen lines I think are
very beautiful.

EYES AND TEARS.

" How wisely Nature did decree
    With the same eyes to weep and see,
    That, having viewed the object vain,
    They might be ready to complain !
    And since the self-deluding sight
    In a false angle takes each height,
    These tears, which better measure all,
    Like watery lines and plummets fall.
    Two tears, which sorrow long did weigh
    Within the scales of either eye,
    And then paid out in equal poise,
    Are the true price of all my joys.
    What in the world most fair appears,
    Yea, even laughter, turns to tears,
    And all the jewels that we prize
    Melt in these pendants of the eyes.
    I have through every garden been
    Amongst the red, the white, the green,
    And yet from all those flowers I saw
    No honey but these tears could draw.
    So the all-seeing sun each day
    Distils the world with chemic ray,
    But finds the essence only showers,
    Which straight in pity back he pours.

Yet happy they whom grief doth bless,
That weep the more and see the less,
And to preserve their sight more true
Bathe still their eyes in their own dew.
So Magdalen in tears more wise
Dissolves those captivating eyes
Whose liquid chains could flowing meet
To fetter her Redeemer's feet.

The incense is to Heaven dear
Not as a perfume, but a tear;
And stars show lovely in the night
But as they seem the tears of light.
Ope, then, my eyes, your double sluice,
And practise so your noblest use;
For others too can see or sleep,
But only human eyes can weep."

Another noted poet of this age is ABRAHAM COWLEY, a trusted servant and secretary of Charles I., and **1618-1667** afterwards devoted to his son, Charles II., who seems to have neglected the poet during his life, and to have contented himself with saying of him after his death, "Mr. Cowley has not left behind him a better man in England."

Milton prized Cowley highly, and thought him one of the greatest among poets; but he is not so much valued now. Much better than his verses I like his prose essays, of which he wrote a dozen or more. The theme of nearly all his essays is a praise of country life, — a life without ambition or cares, led among green fields and beside still waters. The titles of the essays indicate this. They are on Solitude, Gardens, Agriculture, Liberty, and kindred subjects. It seemed as if in all he wrote, Cowley felt the tediousness and hollowness of a life at court, and longed to be free from it. In his essay on Agriculture he exalts above all lives that of the farmer, and in his essay on Greatness he praises a simple house and simple fare above all the luxury of court. His essay on Liberty contains as grand a definition of Freedom as has ever been given. He says, "The liberty of a people consists in being governed by laws which they have made themselves, under whatsoever form it be of government ; the liberty of a private man, in being **master of** his own time and actions, as **far as may** consist with **the laws of** God **and his** country."

Toward **the end of his life Cowley** did attain to a little **estate in the** country, about which he **had** written so much and **had so** longed for. He did not live very long to enjoy **it, and had** suffered so many disappointments before getting **it that he** was not altogether happy in the realization of his **wishes.** After a few years in this retreat, he died suddenly **of** cold caught from getting overheated while working **during the harvest** among his laborers.

Cowley was **a** versatile writer both in prose and verse. **In** poetry he has one long epic, of which the Hebrew king David is the **hero** ; he also wrote several plays. But **of** all his poetry I like much best his shorter pieces. He was very familiar with the Greek and Latin poets, and translated many of **their** verses with such **spirit that** they have the merit of an original. His *Songs from Anacreon* **are** specimens of this easy and free rendering.

Cowley began to write very early, and **tells us** in one **of his essays, entitled "** Myself," **that** he **wrote** verses at thirteen. He says **here : " How this** love of poetry came to be produced in me so **early is a hard** question. I believe I can tell the particular little chance which filled my head first with such chimes **of verse** as have never since left ringing there ; for I remember when I began to read, and to take some pleasure in it, there was wont to lie in my mother's parlor (I know not **by** what accident, for she herself never in her life read any book but of **devotion**), **but** there was **wont** to lie Spenser's works ; this I **happened to** fall upon, and was infinitely delighted with **the** stories of the knights, monsters, and giants, and brave houses which I found everywhere there (though **my** understanding had very little to do **with** all this), **and by** degrees, with the tinkling of the rhymes and the dance of the numbers, I had read him all over before I was twelve years old, **and** was thus made a poet almost immediately."

I think I cannot give you a more characteristic specimen

of Cowley, as showing the bent of his mind as well as his
easy style, than by quoting a story which he borrowed
from one of the Latin authors, and which is added to one
of his essays in praise of a country life. It is *The Country
Mouse* : —

> " At the large foot of a fair hollow tree,
> Close to ploughed ground, seated commodiously,
> His ancient and hereditary house,
> There dwelt a good, substantial country mouse,
> Frugal and grave, and careful of the main,
> Yet one who once did nobly entertain
> A city mouse, well-coated, sleek, and gay,
> A mouse of high degree, who lost his way,
> Wantonly walking forth to take the air,
> And arrived early and alighted there
> For a day's lodging ; the good, hearty host,
> The ancient plenty of his hall to boast,
> Did all the stores produce that might excite,
> With various tastes, the courtier's appetite, —
> Fitches and beans, peason and oats, and wheat,
> And a large chestnut, the delicious meat
> Which Jove himself, were he a mouse, would eat ;
> And for a *hautgout* there was mixed with these
> The swerd of bacon, and the coat of cheese, —
> The precious relics which at harvest he
> Had gathered from the reaper's luxury.
> ' Freely,' said he, ' fall on, and never spare ;
> The bounteous gods will for to-morrow care.'
> And, thus at ease, on beds of straw they lay,
> And to their genius sacrificed the day.
> Yet the nice guest's epicurean mind,
> Though breeding made him civil seem and kind,
> Despised this country feast, and still his thought
> Upon the pies and cakes of London wrought.
> ' Your bounty and civility,' said he,
> ' Which I 'm surprised in these rude parts to see,
> Shows that the gods have given you a mind
> Too noble for the fate that here you find.
> Why should a soul so virtuous and so great
> Lose itself thus in an obscure retreat?
> Let savage beasts lodge in a country den,
> You should see towns, and manners know, and men,
> And taste the generous luxury of the court,
> Where all the mice of quality resort. . . .
> We all, ere long, must render up our breath ;
> No cave nor hole can shelter us from death.

Since life is so uncertain and so short,
Let 's spend it all in feasting and in sport.
Come, worthy sir, come with me, and partake
All the great things that mortals happy make.'
Alas! what virtues hath sufficient arms
T' oppose bright honor and soft pleasure's charms?
What wisdom can their magic force repel?
It draws this reverend hermit from his cell. . . .

" Plainly, the truth to tell, the sun was set
When to the town the weary travellers get.
To a lord's house, as lordly as can be,
Made for the use of pride and luxury,
They come ; the gentle courtier at the door
Stops, and will hardly enter in before.
'But 't is, sir, your command, and, being so,
I 'm sworn t' obedience,' and so in they go.
Behind a hanging in a spacious room,
The richest work of Mortlake's noble loom,
They wait a while, their wearied limbs to rest,
Till silence should invite them to their feast.
About the hour that Cynthia's silver light
Has touched the pale meridies of the night,
At last, the various supper being done,
It happened that the company was gone
Into a room remote, servants and all,
To please their noble fancies with a ball.
Our host leads forth his stranger, and does find
All fitted to the bounties of his mind.
Still on the table half-filled dishes stood,
And with delicious bits the floor was strewed.
The courteous mouse presents him with the best,
And both with fat varieties are blest.
The industrious peasant everywhere doth range,
And thanks the gods for his life's happy change.
Lo! in the midst of a well-freighted pie
They both at last glutted and wanton lie,
When — see the sad reverse of prosperous fate,
And what fierce storms on mortal glories wait —
With hideous noise, down the rude servants come ;
Six dogs before ran barking into th' room.
The wretched gluttons fly with wild affright,
And hate the fulness which retards their flight ;
Our trembling peasant wishes now in vain
That rocks and mountains covered him again.
Oh, how the change of his poor life he curst!
'This, of all lives,' said he, 'is sure the worst.
Give me again, ye gods, my cave and wood ;
With peace, let tares and acorns be my food!'"

One more little bit from Cowley, in a different vein, and we must leave him. This is the ode to *The Grasshopper;* —

"Happy insect, what can be
In happiness compared to thee?
Fed with nourishment divine,
The dewy morning's gentle wine,
Nature waits upon thee still,
And thy verdant cup does fill;
'T is filled wherever thou dost tread,
Nature's self thy Ganymede.
Thou dost drink and dance and sing,
Happier than the happiest king;
All the fields which thou dost see,
All the plants, belong to thee;
All that summer hours produce,
Fertile made with early juice.
Man doth for thee sow and plough;
Farmer he, and landlord thou.
Thou dost innocently enjoy,
Nor does thy luxury destroy.
The shepherd gladly heareth thee,
More harmonious than he.

.   .   .   .   .

To thee, of all things upon earth,
Life is no longer than thy mirth.
Happy insect, happy thou,
Dost neither age nor winter know;
But when thou'st drunk and danced and sung
Thy fill the flowery leaves among
(Voluptuous and wise withal,
Epicurean animal),
Sated with thy summer feast,
Thou retir'st to endless rest."

Of all the poets who supported the Royalist cause at this time, none did it better service than SAMUEL BUTLER. He turned the Puritans into ridicule in 1612–1680 his poem of *Hudibras,* one of the wittiest satires ever written, — and you know that no weapon is more powerful against a foe than ridicule. There were plenty of absurdities in the Puritan manners and dress for ridicule to lay hold of, and for all these Butler had a quick eye. He took for his hero Sir Hudibras, a Presbyterian knight, who, with his squire,

Ralph, goes out to redress all wrongs and correct all abuses in law or religion. If you have read the account of Don Quixote setting out with his squire, Sancho Panza, on his travels, you will be reminded of it by *Hudibras*; but the stories are not much alike, except in the beginning, though Hudibras, like the Don, gets into all sorts of scrapes. He gets beaten, set in stocks, pelted with rotten eggs and all sorts of missiles, and is from first to last a ridiculous object, although he preserves a serene self-conceit, and is unconscious that anybody is laughing at him. You can imagine how much the Cavaliers must have enjoyed this picture of their enemy, the Puritan.

Hudibras is a pattern of clever rhyming, and few poets, before or since, can approach Butler in making difficult words fall easily into rhyme and metre; as thus: —

> " Whatever sceptic could inquire for,
>   For every why he had a wherefore."

Or this : —

> " Alas, what perils do environ
>   The man who meddles with cold iron."

The poem also abounds in lines that have been so much quoted that we use them almost without knowing where we get them.

I shall not attempt to quote from *Hudibras*, because it is difficult to give extracts from it; but I will quote a short satire from Butler which is a capital illustration of his merit : —

THE ELEPHANT IN THE MOON.

> " A learned society of late,
>   The glory of a foreign state,
>   Agreed, upon a summer's night,
>   To search the moon by her own light,
>   To take an inventory of all
>   Her real estate and personal,
>   And make an accurate survey
>   Of all her lands, and how they lay;

> " To observe her country how 't was planted,
>   With what sh' abounded most, or wanted,

And make the properest observations
For settling of new plantations,
If the society should incline
T' attempt so **glorious a design:**
This was the purpose of **their meeting,**
For which they chose a time as fitting, —
When at the full her radiant light,
And influence, too, were at their height.
And now the lofty tube, the scale
With which they heaven itself assail,
Was mounted full against the moon,
And all stood ready to fall on,
Impatient who should have the honor
To plant an ensign **first upon** her, —

"When one, **who,** for his **deep** belief,
Was virtuoso then, in chief,
Approved the most profound and wise,
To **solve impossibilities,**
Advancing gravely, **to apply**
To th' optic **glass his judging eye,**
Cried, ' Strange!' **then reinforced his sight**
Against the moon **with all his might,**
And bent his penetrating **brow**
As if he meant to gaze her through;
When all the rest began t' admire,
And like a train from him took fire.
Surprised with wonder, beforehand,
At what they did not understand,
Cried out impatient to know what
The matter was, they wondered at.

" Quoth he, 'Th' inhabitants o' th' moon,
Who, when the sun shines hot at noon,
Do live in cellars underground,
Of eight miles deep, and eighty round,
Which they count towns and cities there,
Because their people 's civiler
Than the rude peasants that are found
To live **upon** the upper ground,
Called Privolvans, **with whom they are**
Perpetually in open war;
And now **both** armies, highly enraged,
Are in a bloody fight engaged ; . . .
Look quickly, then, that every one
May see the fight before 't is done.'"

On this, one philosopher after the other applies his eye
to the telescope to see the fight in the moon. They all

make some discovery concerning the contending armies and their positions, till at length one of the wisest, after he has looked long and attentively through the glass, cries out, —

" A stranger sight appears
   Than e'er was seen in all the spheres,
   A wonder more unparalleled
   Than ever mortal tube beheld, —
   An ELEPHANT from one of those
   Two mighty armies is broke loose,
   And with the horror of the fight,
   Appears amazed and in a fright ;
   Look quickly, lest the sight of us
   Should cause the startled beast to imboss.
   It is a large one, far more great
   Than e'er was bred in Afric yet,
   From which we boldly may infer
   The moon is much the fruitfuller.
        .   .   .

   And if the moon produce by nature
   A people of so vast a stature,
   'T is consequent she should bring forth
   Far greater beasts, too, than the earth
   (As by the best accounts appears
   Of all our greatest discoverers),
   And that those monstrous creatures there
   Are not such rarities as here."

The appearance of the elephant makes a great sensation in the society ; each member sees it in a different position on the field of battle, sometimes on one side, then shifting to the other. After some consultation, they all agree to draw up a memorial of the transaction, in which a full account of the Elephant in the Moon, proving the existence of gigantic animals there, shall be given. In the mean time, —

" While they were diverted all
   In wording this memorial,
   The footboys, for diversion too,
   As having nothing else to do,
   Seeing the telescope at leisure,
   Turned virtuosi for their pleasure,
   Began to gaze upon the moon, ·
   As those they waited on had done,

　　　　With monkey's ingenuity,
　　　　Who love to practise what they see,
　　　　When one, whose turn it was to peep,
　　　　Saw something in the engine creep,
　　　　And viewing well, discovered more
　　　　Than all the learned had done before;
　　　　Quoth he : 'A little thing is slunk
　　　　Into the long, star-gazing trunk,
　　　　And now is gotten down so nigh,
　　　　I have him just against mine eye.'
　　　　This being overheard by one
　　　　Who was not so far overgrown
　　　　In any virtuous speculation,
　　　　To judge with mere imagination,
　　　　Immediately he made a guess
　　　　At solving all appearances, . . .
　　　　And found, upon a second view,
　　　　His own hypothesis most true ;
　　　　For he had scarce applied his eye
　　　　To the engine, but immediately
　　　　He found *a mouse* was gotten in
　　　　The hollow tube, and shut between
　　　　The two glass windows, in restraint
　　　　Was swelled into an elephant,
　　　　And proved the virtuous occasion
　　　　Of all this learned dissertation."

Meanwhile the wise members of the society had penned
their learned statement, and it was already sealed and
signed, when the elephant was discovered to be a mouse.
A great hubbub of dispute arose, the larger part of the body
refusing to believe that they had been deceived, till, after a
long discussion, some one suggested that the instrument be
taken apart and examined.

　　　　"But when they had unscrewed the glass
　　　　To find out where th' imposter was,
　　　　And saw the mouse that by mishap
　　　　Had made the telescope a trap,
　　　　Amazed, confounded, and afflicted
　　　　To be so openly convicted,
　　　　Immediately they get them gone
　　　　With this discovery alone, —
　　　　That those who greedily pursue
　　　　Things wonderful instead of true,
　　　　That in their speculations choose
　　　　To make discoveries strange news, . . .

Hold no truth worthy to be known
That is not huge and overgrown,
And explicate appearances,
Not as they are, but as they please ;
In vain strive Nature to suborn,
And for their pains are paid with scorn."

XXXII.

THE DIARIES OF SAMUEL PEPYS AND JOHN EVELYN.

IT is one of the weaknesses of human nature to relish gossip ; to be interested in details about one's neighbors ; to want to know what they have been doing, what sort of clothes they wear, and what they had for dinner on a feast-day. The student in history and literature finds just this kind of relish in gossip about people of the past. He likes to know all the little facts about them, as what they wore and what they ate for dinner ; and thus it is quite natural that two old books full of gossip and small-talk about the time of Charles II. have come to be two of the most read books written in that age. These are the diaries of John Evelyn and Samuel Pepys, both of whom kept a careful record of their daily life and all that was going on about them. There is no history of their time which gives such a familiar picture of the life of the day, and the people who figured in it, as either of these two books.

JOHN EVELYN was a gentleman of leisure and fortune, of **1620–1706** rather scholarly habits, and the author of several books, all dignified and learned. He had a fine house and a good library, and his home was resorted to by many literary men and men of learning, who were his friends. Cowley the poet was one of his intimates, and Jeremy Taylor, with whom he kept up many years a correspondence, was a very dear friend. Cowley and Evelyn sympathized in a taste for gardening, and the latter was noted for the beauty of his trees and plants, his fine hedges and smooth lawns. When Peter the Great, Czar of Russia, was in London, in the last part of the century, he rented Evelyn's house for his royal quarters; and the Russian autocrat used to take a barbaric delight in demolishing the fine garden of his landlord. Among other things, he used to amuse himself by driving a wheelbarrow through the thick garden hedge which Evelyn had cultivated with great care.

Evelyn's diary, although it is full of details, is yet dignified, like himself, and makes us respect him in all his goings and comings.

SAMUEL PEPYS, who was his exact contemporary in time, has left a journal less dignified, but a great deal more amusing. Pepys was a Secretary of the **1632–1703** Navy, and was constantly in court circles, so that he knew all that was said and done there. He had an excellent faculty for business, was a good financier, and a man of taste in artistic matters, in books, music, and the drama. He also wrote some books, now almost forgotten, and he kept his journal in a sort of short-hand of his own, which was not deciphered till long after his death. Probably he never would have written with quite the frankness he has shown there if he had known that two hundred years later we should be gloating over his pages. But as he believed it to be solely for his own eye, he wrote down at night all the petty occurrences of his day, mingled with a great deal that goes to make up history. He is a garrulous, delightful old gossip, who tells the color of his silk stockings; how much his new suit cost; when his wife had a new dress and how she looked in it; what play he saw at the theatre, and how he liked it; how King Charles behaved when he was on his most unkingly behavior; and all the scandal of the palace at Whitehall. One gets from this an excellent idea of the manners of the court of Charles II., and can see what very bad manners they were. In order that you may see what a gossip Samuel Pepys was, and how many things, both little and great, he touches on in his diary, I am going to quote most of his entries for the last month of the year 1663, beginning with the last Sunday in November : —

"*Nov. 29th, — Lord's Day.* — This morning I put on my best black-cloth suit, trimmed with scarlet ribbons, very neat, with my cloak lined with velvet, and a new beaver, which altogether is very noble, with my black silk knit canons I bought a month ago. . . .

"*30th.* —. . . At Whitehall, Sir W. Penn and I met the [Duke of York] in the matted gallery, and then he discoursed with us ; and by and by my Lord Sandwich came and stood by and talked ; but it being St. Andrew's Day, he went to the chapel, and we parted.

"*Dec. 1st.*— At noon I home to dinner with my poor wife, with whom nowadays I enjoy great pleasure in her company and learning of arithmetic. After dinner I to the Guildhall to hear a trial at King's Bench before Lord Chief Justice Hyde, about the insurance of a ship ; . . . and it was pleasant to see what mad sort of testimonies the seamen did give, and could not be got to speak in order, and then their terms such as the judge could not understand ; and to hear how sillily the counsel and judge would speak as to the terms necessary in the matter, would make one laugh ; and above all, a Frenchman that was forced to speak in French and took an English oath he did not understand, and had an interpreter sworn to tell us what he said, which was the best testimony of all.

"*7th.* — At Whitehall I hear and find that there was the last night the greatest tide that ever was remembered in England to have been in this river, — all Whitehall having been drowned. . . . To Whitehall, and anon the King, and Duke [of York] and Duchess came to dinner in the vane-room, where I never saw them before ; but it seems since the tables are done he dines there altogether. The Queen is pretty well, and goes out of her chamber to her little chapel in the house. The King of France, they say, is hiring of sixty sail of ships of the Dutch, but it is not said for what design.

"*10th.* — To St. Paul's Churchyard, to my bookseller's. . . . I could not tell whether to lay out my money for books of pleasure, as plays, which my nature was most earnest in ; but at last, after seeing Chaucer, Dugdale's History of Paul's, Stow's London, besides Shakespeare's, Jonson's, and Beaumont's plays, I at last chose Doctor Fuller's Worthies, the Cabbala, or Collection of Letters of State, with another little book or two, all of good use or serious pleasure ; and Hudibras, both parts, **the** book now in greatest fashion for **drollery, though** I cannot, **I confess, see** enough where the wit lies. **My** mind being thus settled, **I went by** link home, **and so to my office, and to read in** Rushworth, and so home to supper and to **bed. Calling at** Wotton's, my shoemaker's, to-day, he tells **me that Sir H. Wright is** dying ; and that Harris **is come to the Duke's** House again ; and of a rare play to be acted this week of Sir **William** Davenant's, the story of Harry the Eighth, with all his **wives.**

" 11*th.* — I to the coffee-house. . . . Then I went and sat by Mr. Harrington and some east-country merchants, and talking of the country about Quinsborough and thereabouts, he told us **himself** that for fish none than the poorest body will buy a dead fish, but must be alive, unless it be in the winter ; and then they told us the manner of putting their nets into the water. Through holes made in the thick **ice they will** spread **a net of** half a mile long ; and he hath **known a** hundred and thirty and a **hundred** and seventy barrels of fish taken out at one draught. **And then** the people come with sledges upon the ice with **snow at the** bottom, **and** lay the fish in **and cover them** with **snow, and so** carry them **to market. And he** hath seen when the said fish have been frozen in **the** sledge so that he hath taken a **fish and broke** a-pieces, so hard it has been ; and yet the **same fishes taken out** of the snow and brought into a hot room will **be alive and leap up** and down. Swallows are often brought up in **their nets out of** the mud from under water, hanging together to some twig or other, dead, in ropes ; and brought to the **fire, will** come to life. Fowl killed in December, Alderman Barker **said** he did buy, and putting **into the box under** his sledge, did forget to take them out till April next, and they then were found there, and were through the frost as sweet and fresh, and eat as well, as at first killed. Young bears are there ; their flesh sold in market as ordinarily as beef here, **and** is excellent sweet meat. They **tell us that bears there never do hurt** anybody, but **fly away from you, unless** you pursue them and set upon them ; but **wolves do much** mischief. **Mr.** Harrington told us how they **do to get so** much honey as they send abroad. **They make hol-**low a great fir-tree, **leaving** only a small slit down **straight in** one place, and this they close up again, only leave a little hole, and there the bees go in and fill the bodies of those trees as full **of wax** and honey as they can hold ; and the inhabitants at times **go** and open the slit and take what they please without killing the bees, and so let them live there still, and make more. . . .

" The great entertainment and sport of the Duke of Corland, and the princes thereabout, is hunting, which is not with dogs, as we, but he appoints such a day, and summons all the country people as to a campagnia, and by several companies gives every one their circuit, and they agree upon a place where the toil is to be set; and so, making fires, every company as they go, they drive all the wild beasts, whether bears, wolves, foxes, swine, and stags and roes into the toil, and there the great men have their stands in such and such places, and shoot at what they have a mind to; and that is their hunting. . . . Against a public hunting the Duke sends that no wolves be killed by the people. And whatever harm they do, the Duke makes it good to the person that suffers it, as Mr. Harrington instanced in the house where he lodged, where a wolf broke into a hog-sty and bit three or four great pieces off the back of the hog before the house could come to help it, and the man of the house told him that there were three or four wolves thereabouts that did get hurt; but it was no matter, for the Duke was to make it good to him, otherwise he would kill them.

" 21*st.* — I did go to Shoe Lane to see a cock-fight at a new pit there, — a spot I never was at in my life; but, Lord! to see the strange variety of people, from parliament men to the poorest prentices, bakers, brewers, butchers, draymen, and what not, and all these fellows one with another in swearing, cursing, and betting. I soon had enough of it. And yet I would not but have seen it once. It is strange to see how people of this poor rank, that look as if they had not bread enough to put into their mouths, shall bet three or four pounds at one bet and lose it, and yet bet as much the next battle, so that one of them will lose £10 or £20 at a meeting.

" 28*th.* — Walking through Whitehall, I heard the King was gone to play at tennis, so I down to the new tennis court and saw him and Sir Arthur Slingsby play against my Lord of Suffolk and my Lord Chesterfield. The King beat three and lost two sets; they all, and he particularly, playing well, I thought. Thence went and spoke with the Duke of Albemarle about his wound at Newhall; but I find him a heavy, dull man, methinks, by his answers to me. The Duchess of York is fallen sick of the measles.

" 31*st.* — To dinner, my wife and I, a fine turkey and a mince pie; and dined in state, poor wretch, she and I, and have thus kept our Christmas together alone almost, having not once been out. . . . I bless God I do, after a large expense, even this month, find that I am worth in money, besides all my household stuff, above £800, whereof in my Lord Sandwich's hand £700, and the rest in my hand. I do live at my lodgings in the Navy Office, my family being, besides my wife and I, Jane Gentleman, Besse, our excellent good-natured cook-maid, and Susan, a little girl, having neither man nor boy, nor like to have again a good while, living now in most perfect content and quiet and very frugally also; my health pretty good. . . . Myself, blessed be God! in a good way, and design and resolution of sticking to my business to get a little money with, doing the best service I can to the King also, which God continue. So ends the old year."

You see from this what a garrulous fellow Pepys was, and on how many subjects his Diary touches; and yet, in the end, you cannot fail to feel a liking for him, and to be sure that, in an age of corruption, he meant, as he says, to "do his duty, whatever come of it." Pepys kept his journal only ten years, — from 1659 to 1669. The fine short-hand, or cipher, in which he wrote it was so trying to his eyesight that he was then obliged to give it up. Evelyn's journal covers a much longer space of time, — from 1641 to 1705. Both of these diaries, however, record the restoration of Charles to the throne, the Great Plague that spread over London in 1665, and the Great Fire which, in 1666, almost consumed the city, and it is interesting to compare the accounts of these events.

We will read from Evelyn the account of the Great Fire, which is a vivid bit of description, and at some time I advise you to read the corresponding account in Pepys; it will give you an excellent idea of the difference in these two characters : —

EVELYN'S DIARY, SEPTEMBER, 1666.

" **2d** *Sept.* — This fatal night, about ten, began the deplorable fire near Fish Steet, in London.

" **3d** *Sept.* — I had public prayers at home. The fire continuing, after dinner I took coach with my wife and son, and went to the Bankside in Southwark, where we beheld that dismal spectacle, the whole city in dreadful flames near the water side ; all the houses from the bridge, all Thames Street, and upwards towards Cheapside, down to the Three Cranes, were now con-

sumed; and so returned, exceeding astonished what would
become of the rest. . . . The conflagration was so universal
and the people so astonished that from the beginning, I know
not by what despondency or fate, they hardly stirred to quench
it, so that there was nothing heard or seen but crying out and
lamentation, running about like distracted creatures, without at
all attempting to save even their goods, such a strange consternation there was upon them; so as it burned in breadth and length,
the churches, public halls, Exchange, hospitals, monuments, and
ornaments, leaping after a prodigious manner from house to
house, and street to street, at great distances one from the
other.   For the heat, with a long set of fair and warm weather,
had even ignited the air, and prepared the materials to conceive
the fire which devoured, after an incredible manner, houses,
furniture, and everything.   Here we saw the Thames covered
with goods floating, all the barges and boats laden with what
some had time and courage to save, as, on the other side, the
carts, etc., carrying out to the fields, which for many miles were
strewn with movables of all sorts, and tents erecting to shelter
both people and what goods they could get away.   Oh, the
miserable and calamitous spectacle! such as haply the world
has not seen since the foundation of it, nor can be out-done
till the universal conflagration thereof.   All the sky was of a
fiery aspect, like the top of a burning oven, and the light seen
above forty miles round about for many nights.   God grant
that mine eyes may never again behold the like, who now saw
above ten thousand houses all in one flame.   The noise and crack-
ing and thunder of the impetuous flames, the shrieking of women
and children, the hurry of people, the fall of towers, houses, and
churches, was like a hideous storm, and the air all about so hot
and inflamed that at the last one was not able to approach it, so
that they were forced to stand still and let the flames burn on,
which they did for near two miles in length and one in breadth.
The clouds of smoke also were dismal, and reached, upon computation, near fifty miles in length.   Thus I left it this afternoon burning, a resemblance of Sodom, or the last day.   It
forcibly called to my mind that passage, *non enim hic habemus
stabilem civitatem;* the ruins resembling the picture of Troy.
London was, but is no more.   Thus I returned.

"*4th Sept.* — The burning still rages, and it is now gotten as
far as the Inner Temple. All Fleet Street, the Old Bailey,
Ludgate Hill, Warwick Lane, Newgate, Paul's Chain, Watling
Street now flaming, and most of it reduced to ashes; the stones
of Paul's flew like grenadoes, the melting lead running down

the streets in a stream, and the very pavements glowing with fiery redness, so as no **horse nor man** was **able to** tread **on** them, . . . the eastern **wind still** more impetuously **driving the** flames forward. Nothing **but the** Almighty power **of God able** to stop them, for vain was **the help of man.**"

On the 6th, however, notwithstanding **Evelyn**'s pious de-claration that nothing but the power of God could arrest **the** flames, the authorities began to blow up some houses by **gun-powder,** and to tear down others, in order to make a gap be-tween the portion unburned and that burning. This, Evelyn said, had been previously proposed, but had met with oppo-sition from some aldermen of the City, whose houses would have been sacrificed **first.** By these means, with the favor of an abating wind, the **fire** was checked on the evening **of the 5th, after it had** burned **three days.** It is interest-ing to note that on the **13th of** September, **eight days after** the fire, Evelyn showed **King** Charles the **survey of the** ruins and the plot for a new city, " **which extremely pleased** the King, Queen, and the Duke of York."

XXXIII.

ON **THE** PROSE WRITERS OF THE SEVENTEENTH CENTURY ;
JOHN BUNYAN AND HIS " PILGRIM'S PROGRESS."

THERE **were not** many prose works produced in the seventeenth century which are interesting to us of the present time. **I have before** spoken of one grand piece of prose, Milton's plea for a free press, whose spirited sen-tences ring like the blasts of a bugle calling to freedom. This **is only** a short tract, but it is one of the noblest pieces of prose to be found in literature. I should not do justice to the prose of this century, however, if I left out the name **of** IZAAK WALTON, who wrote at least one book about which we ought to know something. He was a shopkeeper in London, whose delight and almost sole recreation it was to go fishing whenever he could get away from business, and

he has made **all** the little streams and rivers that flowed in
and around London in his lifetime historical waters by their
mention in his *Complete Angler*. **The** *Angler* **is one** of the
quaintest, most delicious books **in English. It** begins with
a discussion **between** three friends **who are** sportsmen, —
one devoted to hawking, the next to hunting, and the last
to fishing. In the opening chapter **each argues for** the
merit of his favorite sport, till the fisherman's eloquence
convinces the others, and **the hunter concludes to follow
him on his excursion. The two sportsmen wander off on
their day's sport, sometimes** lying along the green banks of
the streams, **sometimes** sheltered by the shade **of** a honey-
suckle hedge, **or by the** branches of a spreading oak, while
Piscator (the fisherman) gives his pupil instructions how to
fish, enlivened **with** story or occasional song or ballad, and
now and then a good moral lesson drawn **from his** rich
stores of experience. At the end of the **day they** adjourn
to the nearest inn, and **have their fish cooked for supper.
In a** succession of **days like** this the *Complete Angler* passes
the time. It is one of the most delightful books to read
under a tree **in a summer afternoon, even if one does** not
carry a rod, and has no taste **for angling.** Walton, who
became a great favorite with **other literary men,** and had
many friends among the divines, **wrote** a number of biogra-
phies, which are very easy and beautiful in style. Among
these are the lives of John Donne and George Herbert, of
whom I have already spoken.

Many of the most famous pieces of prose written at this
time were sermons ; for this was a century which numbered
many great preachers, and some of the most famous English
divines flourished in the reigns of Charles I. and Charles II.
South, Stillingfleet, Barrow, Tillotson, all were distinguished and learned preachers. So were Richard Baxter,
who wrote those celebrated religious books, *The Saints' Rest*
and *Call to the Unconverted ;* Bishop Burnet, who was not
only a clergyman, **but** an historian, and wrote a history of his
own times ; Thomas Fuller, the author of the *Worthies of
England,* — a series of short biographies of great men, which

is full of anecdote and humor, and a charming book to read ; and last and best of all is JEREMY TAYLOR, who has been called the "Shakespeare of divines," because his sermons have the imagery, the grandeur, and the music of a poem. All these preachers, except Baxter, were of the Established Church of England, and all were men of learning and high in the respect of their contemporaries. But one of the greatest books of the century was written by a Dissenting minister, a plain, unlearned man, very different from these dignitaries of the Church. His name is John Bunyan, and his great work is the *Pilgrim's Progress.*

JOHN BUNYAN wrote a great many books and sermons, but the *Pilgrim's Progress* is the only one which has been much read since his death. There are 1628–1688 a few books that go straight to the heart of the world, and never lose their place in it. They may be ever so simple in language, ever so rude in style, but they bear that charm which puts them among the volumes that grace the bookshelves of the scholar, or lie, well-worn and shabby, on the table of the peasant, beside the great Bible. John Bunyan wrote such a book in the intervals of his preaching and labor, while he was part of the time an inmate of a jail where he was shut up for his obstinacy in proclaiming the gospel as it seemed right to him. He had been bred to the trade of a tinker, and accuses himself of being very wicked in his youth, although a habit of swearing and a great love of ringing the church chimes are among the worst faults of which he accuses himself. His strict Puritanism caused him to think his love for ringing the bells a temptation of the devil, and after his conversion he was for a long time tortured by doubts of his salvation. Among other things, he fancied he was tempted, like Judas Iscariot, to betray his Lord, and heard the words, "Sell him, sell him, sell him," ringing like chimes of bells in his ears, day and night. To relieve this morbid state of conscience, he took to preaching, and his plain and homely eloquence was drawing many hearers, when he was arrested for unlawfully proclaiming the gospel, and thrown into jail in his

native **town of Bedford.   Here he** used to join his wife and
children **in the weaving** of tagged lacings to help in their
scanty living, **and here** the idea came to him of writing the
Pilgrim's Progress.   The wretched **old** jail in Bedford is
consecrated as the place whence the Pilgrim set out on that
journey which has never ceased from that time to interest
childhood and age.

More than twelve years **Bunyan** was a prisoner, although
his simple goodness so won upon the heart of his jailer that
after a time he allowed him to leave the prison and go out
to preach on Sundays, returning at night to his jail.

The *Pilgrim's Progress* is an allegory, and ought to be
read for the first time when one is a child, and can enjoy the
story without drawback.   Almost all young people have a
prejudice against **a tale** as soon as they find it is an allegory,
and there is some justice in the feeling, for, as a rule, when
the mind is diverted from a story to guess at its hidden
meaning and keep track of the undercurrent **that flows**
through the book, the effect is tiresome, and often takes
away all our interest.

An allegorical story or poem, therefore, must possess
great **merit in order to** outlive **its age.**   Spenser's *Fairy
Queen* is an allegory, yet very **few** persons think of that
nowadays in reading it ; they find in it a great imaginative
poem, whose characters have **an** existence of their own,
without reference to the abstract virtues they personify, or
the historical characters idealized in the lines.

The *Pilgrim's Progress* also is a story whose incidents
and characters take hold of our interest without reference
to the moral the author intended to convey.   A man sets
out on a perilous journey ; at the outset he sticks fast in a
slough, from which he escapes with difficulty ; he arrives at
a beautiful house where three gracious ladies advise and
comfort him ; he fights with a terrible enemy and gets the
better of him ; he is thrown into prison ; he falls into the
clutches of a giant ; and finally he crosses a swift and
dangerous river into a glorious city, which shines like an
enchanted kingdom in the Arabian tales.   All these events

and the characters that figure in them are as vivid as if there was no under-meaning intended to be conveyed. The battle between the hero and Apollyon in the dark valley is just as honest and fair a battle as was ever told in any tale, and when we are reading it our interest in the result is not harmed by the fact that it was meant for a contest between Good and Evil, and that we may be sure beforehand that good will be victorious. An English critic says, in speaking of this prejudice against allegories, " Some people are as afraid of the allegory as if they thought it would bite them. But if they do not meddle with the allegory, the allegory will not meddle with them." The most devoted reader of the *Pilgrim's Progress* I ever knew was a little girl of six, who never meddled with the allegory, but took it all as a delightful story, in which Giant Despair was as real a giant as those in Jack the Giant-Killer or the other famous Jack of the Bean-stalk.

One great merit of John Bunyan is that he wrote a homely, wholesome style, full of strength and naturalness; and the boy or girl who begins early to read such English as this, taking later the noble works of our great poets, will be able to use our language, either in writing or speaking, with a power which can never be acquired by those who only feed their minds with the flimsy stories in modern newspapers, and magazines written solely for young people. The passage I select to read is that in which Christian, the Pilgrim, and his friend, Hopeful, who is travelling with him, have lost their way on the journey by turning into some by-path which has taken them off the road, and are overtaken by the night in their efforts to find the right way again : —

" Wherefore at last, lighting under a little shelter, they sat down there till the day brake ; but being weary, they fell asleep. Now there was, not far from the place where they lay, a castle called Doubting Castle, the owner whereof was Giant Despair; and it was in his grounds they now were sleeping ; wherefore, he, getting up in the morning early and walking up and down in his fields, caught Christian and Hopeful asleep in his grounds. Then with a grim and a surly voice he bid them awake, and asked them whence they were, and what they did in his grounds.   They told him they were pilgrims, and that they had lost their way.   Then said the Giant, 'You have this night trespassed on me by trampling in and lying on my grounds, and therefore you must go along with me.'   So they were forced to go, because he was stronger than they.   They also had but little to say, for they knew themselves in a fault.   The Giant there-fore drove them before him and put them into his castle into a very dark dungeon, nasty and stinking to the spirits of these two men.   Here, then, they lay from Wednesday morning till Saturday night, without one bit of bread, or drop of drink, or light, or any to ask how they did; they were, therefore, here in evil case, and were far from friends or acquaintance.   Now, in this place Christian had double sorrow, because it was through his unadvised counsel that they were brought into this distress.

"Now, Giant Despair had a wife, and her name was Diffi-dence; so when he was gone to bed he told his wife what he had done, to wit, that he had taken a couple of prisoners and cast them into his dungeon for trespassing on his grounds. Then he asked her, also, what he had best further do to them. She asked what they were, whence they came, and whither they were bound; and he told her.   Then she counselled him that when he arose in the morning he should beat them without mercy.   So when he arose he getteth him a grievous crab-tree cudgel, and goes down into the dungeon to them, and there first falls to rating of them as if they were dogs, although they never gave him a word of distaste.   Then he fell upon them and beat them fearfully, in such sort that they were not able to help themselves or to turn them upon the floor.   This done, he withdraws, and leaves them there to condole their misery and to mourn under their distress, so that all day they spent their time in nothing but sighs and bitter lamentations.   The next night she, talking with her husband further about them, and understanding that they were yet alive, did advise him to counsel them to make away with themselves.   So when morn-ing was come, he goes to them in a surly manner, as before, and perceiving them to be very sore with the stripes that he had given them the day before, he told them that since they were never like to come out of that place, their only way would be forthwith to make an end of themselves, either with knife, halter, or poison; 'For why,' said he, 'should you choose to live, seeing it is attended with so much bitterness?'   But they desired him to let them go.   With that he looked ugly upon them, and rushing to them, had doubtless made an end of them himself, but that he fell into one of his fits (for he sometimes in sunshiny weather fell into fits), and lost, for a time, the use of his hands; wherefore he withdrew, and left them as before, to consider what to do."

Then the prisoners consult together what is best to do. Christian is almost of the opinion that they would better die at once; but Hopeful sustains him, and persuades him to endure a little longer.

"With these words did Hopeful, at present, moderate the mind of his brother; so they continued together in the dark that day in their sad and doleful condition.

"Well, towards evening the Giant goes down into the dungeon again to see if his prisoners had taken his counsel. But when he came there he found them alive; and, truly, alive was all: for now, what for want of bread and water, and by reason of the wounds they received when he beat them, they could do little but breathe. But I say he found them alive; at which he fell into a grievous rage, and told them that, seeing they had disobeyed his counsel, it would be worse with them than if they had never been born.

"At this they trembled greatly, and I think that Christian fell into a swoon; but coming a little to himself again, they renewed their discourse about the Giant's counsel, and whether they had best take it or no. Now Christian again seemed for doing it; but Hopeful made reply as followeth : —

"'My brother,' said Hopeful, 'rememberest thou not how valiant thou hast been heretofore? Apollyon could not crush thee, nor could all thou didst hear or see or feel in the Valley of the Shadow of Death. What hardship, terror, and amazement hast thou already gone through, and art thou now nothing but fears? Thou seest that I am in the dungeon with thee, a far weaker man by nature than thou art. Also, this Giant hath wounded me as well as thee, and hath also cut off the bread and water from my mouth, and with thee I mourn without the light. But let us exercise a little more patience. Remember how thou playedst the man at Vanity Fair, and wast neither afraid of the chain nor cage, nor yet of bloody death; wherefore, let us, at least to avoid the shame that it becomes not a Christian to be found in, bear up with patience as well as we can.'

"Now, night being come again, and the Giant and his wife

being in bed, she asked him concerning the prisoners, and if they had taken his counsel; to which he replied: 'They are sturdy rogues; they choose rather to bear all hardships than make away with themselves.'

"'Take them into the castle-yard to-morrow, and show them the bones and skulls of those thou hast already despatched, and make them believe, ere a week comes to an end, thou wilt tear them in pieces, as thou hast done their fellows before them.'

"So when the morning was come, the Giant goes to them again, and takes them into the castle-yard, and shows them as his wife had bidden him.

"'These,' said he, 'were pilgrims, as you are, once, and they trespassed on my grounds, as you have done; and when I thought fit I tore them in pieces, and so within ten days I will do you; go get you down to your den again.'

"And with that he beat them all the way thither. They lay, therefore, all day on Saturday in a lamentable case as before. Now, when night was come, and when Mrs. Diffidence and her husband the Giant were got to bed, they began to renew their discourse of their prisoners, and withal the old Giant wondered that he could neither by his blows nor counsels bring them to an end. And with that his wife replied, —

"'I fear,' said she, 'that they live in hopes that some will come to relieve them, or that they have picklocks about them, by the means of which they hope to escape.'

"'Sayest thou so, my dear?' said the giant; 'I will therefore search them in the morning.' . . .

"Now, a little before it was day, good Christian, as one half amazed, brake out into this passionate speech: 'What a fool,' quoth he, 'am I, thus to lie in this stinking dungeon, when I may as well walk at liberty. I have a key in my bosom, called Promise, that will, I am persuaded, open any lock in Doubting Castle.'

"Then said Hopeful, 'That is good news, good brother; pluck it out of thy bosom, and try.'

"Then Christian pulled it out of his bosom and began to try at the dungeon door, whose bolt, as he turned the key, gave back, and the door flew open with ease, and Christian and Hopeful both came out. Then he went to the outward door that leads into the castle yard, and with his key opened that door also. After that, he went to the iron gate, for that must be opened too; but that lock went desperately hard, yet the key did open it. Then they thrust open the gate to make their escape with speed; but that gate, as it opened, made such a creaking that it waked Giant Despair, who, hastily rising to pursue his prisoners, felt his limbs to fail, for his fits took him again, so that he could by no means go after them. Then they went on and came to the King's highway, and so were safe, because they were out of his jurisdiction.

" And when they were gone over the stile, they began to contrive with themselves what they should do at that stile to prevent those that should come after them from falling into the hands of Giant Despair. So they consented to erect there a pillar, and to engrave upon the side thereof a sentence : ' Over this stile is the way to Doubting Castle, which is kept by Giant Despair, who despiseth the King of the celestial country, and seeks to destroy his holy pilgrims.' Many, therefore, that followed after, read what was written, and escaped the danger. This done, they sang as follows : —

> " ' Out of the way we went, and then we found
> What 't was to tread upon forbidden ground ;
> And let them that come after, have a care,
> Lest heedlessness makes them as we, to fare,
> Lest they, for trespassing his prisoners are,
> Whose castle 's Doubting, and whose name 's Despair.' "

I cannot better end my praise of this book, for which I have a profound love and reverence, founded on long and very early acquaintance, than by quoting a few words from Macaulay's essay on it : —

" There is no book in our literature on which we would so readily stake the fame of the old unpolluted English language ; no book which shows how rich that language is in its own proper wealth, and how little it has been improved by all it has borrowed. Cowper said, forty or fifty years ago, that he dared not name John Bunyan in his verse, for fear of moving a sneer. . . . We live in better days, and we are not afraid to say that although there were many clever men in England during the latter half of the seventeenth century, there were only two great creative minds : one of those minds produced *Paradise Lost*, and the other, *Pilgrim's Progress*."

XXXIV.

On the Drama of the Restoration; John Dryden
and his Contemporaries.

THERE was a great falling off in dramatic poetry after
Shakespeare's death, and that branch of literature
seemed to decay as quickly as it had grown and blossomed.
The Puritans, while they were in power, opposed the stage
and all work written for it. They were inclined to think
life too serious a business for amusement of any sort. This
gloom and severity helped to cause the great reaction which
followed when the Royalists came back to the control of
affairs. As soon as Charles II. was proclaimed king, a dramatic merry-making began. Sir William Davenant, who
had been poet-laureate to Charles I., took the management
of a theatre, and imported such fine scenery from France
as had never before graced the bare boards of the English
stage. The witty men of the time, many of them nobles of
Charles's court, began to write plays. Everybody thronged
to the theatres, among the rest Samuel Pepys, who in
January, 1661, writes in his diary: "To the theatre, where
was acted *Beggar's Bush*, it being very well done, and here
the first time that ever I saw women come upon the stage."
Up to this date all the women's parts had been acted by
men or boys, and one of the innovations of this new revival
of the drama was to introduce actresses.

Some of the poets I have before mentioned among the
lyric poets were play-writers. Sir John Suckling, Abraham
Cowley, Sir Charles Sedley, all were successful in that line.
In the reign of Charles II. the dramatists were nearly as
plenty as they had been in the Elizabethan age. Many of
their works, which are now worthless as literature, are
written in an easy, natural dialogue, that flows from the
pen just as it falls from the lips; but one finds in these
plays few touches of nobleness, or the indication of any

good purpose in the writing. The worst vices of the dissolute age are faithfully reflected in these comedies. Some of
the more marked names among the dramatists are Davenant, Otway, Lee, Shadwell, Etherege, and Wycherley.

DAVENANT belonged both to the time of Charles I. and
Charles II. He was a fertile writer of plays of the school
founded in the Elizabethan age, and was an imitator of the
great Shakespeare. OTWAY wrote one or two plays showing
a good deal of power, and is interesting from his sad fate.
He died of starvation, after a life of struggle and poverty.
WYCHERLEY was a gifted writer of comedy, sparkling with
wit and full of invention. If he had lived in an age of
better manners and morals, his comedies might have delighted us at the present day ; but as they held the mirror
up to the vices of his own time, and reflected manners that
are disgusting to a purer age, his works are almost entirely
unknown.

The greatest dramatist who appeared after the great line
of Elizabethan dramatists had vanished was JOHN
DRYDEN. And it is not only as a dramatic poet **1631–1700**
that he holds a place in literature. He wrote odes, lyrics,
satires, epics, poetry in almost every vein, and besides this,
vigorous and manly prose.

Dryden holds a high position in the history of literature,
and had an influence over his own age which lasted long
after his death. He helped to form a new taste in poetry,
and to fix rules for poetic art which were more exact and
elegant than had been used before. What we are most
impressed with in the great Elizabethan poets is the spon-
taneity of their genius ; we feel that they were poets born
rather than made. In Dryden's time there was a marked
change : poetry began to be considered an *art* more than
ever before ; rules were laid down, criticism on form was
more severe. This was partly through the influence of
French taste, which had been exerted over the new school
of writers who sprang up in the court of Charles II., many
of whom had lived in France while that prince was exiled
from his country. The French style was an artificial, highly

polished style : in poetry, especially the drama, the French had never **struck out into** original methods, as the English had **done.** Their plays **had** been **modelled on the great** drama of the Greeks, made according to **certain** fixed rules of art. **All French** classic poetry followed the same line-and-plummet **mode of** measure as their **drama ; its** rules were laid out as if verse-making were a craft as exact in its methods as shoemaking. This style now became the fashion in England ; **and** you will perceive that **there** are fashions in literature as well **as** fashions **in** dress. Dryden was a **man** of genius, but of the sort of genius which would **be** likely to adapt itself **to the** taste of his age, not, **like** Milton or Shakespeare, a man who would compel taste to follow him. And Dryden was **also a man** of painstaking and thorough industry, who, having chosen any style, would perfect it and refine it to the uttermost. He accordingly **set to work to** refine and polish his verse **as** no English **poet had done** before. Consequently his poetry was **almost artificially perfect,** although I think we shall agree that **he never touches** the heart as Shakespeare **or** Milton does, **or seizes on** the imagination as Spenser does.

Unlike Milton, Dryden **believed in rhyme.** He said **Milton** did **not** rhyme **in** *Paradise Lost* because **he** could not write smooth and elegant rhymes, and Dryden actually **made** a rhyming opera out of *Paradise Lost,* fancying **it an** improvement on Milton's mighty verse. This is as bad as if he had taken the sonatas of Beethoven and set **them** to **be** ground out by **a** travelling beggar **on a hand-organ. He** had a great fancy for altering **the** older **poets. He** put some of Chaucer's Tales into **his** more fashionable verse, and re-wrote Shakespeare's *Tempest,* adding new characters and scenes **to** this grand play. It is difficult **to** forgive any poet such stupidity. Yet, in spite of this, Dryden was so great a **master** that he compels admiration, and he was also great enough to recognize the grandeur of Shakespeare and Milton when the age around him **was** blind to their superiority.

Dryden wrote such a number **of plays** (twenty-seven in all) that I shall not attempt to mention them. I like best *All for Love, Don Sebastian, The Indian Queen*, and *The Indian Emperor. All for Love* is a play on the same subject as Shakespeare's *Antony and Cleopatra*. Dryden says of this play that it is the one of his works which he wrote purely to please himself; the rest were made to please the people. This is not written in rhyme, as so many of his dramatic works are, and to my taste is the finest of all his plays. I therefore select a scene from this as the best specimen of his dramatic style. You can contrast it, for criticism, with one of Shakespeare's scenes from *Antony and Cleopatra*. Antony has just been told of Cleopatra's death, and is left with his faithful friend Ventidius, one of the generals of his army : —

> *Antony.*   Oh, Ventidius,
> What should I fight for now? my queen is dead.
> I was but great for her; my power, my empire,
> Were but my merchandise to buy her love,
> And conquered kings, my factors. Now she 's dead,
> Let Cæsar take the world,
> An empty circle, since the jewel 's gone
> Which made it worth my strife. My being 's nauseous,
> For all the bribes of life are gone away.
>   *Ventidius.* Would you be taken?
>   *Ant.*   Yes, I would be taken,
> And as a Roman ought, — dead, my Ventidius ;
> For I 'll convey my soul from Cæsar's reach
> And lay down life myself. 'T is time the world
> Should have a lord, and know whom to obey.
> We two have kept its homage in suspense,
> And bent the globe, on whose each side we trod,
> Till it was dented inwards. Let him walk
> Alone upon it. I 'm weary of my part ;
> My torch is out, and the world stands before me
> Like a black desert at the approach of night.
> I 'll lay me down and stray no further on.
>   *Vent.* I could be grieved,
> But that I 'll not outlive you ; choose your death,
> For I have seen him in such various shapes
>   I care not which I take. I 'm only troubled
> The life I bear is worn to such a rag
> 'T is scarce worth giving. I could wish, indeed,
> We threw it from us with a better grace ;
> That, like two lions taken in the toils,

We might at last thrust out our paws and wound
The hunters that enclose us.

Antony.   I have thought on it, —
Ventidius, you must live.

Vent.   I must not, sir.

Ant.   Wilt thou not live, to speak some good of me,
To stand by my fair fame, and guard the approaches
From the ill tongues of men?

Vent.   Who shall guard mine
For living after you?

Ant.   Say I command it.

Vent.   If we die well, our deaths will speak themselves,
And need no living witness.

Ant.   Thou hast loved me,
And fain I would reward thee; I must die.
Kill me! and take the merit of my death
To make thee friends with Cæsar.

Vent.   Thank your kindness;
You said I loved you, and in recompense
You bid me turn a traitor. Did I think
You would have used me thus? That I should die
With a hard thought of you?

Ant.   Forgive me, Roman.
Since I have heard of Cleopatra's death,
My reason bears no rule upon my tongue,
But lets my thoughts break all at random out.
I 've thought better. Do not deny me twice.

Vent.   By Heaven! I will not,
Let it not be to outlive you.

Ant.   Kill me first,
And then die thou: for 't is but just thou serve
Thy friend before thyself.

Vent.   Give me your hand,
We soon shall meet again. Now farewell, Emperor.

                                        [*They embrace.*

Methinks that word 's too cold to be my last;
Since death sweeps all distinctions,
Farewell, *friend!*
That 's all:
I will not make a business of a trifle;
And yet I cannot look on you and kill you.
Pray turn your face.

Ant.   I do; strike home — be sure!

Vent.   Home, as my sword will reach.

                              [*Ventidius kills himself.*

Ant.   Oh, thou mistak'st;
That wound was none of thine; give it me back;
Thou robb'st me of my death.

Vent.   I do indeed ;
But think 't is the first time I e'er deceived you,
If that may plead my pardon.   And, you gods,
Forgive me, if you will, for I die perjured
Rather than kill my friend.   *[Dies.*

   Ant.   Farewell ! Ever my leader, even in death,
My queen and thou have got the start of me,
And I 'm the lag of honor   Gone so soon ?
Is death no more ? he used him carelessly,
With a familiar kindness ere he knocked,
Ran to the door, and took him in his arms,
As who should say, You 're welcome at all hours.
A friend need give no warning   Books had spoiled him,
For all the learned are cowards by profession.   'T is not worth
My further thought, for death, for aught I know,
Is but to think no more.   Here 's to be satisfied
                              [Falls on his sword.
I 've missed my heart.   Oh, unperforming hand,
Thou never could'st have erred in a worse time !
My fortune jades me to the last, and death,
Like a great man, takes state, and makes me wait
For my admittance.   Some perhaps from Cæsar.
                              [Noise heard within.
If he should find me living, and suspect
That I played booty with my life, — I 'll mend
My work ere they can reach me.
      [Rises to his knees. Enter Cleopatra, Charmian, *and Iras.]*
   Cleo.   Where is my lord ? Where is he ?
   Char.   There he lies,
And dead Ventidius by him.
   Cleo.   My fears were prophets.   I am come too late.
Oh ! that accursed Alexas.
                              [She runs to Antony.
   Ant.   Art thou living ?
Or am I dead before I knew, and thou
The first kind ghost that meets me ?
   Cleo.   Help me seat him.
Send quickly, send for help.   *[They place Antony in a chair.*
   Ant.   I am answered.
We live both.   Sit thee down, my Cleopatra.
I 'll make the most I can of life, to stay
A moment more with thee.
   Cleo.   How is it with you ?
   Ant.   'T is as with a man
Removing in a hurry, all packed up
But one dear jewel that his haste forgot,
And he, for that, returns upon the spur.
So I come back for thee.

Cleo. Too long, ye heavens, ye have been **cruel to me;**
Now show your mended faith, and give me back
This fleeting **life.**
   Ant.   **It will not be, my love.**
I keep my **soul** by force.
Say but thou art not false.
   Cleo.   'T is **now** too late
To say I 'm true. I 'll prove it, **and** die with you.

.   .   .   .

   Ant. Enough; my life 's not long enough for **more.**
Thou say'st thou wilt come after; I believe thee,
For I can now believe whate'er thou say'st,
That we may part more kindly.
   Cleo.   I will come;
Doubt not, my life, I 'll come, and quickly too;
Cæsar shall triumph **o'er no** part of thee.
   Ant But grieve not while **thou stayest**
My last disastrous times.
Think we **have** had a clear and glorious day,
And heaven did kindly to delay the storm
Just till **our** close of evening. Ten years' love,
And not a **moment lost,** but all improved
To the utmost joys, — what ages we **have lived!**
And now to die each other's, and so dying,
While hand in hand we walk in groves below,
Whole troops of lovers' ghosts shall flash about **us,**
And all the **train be ours.**
   Cleo. **Your words** are like **the notes of dying swans,** —
Too sweet to last. Were there **so** many hours
For your unkindness, and not **one for** love?
   Ant. No, not a minute. **This** one kiss —
More worth than all I **leave** to Cæsar —

                             [*He dies.*

   Cleo. My lord, my lord! speak, if thou yet have being!
Sign **to me,** if thou cannot speak, or cast
One look. Do anything that shows you **live.**
   Iras. He 's gone too far to hear you,
And this you see, a lump of senseless clay,
The leavings of a soul.

I think that this scene shows Dryden at his very best.
His rhymed dramas **(and over one** third of his plays are
entirely rhyme) do not approach this **in** nobility. I will
give you a few lines from the *Indian Emperor,* the scenes
of which are laid **in** Peru, to show you his rhymed style.
As **the** play opens, the principal characters, Cortez and

Pizarro, the Spanish invaders, thus express their delight at the beauty of this new country on whose shores they have landed : —

[*Enter Cortez and Pizarro, with their company.*]

Cortez. On what new happy climate are we thrown,
So long kept secret and so lately known ?
As if our old world modestly withdrew,
And here in private had brought forth a new.
  Pizarro. Corn, oil, and wine, are wanting to this ground,
In which our countries fruitfully abound,
As if this infant world, yet unarrayed,
Naked and bare in Nature's lap were laid
No useful arts have yet found footing here,
But all untaught and savage doth appear.
  Cortez. Wild and untaught are terms which we alone
Invent for fashions differing from our own ;
For all their customs are by Nature wrought,
But we by art unteach what Nature taught.
  Pizarro. In Spain, our springs, like old men's children, be
Decayed and withered from their infancy.
No kindly showers fall on our barren earth
To watch the season in a timely birth ;
Our summer such a russet livery wears
As in a garment often dyed appears.
  Cortez. Here Nature spreads her fruitful sweetness round,
Breathes on the air, and broods upon the ground ;
Here nights and days the only seasons be.
The sun no climate does so gladly see ;
When forced from hence to view our parts, he mourns,
Takes little journeys and makes quick returns.

And thus the scene continues in praise of this new fairy-land of America, which they are soon to stain with the blood of their conquered victims. I think, even from this little extract, you will decide that tragedy does not move well to alternate rhymes, and that all its grandeur departs when it is set to a see-saw measure.

As a better specimen of his rhymes, I shall quote *Alexander's Feast,* which is thought one of the best things he ever wrote. Dryden said himself that it was "the best ode ever written in English." It was composed for a musical festival held in honor of Saint Cecilia. It is called —

ALEXANDER'S FEAST.

'T was at the royal feast for Persia won
　　By Philip's warlike son .
　　　Aloft in awful state
　　　The godlike hero sate
　　　　On his imperial throne :
　　His valiant peers were placed around,
Their brows with roses and with myrtles bound
　　(So should desert in arms be crowned).
The lovely Thaïs by his side
Sate like a blooming Eastern bride,
In flower of youth and beauty's pride.
　　　Happy, happy, happy pair ;
　　　　None but the brave,
　　　　None but the brave,
　　None but the brave deserves the fair.

　　　　Timotheus, placed on high
　　　　　Amid the tuneful choir,
　　With flying fingers touched the lyre ;
　　　The trembling notes ascend the sky,
　　　　And heavenly joys inspire.
　　The song began from Jove,
　　Who left his blissful seats above, —
　　Such is the power of mighty love.
　　A dragon's fiery form belied the god ;
　　Sublime on radiant spires he rode,
　　When he to fair Olympia pressed,
　　And while he sought her snowy breast ;
Then round her slender waist he curled,
And stamped an image of himself, a sovereign of the world.
　The listening crowd admire the lofty sound,
　A present deity ! they shout around ;
　A present deity ! the vaulted roofs rebound :
　　　　With ravished ears
　　　　The monarch hears,
　　　　Assumes the god,
　　　　Affects to nod,
　　And seems to shake the spheres.

The praise of Bacchus then the sweet musician sung,
　Of Bacchus ever fair and ever young.
　　The jolly god in triumph comes ;
　Sound the trumpets, beat the drums ;
　　　Flushed with a purple grace,
　　　He shows his honest face.
Now give the hautboys breath ; he comes ! he comes !

Bacchus, ever fair and young,
   Drinking joys did first ordain ;
Bacchus' blessings are a treasure,
Drinking is the soldier's pleasure.
     Rich the treasure,
      Sweet the pleasure,
    Sweet is pleasure after pain.

Soothed with the sound, the king grew vain ;
   Fought all his battles o'er again ;
And thrice he routed all his foes, and thrice he slew the slain.
    The master saw the madness rise,
    His glowing cheeks, his ardent eyes ;
    And while he heaven and earth defied,
    Changed his hand and checked his pride.
      He chose a mournful Muse,
      Soft pity to infuse ;
    He sung Darius great and good,
      By too severe a fate
    Fallen, fallen, fallen, fallen,
      Fallen from his high estate,
    And weltering in his blood.
    Deserted at his utmost need
    By those his former bounty fed,
    On the bare earth exposed he lies,
    With not a friend to close his eyes.
With downcast looks the joyless victor sate,
    Revolving in his altered soul
      The various turns of chance below ;
     And, now and then, a sigh he stole,
      And tears began to flow.

    The mighty master smiled to see
    That love was in the next degree ;
    'T was but a kindred sound to move,
    For pity melts the mind to love.
      Softly sweet, in Lydian measures,
      Soon he soothed his soul to pleasures.
    War, he sung, is toil and trouble,
    Honor but an empty bubble,
      Never ending, still beginning,
    Fighting still, and still destroying ;
      If the world be worth thy winning,
    Think, oh, think it worth enjoying.
      Lovely Thaïs sits beside thee,
      Take the good the gods provide thee.
The many rend the skies with loud applause ;
So Love was crowned, but Music won the cause.

The prince, unable to conceal his pain,
  Gazed on the fair
  Who caused his care,
And sighed and looked, sighed and looked,
Sighed and looked, and sighed again;
At length, with love and wine at once oppressed,
The vanquished victor sunk upon her breast.

  Now strike the golden lyre again!
  A louder yet, and yet a louder strain.
  Break his bands of sleep asunder,
    And rouse him, like a rattling peal of thunder.
      Hark! hark! the horrid sound
        Has raised up his head;
        As awaked from the dead,
      And amazed, he stares around.
      Revenge! revenge! Timotheus cries;
        See the Furies arise;
        See the snakes that they rear,
        How they hiss in their hair,
      And the sparkles that flash from their eyes!
        Behold a ghastly band,
        Each a torch in his hand, —
Those are Grecian ghosts that in battle were slain,
        And unburied remain
        Inglorious on the plain.
        Give the vengeance due
        To the valiant crew,
Behold how they toss their torches on high,
      How they point to the Persian abodes,
  And glittering temples of their hostile gods.
  The princes applaud, with a furious joy;
  And the king seized a flambeau with zeal to destroy.
        Thaïs led the way
        To light him to his prey,
And, like another Helen, fired another Troy.

      Thus long ago,
    Ere heaving bellows learned to blow,
      While organs yet were mute,
      Timotheus, to his breathing flute
        And sounding lyre,
  Could swell the soul to rage, or kindle soft desire.
      At last divine Cecilia came,
      Inventress of the vocal frame;
  The sweet enthusiast, from her sacred store,
      Enlarged the former narrow bounds,
      And added length to solemn sounds,
  With Nature's mother-wit, and arts unknown before.

Let old Timotheus yield the prize,
   Or both divide the crown :
He raised a mortal to the skies,
   She drew an angel down.

This ode we have just read is one of the most famous in
our literature. I have told you Dryden's opinion of it.
I leave it now to your own taste to decide whether you
prefer it above some of the lyrics of the time of Shakespeare, or some others of the poets of the nineteenth century whom we shall study later.

Dryden lived to a good old age, and in his last days was
regarded as an authority almost absolute in all matters of
poetry. The place which literary men of his time, and for
some time after, were accustomed to use as their meeting-
place — a sort of headquarters for the wits and poets —
was Will's Coffee-house. Here Dryden used to go almost
every afternoon ; and as he entered, everybody made way
for him to pass to his favorite seat, which was in the warmest
corner near the chimney in winter, and on the coolest end
of the balcony in summer. Here he sat in a sort of state,
the autocrat of letters, and gave his opinions on literary art
till, honored and reverenced by his age, he died in the first
year of the eighteenth century, at the age of sixty-nine.

PART V.

FROM POPE TO WORDSWORTH.

THE EIGHTEENTH CENTURY.

1700 TO 1790.

16

INTRODUCTORY.

DRYDEN'S name stands like a grand landmark at **the** end of the seventeenth century. His life had **cov**-**ered a** period full of changes. Charles I. had been be-headed; Cromwell had held his stern but able rule over the nation; the "merry monarch," as Charles II. was called, had **kept up** his dissolute revels during the fifteen years **he had been king;** James II., his brother, who succeeded **him,** had been forced **to give up** his **crown** and flee to France; and Mary, the daughter of James II., with her politic and wise husband, William of Orange, were reign-ing together **on** the throne of England when Dryden died, just in the opening year of the eighteenth century. **Two** years after his death, Mary's sister, Anne, became queen. Her reign is often called the *Augustan age* of literature, — a title borrowed from a period in Latin history. **During** the reign of the Emperor Augustus Cæsar, **1702** Latin poetry rose to its greatest height **in elegance.** The poets of that day worked to make the language pure and pol-ished, and their verse perfect according to established rules. And **as the** Emperor Augustus **was one of** the patrons of literature, **and it** throve under his fostering care, the age has been known as the Augustan age. And hence it is **that the period in** English which is claimed to resemble **this era in Roman history** received the name of the Au-gustan age.

You will see that the work of Dryden in poetry and criti-cism had been leading up to a new taste in literature. The French have always imitated the ancients, especially in their **work** for the stage. Form and method were **in** their eyes **two of** the most important requirements in poetry. Fol-**lowing** them, the new school **of** English writers began to

consider the artificial finish of a verse the great test of its
merit.   Dryden had made verse in his day more artificially
perfect than it had ever been.   The best writers among
those who followed him improved upon their master.   The
writers of the Elizabethan age, even Shakespeare and Milton,
were looked down upon as poets who did very well in their
day, but did not understand the true art by which poetry
was manufactured.   This was the aspect of the popular
taste towards poetry when Dryden died ; and as he had,
more than most men, set the fashion and laid down the
rules for the time in which he lived, it was natural that his
influence should extend into the age that followed.   That
he did have such an influence we shall recognize in studying the works of Pope, the greatest poet of the Augustan
age.

We shall notice, in reading the leading writers of this
new period in English literature, that many of its greatest
productions in poetry and in prose are *satires*.   Both Latin
and French literature were distinguished for satirical power ;
but until Dryden's time English literature had not been distinguished for its satire.   But with the polish of the French
school, the English writer began to borrow the keenness of
its satire, which held up to laughter anything in art, society,
or politics which he wanted to reform.   Satires against
persons, too, became common, and the poet could in this
way use his talents as a means of defence against those
who were unjust to him, or of revenge against those whom
he disliked.   Dryden's *MacFlecknoe* and Pope's *Dunciad*,
both satires against persons, are two of the most famous
English works of this kind written in verse.

Another marked feature of the age was the *club*, — a
gathering of literary men or politicians, or any group of
men of similar tastes and pursuits, at some general meet-
ing-place where they could discuss subjects most interesting
to them with more freedom than at any private house.   We
have seen that the wits and poets of the sixteenth century
were wont to gather at the Mermaid.   Ben Jonson, a little
later, formed a club at the Devil Tavern, and Dryden

gathered about him the most famous men of the seventeenth century at Will's Coffee-house. In the reign of
Queen Anne these clubs became the rage. They were
generally formed in some of the inns or eating-houses of
the time, and you cannot read the history or the literature
of the age without finding constant mention of them.
Will's Coffee-house continued the chief centre for the men
of letters, and Pope, Gay, Swift, Arbuthnot, and others, who
formed the *Scriblerus Club*,[1] met there. Not far from Will's
was another coffee-house, known as Button's, where Addison
used to have his headquarters, and where his friends sought
him out when they wanted to enjoy the charm of his society.
Then there was the *Kit-Kat Club*, which was formed principally of politicians, but which included also Addison and
Steele. This met at the shop of a pastry-cook, Christopher
Kat, who was celebrated for the excellence of his mutton-
pies. These are two or three among the many meeting-
places of the wits and public men of the day, and you can
see how these gatherings must have fostered the discussions
of all questions which the pens of the writers of the time
took for their theme, and what a strong influence on society
the clubs of the day exercised. With this glimpse into the
Augustan age, we will begin our consideration of some of its
chief writers, — Pope, Prior, and Gay in poetry; Congreve,
its greatest dramatic writer; and De Foe, Swift, Addison,
and Steele, in prose.

---

[1] This club had its name from a satire of the time, written by one of
its members, John Arbuthnot, to ridicule the pedantic and false taste
in literature. The satire was called *Memoirs of Martin Scriblerus.*

XXXV.

On Alexander Pope and his School of Poetry.

ALEXANDER POPE was a boy of twelve when Dryden died. He was a very precocious boy, beginning to write verses at eight years, and lisping rhymes almost from his cradle. He was a great reader, both of English and the classic writers, devouring all kinds of books as soon as he could read. Of course he read and admired Dryden, like all the rest of his age. On one occasion, when eleven or twelve, he induced some friend to take him to Will's Coffee-house, where Dryden sat in state, like a poetical lawgiver, almost every afternoon in the year. With what admiring eyes the little boy, who burned with desire to be one day a great poet, must have looked on the old man in his armchair, surrounded by his courts of wits and admirers! It is related that at this visit some one showed Dryden Pope's translation of some Latin verses, and that he patted the schoolboy on the head in approval, and gave him a shilling. The approval was worth more than the shilling to Pope, we may be sure, and he must have remembered it with pleasure all his life after.

1688-1744

Pope is usually regarded as the founder of the school of poetry which prevailed all through the eighteenth century; but it was a school of which Dryden had laid the corner-stone. Pope could not but be influenced by Dryden, whom he had read so early and admired so much. But in form and execution Pope excelled his master. He had a delicate, musical ear, — an ear that demanded regular cadences; and he wrote lines more regular and smooth than those which contented Dryden and his contemporaries. His rhythm is so regular it sounds to many ears mechanical. His poetry is rhymed, and almost always in couplets; the lines have a see-saw sound, the first half of the verse balancing **the last** like a pair of scales, — as **these,** for instance : —

> " Worth makes the man, **the want of it the fellow.**"
>
> " Slave to no sect, who take no private **road,**
>   But look from Nature up to Nature's **God.**"
>
> " To err is human, to forgive divine."

One can fancy that to read right on, for hours, these smooth, balanced lines would be very tiresome, no matter how excellent the sense. Indeed, it seems to me that much of Pope's meaning would be as good or better in prose, **and** that he might have saved himself the trouble of rhyming. I should claim **that** the true **test** of poetry is that its subject-matter should transcend prose, and flow naturally **into** harmonious numbers ; that the thought **had sought expression in poetry** because prose **had** been a garment **too** mean and poor to clothe its **nobility. If** this be so, Pope **is** not always a poet. But if **poetry be the** art which puts any thought, commonplace **or not, into** regular numbers **and almost** perfect **form, then** Pope **belongs** among the greatest English poets. **He was a man in** miserable health, with a sickly, deformed body ; **yet in** spite of this he did prodigies of work, and elaborated all he did with the patience of the worker in diamonds, who cuts, polishes, and refines till the jewel gives out its fullest lustre.

Pope **wrote no** plays, — the first great poet since Shakespeare's age who did not write in the dramatic form. Instead, he wrote moral essays in verse, — the *Essay on Man* **and the** *Essay on Criticism ;* a few lyrics, as the *Ode on St. Cecilia's Day,* which is not so good as Dryden's ; a great **many** epistles to **different** persons ; satires, in which **he** is a master ; translations and imitations of Greek and Latin authors ; and some miscellaneous poems. His translation of **Homer's** *Iliad* and *Odyssey* alone would have made **him** famous, and he also put Virgil and Horace into English **verse, and** turned some of Chaucer's *Canterbury Tales* into modern **form,** much after **the** manner of a translation.

One of his famous poems (many think it his best) is the *Rape of the Lock*, a lively story in verse. The incident is the stealing of a lock of hair from the head of a belle by one of her admirers. The subject, which is rather artificial, suits Pope's style; there is no other of his poems in which both style and subject are so in harmony, and this, no doubt, is one reason of its success. The heroine, Belinda, has been warned by a sylph of the air, her guardian, who superintends her toilet, that some dread event is to happen; but, undisturbed by the warning, she begins to dress for an excursion up the Thames to Hampton. Her toilet is thus described: —

> "And now unveiled the toilet stands displayed,
> Each silver vase in mystic order laid.
> First, robed in white, the nymph intent adores,
> With head uncovered, the cosmetic powers.
> A heavenly image in the glass appears;
> To that she bends, to that her eyes she rears.
> The inferior priestess, at her altar's side,
> Trembling begins the sacred rites of pride.
> Unnumbered treasures ope at once, and here
> The various offerings of the world appear;
> From each she nicely culls with curious toil,
> And decks the goddess with the glittering spoil.
> This casket India's glowing gems unlocks,
> And all Arabia breathes from yonder box.
> The tortoise here and elephant unite,
> Transformed to combs, the speckled and the white.
> Here files of pins extend their shining rows,
> Puffs, powders, patches, Bibles, billets-doux.
> Now awful beauty puts on all its arms;
> The fair each moment rises in her charms,
> Repairs her smiles, awakens every grace,
> And calls forth all the wonders of her face;
> Sees by degrees a purer blush arise,
> And keener lightnings quicken in her eyes.
>
>   .   .   .   .
>
>   "Not with more glories, in the ethereal plain,
> The sun first rises o'er the purpled main,
> Than, issuing forth, the rival of his beams,
> Launched on the bosom of the silver Thames.
> Fair nymphs and well-dressed youths around her shone,
> But every eye was fixed on her alone.
> On her white breast a sparkling cross she wore,
> Which Jews might kiss, and infidels adore.

Her lively looks a sprightly mind disclose,
Quick as her eyes and as unfixed as those.
Favors to none, to all she smiles extends;
Oft she rejects, but never once offends.
Bright as the sun, her eyes the gazers strike,
And like the sun, they shine on all alike.
Yet graceful ease, and sweetness void of pride,
Might hide her faults, if belles had faults to hide.
If to her share some female errors fall,
Look on her face, and you 'll forget 'em all.
  " This nymph, to the destruction of mankind,
Nourished two locks, which graceful hung behind
In equal curls, and well conspired to deck
With shining ringlets the smooth ivory neck.
Love in these labyrinths his slaves detains,
And mighty hearts are held in slender chains.
With hairy springes we the birds betray;
Slight lines of hair surprise the finny prey;
Fair tresses man's imperial race ensnare,
And beauty draws us with a single hair.
  " The adventurous baron the bright locks admired;
He saw, he wished, and to the prize aspired.
Resolved to win, he meditates the way,
By force to ravish, or by fraud betray.
For when success a lover's toil attends,
Few ask if fraud or force attained his ends."

The *Rape of the Lock* is a poem of society, witty, sparkling, and without earnestness. The poetical essays are in a different vein, and the *Essay on Man* is full of sound philosophy. You may judge of it by this extract : —

  " Heaven from all creatures hides the book of fate,
  All but the page prescribed, their present state :
  From brutes what men, from men what spirits know;
  Or who could suffer being here below?
  The lamb thy riot dooms to bleed to-day,
  Had he thy reason would he skip and play?
  Pleased to the last, he crops the flowery food,
  And licks the hand just raised to shed his blood.
  Oh, blindness to the future, kindly given,
  That each may fill the circle marked by Heaven;
  Who sees with equal eye, as God of all,
  A hero perish or a sparrow fall,
  Atoms or systems into ruin hurled,
  And now a bubble burst, and now a world.
    " Hope humbly, then, with trembling pinions soar,
  Wait the great teacher, Death, and God adore.

What future bliss he gives not thee to know,
But gives that hope to be thy blessing now.
Hope springs eternal in the human breast;
Man never is, but always to be, blessed.
The soul, uneasy, and confined from home,
Rests and expatiates on a life to come.
Lo, the poor Indian! whose untutored mind
Sees God in clouds, or hears him in the wind;
His soul proud science never taught to stray
Far as the solar walk, or milky way;
Yet simple Nature to his hope hath given,
Behind the cloud-topped hill, an humbler heaven, —
Some safer world in depth of woods embraced,
Some happier island in the watery waste,
Where slaves once more their native land behold,
No fiends torment, no Christians thirst for gold.
To be content's his natural desire,
He asks no angel's wing, no seraph's fire,
But thinks, admitted to that equal sky,
His faithful dog shall bear him company."

The measure of Pope's verses is almost always the same,
— in rhymed couplets like these that I have quoted. He
has written, however, a few lyrics, and the best-known of
these, *The Dying Christian to His Soul,* we will read as an
example of his style in the ode : —

"Vital spark of heavenly flame,
Quit, oh, quit this mortal frame!
Trembling, hoping, lingering, flying,
Oh, the pain, the bliss of dying!
Cease, fond Nature, cease thy strife,
And let me languish into life.

"Hark! they whisper; angels say,
'Sister spirit, come away.'
What is this absorbs me quite,
Steals my senses, shuts my sight,
Drowns my spirits, draws my breath?
Tell me, my soul, can this be death?

"The world recedes, it disappears;
Heaven opens on my eyes, my ears
With sounds seraphic ring.
Lend, lend your wings! I mount, I fly!
O Grave, where is thy victory?
O Death, where is thy sting?"

You will notice in reading Pope for the first time how many familiar lines are found in his poetry,— lines, perhaps, which you have heard without knowing whence they came. There are few writers so much quoted; I think that a volume of Pope furnishes more familiar quotations than any other in our language except the Bible or Shakespeare. Lines so even and flowing, and so witty and full of point, are doubly apt to stick in the memory.

Pope's influence on his own age and on the whole century in which he lived was very great. During his life he was a poetical oracle, and he put poetry into a bondage from which it was not freed for a hundred years. Almost every poet up to the last of the eighteenth century was a follower of Pope. During all these years poetry kept a dead level of correctness, until a few men of strong and original genius arose who broke its bonds and gave it again some of the free and untamed spirit that had inspired it in the Elizabethan age.

XXXVI.

On Prior, Gay, and Parnell.

FAR below Pope in rank come Prior, Gay, and Parnell, all of whom were his friends or acquaintances. Matthew Prior, a man of the world and a politican who held several fat offices, found **1664-1721** leisure to write a great deal and in a variety of styles, — lyrics, narrative poems, epitaphs, epistles, and odes. He wrote a dull poem on *Solomon, or the Vanities of the World*, and another, equally tiresome, called *Alma, or the Progress of the Mind*. We shall probably never get farther in our knowledge of these than the titles. His best poems are his shortest ones, and I shall dismiss Prior with one of the prettiest of these short lyrics : —

"The pride of every grove I chose,
   The violet sweet and lily fair,
The dappled pink and blushing rose,
   To deck my charming Chloe's hair.

"At morn the nymph vouchsafed to place
   Upon her brow the various wreath, —
The flower less blooming than her face,
   The scent less fragrant **than** her breath.

"The **flowers she wore** along the day,
   And every **nymph** and shepherd said
That in her **hair** they looked more gay
   Than glowing **in** their native bed.

"Undressed at evening, when she found
   Their odors lost, their colors past,
She changed her look, and on the ground
   Her garland and her eye she cast.

"That eye dropped sense distinct and clear
   As any muse's tongue could speak,
When from its lid a pearly tear
   Ran trickling down her beauteous **cheek.**

"**Dissembling what I knew too well,**
   'My life, my love,' I said, 'explain
This change of humor; prithee tell;
   This falling tear, — what does **it mean?'**

"She sighed, she smiled; and to the flowers
   Pointing, the lovely moralist said,
'**See,** friend, in some few fleeting hours,
   See, yonder, what a change is made.

"'Ah! me, the blooming pride of May
   And that of beauty are but one;
At morn both flourish bright and gay,
   Both fade at evening, pale and gone.

"'At dawn poor Stella laughed and sung;
   The amorous youth around her bowed;
At night her fatal knell **was rung.**
   I saw, **and kissed her in her shroud.**

"'Such as she is who died to-day,
   Such I, alas! may be to-morrow.
Go, Damon, bid thy muse display
   The justice of thy Chloe's sorrow.'"

JOHN GAY, born in the same year with Pope, much beloved by him in life, and mourned by him at his
death, was one of the most amiable of all these **1688-1732**
poets, and was known as a man too good-natured for his
own advantage. He began by writing pastoral poems,
which really contained some natural pictures of country
life, in contrast to most pastorals, which are as stiff and unlike nature as possible. After these, Gay wrote, in contrast
to his earlier works, a long epic called *Trivia, or the Art of
Walking the Streets of London,* in which he describes city
scenes. This last poem is to me exceedingly dull, the only
merit I find in it being that the street scenes it paints are
interesting as a study of the times. After these achieve-
ments in verse he began to write dramas, none of them
drawing much attention till he wrote the *Beggars' Opera,*
which brought him both fame and money. The characters
in this were highwaymen and thieves, the lowest characters
in Newgate prison ; but they were depicted with humor,
accompanied by a biting satire against follies which were
found to exist as well in the highest society as among
thieves. The hero is the highwayman, Macheath, who
narrowly escapes hanging. In one place he says, "As to
conscience and nasty morals, I have as few drawbacks upon my pleasures as any man of quality in England ; in these
I am not in the least vulgar ; " and Polly, the heroine, says
pertly, "A woman knows how to be mercenary, though she
has never been in a court or an assembly." Besides such
hits as these at the follies and vice of the age, some of the
lines contain a vast deal of cynical wisdom. One of the
rogues exclaims over his cups, "The present time is ours,
and nobody alive has more." "Well, I forgive you," says
Mrs. Peachum to Polly, "as far as one woman can forgive
another."

After the great success of the *Beggar's Opera,* Gay wrote
a sequel called *Polly,* which, as almost always happens
when one tries to repeat a success, was greatly inferior to
the first. Yet he made money by it, and was able to retire
in comfortable circumstances, leading a life of retirement

the rest of his days.   His latest works were fables in **rhyme**, inclosing a shrewd and wholesome **moral**.   Here is one of the best :—

THE MAN AND THE FLEA.

Whether on earth, **in air,** or main,
Sure everything alive **is vain.**
Does not the hawk all fowls survey
As destined only for his prey ?
And do not tyrants, prouder things,
Think men were born for slaves to kings ?
When the crab views the pearly strands,
Or Tagus bright with golden sands,
Or crawls beside the coral grove
And hears the ocean roll above, —
" Nature **is too profuse,"** says he,
" Who gave all these to pleasure me."
When bordering pinks and roses bloom,
And every garden breathes perfume ;
When peaches glow with sunny dyes,
Like Laura's cheek when **blushes rise ;**
When with huge figs the branches **bend ;**
When clusters from the vine depend, —
The *snail* looks round on flower and tree,
And cries, " All these were made for me."
   " What dignity 's in human nature ! "
Says Man, the most conceited creature,
As from a cliff he cast his eye,
And viewed the sea and arched sky.
The **sun was sunk** beneath the main ;
The **moon and all** the starry train
Hung **the vast vault of** heaven ; the man
His contemplation **thus began :**
   " When I behold this glorious show,
And the wide watery world below,
The scaly people of the main,
The beasts that range the woods or plain,
The wing'd inhabitants of air,
The night, the day, the various year,
And know all these by heaven designed
As gifts to pleasure humankind, —
I cannot raise my worth too high :
Of what vast consequence am I ! "
   " Not of th' importance you suppose,"
Replies a *flea* upon his nose.
" Be humble ; learn thyself to scan ;
Know pride was never made for **man ;**

'T is vanity that swells thy mind.
What heaven and earth for *thee* designed!
For *thee*, made **only for our need,**
That more important *fleas* might feed."

One of the prettiest things **Gay ever wrote is the** ballad
of *Black-Eyed Susan*, which gave **a later writer,** Douglas
Jerrold, the title for a comedy.   And **let us** note here that
one thing for which Gay deserves credit is that he did not
write, like so many of his compeers, about dukes and duch-
esses, but that in the *Beggar's Opera* he contrives to wake
an interest in the human nature common to all men and
women, just as in the ballad of *Black-Eyed Susan* it is the
common sailor and his love for whom he seeks our sympathy.   This is so much the case **in our day** that it would
not attract notice; **but we must remember that it was** different in the time of Gay, **and that the** humanity that makes
us all akin **was** not **so much the** subject **of the poet's**
verse.

WILLIAM'S FAREWELL TO BLACK-EYED SUSAN.

All in **the Downs the fleet was** moored,
   The streamers waving in the wind,
When Black-eyed Susan came aboard.
   "Oh, where shall I my true love find?
Tell me, ye jovial sailors, tell me true,
If my sweet William sails among the crew."

William, who high upon the yard
   Rocked with the billow to and fro,
Soon as her well-known voice he heard,
   He sighed and cast his eyes below.
The cord slides swiftly through his glowing hands,
And quick as lightning on the deck he stands.

So the sweet lark, high poised in air,
   Shuts close his pinions to his breast
If chance his mate's shrill call he hear,
   And drops at once into her nest.
The noblest captain in the British fleet
Might envy William's lip those kisses **sweet.**

" O Susan, Susan, lovely dear,
   My vows shall ever true remain.
Let **me** kiss off that falling tear;
   We only part to meet again.

Change as ye list, ye winds; my heart shall be
The faithful compass that still points to thee.

. .   .   .

" If to fair India's coast we sail,
 Thy eyes are seen in diamonds bright,
Thy breath is Afric's spicy gale,
 Thy skin is ivory so white.
Thus every beauteous object that I view
Wakes in my soul some charm of lovely Sue.

" Though battle call me from thy arms,
 Let not my pretty Susan mourn;
Though cannons roar, yet, safe from harms,
 William shall to his dear return.
Love turns aside the balls that round me fly,
Lest precious tears should drop from Susan's eye."

The boatswain gave the dreadful word;
 The sails their swelling bosoms spread:
No longer must she stay aboard.
 They kissed, she sighed, he hung his head.
Her lessening boat unwilling rows to land;
" Adieu," she cries, and waved her lily hand.

THOMAS PARNELL was a clergyman and a scholar. He
1679-1718 wrote one piece which has earned him nearly all
the fame he possesses as a poet, — *The Hermit,* —
written in that see-saw rhyme that becomes so tiresome to
the ear when we read much of it. These are the opening
lines : —

" Far in a wild, unknown to public view,
From youth to age a reverend hermit grew.
The moss his bed; the cave his humble cell;
His food the fruits, his drink the crystal well.
Remote from men, with God he passed the days;
Prayer all his business, all his pleasure praise."

I shall not quote *The Hermit* further ; it is a poem which
I think will not find so many readers in the future as it has
found in the past; but there is one little song by Parnell
which we will read, that for melody and archness could
easily be put among the best songs of the earlier singers,
Suckling, Lovelace, or Waller. It is a wonder that a man
who could write such a song could have been tied down to

such stiff models, and **have** trained his muse **to** grind **out** **the** formal **measure** in which *The Hermit* **is** written :

> " When thy beauty appears
>   In its graces and airs,
>   All bright as an angel new dropt from **the sky,**
> At distance I gaze, and am awed by my **fears,**
>   So strangely you dazzle my eye.
>
>   " But when, without art,
>   Your kind thought you impart ;
>   **When** your love runs in blushes through every vein ;
> **When** it darts from your eyes, when it pants in your heart, —
>   Then I **know** you 're a woman again.
>
>   " ' There 's a passion and pride
>   In our sex,' she replied,
>   ' And thus (might I gratify both) I would do, —
>   Still an angel appear to each lover beside,
>   But still be a woman to you.' "

XXXVII.

On the Author of " Robinson Crusoe."

OUR **hearts** will always respond to the mention of the name of **Daniel** De Foe, if **we** have **read** 1661–1731 the story of *Robinson Crusoe* when we were chil- dren, — and **who** of us did not ?

Most of these writers of the Augustan age were men who belonged to the English Church, and were in sympathy with the political party in **power.** De Foe was much of the **time** in opposition **to both.** In religion he belonged **to the Dissenters** ; in **politics he** was a Whig ; and although a few **of his** political **pamphlets** were popular, they brought him, for **the most** part, **only** trouble. He was several times fined ; three **times** set **in the** pillory ; imprisoned in New- gate for **more than** a year, where **he** had an opportunity to **study some of** the types of character he afterwards put into his fictions. **It** was late in life when he gave up po- litical writing and **began** to write novels. Then he seems to have led a more peaceful life, and the success of *Robinson Crusoe* proved that he need not depend on politics for either fame or pecuniary reward.

De Foe's writing is the perfection of realism. When he tells a story we feel that it is true ; we believe it in spite of knowledge to the contrary. In his own time his stories were accepted as fact, and even to this day it is a disputed question whether some of his novels were not drawn from authentic manuscript, or others taken down from the lips of the narrator. The way in which he gives all the little details of the story, the exact dates, the dress of his characters, the minute descriptions, — all make it a reality. Who could ever doubt the truth of a word of *Robinson Crusoe* while reading the story? And the *Account of the Great Plague, The Life of Colonel Jack, The Adventures of Captain Singleton, The Appearance of Mrs. Veal's Ghost to one Mrs. Bargrave*, are all equally realistic.

He wrote two hundred and ten different works, and at last died poor. He was always rising and falling in fortune, one can hardly tell how or why, and says of himself towards the last : —

> " No man has tasted different fortunes more;
> And thirteen times I have been rich and poor."

His style cannot be too much admired in this age of superlatives and exaggerated writing. It is the honest English of every-day life, — simple, direct, and not many-syllabled. And though he wrote on homely matters, and often of vicious men and women, he wrote with good sense and in the interests of morality. His works are accurate as well as realistic, and often are more valuable than history as a picture of the times.

From the great literary men of his time De Foe stands apart. The rest were united by bonds of friendship and interest. Pope, Gay, and Swift were warm friends ; Addison and Steele are almost inseparable in our thoughts. It is true that there was once a quarrel and some coldness between Pope and Addison ; but they still belonged to the same set, and were of one brotherhood. They were all, except De Foe, members of the Scriblerus Club; they hob-nobbed together at Will's Coffee-house. But De Foe stands aloof, an object of ridicule and dislike. Pope satirized him in the *Dunciad;* Gay laughed at him; the Scriblerus Club thought very poorly of his writings; and by those men who should have recognized him as their peer and com-panion, he was underrated and disregarded. For this, as well as for the gratitude we feel to the author of *Robinson Crusoe*, our hearts warm with sympathy towards De Foe, the author of that immortal book of our childhood.

But De Foe has other heroes, besides Robinson Crusoe, whose fortunes we follow with breathless interest through a whole volume. One of these is Colonel Jack, a poor boy, deserted in infancy by heartless parents, and given over to a nurse, at whose death he is thrown helpless and alone on the streets of London. Without a roof over his head, he lives as he can, and thinks himself happy when, on a win-ter's night, he finds lodging in the warm ashes and cinders of a glass manufactory, where he finds a crowd of boys as wretched as himself, who come there to sleep. Here he meets with an older boy, a young pickpocket, precocious in crime, who undertakes to teach little Jack a trade by which he can live like a prince. There are few stories more touch-ing than that of the poor boy's first beginnings in crime. It reminds me very much of the story of Oliver Twist, and his adventure with the Artful Dodger, in Charles Dickens's novel. But I shall let Jack tell a part of his story in his own words : —

COLONEL JACK'S FIRST EXPERIENCE IN CRIME.

"Well, upon the persuasions of this lad, I walked out with him, a poor innocent boy, and (as I remember my very thoughts perfectly well) I had no evil in my intentions. I had never stolen anything in my life; and if a goldsmith had left me in his shop with heaps of money strewed all round me, and bade me look after it, I should not have touched it, I was so honest; but the subtle tempter baited his hook for me, as I was a child, in a manner suitable to my childishness, for I never took this picking

of pockets to be dishonesty ; but, as I have said before, I looked
on it as a kind of trade that I was to be bred up to, and so I
entered upon it till I became hardened in it beyond the power
of retreating; and thus I was made a thief involuntarily, and
went on a length that few boys do without coming to the common period of that kind of life, I mean to the transport-ship or
to the gallows.

"The first day I went abroad with my new instructor, he
carried me directly into the city; and as we went first to the
water-side, he led me into the long room at the custom-house.
We were but a couple of ragged boys at best, but I was much
the worse; my leader had a shirt, a hat and a neckcloth ; as for
me, I had neither of the three, nor had I spoiled my manners
so much as to have a hat on my head since my nurse died,
which was now some years. His orders to me were to keep
always in sight and near him, but not close to him ; nor to take
any notice of him at any time till he came to me; and if any
hurly-burly happened, I should by no means know him, or pretend to have anything to do with him. I observed my orders
to a tittle, while he peered into every corner, and had his eye
upon everybody. I had my eye directly upon him, but went
always at a distance, looking as it were for pins, and picking
them up out of the dust as I found them, and then sticking them
on my sleeve, where I had at last got forty or fifty good pins ; but
still my eye was upon my comrade, who, I observed, was very
busy among the crowds of people that stood at the board doing
business with the officers.

"At length he comes over to me and stooping, as if he would
take up a pin close to me, he put something into my hand
and said, 'Put that up, and follow me downstairs quickly ;'
he did not run, but shuffled along apace through the crowd,
and went down,—not the great stairs which we came in at,
but a little narrow staircase at the other end of the long room.
I followed, and he found I did, and so went on, not stopping
below as I expected, nor speaking one word to me, till through
innumerable narrow passages, alleys, and dark ways, we
were got up into Fenchurch Street, and through Billiter Lane
into Leadenhall Street, and from thence into Leadenhall
Market."

In a quiet place in the market, it not being market-day,
the two boys look over the spoil which the elder thief has
thus thrust into little Jack's hands. It is a gentleman's letter-
case, full of checks and bills, besides many private notes.

Most **of the bills are too large for them, but** they find **one** note, the **smallest of all, which** the elder presents for payment, and gets the **money on it.** Then they divide the spoil, and Jack gets **his share. From** that **hour** trouble begins with **the** poor little vagabond. **He has no** place **to put his** money ; his ragged pockets **are full of holes, and he has no** roof over his head, no box, drawer, or any **crevice to hide** his gains in.

" **Nothing** could be more perplexing than this money was to me all that night. I carried it in my hand a good while, **for it was in** gold, all but fourteen shillings ; and that is to say it was in **four** guineas, and that fourteen shillings was more difficult to carry than **four guineas.** At last I sat down and pulled off one **of my** shoes **and put** the four guineas into that, but after I had gone a **while my shoe** hurt me **so that I could** not go on ; so I was fain to **sit down** again and take it out of my shoe and carry it in my **hand ; then** I found **a dirty linen rag** in the street, and I took that up and **wrapped it up together, and carried** it in that a good **way.** I have often since **heard people say when** they have been talking **of money that they could not** get in, ' I wish I had it in a foul clout.' **In truth** I had mine in a foul clout, for it was foul **according to the letter of that** saying ; **but** it served me till I came to a convenient place, and then I **sat down** and washed the cloth in the kennel, and so then put my **money in** again. Well, I carried it home with me to my **lodging in** the glass house, and when I went to go to sleep I knew **not** what to do with it. If I had let any of the black crew I was with know of it, I should have been smothered in the ashes for it, or robbed of it, or some trick or other put upon me for it ; so I knew **not** what to do, but lay with it in my hand, and my hand in my **bosom,** but then sleep went from my eyes. Oh, the **weight of human** care ! I, a poor beggar boy could not sleep **as soon as** I had but a little money to keep, who before **that, could have slept** upon a heap of brick-bats, stones, **or** cinders or anywhere, **as** sound **as** a rich man does on his **down** bed, and sounder **too.**

" Every now and **then,** dropping asleep, **I would dream** that my money was lost, **and start** like one frighted ; **then,** finding it **fast in my** hand, try to go to sleep again, **but could not for** a long while; then start and drop again. At **last a** fancy came into my head that if I fell asleep I should dream of the money and talk **of** it in my sleep, and tell that I had money ; which if

I should do and one of the rogues should hear me, they would pick it out of my bosom, and out of my hand without waking me; and after that thought I could not sleep a wink more; so that I passed that night over in care and anxiety enough; and this, I may safely say, was the first night's rest that I lost by the cares of this life and the deceitfulness of riches.

"As soon as it was day, I got out of the hole we lay in, and rambled abroad in the fields towards Stepney, and there I mused and considered what I should do with this money, and many a time I wished I had not had it; for after all my ruminating upon it, and what course I should take with it, or where I should put it, I could not hit upon any one thing, or any possible method to secure it, and it perplexed me so that at last, as I said just now, I sat down and cried heartily.

"When my crying was over, the case was the same. I had the money still, and what to do with it I could not tell. At last it came into my head that I would look out for some hole in a tree, and see to hide it there till I should have occasion for it. Big with this discovery, as I then thought it, I began to look for a tree; but there were no trees in the fields about Stepney or Mile-End that looked fit for my purpose; and if there were any that I began to look narrowly at, the fields were so full of people that they would see if I went to hide anything there, and I thought the people eyed me, as it were, and that two men in particular followed me to see what I intended to do.

"This drove me further off, and I crossed the road at Mile-End, and in the middle of the town went down a lane that goes away to the Blind Beggar's in Bethnal Green; when I came a little way in the lane, I found a foot-path over the fields, and in those fields several trees for my turn, as I thought; at last one tree had a little hole in it, pretty high out of my reach, and I climbed up the tree to get it, and when I came there, I put my hand in, and found, as I thought, a place very fit. So I placed my treasure there and was mightily well satisfied with it; but, behold, putting my hand in to lay it more commodiously, as I thought, of a sudden it slipped away from me, and I found the tree was hollow, and my little parcel was fallen in quite out of my reach, and how far it might go in I knew not, so that in a word my money was quite gone, irrevocably lost; there could be no room as much as to hope ever to get it again, for it was a vast, great tree.

"As young as I was, I was now sensible what a fool I was before, that I could not think of ways to keep my money, but I must come thus far to throw it into a hole where I could not reach it. Well, I thrust my hand quite up to my elbow, but no bottom was to be found, or any end of the hole or cavity; I got a stick of the tree, and thrust it in a great way, but all was one. Then I cried, nay, roared out, I was in such a passion; then I got down the tree again, then up again; I thrust in my hand again till I scratched my arm and made it bleed, and cried all the while most violently; then I began to think I had not so much as a halfpenny left for a halfpenny roll, and I was hungry, and then I cried again; then I came away in despair, crying and roaring like a little boy that had been whipped; then I went back again to the tree and up the tree again, and this I did several times.

"The last time I had gotten up the tree I happened to come down not on the same side that I went up and came down before, but on the other side of the tree, and on the other side of the bank also; and behold the tree had a great open place in the side of it close to the ground, as old hollow trees often have; and, looking into the open place, to my inexpressible joy there lay my money and my linen rag, all wrapped up just as I had put it into the hole; for, the tree being hollow all the way up, there had been some moss or light stuff, which I had not judgment enough to know was not firm, and had given way when it came to drop out of my hand, and so it had slipped quite down at once. . . .

"It would tire the reader should I dwell on all the little boyish tricks that I played in the ecstasy of my joy and satisfaction when I found my money. Joy is as extravagant as grief; and since I've been a man I have often thought that had such a thing befallen a man so to have lost all he had, and not have a bit of bread to eat, and then so strangely to find it again, after having given it effectually over, — I say, had it been so with a man, it might have hazarded his using some violence upon himself."

We cannot follow any further in detail the fortunes of little Jack. Before he gets deep enough in his career of a pickpocket to be arrested by the law, he is kidnapped by the captain of a vessel who has given him some drugged liquor, and, while insensible, he is carried off to the colony of Virginia, in America, where he is sold to a master, an English planter who is cultivating lands in these new colonies belonging to England. The time of servitude for which he is sold is five years, and, after he recovers his liberty, Jack manages so well that he himself becomes a landholder and a prosperous man, and ends his story in great peace and contentment.

During his period of imprisonment in Newgate, De Foe began the publication of a sort of journal called the *Review*, published twice a week, which was somewhat on the plan of the modern newspaper. In this he gave such news, foreign and native, as he could get hold of, and criticisms on politics at home and abroad. Finding that politics alone would not interest his readers, he formed the idea of a Scandal Club, whose members should discuss all the topics of the day in his paper. Like most of De Foe's works, the *Review* has passed into obscurity; but I refer to it because this was the forerunner of *The Tatler*, *The Spectator*, and other series written by the two famous English writers who are the subjects of our next Talk.

XXXVIII.

ON ADDISON AND STEELE, EDITORS OF "THE SPECTATOR."

THE names of JOSEPH ADDISON and RICHARD STEELE are almost as closely interwoven in friendship as those
1672–1719 of Beaumont and Fletcher, and their lives were
united for a much longer period than those of
1671–1729 the two dramatists. They were schoolboys together in the Charterhouse School, — Addison the head boy in his class, grave, studious, painstaking; Steele a merry youngster who got whipped as often as praised, and was gay and light-hearted in spite of the rod and his unmastered lessons. There was always the same difference between them in after life, and to the last of his days Steele seemed to regard Addison with the same sort of awe he had felt for the boy who was always above him in school.

Joseph Addison was one of the most gifted men of his age. He wrote sufficiently well in college to attract attention, and almost as soon as he left his studies he was offered a position in public life. But politics did not suit his taste, and he came back to his books and his pen rather soured and disappointed by his experience. His earlier works were nearly all of them in verse, and his first success was the tragedy of *Cato*, which had a run at the theatre only equalled by Gay's *Beggar's Opera*. But it was as a prose-writer, and particularly as the writer of prose essays, that Addison made his reputation.

It was Steele, not Addison, who began the enterprise that made them both honored among English essayists. While Addison had been trying political life, Steele had enlisted as a soldier, beginning at the very bottom of the military ladder, but rising rapidly in the scale of promotion, largely from his personal popularity. After he entered the army he discovered his gifts as a writer. In the midst of a wild career he was suddenly checked by a burst of repentance, in which he wrote a tract called the *Christian Hero*, which excited the amazement of his comrades that a man who practised so badly could preach so well. Very soon after this he wrote a brilliant comedy, *The Funeral, or Grief à la Mode*. The *Christian Hero* had given him a reputation for piety which, as he says, he felt he did not deserve, and so he struck the balance by a rattling comedy. This was characteristic of good-natured Dick Steele, who was never moderate in anything, and, as he says, "was always sinning and repenting."

This first comedy was followed by others, which gave him a reputation as a man of wit and genius. He had arrived at middle age, and was living in London, a gay man of the world, a frequenter of clubs, welcome in the best society, a man well fitted to hold the mirror up to the virtues for which he had a hearty respect, and the vices he was never quite strong enough to withstand, when the idea of *The Tatler* came to him.

The Tatler was in plan not unlike De Foe's *Review*.

It was a tri-weekly paper, with a small portion devoted to news; but the larger part of its space was given to a daily essay on subjects most interesting to its readers.

These essays were in the main on social topics; they criticised reigning follies in taste and manners; they exalted what was best and noblest in human nature; "they advocated a general simplicity in dress, conversation, and behavior." The purpose was good, and there are few literary works which have had so wholesome and so immediate an influence on the time as these essays of Steele and Addison.

Addison was in Ireland when Steele began this new enterprise; but he thought, on first seeing it, that he recognized Steele's hand in *The Tatler;* and convinced that this mode of writing was the one of all others best suited to his own genius, he sent some contributions to Steele. *The Tatler* lived about two years, and when it was dropped, it was almost immediately succeeded by *The Spectator*, in which the two friends united as partners in full, writing nearly an equal share. This is the longest sustained and the most famous of all their papers. For the greater part of the time it was issued daily, and was published solely as a series of essays, without news or politics. It was followed by *The Guardian* and by two or three other journals, none of them so long-lived or successful as *The Spectator*, and that stands as the chief among all works of its kind.

I know at this day no more delightful reading than *The Spectator*. Addison and Steele formed just such an admirable contrast to each other as would make the papers a constant variety. Addison, more profound and thoughtful than Steele, had a fund of quaint humor, a little satirical, which touched genially but keenly on all the follies of the time. He was also a critic of merit, and his series of essays on Milton in *The Spectator* drew attention to the unheeded beauty of *Paradise Lost.* Steele, with less judgment than Addison, had abundant wit and pathos, and could move to tears and laughter. They also worked readily together on one conception, as did Beaumont and

Fletcher. The delightful characters of the Spectator's Club, Sir Roger de Coverley, Will Honeycomb, Captain Sentry, and the rest, were first drawn by Steele; but Addison entered fully into his conception of them, and made Sir Roger one of his favorite characters, adding to him some of those traits that make the dear old gentleman so delightful to those who have ever read *The Spectator*.

I have just hinted that Steele was not moderate either in his good or bad qualities, — he was always at an extreme in both; but as an offset to his vices, he had always generous and noble words for woman. Up to his time, little appeal had been made to the higher virtues in woman, and the fashionable comedies painted her as a creature without heart or brains. The service Steele did in writing for women and about them as if they were reasonable beings, is one of the best traits of his essays. As one of his characteristic pieces of writing, I have selected for your reading, Paper XXXIII. of *The Spectator* : —

THE STORY OF LÆTITIA AND DAPHNE, OR THE ART OF IMPROVING BEAUTY.

A friend of mine has two daughters, whom I will call Lætitia and Daphne; the former is one of the greatest beauties of the age in which she lives, the latter no way remarkable for any charms in her person. Upon this one circumstance of their outward form the good and ill of their life seems to turn. Lætitia has not, from her very childhood, heard anything else but commendations of her features and complexion, by which means she is no other than nature made her, — a very beautiful outside. The consciousness of her charms has rendered her insupportably vain and insolent towards all who have to do with her. Daphne, who was almost twenty before one civil thing had been said to her, found herself obliged to acquire some accomplishments to make up for the want of those attractions which she saw in her sister. Poor Daphne was seldom admitted to a debate wherein she was concerned; her discourse had nothing to recommend it but the good sense of it, and she was always under a necessity to have very well considered what she was to say before she uttered it; while Lætitia was listened to with partiality, and approbation sat in the countenances of

those she conversed with, before she communicated what she
had to say. These causes have produced suitable effects, and
Lætitia is as insipid a companion as Daphne is an agreeable
one. Lætitia, confident of favor, has studied no arts to please;
Daphne, despairing of any inclination towards her person, has
only depended on her merit. Lætitia has always something in
her air that is sullen, grave, and disconsolate. Daphne has a
countenance that appears cheerful, open, and unconcerned. A
young gentleman saw Lætitia this winter at a play, and became
her captive. His fortune was such that he wanted very little
introduction to speak his sentiments to her father. The lover
was admitted with the utmost freedom into the family, where
a constrained behavior, severe looks, and distant civilities
were the highest favors he could obtain from Lætitia; while
Daphne used him with the good humor, familiarity, and innocence of a sister, insomuch that he would often say to her,
"Dear Daphne, wert thou but as handsome as Lætitia." She
received such language with that ingenuous and pleasing mirth
which is natural to a woman without design. He still sighed in
vain for Lætitia, but found certain relief in the agreeable conversation of Daphne. At length, heartily tired with the haughty
impertinence of Lætitia, and charmed with the repeated instances of good humor he had observed in Daphne, he one day
told the latter that he had something to say to her that he
hoped she would be pleased with, — "Faith, Daphne," continued he, "I am in love with *thee*, and despise thy sister sincerely." The manner of his declaring himself gave his mistress
occasion for a very hearty laughter. "Nay," said he, "I knew
you would laugh at me, but I will ask your father." He did
so; the father received his intelligence with no less joy than
surprise, and was very glad: he had no care now left but for
his beauty, which he thought he could carry to market at his
leisure. I do not know anything that has pleased me so much
in a great while as this conquest of my friend Daphne's. All
her acquaintance congratulate her upon her chance-medley, and
laugh at that premeditating murderer, her sister. As it is an
argument of a light mind to think the worse of ourselves for
the imperfection of our persons, it is equally below us to value
ourselves upon the advantages of them. The female world
seems to be almost incorrigibly gone astray in this particular,
for which reason I shall recommend the following extract out
of a friend's letter to the professed beauties, who are, as a
people, almost as insufferable as the professed wits: —

"M. St. Evremond has concluded one of his essays with

affirming that the last sighs of a handsome woman are not so much for the loss of her life as of her beauty. Perhaps this raillery is pursued too far ; yet it is turned upon a very obvious remark, that woman's strongest passion is for her own beauty, and that she values it as her favorite distinction. From hence it is that all arts which pretend to improve or preserve it meet with so general a reception among the sex. To say nothing of many false helps and contraband wares of beauty which are daily vended in this great mart, there is not a maiden gentle-woman of a good family in any county of South Britain who has not heard of the virtues of May-dew, or is unfurnished with some receipt or other in favor of her complexion ; and I have known a physician of learning and sense, after eight years' study in the University, and a course of travels in most countries in Europe, owe the first raising of his fortunes to a cosmetic wash.

" This has given me occasion to consider how so universal a disposition in womankind, which springs from a laudable motive, the desire of pleasing, and proceeds upon an opinion not altogether groundless, that nature may be helped by art, may be turned to their advantage. And, methinks, it would be an acceptable service to take them out of the hands of quacks and pretenders, and to prevent their imposing on themselves, by discovering to them the *true secret and art of improving* beauty.

" In order to do this, before I touch upon it directly, it will be necessary to lay down a few preliminary maxims, viz. :

" That no woman can be handsome by the force of features alone, any more than she can be witty only by the help of speech.

" That pride destroys all symmetry and grace, and affectation is a more terrible enemy to fine faces than the small-pox.

" That no woman is capable of being beautiful who is not incapable of being false.

" And that what would be odious in a friend is deformity in a mistress.

" From these few principles thus laid down, it will be easy to prove that the true art of assisting beauty consists in embellishing the whole person by the proper ornaments of virtuous and commendable qualities. By this help alone it is that those who are the favorite works of nature, or, as Mr. Dryden expresses it, the porcelain clay of humankind, become animated, and are in a capacity of exerting their charms ; and those who seem to have been neglected by her, like models wrought in haste, are capable in a great measure of finishing what she has left imperfect.

"It is, methinks, a low and degrading idea of that sex, which was created to refine the joys and soften the cares of humanity, to consider them merely as objects of sight. This is abridging them of the natural extent of their power, to put them on a level with the pictures at Kneller's. How much nobler is the contemplation of beauty, heightened by virtue, and commanding our esteem and love, while it draws our observation! How faint and spiritless are the charms of a coquette, when compared with the real loveliness of Sophronia's innocence, piety, good humor, and truth, — virtues which add a new softness to her sex, and even beautify her beauty! That agreeableness which must otherwise have appeared no longer in the modest virgin is now preserved in the tender mother, the prudent friend, and the faithful wife. Colors artfully spread upon canvas may entertain the eye, but not affect the heart; and she who takes no care to add to the natural graces of her person any excelling qualities may be still allowed to amuse as a picture, but not to triumph as a beauty."

XXXIX.

ON JOSEPH ADDISON'S ESSAYS.

THERE are so many noble pieces of writing among Addison's essays that one hesitates in choosing an extract. I advise every one to keep a volume of *The Spectator* at hand, and cull for himself. In the mean time, I will give some short extracts which show in brief the variety of his humor, and how easily he passes from grave to gay, from lively to severe.

The first is from —

POPULAR SUPERSTITIONS.

"Going yesterday to dine with an old acquaintance, I had the misfortune to find his whole family very much dejected. Upon asking him the occasion of it, he told me that his wife had dreamt a strange dream the night before, which they were afraid portended some misfortune to themselves or to their children. At her coming into the room I observed a settled melancholy in her countenance, which I should have been troubled for had I not heard from whence it proceeded. We were no sooner sat down, but after having looked upon me a little while, 'My dear,' says she, turning to her husband, 'you may now see the stranger that was in the candle last night.' Soon after this, as they began to talk of family affairs, a little boy at the lower end of the table told her that he was to go into join-hand on Thursday. 'Thursday!' says she. 'No, child, if it please God you shall not begin upon Childermas day; tell your writing-master that Friday will be soon enough.' I was reflecting with myself upon the oddness of her fancy, and wondering that anybody could establish it as a rule to lose a day in every week. In the midst of these my musings, she desired me to reach her a little salt upon the point of my knife, which I did in such a trepidation and hurry of obedience that I let it drop by the way; at which she immediately started, and said it fell towards her. Upon this I looked very blank, and observing the concern of the whole table, began to consider myself, with some confusion, as a person that had brought a disaster upon the family. The lady, however, recovering herself after a little space, said to her husband, with a sigh, 'My dear, misfortunes never come single.' My friend, I found, acted but an under part at his table, and being a man of more good-nature than understanding, thinks himself obliged to fall in with all the passions and humors of his yoke-fellow. 'Do not you remember, child,' says she, 'that the pigeon-house fell the very afternoon that our careless wench spilt the salt upon the table?' 'Yes,' says he, 'my dear, and the next post brought us an account of the battle of Almanza.' The reader may guess at the figure I made after having done all this mischief. I despatched my dinner as soon as I could, with my usual taciturnity, when, to my utter confusion, the lady, seeing me quitting my knife and fork, and laying them across one another on my plate, desired me that I would humor her so far as to take them out of that figure and place them side by side. What the absurdity was which I had committed, I did not know; but I suppose there was some traditionary superstition in it, and therefore, in obedience to the lady of the house, I disposed of my knife and fork in two parallel lines, which is the figure I shall always lay them for the future, though I do not know any reason for it.

"It is not difficult for a man to see that a person has conceived an aversion to him. For my own part, I quickly found, by the lady's looks, that she regarded me as a very odd kind of fellow, with an unfortunate aspect. For which reason I took my leave immediately after dinner, and withdrew to my old lodgings. Upon my return home I fell into a profound contemplation on the evils that attend these superstitious follies of mankind; how they subject us to imaginary afflictions, and additional sorrows that do not properly come with our lot. As if the natural calamities of life were not enough for it, we turn the most indifferent circumstances into misfortune, and suffer as much from trifling accidents as from real evils. I have known the shooting of a star spoil a night's rest, and have seen a man in love grow pale and lose his appetite upon the plucking of a merry-thought. A screech-owl at midnight has alarmed a family more than a band of robbers, — nay, the voice of a cricket has struck more terror than the roaring of a lion. There is nothing so inconsiderable which may not appear dreadful to the imagination that is filled with omens and prognostics. A rusty nail or a crooked pin shoot up into prodigies."

The following essay from Addison gives a humorous description of *Clubs*, which in Queen Anne's time sprang up in such numbers and with such a variety of objects : —

ACCOUNTS OF VARIOUS CLUBS.

"Man is said to be a sociable animal; and as an instance of it, we may observe that we take all occasions and pretences of forming ourselves into those little nocturnal assemblies which are commonly known by the name of clubs. When a set of men find themselves to agree in any particular, though never so trivial, they establish themselves into a kind of fraternity, and meet once or twice a week, upon the account of such a fantastic resemblance. I know a considerable market-town, in which there was a club of fat men, that did not come together (as you may well suppose) to entertain one another with sprightliness and wit, but to keep one another in countenance. The room where the club met was something of the largest, and had two entrances, the one by a door of moderate size, and the other by a pair of folding-doors. If a candidate for this corpulent club could make an entrance through the first, he was looked upon as unqualified; but if he stuck in the passage and could not force his way through it, the folding-doors were immediately thrown open for his reception, and he was saluted as a brother. I have heard that this club, though it consisted of but fifteen persons, weighed above three ton.

"In opposition to this society, there sprang up another, composed of scarecrows and skeletons, who, being very meagre and envious, did all they could to thwart the designs of their bulky brethren, whom they represented as men of dangerous principles, till at length they worked them out of the favor of the people, and, consequently, out of the magistracy. These factions tore the corporation in pieces for several years, till at length they came to this accommodation: that the two bailiffs of the town should be annually chosen out of the clubs, by which means the principal magistrates are at this day coupled like rabbits, one fat and one lean. . . .

"The Humdrum club, of which I was formerly an unworthy member, was made up of very honest gentlemen of peaceable disposition, that used to sit together, smoke their pipes, and say nothing till midnight. The *Mum* club (as I am informed) is an institution of the same nature, and as great an enemy to noise.

"After these two innocent societies, I cannot forbear mentioning a very mischievous one that was erected in the time of King Charles II.: I mean the club of duelists, into which none was to be admitted who had not fought his man. The president of it was said to have killed half a dozen in single combat; but as for the other members, they took their seats according to the number of their slain. There was likewise a side-table, for such as had only drawn blood, and shown a laudable ambition of taking the first opportunity to qualify themselves for the first table. This club, consisting only of men of honor, did not continue long, most of the members of it being put to the sword, or hanged, a little after its institution.

"Our modern celebrated clubs are founded upon eating and drinking, which are points wherein most men agree, and in which the learned and the illiterate, the dull and the airy, the philosopher and the buffoon, can all of them bear a part. . . . When men are thus knit together by a love of society, not a spirit of faction, and do not meet to censure or annoy those that are absent, but to enjoy one another; when they are thus combined for their own improvement, or for the good of others, or at least to relax themselves from the business of the day by an innocent and cheerful conversation, — there may be something very useful in these little institutions and establishments."

Addison's prose style has ever since his day been regarded as a model, and stands for that which is most stately and polished in English prose. In spite of the fact that his carefully worded sentences sound a little stiff and old-fash-

ioned, we cannot help feeling their charm as they flow from
his pen ; and there are few names in literature that excite
a warmer personal interest in those who are familiar with
his life and his writings than the name of Joseph Addison.

XL.

ON THE GREAT DEAN SWIFT.

THE last writer whom we shall include in the *Augustan
age* is JONATHAN SWIFT, who was a clergyman of the
English Church and was appointed to the deanery
1667-1745 of the Cathedral of St. Patrick's, in Ireland,
which gave him the title of *Dean Swift*, by which he
is best known.   He began life, like so many other great
men, without fortune, and as a young man was a secretary
and a poor dependent in the family of Sir William Temple.
Swift seems to have felt poverty and dependence on a rich
patron very bitterly.   It soured him, and spoiled his
manners all his life long, — at least, this is the only explanation, except natural ill-temper, of the fact that his
manners were brusque and disagreeable to the worst degree, although, in spite of this, he had many friends, and won
the affection of two lovable and accomplished women.   His
conduct to these two women, both of whom were devoted
to him, was heartless ; his behavior to people who befriended
him was often rude and uncivil ; and if we may judge of him
through his biographies, he is a man whom we should prefer
to know only in his writings.   But there he appears a great
man.   He was a versatile writer, and whatever he wrote
was at once noted.   His satires in prose were as keen as
Pope's rhymed satires ; he was as shrewd an observer and
could hit off the follies of the age as cleverly as Addison
or Steele ; he almost rivalled De Foe in his power of painting fiction with the hues of truth ; and he was a clever poet
besides.   Whatever he does, the quality that impresses one
in his work is *power*.

The first work which drew notice was *The Battle of the Books*. The question had been raised in France whether modern writers were not as great as the ancient writers. This dispute spread to England. Naturally, in the state of public taste, the greater part of the reading world thought it a dangerous heresy to assert that a modern writer could equal those of Greece and Rome, and the valiant few who dared to stand by this idea were hooted at in disdain. In *The Battle of the Books*, Swift sided with the majority, and assailed with the arrows of his satire those who ventured to plead for the moderns.

The Battle of the Books was soon followed by the *Tale of a Tub*, which made a sensation in literary circles that we could hardly appreciate in reading it nowadays. This was the story of three sons who, on the death of their father, are each bequeathed a coat that, with proper usage, should last a lifetime. These three sons are Peter (the Papist), Martin (the English Church), and Jack (the Dissenter). In those days the pulpits of Dissenting preachers were called "tubs," in derision, — whence Swift got the title for his book of *The Tale of a Tub*.

The trouble that these three brothers have with their coats, and the shifts they are put to to wear them in conformity to their father's will, is very droll to read about, even when we do not care to follow out the satire. I hardly need tell you that although Martin has some share in the ridicule, yet his coat is in very good condition, and comes out bravely beside those of his brothers, Jack and Peter.

Gulliver's Travels appeared about twenty years after *The Tale of a Tub*. In the mean time, Swift had written many prose tracts and several poems. During this time he was made Dean of St. Patrick's. He was one of those men who, like Dryden, exercised a power over their age. He could wield this power over men and affairs even from his remote post in Ireland ; and when he went to London (and his visits there were frequent) the great metropolis felt his presence. He was a guest at the houses of the great, the Scriblerus Club were honored to have him as a member, and he was the friend of Pope, Gay, Addison, and of all the famous men of this Augustan age.

Gulliver's Travels will live when all the religious and political quarrels that it laughs at are altogether forgotten. It is the account of the travels of a respectable Englishman who meets with most extraordinary adventures, which are related in the same realistic way in which De Foe tells his stories. Gulliver is first shipwrecked in the country of the Lilliputians, or little people. Finding himself safe from the sea, and once more on firm earth, he lies down, overpowered with fatigue, and falls into a deep sleep. When he wakes he finds himself besieged by an army of little beings three inches in height, who have erected scaling-ladders to climb upon his body, and are walking about all over him. They have brought their ropes and cables (of the size of common thread), and made an ingenious array of bonds to fasten him to the earth. At the first movement he makes on waking, he breaks a great part of the network of bonds that fastens him; then the little army discharge a flight of arrows, which prick him like needles. Finding, however, that he is not disposed to harm them, they at last lead the "man-mountain," as they call him, to the presence of their emperor, and he is entertained with princely hospitality in the kingdom of Lilliput. He thus gives an account of his manner of living : —

"And here it may perhaps divert the curious reader to give some account of my domestics and my manner of living in this country during a residence of nine months and thirteen days. Having a head mechanically turned, and being likewise forced by necessity, I had made for myself a table and chair, convenient enough, out of the largest trees in the royal park. Two hundred seamstresses were employed to make me shirts and linen for my bed and table, all of the strongest and coarsest kind they could get; which, however, they were forced to quilt together in several folds, for the thickest was some degrees finer than lawn. Their linen is usually three inches wide, and three feet make a piece. The seamstresses took my measure as I lay on the ground, one standing at my neck and another at my mid-leg with a strong cord extended that each held by the end,

while a third **measured** the length of the cord with a rule of **an**
inch long. Then they measured my right thumb, and desired
no more, for, **by** mathematical computation, **that twice round**
the thumb is once round the wrist, and **so on to the neck** and
waist; and by the help of my old shirt, which I displayed before
them on the ground for a pattern, they fitted **me exactly.**
Three hundred tailors were employed in **the same manner to**
make me clothes; but they had another contrivance for taking
my measure. I kneeled down, and they raised a ladder from
the ground to my neck; upon this ladder one of them mounted,
and let fall a plumb-line from my collar to the floor, which just
answered the length of my coat; but my waist and arms I
measured myself. When my clothes were finished (which was
done in my house, for the largest of theirs would not have been
able to hold them) they looked like the patchwork made by the
ladies in England, only that mine **were** all of a color.

"I had three hundred cooks **to dress my** victuals in little
convenient huts built about **my house, where they and** their
families lived and prepared **me two dishes apiece;** I took **up**
twenty waiters in my hand, **and placed them on** the **table; a**
hundred more attended below **on the** ground, some with dishes
of meat, and some with barrels **of wine and** other liquors **slung**
on their shoulders, all which **the** waiters above drew up, **as**
I wanted, in a very ingenious manner, by certain cords, as **we**
draw the bucket up a well in Europe. A dish of their meat
was a good mouthful, and a barrel of their liquor a reasonable
draught. Their mutton yields to ours, but their beef is excel-
lent. I have had a sirloin so large that I have been forced to
make three bites of it; but this is rare. My servants were
astonished to see me eat it, bones and all, as in this country we
do the leg of a lark. Their geese and turkeys I usually eat at
a mouthful, and I confess they far excel ours. Of their smaller
fowls I could take up twenty or thirty at the end of my knife.

"One day his imperial majesty [the Emperor of Lilliput], being informed of my way of living, desired 'that himself and **his**
royal consort, with the young princes of the blood of both sexes,
might have the happiness,' as he pleased to call it, **'of dining**
with me.' They came accordingly, and I placed them **in chairs**
of state upon my table, just over against me, with **their guards**
about them. Flimnap, the lord high **treasurer, attended** them
likewise with his white staff; and I observed he **often** looked on
me with a sour countenance, which I would not seem to regard,
but eat more than usual, in honor of my dear country, as well
as to fill the court with admiration. **I** have some private

reasons to believe that this visit from his Majesty gave **Flimnap** an opportunity of doing me ill offices to his master. The minister had always **been** my secret enemy, though he outwardly caressed me more than was usual to the moroseness of his nature. He represented to the emperor the condition of his treasury   that he was forced to **take** up money at a great discount; that exchequer bills would not circulate under nine per cent below par; that I had cost his Majesty above a million **and a half of** *sprugs* (their greatest gold coin, about the bigness **of a spangle);** and upon the whole, **that it** would be advisable in **the emperor to take the first fair** occasion of dismissing me."

On his next voyage after his return from Lilliput, Gulliver encounters a shipwreck which throws him on the coast of Brobdingnag, or the giants' country. In saving himself from the wreck, he has seen a huge monster wading in the surf, but escapes from him and makes his way to a field of gigantic grain, whose stalks are forty feet high. As he is floundering about in this field of grain like a man in a pathless forest, there come into it a party of reapers, each as high as an ordinary church steeple, who stride ten yards at each step. Gulliver at once reflects that he would be as much of a pygmy to these people as the Lilliputians had been pygmies to him ; and hiding in the grain, he begins to philosophize that nothing is either great or little except by comparison. He goes on thus : —

" Scared and confounded as I was, I could not forbear going on with these reflections, when one of the reapers approaching within ten yards of the ridge where I lay, made me apprehend that with the next step I should be squashed to death under his foot, or cut in two with his reaping-hook ; and, therefore, when he was again about to move, I screamed as loud as fear could make me; whereupon the huge creature stopped short, and looking round about under him for some time, at last espied me as I lay on the ground. He considered awhile, with the caution of one who endeavors to lay hold on a small, dangerous animal in such a manner that it shall not be able either to scratch or bite him, as I myself have sometimes done with a weasel in England. At length he ventured to take me behind, by the middle, between his finger and thumb, and brought me within three yards of his eyes, that he might behold my shape more perfectly. I guessed his meaning, and my good fortune gave me so much presence of mind that I resolved not to struggle in the least, as he held me in the air above sixty feet from the ground, though he grievously pinched my sides, for fear I should slip through his fingers. All I ventured was to raise mine eyes towards the sun, and place my hands together in a supplicating posture, and to speak some words in a humble, melancholy tone, suitable to the condition I was now in; for I apprehended every moment that he would dash me against the ground, as we do some hateful little animal which we have a mind to destroy. But my good star would have it that he appeared pleased with my voice and gestures, and begun to look on me as a curiosity, much wondering to hear me pronounce articulate words, although he could not understand them. In the mean time I was not able to forbear groaning and shedding tears, and turning my head towards my sides, letting him know, as well as I could, how cruelly I was hurt by the pressure of his thumb and finger. He seemed to apprehend my meaning, for, lifting up the lappet of his coat, he put me gently into it, and immediately ran along with me to his master, who was a substantial farmer, and the same person I had first seen in the field.

" The farmer, having (as I suppose by their talk) received such an account of me as his servant could give him, took a piece of small straw about the size of a walking-staff, and therewith lifted up the lappets of my coat, which it seems he thought to be some kind of covering that nature had given me. He blew my hair aside to get a better view of my face; he called his hinds about him and asked them, as I afterwards learned, ' whether they had ever seen in the fields any little creature that resembled me;' he then placed me softly on the ground on all fours; but I immediately got up and walked slowly backward and forward to let him see I had no intent to run away. They all sat down in a circle about me, the better to observe my motions. I pulled off my hat and made a low bow to the farmer; I fell on my knees, lifted up my hands and eyes, and spoke several words as loud as I could; I took a purse of gold out of my pocket and humbly presented it to him. He received it on the palm of his hand, then applied it close to his eye, to see what it was, and afterwards turned it several times with the point of a pin, but could make nothing of it; whereupon I made a sign that he should put his hand upon the ground; I then took the purse, and opening it, poured all the gold into his palm. I saw him wet the tip of his finger upon his tongue and take up one of my largest pieces, and then another; but he seemed to be wholly ignorant what they were. He made me a sign to put them again into my purse, and the purse again into my pocket, which, after offering it to him several times, I thought it best to do.

" The farmer by this time was convinced I must be a rational creature. He spoke often to me, but the sound of his voice pierced my ears like that of a water-mill; yet his words were articulate enough. I answered as loud as I could in several languages, and he often laid his ear within two feet of me; but all in vain, for we were wholly unintelligible to each other. He then sent his servants to their work, and taking his handkerchief out of his pocket, he doubled it and spread it on his left hand, which he placed flat on the ground, with palm upwards, making me a sign to step into it, as I could easily do, for it was not above a foot in thickness. I thought it my part to obey; and for fear of falling, laid myself at full length upon the handkerchief, with the remainder of which he lapped me up to the head for further security, and in this manner he carried me home to his house. There he called his wife and showed me to her; but she screamed and ran back, as women in England do at the sight of a toad or spider. However, when she had awhile seen my behavior and how well I observed the signs her husband made, she was soon reconciled, and by degrees became extremely tender to me.

" It was about twelve at noon, and a servant brought in dinner. It was only one substantial dish of meat (fit for the plain condition of a husbandman), in a dish of about four and twenty feet diameter. The company were the farmer and his wife, three children, and an old grandmother. When they sat down, the farmer placed me at some distance from him on the table, which was thirty feet high from the floor. I was in a terrible fright, and kept as far as I could from the edge, for fear of falling. The wife minced a bit of meat, then crumbled some bread on a trencher, and placed it before me. I made her a low bow, took out my knife and fork, and fell to eat, which gave them exceeding delight. The mistress sent her maid for a small dram-cup which held about two gallons, and filled it with drink; I took up the vessel with much difficulty in both hands, and in a most respectful manner drank to her ladyship's health, expressing the words as loud as I could in English, which made the company laugh so heartily that I was almost deafened with the noise. This liquor tasted like a small cider, and was not unpleasant. Then the master made me a sign to come to his trencher side; but as I walked on the table, being in great surprise all the time, as the indulgent reader will easily conceive and excuse, I happened to stumble against a crust and fell flat on my face, but received no hurt. I got up immediately, and observing the good people to be in much concern, I took my hat (which I held under my arm out of good manners), and waving it over my head, made three huzzas to show that I had got no mischief by my fall.

"But advancing forward towards my master (as I shall henceforth call him), his youngest son, who sat next to him, an arch boy of about ten years old, took me up by the legs and held me so high in the air that I trembled in every limb; but his father snatched me from him, and at the same time gave him such a box on the left ear as would have felled a European troop of horse to the earth, ordering him to be taken from the table. But being afraid the boy might owe me a spite, and well remembering how mischievous all children among us are to sparrows, rabbits, young kittens, and puppy dogs, I fell on my knees, and pointing to the boy, made my master to understand as well as I could that I desired his son should be pardoned. The father complied, and the lad took his seat again; whereupon I went to him and kissed his hand, which my master took, and made him stroke me gently with it.

"In the midst of dinner my mistress' favorite cat leaped into her lap. I heard a noise behind me like that of a dozen stocking-weavers at work, and turning my head, I found it proceeded from the purring of that animal, who seemed to be three times larger than an ox, as I computed by the view of her head and one of her paws, while her mistress was feeding and stroking her. The fierceness of this creature's countenance altogether discomposed me, though I stood at the further end of the table, above fifty feet off, and although my mistress held her fast, for fear she would spring and seize me in her talons. But it happened there was no danger, for the cat took not the least notice of me when my master placed me within three yards of her. And, as I have been always told, and found true by experience in my travels, that flying or discovering fear before a strange animal is a certain way to make it pursue or attack you, so I resolved in this dangerous juncture to show no manner of concern. I walked with intrepidity five or six times before the very head of the cat, and came within half a yard of her, whereupon she drew herself back as if afraid of me. I had less apprehension concerning the dogs, whereof three or four came into the room, as is usual in farmers' houses, one of which was a mastiff, equal in bulk to four elephants, and a greyhound, somewhat taller than the mastiff, but not so large."

It must be kept in mind while reading the account of Gulliver's life in Brobdingnag that he was a man six feet in height, and proportionately large, otherwise he will assume to us only Lilliputian size. The whole account of his life there is very amusing, — how he was made a pet of by his master's little daughter Glumdalclitch, who fitted up her doll's cradle for him ; how he had a padded box to travel in, which was carried about by Glumdalclitch ; how his master made a show of him through the kingdom of the Brobdingnagians ; together with many other interesting adventures, till he finally escapes and gets home again.

Gulliver makes several other voyages besides these which we have read of, — one to a flying island called Laputa ; another to the land of the Houyhnhnms and the Yahoos, in which horses are the superior race of animals, and man the inferior. But none are so interesting as those to Lilliput and Brobdingnag, and the story of Gulliver will always be that by which the great Dean Swift will be longest remembered.

XLI.

ENGLISH COMEDY WRITERS, — CONGREVE, VANBRUGH, AND FARQUHAR.

THREE of the most brilliant comedy writers in English were contemporaries of Pope, Swift, and Addison ; these were Congreve, Vanbrugh, and Farquhar, whose lively, brilliant, pointed style in their dialogue comes nearest to the brightness of French comedy, of anything we have ever had in our literature. Almost every sentence spoken by their characters is so sharp with wit that the dialogue reads like a string of epigrams. It is a pity that so much genius was lavished on works of which the motive is coarse and repulsive. Not one of the comedies of this age is now acted, and few can be read with either profit or pleasure.

WILLIAM CONGREVE, the earliest of this trio, was also the most distinguished. He was a man of the world, and thus the better fitted to write comedies which 1670-1729 were pictures of the world in which he lived. Nearly all his works were comedies, although his one tragedy, the *Mourning Bride*, was that of which Dr. Johnson said : "If I were requested to select from the whole mass of English poetry the most poetical paragraph, I know not what I should prefer to an exclamation in the *Mourning Bride.*" Here is the "paragraph" to which Johnson refers, — the description of the cathedral at night :—

[*Almeria and Leonora in the cathedral.*]

Alm. It was a fancied noise, for all is hushed.
Leon. It bore the accent of a human voice.
Alm. It was thy fear, or else some transient wind
    Whistling through hollows of this vaulted aisle.
    We 'll listen.
Leon. Hark!
Alm. No, all is hushed and still as death. 'T is dreadful!
    How reverend is the face of this tall pile,
    Whose ancient pillars rear their marble heads
    To bear aloft its arched and ponderous roof,
    By its own weight made steadfast and immovable,
    Looking tranquillity. It strikes an awe
    And terror on my aching sight. The tombs
    And monumental caves of death look cold,
    And shoot a chillness to my trembling heart.
    Give me thy hand, and let me hear thy voice ;
    Nay, quickly speak to me, and let me hear
    Thy voice ; my own affrights me with its echo.

Let me say, after reading this, that I know of no subject on which I would not rather take Dr. Johnson's opinion, than upon that of poetry.

But Johnson's verdict was that of Congreve's own time. Congreve had places of profit and honor in abundance ; great men were proud to call on him ; Pope dedicated to him his translation of the *Iliad;* and after his death, a great lady had a wax figure made to resemble him, laid out in state in her drawing-room, that she might lavish on it the affection she had felt for Congreve himself.

His comedies are all that can be desired in sparkle and brilliancy of style. Hazlitt, a very good critic, who wrote in the early part of this century, says that "They are full of the niceties of English style, and there is even a peculiar flavor in the words not to be found in another writer." It is their grossness which makes them now so fortunately unknown. Here is a scene from the opening of *Love for Love,* one of the most famous of the comedies: —

(*Valentine, who has fallen under his father's displeasure by his extravagant way of living, and is in love with Angelica, who is also displeased with him, has shut himself up in his lodgings and taken to study. He is at his table reading, and Jeremy, his valet, is standing near him.*)

Val. Jeremy —.

Jer. Sir?

Val. [*Throwing the book at him*]. Here, take away. I'll walk a turn, and digest what I've read.

Jer. [*Taking the book, mutters*]. You'll grow devilish fat upon this paper diet.

Val. And d'ye hear, go you to breakfast. There's a page doubled down in Epictetus that is a feast for an emperor.

Jer. Was Epictetus a real cook, or did he only write receipts?

Val. Read, read, sirrah! and refine your appetite; learn to live upon instruction; feast your mind and mortify your flesh; read, and take your nourishment in at your eyes, shut up your mouth and chew the cud of understanding: so Epictetus advises

Jer. Oh, Lord, I have heard much of him when I waited on a gentleman at Cambridge. Pray, what was that Epictetus?

Val. A very rich man, not worth a groat.

Jer. Humph! and so he has made a very fine feast where there is nothing to be eaten?

Val. Yes.

Jer. Sir, you are a gentleman, and probably understand is fine feeding; but, if you please, I'd rather live on board wages. Does your Epictetus, or your Seneca here, or any of these poor rich rogues teach you how to pay your debts without money? Will they shut up the mouths of your creditors? Will Plato be bail for you; or Diogenes, because he understands confinement and lived in a tub, go to prison for you? S'life, sir, what do you mean? to mew yourself up here with three or four musty books, in commendation of starving and poverty?

Val. Why, sirrah, I have no money, you know it, and therefore resolve to rail at all who have; and in that I but follow the example of the wisest and wittiest men in all ages, those poets and philosophers whom you naturally hate for just such another reason, because they abound in sense, and you are a fool.

Jer. Ay, sir, I am a fool, and I know it; and yet, Heaven help me, I 'm poor enough to be a wit. But I was always a fool when I told what your expenses would bring you to, — your coaches and your liveries, your treats and your balls, your being in love with a lady that did not care a farthing for you in your prosperity; and keeping company with wits that cared for nothing but your prosperity; and now, when you are poor, hate you as much as they do one another.

Val. . . . For the wits, I am in a condition to be even with them. . I 'll take some of their trade out of their hands.

Jer. Now, Heaven of mercy, continue the tax on paper. You don't mean to write?

Val. Yes, I do; I 'll write a play.

Jer. Hem! Sir, if you please to give me a small certificate, of three lines only, to certify those whom it may concern that the bearer hereof, Jeremy Fetch by name, has for the space of seven years truly and faithfully served Valentine Legend, Esq., and that he is not now turned away for any misdemeanor, but does voluntarily dismiss his master from any further authority over him.

Val. No, sirrah, you shall live with me still.

Jer. Sir, it 's impossible. I may die with you, starve with you, or be damned with your works; but to live even three days the life of a play, I no more expect it than to be canonized for a muse after my death.

Val. You are witty, you rogue! I shall want your help. I 'll have you learn to make couplets to tag the ends of acts. .

Jer. You 're undone, sir, you 're ruined; you won't have a friend in the world if you turn poet. Confound that Will's Coffee-house; it has ruined more young men than the Royal Oak Lottery, — nothing thrives that belongs to it. . .

[*Enter Mr. Scandal.*]

Scan. What, Jeremy holding forth?

Val. The rogue has, with all the wit he could muster up, been declaiming against wit.

Scan. Ay? Why, then, I 'm afraid Jeremy has wit, for wherever it is, it 's always contriving its own ruin.

Jer. Why, so I 've been telling my master, sir. Mr. Scandal, for Heaven's sakes, try, if you can, to dissuade him from turning poet.

Scan. Poet! He shall turn soldier first, and rather depend upon the outside of his head than the lining. What! has not your poverty made you enemies enough, but you must needs show your wit to get more? . .

Val. Therefore I would rail in my writings and be revenged.

Scan. Rail — at whom? — the whole world? Impotent and vain! Who would die a martyr to sense, in a country where the religion is folly? You may stand at bay for a time, but when the full cry is against you, you sha'n't have fair play for your life. No, turn flatterer, quack, lawyer, parson, — anything but poet.

SIR JOHN VANBRUGH was an architect as well as a play-
writer, and so his reputation was built on two
1666–1726 foundations, for some of his buildings are almost
as famous as his plays. His comedies have many of the
merits of Congreve's; the situations in the dramas are
even more full of fun, although his style is less refined. In
this he more resembles Farquhar, who came a little later
than either.

GEORGE FARQUHAR was an actor, who, like the Elizabethan
dramatists, united play-writing to play-acting.
1678–1707 Hazlitt says of this trio: "We should have
courted Congreve's acquaintance most for his wit and the
elegance of his manners; Vanbrugh's for his power of far-
cical description, and telling a story; Farquhar's, for the
pleasure of his society and the love of good fellowship."

These old comedies held up so clear a mirror to the
vices of their time that they are now unfit to read. Had
the times been more decent and refined, comedy would
have reflected this refinement. But as manners improved,
wit declined; and we have not since had so witty and brilliant comedies in English literature as those of the time of
these three writers.

XLII.

A GROUP OF EIGHTEENTH CENTURY POETS, — YOUNG, THOMSON, AND SHENSTONE.

I CANNOT promise that you will find the poets who
follow Pope through the eighteenth century very interesting; they continue on in a path of dead-level merit,
from which they rarely diverge to produce anything that
deeply touches the heart or the imagination. For my own
part, I much prefer the untamed originality of the earlier

poets. There is a charm in their freedom and naturalness which is never failing. The constant see-saw rhymes, almost always in couplets, which Pope had made the fashion, when used by poets less gifted than Pope become so tiresome that I think if I were obliged to accept them as poetry, I should henceforth read nothing but prose.

I will not dwell long, therefore, on the poetry of this period, but will run over for you the names of the most noted poets and their greatest works, from the time of Pope to the last quarter of the century.

EDWARD YOUNG is best known as the author of *Night Thoughts,* a serious and sombre poem which was much read by our grandfathers and grand- 1684–1765 mothers, and is likely to be read very little hereafter. Young seems to have been a worldly man who wrote very unworldly poetry. He was gay and rather dissipated in youth, entered the Church at fifty, was disappointed that he did not attain to a bishopric, and at sixty wrote his *Night Thoughts* to express his dissatisfaction with life and the way it had used him. His verse sounds more like complaining over disappointments than the lofty musings of a mind enriched by long experience.

Young wrote other poems than this, but they are so far forgotten that he is known only as the author of *The Night Thoughts;* and although this poem will never again be valued as highly as it once was, there are in it many lines which have been so frequently quoted that they have become a part of the language ; and there are also occasional passages good enough to be remembered as long as literature exists, — I mean such lines as these : —

> " Procrastination is the thief of Time."
> " Tired Nature 's sweet restorer, — balmy sleep."
> " Death loves a shining mark."
> " How blessings brighten as they take their flight ! "

These lines I have quoted are like proverbs, and have become crystallized in our daily speech.

Let me give one short passage, to show the style of *The Night Thoughts :* —

> " Self-flattered, unexperienced, high in hope,
> When young, with sanguine cheer and streamers gay,
> We cut our cable, launch into the world,
> And fondly dream each wind and star our friend,
> All in some darling enterprise embarked.
> But where is he can fathom its event?
> Amid a multitude of artless hands,
> Ruin's sure perquisite, her lawful prize!
> Some steer aright; but the black blast blows hard,
> And puffs them wide of hope; with hearts of proof
> Full against wind and tide, some win their way;
> And when strong effort has deserved the port,
> And tugged it into view, 't is won; 't is lost!
> Though strong their oar, still stronger is their fate;
> They strike, and while they triumph, they expire,
> In stress of weather, most: some sink outright;
> O'er them, and o'er their names, the billows close
> To-morrow knows not they were ever born.
> Others a short memorial leave behind,
> Like a flag floating when the bark's engulfed,
> It floats a moment and is seen no more.
> One Cæsar lives; a thousand are forgot.
> How few, beneath auspicious planets born,
> Darlings of Providence, fond Fate's elect,
> With swelling sails, make good the promised port,
> With all their wishes freighted; yet even these,
> Freighted with all their wishes, soon complain;
> Free from misfortune, not from nature free,
> They still are men, and when is man secure?
> As fatal time, as storm, the rush of years
> Beats down their strength; their numberless escapes
> In ruin end; and, now, their proud success
> But plants new terrors on the victor's brow;
> What pain to quit the world just made their own!
> Their nest so deeply drowned, and built so high!
> Too low they build who build beneath the stars."

This is a fair specimen of Young's manner and his philosophy. I think we should not greet it as great poetry if it were published for the first time to-day.

In strong contrast to Young is JAMES THOMSON. To read his poetry after the *Night Thoughts* is like coming from thickest gloom to genial sunshine. Thomson's *Seasons,* in four parts, treats of the Spring, Summer, Autumn, and Winter. They are like a series of pictures of the year, each with the color and atmosphere of the sea-

1700–1748

son they describe. In Spring we see the tender green of budding plants and trees; in Summer, the brightness of blossoms; the Autumn is russet and purple, with ripened grain and fruits; and the Winter is gray, cold, and comfortless, with mud, sleet, and bare boughs. No man could have written thus if he had not been an acute observer of Nature and in close sympathy with her.

He wrote his *Winter* when in college, and it aided him to gain the notice of a rich patron. In those days the patronage of a great man was as necessary to a poet as a good publisher is in these days. Thomson had the usual ups and downs of a man of talent who is poor: he went abroad as tutor to a rich man's sons; he acted as secretary to a lord; he wrote for the stage; and at length got a pension from Frederic, Prince of Wales (the son of George II.), after which he lived in comparative ease.

He spent the last of his life in a pleasant home on the Thames, and died, when forty-eight, of a cold and fever brought on by a row on the river, taken when he was overheated. He was a popular man, beloved by his friends, among whom was Pope, who had given the *Seasons* encouraging praise, and had added to it a few lines when Thomson sent it to him for friendly criticism. In his retirement Thomson wrote *The Castle of Indolence*, a poem in Spenser's measure, which has some very fine bits of description, but is rather a close imitation of the older poet. His plays had some success, but have not added much of value to literature. *Sophonisba*, his chief tragedy, is remembered by a ridiculous incident on its first performance. In one sentimental line the hero exclaims, —

"O Sophonisba! Sophonisba, O!"

As the actor uttered this on the first night, a mischievous person in the gallery groaned, "O Jemmy Thomson! Jemmy Thomson, O!" which threw the audience into a fit of laughter, and spoiled the effect of the scene.

The Seasons is a book which, like Izaak Walton's *Angler*, I like to read out of doors under the trees; and I advise you to make it your companion some summer's day, and read to

19

the acompaniment of birds and rippling water, as you recline under trees by the bank of a running stream.

The *Hymn to the Seasons* gives a summing up of the longer poem, and we will read the opening lines from this:

"These as they change, Almighty Father, these
Are but the varied God. The rolling year
Is full of Thee. Forth in the pleasing Spring,
Thy beauty walks, Thy tenderness and love
Wide flush the fields; the softening air is balm;
Echo the mountains round; the forest smiles,
And every sense and every heart is joy.
Then comes Thy glory in the Summer months,
With light and heat refulgent. Then Thy sun
Shoots full perfection through the swelling year;
And oft thy voice in dreadful thunder speaks;
And oft at morn, deep noon, or falling eve,
By brooks and groves, in hollow whispering gales.
Thy bounty shines in Autumn unconfined,
And spreads a common feast for all that lives.
In Winter awful Thou! with clouds and storms
Around Thee thrown, tempest o'er tempest rolled,
Majestic darkness! On the whirlwind's wing
Riding sublime, Thou bid'st the world adore,
And humblest nature with Thy northern blast.
Mysterious round, what skill, what force divine,
Deep felt, in these appear! a simple train,
Yet so delightful mixed, with such kind art,
Such beauty and beneficence combined;
Shade unperceived so softening into shade,
And all so forming an harmonious whole,
That, as they still succeed, they ravish still.
But wandering oft with brute unconscious gaze,
Man marks Thee not; marks not the mighty hand,
That, ever busy, wheels the silent spheres,
Works in the secret deep, shoots steaming thence
The fair profusion that o'erspreads the Spring;
Flings from the sun direct the flaming day;
Feeds every creature; hurls the tempest forth;
And as on earth this grateful change revolves,
With transport touches all the springs of life"

WILLIAM SHENSTONE lived the sort of life that the poet Cowley longed for, while he aspired to the life
1714-1763 that Cowley despised. You remember that Cowley, who was a courtier, was always picturing the delights of

a little estate in the country which he could adorn as he chose, and where he might spend his days in peaceful quiet. Shenstone had just such a little estate inherited from his father, and spent all his time and fortune embellishing it in the most fanciful style of landscape gardening, till he made it a wonder of walks, mazes, arbors, gardens, and running waters. But although he amused himself with these occupations, he was ambitious for political honors, and a little soured and disappointed that he could never attain to them.

He wrote his poetry chiefly, it seems, for his amusement, and not in the hope of any special reward. In his childhood he had been sent to a village school (called in England a *dame school*), and his most noted poem, *The Schoolmistress*, written in Spenserian stanza, pictures the dame and her school. Here are a few verses from his description of the schoolmistress : —

> " Her cap, far whiter than the driven snow,
> Emblem right meet of decency does yield;
> Her apron dyed in grain as blue, I trow,
> As in the harebell that adorns the field;
> And in her hand, for sceptre, she does wield
> Tway birchen sprays, with anxious fear entwined,
> With dark distrust, and sad repentance filled,
> And steadfast hate, and sharp affection joined,
> And fury uncontrolled, and chastisement unkind.

> " A russet stole was o'er her shoulders thrown;
> A russet kirtle fenced the nipping air.
> 'T was simple russet, but it was her own;
> 'T was her own country bred the flock so fair;
> 'T was her own labor did the fleece prepare;
> And sooth to say, her pupils ranged around,
> Through pious awe, did term it passing rare;
> For they in gaping wonderment abound,
> And think, no doubt, she been the greatest wight on ground.

> " One ancient hen she took delight to feed,
> The plodding pattern of the busy dame,
> Which ever and anon, impelled by need,
> Into her school, begirt with chickens, came, —
> Such favor did her past deportment claim;

And if neglect had lavished on the ground
   Fragment of bread, she would collect the same ;
   For well she knew, and quaintly could expound,
What sin it were to waste the smallest crumb she found.

   .   .   .   .

" Right well she knew each temper to descry,
   To thwart the proud and the submiss to raise ;
   Some with vile copper-prize exalt on high,
   And some entice with pittance small of praise ;
   And other some with baleful sprig she 'rays.
   Even absent she the reins of power doth hold,
   While with quaint arts the giddy crowd she sways,
   Forewarned, if little bird their pranks behold,
'T will whisper in her ear, and all the scene unfold."

This picture of the old dame is very real ; but better than
The Schoolmistress I like a pastoral by Shenstone, which,
although written in a jingling, rather commonplace measure, has a taste of the old ballad in it, and recalls the fresh
days of poetry. This pastoral is in four parts, — Absence,
Hope, Solicitude, Disappointment, — and is addressed to
Phyllis by the Shepherd Corydon. These are a few stanzas from Part II. : —

" My banks they are furnished with bees,
   Whose murmur invites one to sleep ;
My grottos are shaded with trees,
   And my hills are white over with sheep ;
I seldom have met with a loss,
   Such health do my fountains bestow, —
My fountains, all bordered with moss
   Where the harebells and violets grow.

" Not a pine in my grove is there seen,
   But with tendrils of woodbine is bound ;
Not a beech's more beautiful green
   But a sweetbrier entwines it around ;
Not my fields in the prime of the year
   More charms than my cattle unfold ;
Not a brook that is limpid and clear,
   But it glitters with fishes of gold.

   .   .   .   .

" I have found out a gift for my fair,
   I have found where the wood-pigeons breed ;
But let me that plunder forbear,
   She will say 't was a barbarous deed.

For he ne'er **could be true,** she averred,
  Who could rob **a poor bird of** his young,
And I loved her the more when I heard
  Such tenderness fall **from** her tongue.

"I have heard her with sweetness unfold
  How that pity was due to a dove,
That it ever attended the bold,
  And she called it the sister of Love;
But her words such a pleasure convey,
  So much I her accents adore,
Let her speak, and whatever she say,
  Methinks I should love her the more.

"Can a bosom so gentle remain
  Unmoved when her Corydon sighs?
Will a nymph that is fond of the plain
  These plains and this valley despise?—
Dear regions of silence and shade,
  Soft scenes of contentment and ease,
Where **I** could have pleasingly strayed,
  If **aught in her** absence could please."

XLIII.

OTHER EIGHTEENTH CENTURY POETS, — GRAY, COLLINS, AKENSIDE, BEATTIE.

NEAR Shenstone in age was THOMAS GRAY, who has made himself immortal by one poem, and that one of the best in our language, — the *Elegy in a Country Churchyard*. He has written several odes, one **1716–1771** to *Adversity,* another *On a Distant Prospect of Eton College,* **both far above** the average in merit. But the *Elegy* overshadows all else he has done, and **is dear to** all lovers of good poetry. Its merit was recognized, **too,** from the time it first appeared, — **which is a** little unusual. It nearly always happens that really great **works** are not known **to** be great till time has sat in judgment upon **them;** it **takes** distance to show men how great they really are.

Gray seems to have been like the youth described in his

Elegy, contemplative, **sad**, **a** man of fastidious **tastes, and** not quite at home **in** a rough world. **His early** life had been clouded **by** unhappiness; **and when** childhood, the **background of life**, is obscured by sadness, **the** after-life often takes on a tinge of gloom. The *Elegy* is doubtless a poem that you already know **by** heart. Not-so familiar, perhaps, are two other fine **odes** of his, *The Bard* and *The Progress of Poetry*. These **are**, however, much more arti-ficial **than** the *Elegy*, which **owes its power to** the fact that it touches so **many** responsive **chords in the** human heart. Another little **poem**, one **of his** shortest odes, *To Spring*, has something **of this same** sympathetic quality, and also has those **touches descriptive of** scenes and sounds in nature, which **are** such marked beauties of the *Elegy*. For instance, the description of the insect youth upon the wing is a dainty bit of word-painting; while " through **the** *peopled* air the busy murmur glows," almost equals the lines, " The beetle wheels **his** droning flight, While drowsy tinklings lull the distant fold," in the *Elegy*. But we will read the *Ode on the Spring* : —

> " Lo! where the rosy-bosomed **Hours**,
>   Fair Venus' train, appear,
> Disclose the long-expected flowers,
>   **And wake** the purple year!
> The Attic warbler pours her throat,
> Responsive **to the** cuckoo's note,
>   The untaught harmony of Spring;
> While, whispering pleasure **as they** fly,
> Cool Zephyrs through the clear blue sky
>   Their gathered fragrance fling.
>
> " **Where'er** the oak's **thick branches** stretch
>   A broader, browner **shade**;
> Where'er the rude and moss-grown beech
>   O'er-canopies the glade, —
> **Beside some** water's rushy **brink**
> With me **the** Muse shall sit, and think
>   (At ease reclined in rustic **state**)
>   How **vain the** ardor of **the crowd**,
>   How low, how little **are the** proud,
>   How indigent the great!

" Still is the **toiling hand of Care**;
   The **panting herds repose**:
Yet hark, **how** through **the** peopled **air**
   The busy **murmur** glows!
The insect youth are **on the wing**,
Eager to taste the honied spring,
And float amid the liquid noon :
   Some lightly o'er the current skim,
   Some show their gayly-gilded trim,
Quick glancing to the sun.

" To Contemplation's sober eye
   Such is the race of man :
And they that creep, and they that fly,
   Shall end where they **began**.
Alike the busy and the gay
But **flutter** through life's little day,
In Fortune's varying colors drest;
   Brushed by the hand of rough **Mischance**,
   Or chilled by Age, their **airy dance**
They leave, in dust to rest.

" Methinks I **hear in accents low**
   The sportive kind reply :
' Poor moralist! and what art thou ?
   A solitary fly!
Thy joys no glittering female meets,
No hive hast thou of hoarded sweets,
No painted plumage to display ;
   On hasty wings thy youth is flown,
   Thy sun is set, thy spring is gone, —
We frolic, while 't is May.' "

WILLIAM **COLLINS** had one of those natures that so often form a poet : he had a head full of fancies, but an organization too delicate to bear the hard uses **1720–1756** of the world. **While** in college he wrote a series of *Oriental Eclogues,* which he laughed at **himself** in later years, saying they might **just as** appropriately have **been** called " Irish Eclogues." **After this** he wrote and published **his** *Odes,* which fell **dead from the press.** The **unhappy poet,** disregarded and **poor,** never recovered **from** this disappointment. He led a gloomy, morbid life for several years, often in debt, and sometimes in dissipation. Samuel Johnson (the great **Dr. Johnson**) tells us that **once** when he went to see the poet, a bailiff was lurking outside his lodgings, ready to arrest him for debt. Yet Collins was a man as profound in learning as he was rich in fancy. Thus the world often uses the men best able to serve it. In the midst of his distress an uncle left him a legacy of two thousand pounds. But it was too late. He showed his bitterness by buying the edition of his *Odes* which had been published, and putting it into the flames. Not long after, he became insane, so that he was obliged to be shut up in a madhouse. Death came mercifully when he was thirty-six years old, — ten years after he had published his volume of poetry.

His *Odes* are on divers subjects, — *Pity, Fear, Liberty, Simplicity*, etc. The one best known is the *Ode to the Passions*, which is in almost every poetical collection; that which I like best is on *Evening*, and I quote it for you. It is a very delicate and tender poem, like the hues of a soft sunset. In those days of artificial poetry there are few poems that can compare with this for natural grace; and some of the lines, as where he speaks of Evening with dewy fingers drawing "the gradual, dusky veil," remind one of Milton's early poems : —

ODE TO EVENING.

If aught of oaten stop, or pastoral song,
May hope, oh, pensive Eve, to soothe thy modest ear
　　Like thy own brawling springs,
　　Thy springs and dying gales,

O nymph reserved, while now the bright-haired sun
Sits in yon western tent, whose cloudy skirts,
　　With brede ethereal wove,
　　O'erhang his wavy bed · —

Now air is hushed, save where the weak-eyed bat,
With short, shrill shriek flies by on leathern wing;
　　Or where the beetle winds
　　His small but sullen horn,

As oft he rises midst the twilight path,
Against the pilgrim borne in heedless hum.
　　Now teach me, maid composed,
　　To breathe some softened strain,

Whose numbers, stealing through thy darkening vale,
May not unseemly with its stillness suit,
    As, musing slow, **I hail**
    Thy genial loved return!

For when thy folding star, arising, shows
His paly circlet, at his warning lamp,
    The fragrant Hours, and elves
    Who slept in buds the day,

And many a nymph who wreathes her brows with sedge,
And sheds the freshening dew, and, lovelier still,
    The pensive Pleasures sweet,
    Prepare thy shadowy car.

Then let me rove some wild and heathy scene,
Or find some ruin midst its **dreary dells,**
    Whose walls more awful nod,
    By thy religious gleams.

Or, if chill blustering winds, or **driving rain,**
Prevent my willing feet, be mine the **hut**
    That from the mountain's side
    Views wilds and swelling floods,

And hamlets **brown, and** dim-discovered spires,
And hears their simple bell, and marks o'er all,
    Thy dewy fingers draw
    The gradual dusky veil.

While Spring shall pour his showers, as oft he wont,
And bathe thy breathing tresses, meekest Eve!
    While Summer loves to sport
    Beneath thy lingering light;

While sallow **Autumn** fills thy lap with leaves;
Or Winter, yelling through the troublous air,
    Affrights thy shrinking train,
    And rudely rends thy robes :

So long, regardful of thy quiet rule,
Shall Fancy, Friendship, Science, smiling Peace,
    Thy gentlest influence own,
    And love thy favorite name."

The Pleasures of the Imagination, by Dr. MARK AKEN-
SIDE, and *The Minstrel*, by Dr. JAMES BEATTIE,
deserve at least a passing mention. *The Pleasures*   1721–1770
of the Imagination is a blank-verse poem from which we

could cull fine passages, although it is stiff, and dull to read
all through.   *The Minstrel* is in Spenserian measure ; its
hero, Edwin, a youth full of aspiration and good-
1735–1803   ness, is tutored by an old hermit, who discourses
to him on all noble themes.   Beattie also wrote that ballad
of *The Hermit* whose opening lines are so familiar : —

> " At the close of the day, when the hamlet is still,
>   And mortals the sweets of forgetfulness prove."

Beattie published his works as the last quarter of the
century began.   Before we enter upon a period full of
events, I wish to go back a space and trace for you the
history of the novel in the eighteenth century.

XLIV.

On the Birth of the English Novel ; Richardson and Fielding.

THE novel, which in the present is the most widely read
of any kind of book that issues from the printing-
press, is really a plant of comparatively recent growth in
literature.   In my Talks thus far, I have been able to show
you very few works of prose fiction.   In the sixteenth
century there were occasional long and rather tedious
romances, among the best of which are Sidney's *Arcadia*
and Lyly's *Euphues*.   In the seventeenth century we have
no great work that can be called a novel, unless we should
reckon John Bunyan's *Pilgrim's Progress* in the list.

The nearest approach to the prose fiction of the present,
previous to the middle of the eighteenth century, is found
in De Foe's works, which are nearly all biographical rela-
tions, like *Robinson Crusoe* and *Colonel Jack*.

I think, therefore, the birth of the modern novel of society,
reflecting the life, manners, and conversation of the age, is
usually dated from the middle of the eighteenth century,
when Richardson and Fielding began to write.

The pioneer in the novel of sentiment, which has for its subject the various distresses and moving situations in the lives of a pair of lovers, is SAMUEL RICHARDSON. The first fifty years of his life seem to have been a slow preparation for the work which filled his later **1689–1761** years. He was a delicate and rather shy boy, who sought the society of women and girls rather than of boys of his own age.

He showed early an ability for letter-writing, and when a boy was largely employed by the young women of his acquaintance in writing their love-letters. In this way, no doubt, the style afterwards used in his novels — all of which are written in the form of letters — was first formed. But notwithstanding his early experience with the pen, Richardson was not drawn from the ordinary pursuits of life by it. He was bred a printer, learned his trade thoroughly, and when he had served a seven years' apprenticeship married his master's daughter and went into business for himself, in the good old orthodox style of doing things. He was over fifty years old, in easy circumstances, living in a snug little villa, the fruit of his honest labors, when he began to write his first novel. He says that two publishers, business friends, whom he had often furnished with prefaces and other garnishes to the works he printed for them, asked him why he did not write some letters in the form of a novel, illustrating scenes in real life. They probably saw his talent in that direction, and thought that by means of it they might turn an honest penny for themselves and him. He took their advice, and his first famous novel, *Pamela,* was the result.

Were we to read *Pamela* to-day, knowing nothing of its history, the excitement and delight it caused on its first appearance would be incredible. While he was writing it he began by reading a little to his wife and a young lady visitor; and after that he says they came every night to his study, saying, " Have you any more of *Pamela,* Mr. Richardson? We have come to have a little more of *Pamela.*"

On its publication the story took every woman's heart by

storm; nor was the admiration of the book confined to
women only : it was read by men of the world as well as by
scholars and critics.   It created a sensation almost as great
in France as in England, and the greatest thinkers in
France, who were laying the foundations of ideas that were
soon to appear in the French Revolution, left off for the
time discussion of graver matters, while they read with delight Samuel Richardson's novels.

It was several years after *Pamela* that *Clarissa Harlowe*
appeared.   This was his greatest success, and carried him
to a height of fame that might have turned a stronger head
than his.   In both novels the plot had the same mainspring.
Each heroine is subjected to the persecutions of an unprincipled lover, through whose baseness she suffers all kinds of
trials ; in the end the servant-maid, Pamela, turns her suitor
into a good husband by force of her beauty and virtues,
while the gifted Clarissa sinks under the wrongs she suffers
from the depraved Lovelace, and after calmly arranging her
funeral, even to the fitting up of her coffin, she passes
away amid the lamentations of friends and relatives.

Richardson has been specially praised because he drew
his characters from life, and brought fiction from the regions of stilted romance into the ordinary walks of human
life.   This is one of his merits, although in endeavoring to
be realistic he is sometimes ludicrous.   When Lovelace
goes to see Clarissa, he writes to Belford the following account of her dress, for which we ought to be obliged to
him, since it gives us a picture of a well-dressed woman in
the year 1750 ; but it seems a little out of place from a man
who is in a delirium of joy at meeting his beloved : —

"Thou shalt judge of her dress.   I am a critic, thou know'st,
in women's dresses.   There is such a native elegance in this
lady that she surpasses all that I could imagine surpassing.   But
then her person adorns what she wears, more than dress can
adorn her. . . . . Her headdress was Brussels lace, peculiarly
adapted to the charming air and turn of her features ; a sky-blue
ribbon illustrated that. . . . Her gown was a pale primrose,
colored paduasoy, the cuffs and robings curiously embroidered
by the fingers of this ever-charming Arachne in a running

pattern of violets and **their leaves**; a pair of **diamond snaps** in her ears. Her ruffles were the same as her **cap, her apron** flowered lawn, her petticoat white satin quilted, **her shoes blue** satin braided with the **same color, without lace,** — for what need **has the** prettiest foot in the world **of ornament? Neat buckles on** them, and on her charming arms **a pair of black velvet** glove-like muffs."

But it is his description **of** Clarissa's preparations for her death, and all the circumstances attending it, that Richardson's genius **rises** to its full height. All preparations for the burial are described with the minuteness of a fashionable auctioneer's catalogue. Belford, the friend of Lovelace, **writes thus to** him after **a** visit to Clarissa, who is sinking rapidly into a decline : —

"She had slept **better, I found, than I, though her solemn re**pository [her coffin, **which** Clarissa ordered **some time before** death] was under her window **not far from her bedside. I was** prevailed on to go up **and** look **at the devices. Mrs. Lovick** has since shown me **a copy of the** draught **by which all was** ordered, and I will give thee a sketch **of** the symbols.

"The principal device, neatly etched, on a plate **of white** metal, is a crowned serpent with its tail in its mouth, forming **a ring, the** emblem of eternity ; and in the circle made by it is this inscription :—

"CLARISSA **HARLOWE,**

" April X.;

[Then the year]

" Ætat. XIX.

" For ornaments: **at** top an hour-glass, winged ; at bottom, an **urn.** Under the hour-glass, on another plate, this inscription :

" ' *Here the wicked cease from troubling, and here the weary* **be at** *rest.*' JOB 3–17.

" Over the urn, near the bottom : —

"Turn again unto thy rest, O my **soul ! For the** Lord **hath** rewarded thee; and why ? ' *Thou hast delivered my soul* **from** *death, mine eyes from tears, and my feet from falling.*' **Ps.** cxvi. 7, 8.

"Over this text is the head of a **white lily snapped short off** and just falling from the stalk ; and **this inscription over that, between** the principal plate and the lily : —

"'The days of man are but as grass: for he flourisheth as a flower of the field. For as soon as the wind goeth over it, it is gone: and the place thereof shall know it no more." Ps. ciii 15, 16.

"She excused herself to the women on the score of her youth, and being used to draw for her needle-works, for having shown more fancy than would perhaps be thought suitable on so solemn an occasion. The date, April 10th, she accounted for as not being able to tell what her closing day would be, and as that was the fatal day of her leaving her father's house. . . . The burial dress was brought home with it [the coffin]. The women had curiosity enough, I suppose, to see her open that. And, perhaps, thou wouldst have been glad to have been present to have admired it too."

If Clarissa had been a female undertaker, she could not more admirably have arranged for her death and burial; yet all this, which seems to the modern reader overstrained sentimentality, sent the readers of that age weeping to their beds.

It is said that so many young women of the time fell in love with Lovelace, in spite of his vices, that Richardson felt as if he must write a novel which should contain an antidote to the dangerous fascinations of the hero of *Clarissa*. He accordingly constructed the character of Sir Charles Grandison, who was rich, well-born, well-bred, and a walking encyclopædia of all the virtues. You remember the hero in the fairy tale, whose gifts from eleven good fairies are at last made null and void by the curse of one evil fairy. This evil fairy came in at Sir Charles Grandison's baptism to endow him with insupportable priggishness; so that in spite of his virtues one can hardly endure him through the seven volumes that make this formidable story, which, I fancy, very few readers of modern novels will ever read through. Walter Scott tells a story of an old lady of advanced age who preferred to have *Sir Charles Grandison* read aloud to her above all other books, "Because," she said, "should I fall asleep in the course of the reading, I am sure I shall have lost none of it, but shall find the characters where I left them, talking together in the cedar parlor."

HENRY FIELDING, the greatest novelist of the group, owed his first success to a desire to satirize Richardson. His first novel, *Joseph Andrews*, was written to ridicule Richardson's *Pamela*; but it was so interesting and witty that readers forgot it was intended for a burlesque, and read the story for its own sake.

1707–1754

Fielding is as hearty and vigorous as Richardson is sentimental. The two authors evidently did not like each other, and the reason was grounded in nature, and not in any rivalry as authors. Fielding's novels are the first novels in literature at once powerful, dramatic, and realistic. Yet it is difficult for any one bred in an age more refined, and especially for a woman, to enjoy heartily a story which depicts characters so immoral, or scenes so repulsive as are found in *Tom Jones*, Fielding's greatest novel. It hardly lessens our distaste to know that it is true to the life of the eighteenth century, when we like so little the kind of life it depicts. Yet their overflowing humor, their keen insight into human nature, and their fresh, wholesome style, have kept the novels of Fielding at the very top of English fiction; and the debt our modern novelists, Thackeray, Dickens, and many of lesser note, owe to him, is never to be reckoned. I cannot do better justice to Fielding than by quoting a paragraph from what Thackeray says of him :[1]

"What a genius! what a vigor! what a bright-eyed intelligence and observation! what a wholesome hatred for meanness and knavery! what a vast sympathy! what a cheerfulness! what a manly relish of life! what a love of human kind! what a POET is here! watching, meditating, brooding, creating! what multitudes of truths has that man left behind him! what generations he has taught to laugh wisely and fairly! what scholars he has formed and accustomed to the exercise of thoughtful humor and the manly play of wit! what a courage he had! what a dauntless and constant cheerfulness of intellect, that burned bright and steady through all the storms of his life and never deserted its last wreck. It is wonderful to think of the pains and misery which the man suffered, the pressure of want, illness, remorse, which he endured, and that the writer was

[1] Lectures on the English Humorists.

neither malignant **nor** melancholy, his view of truth never warped, and his generous human kindness never surrendered."

On such a tribute, from such a man, I think we may fairly let Fielding's merits rest.

XLV.

The Novelists Smollett and Sterne.

TOBIAS SMOLLETT is another of the great novelists of the period. *Roderick Random, Peregrine Pickle,* and *Humphrey Clinker* are the titles of his **most** famous fictions. But his pages are disfigured by the same coarseness that repels us in Fielding, and he has not nearly **as** much genius. Thackeray, **whose opinion of** Fielding we have just quoted, says he thinks *Humphrey Clinker* the most laughable story ever written since the **goodly** art of novel-writing began ; and Dickens has borne testimony to **Smollett's power in his** own novel of *David Copperfield,* where he relates how David kept Steerforth and **the** other boys awake in the dormitory while he narrated the **adventures** of **Roderick or** Peregrine or Humphrey.

1721-1771

Laurence Sterne, author of *Tristram Shandy,* was only **second** to Richardson in sentimentality, and to **Fielding in wit.** He has the same faults of grossness that we complain of in the others, and he is, on the whole, less wholesome than any **of them.** But some of the characters in *Tristram Shandy* will **always** live in literature, particularly **that of** good Uncle **Toby,** who is one of **the** most delightful personages of fiction. You all have heard of Uncle Toby, — of his goodness to Le **Fevre ; his** embarrassments with the Widow Wadman ; his humane little speech when he takes out the fly from the milk-jug and sets it to **dry in** the sun, "There is room enough in the world for **thee** and for me." All these characteristics make him an

1713-1768

immortal figure in literature, one to set beside Addison's Sir Roger de Coverley, or our own dear Mr. Pickwick.

The *Sentimental Journey* is the record of a tour which Sterne made on the Continent ; and here is an extract from it, which is a good illustration of Sterne's style. He has been to visit the Bastile, and is seized with these reflections:

" ' And as for the Bastile,' said I to myself, ' the terror is in the word. Make the most of it you can, the Bastile is but another word for a tower; and a tower is but another word for a house you can't get out of. Mercy on the gouty, they are in it twice a year; but with nine livres a day, and pen and ink and paper, and patience, albeit a man can't get out, he may do very well within, at least for a month or six weeks; at the end of which, if he is a harmless fellow, his innocence appears, and he comes out a better and wiser man than when he went in.' I had some occasion (I forget what) to step into the courtyard as I settled this account; and remember I walked downstairs in no small triumph with the conceit of my reasoning. ' Beshrew the sombre pencil,' said I, vauntingly ; ' for I envy not its powers, which paints the evils of life with so hard and deadly a coloring. The mind sits terrified at the objects she has magnified herself and blackened; reduce them to the proper size and hue, and she overlooks them. 'Tis true,' I said, correcting the proposition, ' the Bastile is not an evil to be despised; but strip it of its towers, fill up the fosse, unbarricade the doors, call it simply a confined place, and suppose it is some tyrant of a distemper, and not of a man, which holds you in it, half the evil vanishes, and you bear the other half without complaint.' I was interrupted in the heyday of this soliloquy with a voice which I took to be that of a child, which complained it could not get out. I looked up and down the passage, and seeing neither man, woman, nor child, I went out without further attention. In my return back through the passage, I heard the same words repeated twice over and looking up, I saw it was a starling hung in a little cage. ' I can't get out; I can't get out,' said the starling. I stood looking at the bird, and to every person who came through the passage it ran fluttering to the side towards which they approached it with the same lamentation of its captivity.

" ' *I can't get out*,' said the starling. ' God help thee,' said I ; ' but I 'll let thee out, cost what it will ; ' so I turned about the cage to get the door. It was twisted and double-twisted so fast with wire that there was no getting it open without pulling the cage to pieces. I took both hands to it. The bird flew to the place where I was attempting his deliverance, and thrusting his head through the trellis, pressed his breast against it as if impatient. 'I fear, poor creature,' said I, 'I cannot set thee at liberty.' 'I can't get out; I can't get out,' said the starling. I vow, I never had my affections more tenderly awakened, nor do I remember an incident in my life where the dissipated spirits, to which my reason had been a bubble, were so suddenly called home. Mechanical as the notes were, yet so true in tune to Nature were they chanted that in one moment they overthrew all my systematic reasonings upon the Bastile; and I walked heavily upstairs, unsaying every word I had said in going down them.

"'Disguise thyself as thou wilt, still, Slavery,' said I, 'thou art a bitter draught; and though thousands in all ages have been made to drink of thee, thou art no less bitter on that account. 'T is *thou*, thrice sweet and gracious goddess,' addressing myself to Liberty, 'whom all, in public or in private, worship, whose taste is grateful, and ever will be so till Nature herself shall change; no tint of words can spot thy snowy mantle, or chemic power turn thy sceptre into iron; with thee to smile upon him as he eats his crust, the swain is happier than the monarch, from whose court *thou* art exiled. 'Gracious Heaven!' cried I, kneeling down on the last step but one in my ascent, 'grant me but health, thou great bestower of it, and give me but this fair goddess as my companion, and shower down thy mitres, if it seem good unto thy divine providence, upon those heads that are aching for them.'

"The bird in his cage pursued me into my room. I sat down close to my table, and leaning my head upon my hand, I began to figure to myself the miseries of confinement. I was in a right frame for it, and so I gave full scope to my imagination; I was going to begin with the millions of my fellow-creatures born to no inheritance but slavery; but finding, however affecting that picture was, that I could not bring it near me, and that the multitude of sad groups in it did but distract me, I took a single captive, and having first shut him up in his dungeon, I then looked through the twilight of his grated door to take his picture. I beheld his body half wasted away with long expectation and confinement, and felt what kind of sickness of the heart it was that arises from hope deferred. Upon looking nearer I saw him pale and feverish; in thirty years the western breeze had not once fanned his blood; he had seen no sun, no moon, in all that time, nor had the voice of friend or kinsman breathed through his lattice; his children — But here my heart began to bleed, and I was forced to go on with another part of the portrait. He was sitting upon the ground upon a little straw in the furthest corner of his dungeon, which was alternately his chair and his bed; a little calendar of small sticks lay at the head, notched all over with the dismal nights and days he had passed there; he had one of these little sticks in his hand, and with a rusty nail he was etching another day of misery to add to the heap. As I darkened the little light he had, he lifted up a hopeless eye towards the door, then cast it down, shook his head, and went on with his work of affliction. I heard his chains upon his legs as he turned his body to lay his little stick upon the bundle. He gave a deep sigh; I saw the iron enter into his soul. I burst into tears. I could not sustain the picture of confinement which my fancy had drawn."

It seems a pity to end by saying that the man who could *write* thus feelingly seems to have had very little real feeling in his nature, and that by all accounts he was selfish and cold-hearted.

XLVI.

ON DR. SAMUEL JOHNSON.

IN several of the notable periods in literature you will find some one man who, by force of his genius or his character, exercises a sort of royal rule over his fellows. In the Elizabethan age Ben Jonson held such a sway over his literary circle, partly because he had great ability, and partly because his good opinion of himself was so strong that he was able to impress it upon other men. In the last quarter of the seventeenth century Dryden exercised an almost unlimited power. Sitting in his chair at Will's Coffee-house, he appears as much of an autocrat as if he had been a crowned king of letters. Something of the same sway over men and affairs Dean Swift held in the Augustan age. But none of these wielded a power so absolute or of so long duration as did Samuel Johnson, who for many years of his life and long after his death was a sort of despot, from whom there was no appeal.

Of all the men of the past whose acquaintance we make through books, I do not remember one whom we know so much about, or can see so vividly, as DR. SAMUEL JOHNSON. Our thanks for this are due to the man who wrote his life, James Boswell, a Scotchman, familiarly called " Bozzy," who for years was happy to stand in the background of Johnson's greatness, looking at him with reverent admiration, eagerly waiting upon every word that fell from his lips, that he might treasure it up to send down to posterity. Nothing was too trivial for Boswell; if Dr. Johnson sneezed, down went the fact in Boswell's notebook. The result is that Boswell's *Life of Johnson* is one of the most minute and most entertaining biographies ever written; and although we laugh at the author, we shall be always grateful to him.

1709–1784

It was the strong and sterling forces of character that got Dr. Johnson his footing in the world. He had neither good looks, elegant manners, fine tact, nor any personal graces to help him. Lacking all these, he yet rose from obscurity to a very high place in his day and generation.

He was born in the little town of Lichfield, and was twenty-eight years old when he started for London, to begin there his literary career. David Garrick, afterwards the great actor, who had been Johnson's schoolfellow and later his pupil, was his companion in this journey. Johnson's capital in trade was his tragedy of *Irene*, which he carried in his pocket, while Garrick had little more than a gay heart and his dramatic genius to start with. The tragedy of *Irene* never made a success, even with Garrick's genius to uphold it; but Johnson climbed steadily to power.

His early days in London are pathetic to read about. He was very poor, sometimes so poor that he walked the streets at night because he had no money to pay his lodging. His clothes were often so shabby that he could not appear in respectable society. After he had written some articles which attracted notice, in the *Gentleman's Magazine,* the publisher, Mr. Cave, invited him to dinner to meet some friends who were anxious to see a man who could write with such power. Johnson came to the dinner; but his clothes were so poor that he dined behind a screen out of sight of the guests. But nothing could crush him, although once in after life, when he was prosperous and honored, in recalling the miseries of a poor author he burst into tears at the sharp remembrance of them. By and by his articles, which he wrote for newspapers and magazines, began to attact attention. Pope praised him; Richardson the printer (who afterwards wrote *Clarissa Harlowe*) admired him; the publishers began to inquire him out; and soon his lot grew easier.

His first notable work was a *Dictionary of the English Language,* which his publisher engaged him to make, agreeing to pay him fifteen hundred and seventy-five pounds for the work, paid in instalments, a guinea at a time, as he furnished the copy. He agreed to complete the work in three years; but although begun in 1747, it was not published till 1755. In the mean time he did other work. It occurred to him in his intervals of compiling the dictionary to edit a paper on the plan of Addison and Steele in *The Spectator,* and thus he began *The Rambler,* writing a series of two hundred papers by that name. Of all his works none was so popular as this. Goldsmith gives the general opinion about it in one of his essays called *The Fame Machine,* in which he represents a small carriage as taking passengers to the Temple of Fame. As Goldsmith is talking to the coachman, he says, a grave personage appeared, —

"Whom at some distance I took for one of the most reserved and even disagreeable figures I had ever seen; but as he approached, his appearance improved, and when I could distinguish him thoroughly, I perceived that in spite of the severity of his brow, he had one of the most good-natured countenances that could be imagined. Upon coming to open the stage-door, he lifted a parcel of folios into the seat before him; but our inquisitorial coachman at once shoved them out again. 'What, not take in my Dictionary?' exclaimed the other, in a rage. 'Be patient, sir,' replied the coachman; 'I have drove a coach, man and boy, these two thousand years; but I do not remember to have carried above one dictionary during the whole time. That little work which I perceive peeping from one of your pockets, may I presume to ask what it contains?' 'A mere trifle,' replied the author; 'it is called *The Rambler.*' '*The Rambler!*' cries the coachman; 'I beg, sir, you'll take your place. I have heard our ladies in the court of Apollo frequently mention it with rapture, and Clio, who happens to be a little grave, has been heard to prefer it to *The Spectator;* though others have observed that the reflections, by being refined, sometimes become minute."

Besides the works which I have mentioned, Johnson wrote a series of *Lives of the Poets,* which were written as prefaces to an edition of the works of the English poets. These were so much esteemed as criticism that they took their place in literature as critical biographies, independent of the work for which they were written. They included the lives of Milton, Parnell, Waller, Dryden, Pope, Thomson, Gray, and many others. He also edited Shakespeare, with criticisms on the plays. Of the poets of his own time, and of the school which he had been educated to believe was the correct school in poetry, he could write with excellent judgment; but Milton, Shakespeare, the poets of the Elizabethan age, were too great for him, and the present age does not accept his criticism of them.

His story of *Rasselas,* a little work which has taken a place among English classics, is the most readable of all his works. It is the account of an Eastern prince who is reared in a happy valley and guarded from all knowledge of evil, but finally grows weary of the monotony of his life, and wanders through the world in the vain search after happiness. It was written, so Johnson said, to pay the funeral expenses of his mother and some little debts she left at death, and the author got for it one hundred and twenty-five pounds.

Here is a short extract from *Rasselas*, — the speech of the young prince when he discovers that, in spite of the felicities of the " Happy Valley," he is not content with it, nor with himself : —

" ' What,' said he, 'makes the difference between man and all the rest of the animal creation? Every beast that strays beside me has the same corporeal necessities with myself ; he is hungry, and crops the grass ; he is thirsty, and drinks the stream ; his thirst and hunger are appeased ; he is satisfied, and sleeps ; he arises again, and is hungry ; he is again fed, and is at rest. I am hungry and thirsty like him ; but when thirst and hunger cease, I am not at rest ; I am, like him, pained with want, but am not, like him, satisfied with fulness. The intermediate hours are tedious and gloomy ; I long again to be hungry, that I may again quicken my attention. The birds peck the berries or the corn, and fly away to the groves, where they sit in seeming happiness on the branches, and waste their lives in tuning an unvaried series of sounds. I likewise can call the lutanist and the singer ; but the sounds that pleased me yesterday weary me to-day, and will grow yet more wearisome to-morrow. I can discover within me no power of perception which is not glutted with its proper pleasure, yet I do not feel myself delighted. Man surely has some latent sense for which this place affords no gratification ; or he has some desires, distinct from sense, which must be satisfied before he can be happy.' . . .

" With observations like these the prince amused himself as he returned, uttering them with a plaintive voice, yet with a look that discovered him to feel some complacence in his own perspicuity, and to receive some solace of the miseries of life from consciousness of the delicacy with which he felt, and the eloquence with which he bewailed them."

The Johnsonian style is in pompous and long-syllabled words, overloaded with words of Latin origin. Johnson underrated the value of strong, homely English ; and when he had expressed himself in plain, direct words, he was apt to translate himself into a more verbose style. Boswell gives some good instances, as once when the great Doctor had said vigorously, speaking of one of the comedies of the time of Charles II. : " It had not wit enough to keep itself sweet ; " and immediately changed it to " It had not enough vitality to preserve it from putrefaction." Macaulay finds a still better instance from one of Johnson's familiar letters when he was travelling in the Hebrides. He writes : " When we were taken upstairs, a dirty fellow bounced out of the bed in which we were to lie." Afterwards, when he printed the journal of these travels, he gave the account thus : " Out of one of the beds in which we were to repose, started up, at our entrance, a man black as Cyclops from the forge." This is what Macaulay wittily calls " putting a sentence out of English into Johnsonese."

In person Johnson was awkward, stooping, with shambling gait, head rolling from side to side, and face disfigured with marks of scrofula. In manners he must have been very disagreeable, as he was often intolerant, overbearing in conversation, and regardless of the feelings of others. He was extremely narrow-minded in some of his views : a Tory who could hardly bear the name of Whig ; an Englishman who hated all foreigners, and declared the Americans, at the outbreak of their Revolution, " A party of convicts who ought to be hanged ; " a Churchman who had no sympathy with Dissenters ; and a partisan in most of his literary opinions. Yet, with so much to be disliked, he was a generous man, whose house was filled with poor people who lived on his bounty ; he was very tender to distress, and was a truthful, honest, independent man.

Johnson was the centre of the *Literary Club* started in his day, which had Goldsmith, Edmund Burke, Joshua Reynolds the artist, David Garrick, and other famous men among its members. This club was one of his haunts, and another was the house of Mr. Thrale, a wealthy gentleman who befriended him, where he took tea once a week, till for a time he took up his abode in the house altogether. Mrs. Thrale, who was a lively, sweet-tempered woman, made much of him and poured his tea cheerfully, — not a light office ; for he drank a dozen cups at a sitting, and once took twenty-five at one tea-drinking, — rather to the disgust of his hostess.

Johnson did **more than any** other one man in **English** letters to make literature a working profession, — to take it **out** of the hands of patrons, and make the **dealings of** author and publisher a substantial business relation. **He was** one of the first English **authors who lived** by his work ; and the honest independence **with which** he inspired the profession has been a help to authors ever since his time.

His dictionary, too, was one of the great works of the century. While we cannot help wishing that the Johnsonian tendency in language had been towards greater simplicity, and not towards the introduction of so many Latin words, still **we** must see that he did a great work for the language. **In his** time there **was no** standard **dictionary,** and Johnson, **in arranging** and defining **the words of the** language, brought it **into** order and gave it form. **He singly** and alone attempted **to do for** England **what the French** Academy did for **France ; and** although **it is a** question whether it is not better **to** have so important a **work** done by a body of scholars rather than by one man, **yet nobody** in raising that question will doubt the **value and** honesty **of** Samuel Johnson's labors.

XLVII.

ON OLIVER **GOLDSMITH** AND " **THE VICAR** OF WAKEFIELD."

THE name of OLIVER GOLDSMITH is often heard in connection with that of **Dr.** Johnson, and the **two** men were excellent friends, although John- 1728–1774 son was twenty years older than Goldsmith, and, in a kindly way, disposed to patronize his young friend.

Goldsmith's early life was a checkered one. After leaving college he made attempts to enter life at most of its **principal** gates. He tried teaching, the law, the Church, medicine, until, throwing up all the professions, he started on a vagabond tour through Europe, from which he returned to London poor, alone, unfriended, and with no settled calling in life. He began his literary career by writing for a magazine, the drudge of a publisher who worked him hard and paid him little. But in this work Goldsmith first discovered what he was capable of doing, and this was the first step in the ladder he climbed so rapidly. His literary life lasted about fifteen years; and in this time he produced poetry, history, biography, works on natural science, essays, novels, and comedies, with wonderful versatility, and with success in almost every style. With work or without it, he was always in debt, for he was reckless and improvident in his habits, and never could resist the passion for gambling, which in early youth was nearly his ruin.

His first success was in essay writing. He published *The Bee*, which in lightness and vivacity was in strong contrast to the dignity and weight of Johnson's *Rambler*. If Johnson and Goldsmith had united their powers, as Addison and Steele had done forty years earlier, they would have made a paper almost, if not quite, as good as *The Spectator*.

After *The Bee*, Goldsmith contributed to a newspaper *The Letters of a Chinese Philosopher*, professedly written by a Chinese gentleman travelling in England, who notes all that impresses him as odd in government, society, and morals, and compares them, favorably or unfavorably, with Eastern customs. You can fancy what an opportunity Goldsmith found in the person of the Chinese gentleman for good-natured satire against whatever in politics or manners deserved it.

His first fame was won by his poem *The Traveller*, in which he put the impressions and memories of his tour in Europe into verse. This brought him reputation among literary men; and the praise with which it was received encouraged the publishers to bring out *The Vicar of Wakefield*, which had been some time in their hands. This story is, of all his works, the one which brings him closest to his readers of the present. I have never seen any one, young or old, who did not read it with delight, and I believe it will continue to be read as long as the eighteenth century is remembered in literature. Dr. Johnson gives this account of how the *Vicar* came to be published :—

"I received one morning a message from poor Goldsmith that he was in great distress, and as it was not in his power to come to me, begging that I would come to him as soon as possible. I sent him a guinea, and promised to come to him directly; I accordingly went as soon as I was dressed, and found that his landlady had arrested him for his rent, at which he was in a violent passion. I perceived that he had already changed my guinea, and had got a bottle of Madeira and a glass before him ; I put the cork into the bottle, desired he would be calm, and began to talk to him of the means by which he might be extricated. He then told me that he had a novel ready for the press, which he produced to me. I looked into it, and saw its merit; told the landlady I would soon return; and having gone to a bookseller, sold it for sixty pounds. I brought Goldsmith the money, and he discharged his rent, not without rating his landlady in a high tone for having used him so ill."

Goldsmith's *Vicar of Wakefield* appeared after Richardson, Fielding, and Smollett had gained their fame as novelists, and was the purest and most wholesome of English stories yet written. The scenes of Fielding and Smollett are too frequently vicious, or are carried on in the haunts of vice.

Goldsmith took his reader into rural English life, among characters who at once get a hold on our hearts which they never lose. We learn to love them all, from artless Dr. Primrose to the pedantic, yet easily humbugged, Moses. We enjoy all the amusements of the family when they are living in competency — their tea-drinkings, out-door dances, their social commerce with neighbors — as if we were taking part in them ; and their revulsion from a comfortable estate to poverty we feel as if it were our own. How delightfully Mr. Burchell, the lord in disguise, comes into the story; we guess, long before the artless Primroses do, that he is to be their benefactor. And when the bad young squire comes upon the scene, I tremble for Olivia's peace of mind even when I read the novel for the twentieth time.

How wise good Dr. Primrose is in all his little discourses, although we see that he is, in all minor matters, led by his wife and daughters very tenderly by the nose! Yet he sometimes gets the better of them. One day, he says, —

" My wife went to make the venison pasty, Moses sat reading, while I taught the little ones. My daughters seemed equally busy with the rest, and I observed them for a good while cooking something over the fire. I at first supposed they were assisting their mother; but little Dick informed me, in a whisper, that they were making a wash for the face. Washes of all kinds I had a natural antipathy to, for I knew that instead of mending the complexion they spoiled it. I therefore approached my chair by slow degrees to the fire, and grasping the poker, as if it wanted mending, seemingly by accident overturned the whole composition, and it was too late to begin another."

One of the most delicious bits of humor in the book is the good old Doctor's account of the way in which the family had their portraits painted : —

" My wife and daughters happening to return a visit at neighbor Flamborough's, found that family had lately got their pictures drawn by a limner who travelled the country and took likenesses for *fifteen shillings a head*. As this family and ours had long a sort of rivalry in point of taste, our spirit took the alarm at this stolen march upon us, and notwithstanding all I could say (and I said much), it was resolved that we should have our pictures done too. Having, therefore, engaged the limner (for what could I do?), our next deliberation was to show the superiority of our taste in the attitudes. As for our neighbor's family, there were seven of them, and they were drawn with seven oranges, — a thing quite out of taste, no variety in life, no composition in the world. We desired to have something in a brighter style ; and after many debates, at length came to the unanimous resolution of being drawn together in one large historical family piece. This would be cheaper, since one frame would serve for all, and it would be infinitely more gen-

teel; for all families of any taste were now drawn in the same
manner. As we did not immediately recollect an historical subject to hit us, we were contented each with being drawn as independent historical figures. My wife desired to be drawn as
Venus, and the painter was requested not to be too frugal of his
diamonds in her stomacher and hair. Her two little ones were
to be as Cupids by her side; while I, in my gown and band, was
to present her with my books on the Whistonian controversy.
Olivia would be drawn as an Amazon, sitting on a bank of
flowers, dressed in a green joseph richly laced with gold, and a
whip in her hand; Sophia was to be a shepherdess, with as
many sheep as the painter could put in for nothing; and Moses
was to be dressed out with a hat and white feather.

". . . The painter was therefore set to work; and as he wrought
with assiduity and expedition, in less than four days the whole
was completed. The piece was large, and it must be owned he
did not spare his colors, for which my wife gave him great en-
comiums. We were all perfectly satisfied with his performance;
but an unfortunate circumstance, which had not occurred till the
picture was finished, now struck us with dismay. It was so
very large that we had no place in the house to fix it! . . . This
picture, therefore, instead of gratifying our vanity, as we hoped
it would, leaned in the most mortifying manner against the
kitchen wall, where the canvas was stretched and painted,
much too large to be got through any of the doors, and the jest
of all our neighbors."

Goldsmith's poem, *The Deserted Village*, breathes something of the same spirit as *The Vicar of Wakefield.* It
shows the same sympathy with the simple life of rural England; and the character of the village preacher, who reminds us of Dr. Primrose, is said to be a genuine portrait of
the poet's father :—

> " Near yonder copse, where once the garden smiled,
> And still where many a garden flower grows wild,
> There, where a few torn shrubs the place disclose,
> The village preacher's modest mansion rose.
> A man he was to all the country dear,
> And passing rich with forty pounds a year ;
> Remote from towns he ran his godly race,
> Nor e'er had changed, nor wished to change his place ;
> Unskilful he to fawn, or seek for power,
> By doctrines fashioned to the varying hour ;

Far other aims his heart had learned to prize,
More bent to raise the wretched than to rise.
His house was known to all the vagrant train ;
He chid their wanderings, but relieved their pain.
The long-remembered beggar was his guest,
Whose beard descending swept his aged breast ;
The ruined spendthrift, now no longer proud,
Claimed kindred there, and had his claims allowed ;
The broken soldier, kindly bade to stay,
Sat by his fire, and talked the night away,
Wept o'er his wounds, or tales of sorrow done,
Shouldered his crutch, and showed how fields were won.
Pleased with his guests, the good man learned to glow,
And quite forgot their vices in their woe ;
Careless their merits or their faults to scan,
His pity gave ere charity began.

"Thus to relieve the wretched was his pride,
And e'en his failings leaned to Virtue's side ;
But, in his duty prompt at every call,
He watched and wept, he prayed and felt for all ;
And, as a bird each fond endearment tries
To tempt its new-fledged offspring to the skies,
He tried each art, reproved each dull delay,
Allured to brighter worlds, and led the way.

" Beside the bed where parting life was laid,
And sorrow, guilt, and pain, by turns dismayed,
The reverend champion stood.   At his control
Despair and anguish fled the struggling soul ;
Comfort came down the trembling wretch to raise,
And his last faltering accents whispered praise.

" At church, with meek and unaffected grace,
His looks adorned the venerable place ;
Truth from his lips prevailed with double sway,
And fools, who came to scoff, remained to pray.
The service past, around the pious man,
With steady zeal, each honest rustic ran ;
E'en children followed with endearing wile,
And plucked his gown to share the good man's smile.
His ready smile a parent's warmth expressed ;
Their welfare pleased him, and their cares distressed.
To them his heart, his love, his griefs were given,
But all his serious thoughts had rest in heaven.
As some tall cliff that lifts its awful form,
Swells from the vale, and midway leaves the storm,
Though round its breast the rolling clouds are spread,
Eternal sunshine settles on its head."

Probably *The Vicar of Wakefield* and *The Deserted Village* will outlive all else that Goldsmith ever wrote, but neither of these won him such success during his life as his comedies, *She Stoops to Conquer* and *The Good-Natured Man*. Best of these is *She Stoops to Conquer*, which deserved its success. It is a play whose situations are mirthful and innocent, and whose characters are laughable, without being coarse. The drama had made great improvement in purity during the century which began with Congreve and Farquhar ; and the work of Gold- 1751–1816 smith in *She Stoops to Conquer* and *The Good-Natured Man*, followed by RICHARD BRINSLEY SHERIDAN'S plays, *The Rivals* and *The School for Scandal*, did more to elevate the stage than many sermons had yet been able to do. And we may count it as one of the chief merits of a writer so versatile as Goldsmith that his wit was pure and wholesome, his pathos true and not morbid, and that few men have written so little that in the interests of morality we could wish to blot.

XLVIII.

ON THE FIRST WOMAN NOVELIST.

IN the year 1778 the whole reading world was agitated by the appearance of an anonymous novel called *Evelina*. Everybody read it with delight, and it was pronounced a wonderful picture of the times. All London was occupied in guessing what new author had burst into fame, and everybody was praising *him*, and wondering about *him*, when it was whispered from one to another that a young lady, MISS FANNY BURNEY, had 1752–1840 written this book, and Miss Burney at once became the heroine of the hour. Dr. Johnson's friend Mrs. Thrale sent and invited her to tea, where the great Doctor sat beside her and paid her extravagant compliments.

Edmund Burke, the statesman, sat up all night to read her book; Sir Joshua Reynolds, the painter, declared he would give fifty pounds to know the author; and praises were showered upon her by readers great and little. We, who read every year dozens of novels far cleverer than *Evelina*, may find it difficult to understand this *furor*. But we must remember that no English *woman* had ever before written a novel, and that *Evelina* was more natural in style than were Richardson's novels, and much more delicate and refined than Fielding's; and then we shall not be surprised at the wonder as well as the delight with which it was welcomed. The young ladies who had been reading *Tom Jones* or the more delicate pages of *Clarissa Harlowe* could read *Evelina* without a blush; and the artlessness and innocence of the heroine would win the heart of the severest critic.

Evelina, a girl of sixteen, bred in a country parsonage, is taken to London by some friends, and all at once ushered into the gay life of that city as it was a century ago. Soon after her arrival in London, Evelina goes with her friends, Mrs. Mirvan and her daughter Maria, to a ball, of which she writes next day the following account to her guardian in the country : —

" We came home from the *ridotto* so late, or rather so early, that it was not possible for me to write. Indeed, we did not *go* — you will be frightened to hear it — till past eleven o'clock; but nobody does. A terrible reverse of the order of nature ! We sleep with the sun, and wake with the moon.

" The room was very magnificent, the lights and decorations were brilliant, and the company gay and splendid. But I should have told you that I made many objections to being of the party, according to the resolution I had formed. However, Maria laughed me out of my scruples, and so once again I went to an assembly. . . .

" Miss Mirvan was soon engaged; and presently after, a very fashionable, gay-looking man, who seemed about thirty years of age, addressed himself to me, and begged to have the honor of dancing with me. Now, Maria's partner was a gentleman of Mrs. Mirvan's acquaintance; for she had told us it was highly improper for young women to dance with strangers at any public assembly. Indeed, it was by no means my wish so to do;

yet I did not like to confine myself from dancing at all; neither did I dare refuse this gentleman, and then, if any acquaintance should offer, accept him; and so, all these reasons, combining, induced me to tell him — yet I blush to write it to you! — that I was *already engaged;* by which I meant to keep myself at liberty to dance or not, as matters should fall out.

"I suppose my consciousness betrayed my artifice, for he looked at me as if incredulous; and, instead of being satisfied with my answer, and leaving me, according to my expectation, he walked at my side, and, with the greatest ease imaginable, began a conversation in the free style which only belongs to old and intimate acquaintance. But, what was most provoking, he asked me a thousand questions concerning *the partner to whom I was engaged.* And at last he said, 'Is it really possible that a man whom you have honored with your acceptance can fail to be at hand to profit from your goodness?'

"I felt extremely foolish, and begged Mrs. Mirvan to lead me to a seat; which she very obligingly did. The captain (her husband) sat next her; and, to my great surprise, this gentleman thought proper to follow and seat himself next to me.

"'What an insensible!' continued he; 'why, madam, you are missing the most delightful dance in the world! The man must be either mad or a fool. Which do you incline to think him yourself?'

"'Neither, sir,' answered I, in some confusion.

"He begged my pardon for the freedom of his supposition, saying, 'I really was off my guard, from astonishment that any man can be so much and so unaccountably his own enemy. But where, madam, can he possibly be? Has he left the room? or has not he been in it?"

"'Indeed, sir,' said I, peevishly, 'I know nothing of him.'

"'I don't wonder that you are disconcerted, madam; it is really very provoking. The best part of the evening will be absolutely lost. He deserves not that you should wait for him.'

"'I do not, sir,' said I, 'and I beg you not to —'

"'Mortifying indeed, madam,' interrupted he; 'a lady to wait for a gentleman! Oh, fie, careless fellow! What can detain him? Will you give me leave to seek him?'

"'If you please, sir,' answered I, quite terrified lest Mrs. Mirvan should attend to him; for she looked very much surprised at seeing me enter into conversation with a stranger.

"'With all my heart,' cried he; 'pray, what coat has he on?'

"'Indeed, I never looked at it.'

"'Out upon him!' cried he; 'what! did he address you in a coat not worth looking at? What a shabby wretch!'

"How ridiculous! I really could not help laughing, — which, I fear, encouraged him, for he went on, —

"'Charming creature! and can you really bear ill-usage with so much sweetness? Can you, *like Patience on a monument*, smile in the midst of disappointment? For my part, though I am not the offended person, my indignation is so great that I long to kick the fellow round the room! — unless, indeed' (hesitating, and looking earnestly at me), 'unless, indeed, it is a partner of your own *creating*.'

"I was dreadfully abashed, and could not make any answer.

"'But no!' cried he again, and with warmth, 'it cannot be that you are so cruel! Softness itself is painted in your eyes. You could not, surely, have the barbarity so wantonly to trifle with my misery.'

"I turned away from this nonsense with real disgust. Mrs. Mirvan saw my confusion, but was perplexed what to think of it, and I could not explain to her the cause, lest the captain should hear me. I therefore proposed to walk; she consented, and we all rose. But — would you believe it? — this man had the assurance to rise too, and walk close by my side, as if of my party!

"'Now,' cried he, 'I hope we shall see this ingrate. Is that he,' pointing to an old man who was lame, 'or that?' And in this manner he asked me of whoever was old or ugly in the room. I made no sort of answer; and when he found that I was resolutely silent, and walked on as much as I could without observing him, he suddenly stamped his foot, and cried out in a passion, 'Fool! Idiot! Booby!'

"I turned hastily toward him. 'Oh, madam,' continued he, 'forgive my vehemence; but I am distracted to think there should exist a wretch who can slight a blessing for which I would forfeit my life! Oh that I could but meet him! I would soon — But I grow angry; pardon me, madam: my passions are violent, and your injuries affect me!'

"I began to apprehend he was a madman, and stared at him with the utmost astonishment. 'I see you are moved, madam,' said he; 'generous creature! — but don't be alarmed; I am cool again, I am indeed, — upon my soul, I am; I entreat you, most lovely of mortals! I entreat you to be easy.'

"'Indeed, sir,' said I, very seriously, 'I must insist upon your leaving me; you are quite a stranger to me, and I am both unused and averse to your language and your manners.'

" This seemed to have some effect on **him.** **He made me a low bow,** begged my pardon, **and vowed he would not for the** world offend me.

" 'Then, **sir, you must** leave me,' cried I.

" ' I am gone, madam, I am gone !' with a most tragical air, and he marched away at a quick pace out of sight in a moment; but before I had time to congratulate myself, he was again at my elbow.

" 'And could you really let me go, and not be sorry? Can you see me suffer torments inexpressible, and yet retain all your favor for that miscreant who flies you? Ungrateful puppy! I could bastinado him !'

" 'For Heaven's sake, my dear,' cried Mrs. Mirvan, 'who is he talking of?'

" 'Indeed, I do not know, madam,' said I; 'but I **wish he** would leave **me.'**

" 'What 's **all that there?'** cried the captain.

" The man made **a low bow,** and said, 'Only, **sir, a** slight objection which this **young lady** makes to dancing with me, and which I am endeavoring **to obviate.** **I shall think myself** greatly honored if you will intercede **for me.'**

" 'That lady, sir,' said the captain, coldly, **'is her own mis-tress.'** And he walked sullenly on.

" 'You, madam,' said the man, who looked delighted, to **Mrs.** Mirvan, ' you, I hope, will have the goodness to speak for me.'

" 'Sir,' answered she, gravely, 'I have not the pleasure of being acquainted with you.'

" 'I **hope when** you have, ma'am,' cried he, undaunted, 'you will honor me with your approbation; but while I am yet unknown to you, it would be truly generous in you to countenance me; and I flatter myself, madam, that you will not have cause to repent it.'

" Mrs. Mirvan, with an embarrassed air, replied, ' I do not at all mean, **sir, to** doubt your being a gentleman, but —'

" 'But *what*, **madam?** That doubt removed, why a *but?*'

" 'Well, sir,' said Mrs. Mirvan, with a good-humored smile, 'I will even treat you with your own plainness, and try what effect that will have on you; I **must** therefore tell **you, once for** all —'

" 'Oh, pardon me, madam!' interrupted he, **eagerly,** 'you must not proceed with those words *once for all;* no, if *I* have been too *plain*, and, though a *man*, deserve a rebuke, remember, dear ladies, that if you copy, you ought, in justice, to excuse me.'

" We both stared at the man's strange behavior.

"'Be nobler than your sex,' continued he, turning to me; 'honor me with one dance, and give up the ingrate who has merited so ill your patience.'

" Mrs. Mirvan looked with astonishment at us both.

"'Whom does he speak of, my dear? You never mentioned —'

"'Oh, madam,' exclaimed he, 'he was not worth mentioning, — it is pity he was ever thought of; but let us forget his existence. One dance is all I solicit. Permit me, madam, the honor of this young lady's hand; it will be a favor I shall ever most gratefully acknowledge.'

"'Sir,' answered she, 'favors and strangers have with me no connection.'

"'If you have hitherto,' said he, 'confined your benevolence to your intimate friends, suffer me to be the first for whom your charity is enlarged.'

"'Well, sir, I know not what to say to you, but —'

" He stopped her *but* with so many urgent entreaties that she at last told me I must either go down one dance or avoid his importunities by returning home. I hesitated which alternative to choose; but this impetuous man at length prevailed, and I was obliged to consent to dance with him.

" And thus was my deviation from truth punished, and thus did this man's determined boldness conquer."

Into such scrapes as these do Evelina's inexperience and thoughtlessness constantly lead her; and the case is made still worse by the fact that her vulgar grandmamma, who returns from a long residence in France, takes her from her friends and attempts to chaperone her. The whole tone of the society is so vulgar, the manners of the persons who pass for well-bred are so bad, that one is almost inclined to doubt what was said of the novel, — that it was a perfect picture of fashionable life in its time.

Miss Burney wrote several other novels after *Evelina*, one of which, *Cecilia*, had almost as great a success even as *Evelina*. Her fame led to her appointment as one of the ladies-in-waiting to the queen of George III., — a position which was much more respectable than it was pleasant. When about forty she married a French officer, M. d'Arblay, and after that, published an account of her own life,

The Memoirs of Mme. d'Arblay, which is one of the most sincere and entertaining books in literature. She begins with the account of her writing *Evelina ;* tells all the triumphs of her authorship ; gives striking and life-like pictures of Dr. Johnson and the other great men and women she met ; and finally takes us into the court of George III., and shows us her very uncomfortable life there among the royal personages. These memoirs are most delightful reading, and give one a very vivid idea of the society of which Miss Burney was a part.

By the time *Evelina* appeared, the novel had begun to be felt as one of the strongest forces in literature. Miss Burney led a crowd of woman-writers who appeared rapidly during the last years of the last century. For the first time in the history of English literature a field was opened where woman could work in rivalry with man. In the novel she could equal, and sometimes surpass him ; and from that time to this, the woman-writer of novels has held her place among the best.

MRS. ANNE RADCLIFFE was famous as a writer of high-wrought fictions. Chief among these are the *Romance of the Forest* and *The Mysteries of* 1764–1823 *Udolpho.* White-robed figures walking by moonlight, black-robed men, ruined castles, midnight groans, — all these were part of the machinery of her stories. They were no doubt very thrilling and sensational in their day, but beside more modern successes in that line they appear quite tame and harmless.

MRS. AMELIA OPIE was a writer of different character from Mrs. Radcliffe. Her stories, *Father and Daughter, Tales of the Heart, Temper,* etc., as 1769–1853 their titles show, were tales of real life, written with a rather too obvious moral, and with hardly vigor enough to keep them alive.

MISS MARIA EDGEWORTH, who was a native of Ireland, laid most of the scenes of her books in that country. 1767–1849 Her stories for children in *The Parent's Assistant,* of *Lazy Lawrence, Simple Susan,* and her tale of

Rosamund, *Frank*, *Harry and Lucy*, pleased the children of a generation ago, but are now very little read.

Then came the PORTER sisters, JANE and ANNA MARIA, the first of whom wrote those stately old-fashioned novels *Thaddeus of Warsaw* and *The Scottish Chiefs*, over which our grandmothers hung enraptured. And at the beginning of

1775–1817 our century appeared JANE AUSTEN, the author of *Pride and Prejudice, Mansfield Park, Sense and Sensibility*, who wrote with a naturalness and good sense which has made her a favorite with readers even to our time. These, with many others, kept the circulating libraries of the time supplied with new books, till early in this century the fame of all others was almost lost in the great splendor of Walter Scott's success as the novelist of history.

XLIX.

THE WORK OF THOMAS PERCY AND JAMES MACPHERSON, AND THE SAD STORY OF THOMAS CHATTERTON, THE BOY-POET.

IN 1765, about the time that Goldsmith published the artless story of dear old Dr. Primrose, Bishop Percy, who was a friend of both Goldsmith and Dr. Johnson, published a collection of old English ballads, which he called *Reliques of Ancient English Poetry*. I can fancy that the readers of the time were growing tired of the exact and didactic sort of verses which had been fashionable for so many years, and welcomed a draught from the pure springs of English poetry which lay hidden in those old songs.

THOMAS PERCY, a scholar of elegant tastes, was already known as a writer of some merit, when the design of publish-

1728–1811 ing a collection of English ballad poetry occurred to him. He had in his library an old manuscript containing songs and ballads, some of them of earlier date

than Chaucer, while **others were** written **as late as the seventeenth century.** This manuscript had been marred by time
and mould and mutilation **until in some places words or**
whole lines were illegible ; in others, half a leaf was wanting.
To many men it would have seemed a hopeless task to de-
cipher the tattered and time-stained pages ; **but** Dr. Percy
had just the taste and skill for the work he undertook. He
seems to have had a knack at renovation which certain
menders of old pictures have shown, and to have been able
to supply missing words and lines, and to patch up an old
ballad out of detached fragments with such skill that one
could not detect his handiwork from the original. Adding
to his own manuscript old ballads from many other sources,
he **at last** produced the three volumes of *Reliques of Ancient English Poetry*, **for** which every lover of ballads **has**
been grateful **to** him from that time to this. **Here are to be**
found the old rhymes **of** *Chevy Chase*, the *Battle of Otter-
bourne*, *Sir Patrick Spence*, **the** *Babes in the Wood*, **some**
of the ballads of *Robin Hood*, and many more dear **old**
rhymes, which in our childhood we learned by heart. The
interest which this work excited was as great as it deserved
to be, and Percy won by it a place in literature which none
of his other works could have gained for him.

While Bishop Percy was making his collection of antique
English **poetry,** JAMES MACPHERSON was working in a similar
field. A native of Scotland, he had become greatly interested in the Gaelic speech of his forefathers. He claimed
that he had discovered some remains in manuscript of the
ancient Gaelic bard Ossian, and gave them to the world in
a poetical-prose translation of his own. This
poetry, which was wild and picturesque, like the   1762
early bardic poetry, was at once read and admired. A **very**
few lines will give an idea of the style of *Ossian.* I select
these from the longest poem, *Fingal*, which celebrates the
deeds of the famous Gaelic warrior, *Fingal :* —

" Fingal, like a beam from heaven, shone in the midst of his
people. His heroes gather round him. He sends forth the
voice **of his** power. ᾿Raise my standards on high ; spread them

on Lena's wind like the flames of an hundred hills. Let them
sound on the winds of **Erin** and remind us **of the fight. Ye
sons of** the roaring streams that pour **from a thousand hills,**
hear ye the king of Morven; attend **to the** words of his power.
Gaul, strongest **arm** of death; Oscar **of the** future fights; Con-
nal, son of the blue shields **of Sora; Dermid** of the dark-brown
hair; Ossian, **king of** many songs, — **be** near your father's arm.'
We reared the sunbeam of battle, the standard of the king.
Each hero exulted with joy as waving it flew in the wind. It
was studded with gold above as the blue wide shell of the
mighty sky. Each hero had **his standard too, and** each his
gloomy men. . . . Now, like an **hundred different** winds that
pour through many vales, divided, **dark the sons** of Selma
advanced. Cromla echoed around. **How can I** relate the
deaths when we closed in the strife of arms ? O daughter of
Toscar, bloody were **our hands!** The gloomy ranks of Lochlin
fell like the banks of the roaring Cona ! **Our arms were** victo-
rious on Lena. Each chief fulfilled his promise. . . . **Thou
hast seen the sun** retire **red** and slow behind **his cloud, night**
gathering round on the mountain, while the **unfrequent blast**
roars in the narrow vale. At length the rain beats **hard; thunder**
roars in peals; lightning glances on the rocks; **spirits ride on**
beams of fire. The strength of the **mountain** streams comes
roaring down the hills. Such was the noise of battle, maid of
the arms of snow! **Why, daughter of** Toscar, why that tear?
The maids of Lochlin have cause **to weep.** The people of their
country **wail.** Bloody **are** the blue **swords of** the race of **my**
heroes."

The work of both **Percy and** Macpherson caused hot dis-
cussion in literary circles. Bishop Percy's collection had
aroused a dispute among other scholars of ancient poetry
concerning his right to amend the old ballads by adding or
supplying his own words or lines where the originals were
missing. Although Percy had done his work in the **best of**
faith and in all honesty, telling just what part of the **work**
was his own, yet the criticism upon him for these interpolations into the old text was so sharp that the poor bishop
must have felt as if he had unexpectedly put his head into
a hive of stinging-bees.

In the case of Macpherson and his Ossianic poems, the
dispute ran higher. One party believed that these poems

were really translations from the Gaelic; another party declared that Macpherson had composed them himself; and the two factions belabored each other with arguments and abuse. During most of the discussion, Macpherson maintained a silence which seems rather obstinate; and there never was any absolute settlement of the inquiry as to the originality of the poems. It seems probable, however, that although they were, in the main, written by Macpherson, they were founded on fragments of old songs of the Celtic bards which had been preserved by tradition in the Highlands of Scotland.

But the dispute about the work of Percy and Macpherson was slight compared with that which arose concerning the writings of Thomas Chatterton, the boy-poet, one of the greatest prodigies in the whole history of our literature.

THOMAS CHATTERTON was born in the interesting old town of Bristol. His mother, left a widow just before the birth of this son, started a milliner's shop, and bravely took upon herself the burden of support- **1752-1770** ing and educating her family. When five years old, Chatterton was sent to school; but as the manner of imparting instruction does not seem to have taken hold of his infant mind, he stayed there a year without learning his letters; and at six the teacher reported him to his mother as a hopeless dunce. Just before this time he saw an old French book with illuminated letters, and fell so in love with it that his mother conceived the idea of teaching him his letters from another ancient book which she owned, — an old copy of the Bible in the black-letter text in which the early English books were printed. From this old text he learned to read; and when once he had mastered the alphabet, books became his delight. By the time he was eight, this hopeless dunce had devoured every book he could lay hands upon. He went to a free school in his town, and had for tutor a man named Phillips, who sometimes wrote verses for the current newspapers. For him Chatterton felt a warm friendship, and Phillips seems to have been the only person about him able in the least to sympathize with his genius.

The old church of St. Mary's, at Bristol, in which one of Chatterton's uncles had been a sexton, was an ancient and interesting old building. In the fifteenth century it had been repaired and partly rebuilt by worthy Mr. William Cannynge, a rich citizen of Bristol. In the time of Chatterton's father, a chest in a room over the church porch had been opened, and a quantity of old papers, among them the deeds of the church and other papers relative to William Cannynge's bequest, had been taken out and removed for safe keeping. Some of these old parchments, considered worthless, had fallen into the hands of Chatterton's father, who carried off a quantity to his house.

Chatterton had grown to be eleven or twelve, and had already begun to write verses, when one day he came upon some pieces of this old manuscript. He was at once interested in its history, and collecting all he could find, he carried his treasures off to a room in his mother's house of which he kept the key, and locked them up there, guarding them henceforth from all eyes. He seems to have spent all his leisure poring over and imitating the writing of the manuscript. He kept his writing materials in this room, and he added to these ochre and lampblack, to counterfeit the yellow and grimy look of the parchment.

At fifteen the boy was apprenticed to an attorney, who proved a very disagreeable and exacting master. Here Chatterton was set to work as copying-clerk, and employed in all the various capacities of an office drudge. Yet he still found time for his work with the old manuscripts, and at length wrote to Dodsley, a bookseller in London, that he had a valuable collection of poems for publication, written by Thomas Rowley, a priest of Bristol, in the fifteenth century, and a friend of Mr. Cannynge, the benefactor of the Bristol church.

These poems were written in wonderful imitation of old black-letter manuscript in text, in spelling, and in style. But the poor boy could get little notice from either the bookseller or the rich patrons of literature to whom he sent an account of these treasures. Discouraged at his want of success in Bristol, he resolved to go **to London and live by** his pen.

Chatterton was only a little more than seventeen when, in the spring of 1770, he came up to the great city with high hopes and full of courage. He began at once to write for magazines and newspapers, and at first met with enough success to encourage him in splendid dreams of fame and fortune. He wrote glowing accounts to his mother and **sister of** what he intended to achieve; he spent his **earn**ings in presents for them, — a set of china for his mother, a **fan** for his sister, and other trinkets to send home to Bristol. **But** his bright **hopes** faded; the little money he could earn was barely enough for **his** scanty support, and he gradually fell **from his** lofty mood to one of despair. Forced by necessity, **he went** in midsummer **to** take a cheap **lodging in the house** of a dressmaker **in London. Too proud to** make known his wants or ask **assistance, he was soon on** the verge of starvation. One evening **in August, when he had been for** two or three days without **his dinner, his landlady, mistrust**ing his condition, **invited him to dine with her.** With characteristic pride, he refused the dinner, and shutting **him**self up in his room, he ended his short, sad life with a **dose of arsenic.** He was found dead next morning **in his room,** among **a** litter of papers torn into bits, which he **had de**stroyed before taking the poison, without a word of farewell or explanation. Thus ended, in suicide and despair, the brief life **of the greatest** prodigy in the history of English literature.

It was after his **death that the** discussion about the poetry which he claims **was written by** Thomas Rowley began. It **was a** controversy **much** hotter, and engaged men more eminent, than even Percy's ballads or Macpherson's translations. But the best authorities agreed that the old **poems** must have been written by Chatterton only, and **that** Row**ley** was the pseudonym **under** which **he had** sought **to** hide his own work, believing, no doubt, that more **fame** would **attach** to them with Rowley's name **than the works** themselves would **bring.**

The most remarkable among the poems ascribed to **Row-**
ley are a ballad on the *Execution of Sir Charles Bawdin ;
The Tragedy of Ella ; The Battle of Hastings ; The Tournament ;* and *A Description of Cannynge's Feast.*

The *Execution of Sir Charles Bawdin,* although it has
less poetical merit than *Ella,* is **most in** keeping with the an-
tique style **Chatterton** strove to imitate, and has in it a good
deal of the ring of the early ballad. It begins thus : —

> " **The** feathered songster chanticleer [1]
>   Had wound his bugle **horn,**
> And told the early villager
>   The coming of the morn.

> " **King** Edward saw the ruddy streaks
>   Of light eclipse the gray,
> And heard the raven's croaking throat
>   Proclaim the fated day.

> " ' Thou 'st right,' quoth he ; ' for **by the God**
>   **That** sits enthroned on high,
> Charles Bawdin and his fellows twain
>   To-day shall surely die ! '

> " Then with a jug of nappy ale
>   His knights did on him wait :
> ' Go tell the traitor that to-day
>   He leaves this mortal state.'

> " Sir Canterlone then bended low,
>   With heart brimful of woe ;
> He journeyed to the castle-gate,
>   And to Sir Charles did go.

[1] **As** the ancient spelling which Chatterton used was merely the
artificial form into which he put his verses, and it would make it more
difficult to read if I followed it, I give it to you in ordinary **spelling.**
This is **a** specimen of the stanzas in antique spelling : —

> " **The** feathered chanti cleere
>   Han wounde hys bugle **horn,**
> And tolde the earlie villager
>   The commynge of the morn.

> " King Edward saw the ruddie streakes
>   Of lyghte eclypse the greie,
> And herde the raven's crokynge throte
>   Proclaime the fated daye."

> " But when he came, his children twain,
>   And eke his loving wife,
> With briny tears did wet the floor
>   For good Sir Charles's life.
>
> "' Oh, good Sir Charles,' said Canterlone,
>   ' Bad tidings I do bring.'
> ' Speak boldly, man,' said brave Sir Charles,
>   ' What says the traitor king ?'
>
> "' I grieve to tell, before yon sun
>   Does from the welkin fly,
> He hath upon his honor sworn
>   That thou shalt surely die.'
>
> "' We all must die,' said brave Sir Charles, —
>   ' Of that I am not afeared.
> What boots to live a little space?
>   Thank Jesus, I 'm prepared.' "

In spite of the intercession of Sir Charles's friends, among whom is worthy Mr. Cannynge of Bristol, the king refuses to repeal his sentence, and the knight, after an affecting leave-taking with his wife and children, is led out to execution.

> " Before him went the councilmen
>   In scarlet robes and gold,
> And tassels spangling in the sun,
>   Much glorious to behold.
>
> "The friars of St. Augustine next
>   Appeared to the sight,
> All clad in homely russet weeds
>   Of godly monkish plight.
>
> "In different parts a godly psalm
>   Most sweetly they did chant;
> Behind their backs six minstrels came,
>   Who tuned the strange bataunt.
>
> " Then five and twenty archers came ;
>   Each one the bow did bend,
> From rescue of King Henry's friends,
>   Sir Charles for to defend.
>
> " Bold as a lion came Sir Charles,
>   Drawn on a cloth-laid sled
> By two black steeds in trappings white,
>   With plumes upon their head.

> " Behind him five and twenty more
>   Of archers strong and stout,
> With bended bow each one in hand,
>   Marched in goodly rout.
>
> " Saint James's friars marched next,
>   Each one his part did chant ;
> Behind their backs six minstrels came,
>   Who tuned the strange bataunt.
>
> " Then came the mayor and aldermen,
>   In cloth of scarlet decked ;
> And their attending men, each one
>   Like eastern princes tricked.
>
> " And after them a multitude
>   . Of citizens did throng ;
> The windows were all full of heads
>   As he did pass along."

In the midst of this gorgeous procession the knight goes on to death steadfast and unafraid ; he mounts the scaffold without trembling, and beards the king as a traitor ; and with a prayer, —

> " Then kneeling down, he laid his head
>   Most seemly on the block ;
> Which from his body fair at once
>   The able headsman stroke.
>
> " And out the blood began to flow,
>   And round the scaffold twine ;
> And tears enough to wash 't away
>   Did flow from each man's eyen.
>
> .   .   .
>
> " Thus was the end of Bawdin's fate.
>   God prosper long our king,
> And grant he may with Bawdin's soul
>   In heaven God's mercy sing ! "

Besides the poems which Chatterton pretended were written by Rowley, he published almost as many others under his own name. These are not equal in merit to the Rowley poems, but they show promise of a genius which would have grown and ripened with age. As a specimen of his style when he was not trying to conceal himself behind the name of the fifteenth century monk, we will read a few stanzas from an *Elegy* he wrote on Mr. Phillips, his teacher in Bristol Free School, whose death he laments in a measure like that of Gray's *Elegy*. He begins by praising Phillips as a poet (Phillips had written verses while Chatterton was his pupil), and then bewails his loss as a friend in these lines : —

> " Wet with the dew, the yellow hawthorns bow ;
>   The loud winds whistle through the echoing cave ;
> Far o'er the lea the breathing cattle low,
>   And the full Avon lifts the darkened wave.
>
> " Now as the mantle of the evening swells,
>   Upon my mind I feel a thickening gloom ;
> Ah ! could I charm by necromantic spells
>   The soul of Phillips from the deathly tomb !
>
> " Then would we wander through this darkened vale
>   In converse such as heavenly spirits use, ·
> And, borne upon the pinions of the gale,
>   Hymn the Creator and invoke the muse.
>
> .   .   .   .   .
>
> " Now rest, my muse, but only rest to weep
>   A friend most dear by every sacred tie ;
> Unknown to me be comfort, peace, or sleep ;
>   Phillips is dead, — 't is pleasure then to die.
>
> " Few are the pleasures Chatterton e'er knew,
>   Short were the moments of his transient peace ;
> But melancholy robbed him of those few,
>   And this hath bid all future comfort cease."

These verses are crude and boyish ; but it is the crudity of genius, not the sort of precocity that exhausts itself in one or two efforts. We must believe that if Chatterton had only been strong and patient enough to wait a little longer, or if he had found one helping hand stretched out to hold him up in time of sorest need, he might have stood in the front rank of poets.

The works of Percy, Macpherson, and Chatterton were all published within a period of less than ten years. These reprints of old English songs, these fragments restored from old Celtic bards, even the ballads in which poor Chatterton imitated the lays of an elder age, — all indicated a return to a fresher and more natural school of poetry. For almost a century popular taste had been held in a sort of bondage by Dryden and Pope and the poets who followed them. Even the untaught lay of the earliest minstrel was refreshing to ears which were tired of the see-saw verses, rhymed in pairs, which had so long been heard. Thus we see it is quite natural that this should lead finally to a reaction towards something new and fresh in poetic treatment, and to a change in popular taste.

L.

ON WILLIAM COWPER AND ROBERT BURNS.

WILLIAM COWPER stands midway between two events in the history of poetry, — the going out of Pope, and the coming in of Wordsworth. He was 1731–1800 a boy of thirteen when Pope died, with the reputation of being the greatest of English poets ; and in 1800, the year of Cowper's death, a few persons were beginning to suspect that Wordsworth was the foremost poet of a new order. If we look closely into Cowper's poetry, I think we shall find in it a remembrance of Pope, and a prophecy of Wordsworth.

His life was early clouded with a great sorrow. At six years, he lost his mother. One of his most feeling poems, *Lines on Receipt of my Mother's Picture*, speaks of this grief : —

> " My mother ! when I learned that thou wast dead,
> Say, wast thou conscious of the tears I shed ?
> Hovered thy spirit o'er thy sorrowing son,
> Wretch even then, life's journey just begun ?
> Perhaps thou gav'st me, though unfelt, a kiss ;
> Perhaps a tear, if souls can weep in bliss.

> " I heard the bell tolled on thy burial day,
> I saw the hearse that bore thee slow away,
> And, turning from my nursery window, drew
> A long, long sigh, and wept a last adieu."

The sadness which began so young was made deeper by his fear of becoming insane, — for insanity threatened him early in life, — and also by his morbid religious fears. Although a pious, pure-souled man, the gloomy doctrines of his belief took such hold on his mind that they made him miserable through life, and hung like a black pall over the future.

Yet his poetry is by no means all sadness, and is sometimes bright and gay. He began to write later than most poets, and writing became his chief pleasure, helping to avert that insanity which had twice attacked him. He published first a volume of short poems. Later appeared *The Task*, the longest and most famous of all his works. This begins with the praise of the sofa ; traces its growth from a three-legged stool to a luxurious couch ; and then, leading away from the fireside by which the sofa is placed, the poem leads into rural wanderings, in which the poet talks of Nature and her lessons. The measure is blank verse, and although in subject it is not unlike some of those long didactic poems written earlier than Cowper, it is in a natural and hearty tone that makes it far superior to most poetry of the didactic style.

Perhaps Cowper's most widely read poem is the ballad of *John Gilpin*. The story was told him one evening by a lady who had encouraged him to write, and who suggested the subject of *The Task* to him. The picture of Gilpin galloping off on a horse that would not be stopped so touched Cowper's sense of humor that he could hardly sleep for laughter the night after hearing it, and could not rest till he had put it into a ballad.

The last poem he wrote was *The Castaway*, — one of the dreariest and saddest of poems. This seems like a picture of Cowper's own mind, and he himself traces the likeness in the first and last stanzas : —

> "Obscurest night involved the sky,
> The Atlantic billows roared,
> When such a destined wretch as I,
> Washed headlong from on board,

22

Of friends, of hope, of all bereft,
His floating home forever left.

. . . . . .

" Not long beneath the whelming brine,
    Expert to swim, he lay,
Nor soon he felt his strength decline,
    Or courage die away,
But waged with death a lasting strife,
Supported by despair of life.

" He shouted ; nor his friends had failed
    To check the vessel's course ;
But so the furious blast prevailed
    That, pitiless perforce,
They left their outcast mate behind,
And scudded still before the wind.

" Some succor yet they could afford,
    And such as storms allow, —
The cask, the coop, the floated cord, —
    Delayed not to bestow ;
But he, they knew, nor ship, nor shore,
Whate'er they gave, should visit more.

" Nor cruel, as it seemed, could he
    Their haste himself condemn,
Aware that flight, in such a sea,
    Alone could rescue them ;
Yet bitter felt it still to die
Deserted, and his friends so nigh.

" He long survives who lives an hour
    In ocean self-upheld ;
And so long he, with unspent power,
    His destiny repelled,
And ever, as the minutes flew.
Entreated help, or cried, ' Adieu ! '

" At length, his transient respite past,
    His comrades, who before
Had heard his voice in every blast,
    Could catch the sound no more ;
For then, by toil subdued, he drank
The stifling wave, and then he sank.

. . . . .

" I therefore purpose not, or dream,
    Descanting on his fate,
To give the melancholy theme
    A more enduring date ;

> But misery still delights to trace
> Its semblance in another's case.

> " No voice divine the storm allayed,
>   No light propitious shone,
> When, snatched from all effectual aid,
>   We perished, each alone, —
> But I beneath a rougher sea,
> And whelmed in deeper gulfs than he."

One noticeable thing in Cowper's verses is his sympathy with the humanity of which he was part, — a feeling for the suffering and oppressed everywhere. There is hardly a poem of his which does not speak this. *The Task* is full of such lines : —

> " My soul is sick with every day's report
> Of wrong and outrage, with which earth is filled."

And again, —

> " I would not have a slave to till my ground,
> To carry me, to fan me while I sleep,
> And tremble when I wake, for all the wealth
> That sinews bought and sold have ever earned."

This tenderness in Cowper breaks out even for the most helpless animal, —

> " I would not enter on my list of friends
> (Though graced with polished manners and fine sense,
> Yet wanting sensibility), the man
> Who needlessly sets foot upon a worm."

This spirit of humanity, of sympathy for the sorrows and ardor for the rights of man, had long needed a voice among the poets, and it was only a year later than Cowper's *Task* when a little volume of poems apppeared, in which this voice spoke with a power it had never before possessed.

This volume was published in Scotland, and written by ROBERT BURNS, a poet of the people. He was   **1759-1796** the son of a farmer, and was himself a farm laborer till manhood. Without training or the culture of the schools, he was a born poet, singing his songs in the dialect of Scotland, — the homely English spoken by the Scottish people, often inelegant and full of roughness, but rich in expression and feeling. As he was fettered with no rules of verse-making, Burns sang with an ease and freedom that brought back the earlier days of song. Yet his poetry had also a ring in it that was the echo of the modern spirit. It was ten years after the American Revolution, which had declared that men were equal in rights; it was on the very threshold of the French Revolution, — an outburst of democracy that revenged the wrongs the French people had suffered for centuries, — that Burns began to sing. It is not strange that from lips like his, his voice rang like a slogan-cry when he spoke for humanity.

Poetry had not before found vent in words like these:

HONEST POVERTY.

Is there, for honest poverty,
　That hangs his head an' a' that?
The coward slave, we pass him by,
　We dare be poor for a' that!
For a' that, an' a' that;
　Our toils obscure, an' a' that;
The rank is but the guinea's stamp!
　The man 's the goud for a' that.

What though on hamely fare we dine,
　Wear hoddin grey, and a' that!
Gie fools their silks, and knaves their wine,
　A man 's a man for a' that!
For a' that, an' a' that;
　Their tinsel show an' a' that:
The honest man, though e'er sae poor,
　Is king o' men for a' that.

A prince can mak a belted knight,
　A marquis, duke, an' a' that;
But an honest man 's aboon his might,
　Guid faith! he maunna fa' that.
For a' that, an' a' that,
　Their dignities an' a' that,
The pith o' sense an' pride o' worth
　Are higher ranks than a' that.

Then let us pray that, come it may,
　As come it will for a' that,

> That sense and worth o'er a' the earth
>   May bear the gree an' a' that !
> For a' that, an' a' that ;
>   It 's coming yet, for a' that,
> That man to man, the warld o'er,
>   Shall brothers be for a' that.

These **were** noble lines, and Burns wrote many such. He is also full **of** the true spirit of song,— arch, tender, exquisite. Never, since the early song-writers, had there been anything more natural than his little love-songs :

> " She is a winsome wee thing,
> She is a handsome wee thing,
> She is a bonnie wee thing,
> This sweet wee wife of mine.

> " I never saw a fairer,
> I never lo'ed a dearer,
> And neist my heart I 'll wear her,
> For fear my jewel tine.

> " The warld's wrack, **we share it,**
> The wrastle and **the care** o't
> Wi' her I 'll blithely **bear** it,
> And think my lot sublime."

Or this : —

> " Oh, my luve is like the red, red rose
>   That 's newly sprung in June ;
> Oh, my luve is like the melodie
>   That 's sweetly played in **tune.**
> As fair thou art, my bonnie lass,
>   **So** deep in luve am I,
> **And I** will luve thee still, my dear,
>   **Till a'** the seas gang dry "

Of **such songs as these** Burns wrote scores ; and yet, in **the** midst **of their careless** music, the deeper undersong constantly **makes itself heard,** as this plea for **human** charity : —

> " Then gently scan your brother-man,
>   Still gentler sister-woman ;
> Tho' they may gang a kennin' wrang,
>   To step aside is human.

> .   .   .   .   .   .

> " Who made the heart, 't is He alone
>   Decidedly can try us ;
>   He knows each chord, its various tone ;
>   Each spring, its various bias.
>   Then at the balance let 's be mute, —
>   We never can adjust it, —
>   What 's done we partly may compute,
>   But know not what 's resisted."

Just about the same time with Cowper and Burns came
GEORGE CRABBE, whose first poem of any note, *The
Village*, was published a year or two before Cowper's *Task*. There is something in Crabbe which reminds
one of Cowper, and something, besides the title, which recalls Goldsmith's *Deserted Village*. He paints scenes of
nature, and domestic life among the poor. His *Tales* in
verse, which were taken from humble life, first gave him a
name among poets. Then he wrote *Tales of the Hall*, and
drew his characters from a higher rank ; but these were not
nearly so happy in their description as the first. They were
very much read and liked in the early part of this century ;
but I think Crabbe's day as a poet is past, and that he is
one whose name will remain in the archives of the poets
long after his poetry has ceased to be read. He was too
realistic to be a great poet ; every line he wrote was true to
nature. But Poetry must not be the naked Truth : Truth's
fair form must be veiled by Fancy, in order to enter the
ideal world of Poetry. Although there never was a measure
so well adapted to commonplace subjects as that he used,
yet in Crabbe's hands it sometimes is more than commonplace, it is comically matter-of-fact. This, in his best style,
is the opening of one of the Tales : —

> " Genius, thou gift of heaven, thou light divine,
>   Amid what dangers art thou doomed to shine !
>   Oft will the body's weakness check thy force,
>   Oft damp thy vigor and impede thy course ;
>   And trembling nerves compel thee to restrain
>   Thy nobler efforts, to contend with pain ;
>   Or Want (sad guest) will in thy presence come,
>   And breathe around her melancholy gloom ;
>   So life's low cares will thy proud thought confine,
>   And make her sufferings, her impatience, thine."

1754–1832

It is difficult to decide among what group of poets to class SAMUEL ROGERS. He was contemporary with the whole line, from Cowper almost to our own time. His first poems appeared when Cowper began to write; his *Pleasures of Memory* was published about the time Wordsworth was bringing out the **Lyrical Ballads**; his *Italy* was nearly contemporary with the death of Shelley; and he lived to see Tennyson called the greatest poet of this generation. At his hospitable home, the abode of good taste in literature and art, one might have met the finest wits of more than half this century.

1762-1855

Rogers's **Pleasures** *of Memory* is one of those didactic poems, such as Akenside's *Pleasures of the Imagination*, which appeared **fifty years earlier,** or Campbell's *Pleasures of Hope*, written a little later, in which the poet exalts one quality of the mind **over** all the others, and makes it the theme on which to **hang** his **musings** on nature **and human** life. A dozen lines of his apostrophe to Memory will suffice to show the poet's style :—

> " Hail, Memory, hail! in thy exhaustless mine
> From age to age unnumbered treasures shine!
> Thought and her shadowy brood thy call obey,
> And place and time **are** subject to thy sway!
> **Thy** pleasures most we feel when most alone,—
> **The** only pleasures we can call our own.
> Lighter than air, Hope's summer visions die,
> If but a fleeting cloud obscure the sky;
> **If** but a beam of sober reason play,
> **Lo,** Fancy's fairy frost-work **melts** away!
> **But can** the wiles of art, the grasp of power,
> **Snatch the rich relics of a** well-spent hour?
> **These, when** the trembling spirit wings her flight,
> Pour round her path a stream of living light,
> And gild those pure and perfect realms of rest
> Where virtue triumphs, and her sons are blest!"

This poem on *Italy* is **in** blank **verse,** with now and **then a** fragment in prose, **and is a** sort **of poetical** journal **of a** tour **in** Italy, in which he puts down descriptions of **places,** the impressions made **on** his **mind** by the new scenes, and various tales or adventures he met with in the

travels.   The story of Genevra, the bride who was hidden in
the oak chest on her bridal day, and was never found till
years after, when her skeleton was discovered in decayed
bridal robes, is one of the best-known episodes of the
poem.

These poets, Cowper, Burns, Crabbe, and Rogers, may be
said to stand midway between the old and the new in
poetry.   Crabbe and Rogers were not men to make any
revolution, and were poets who would take their color from
the greater geniuses around them ; but Cowper showed
signs of a change, while Burns's songs may be said to be the
first awaking of a new spirit in English poetry.   Although
he founded no school and made no revolution in literature,
he is the minstrel of a new order.   Hitherto the minstrel
sits in the court of the king, and sings only to the ear of
royalty.   He has gone to battle with the king's hosts, and
sometimes fallen in the king's hour of triumph.   But this
new minstrel, who sings songs to poverty and honest manhood, whose love is in no royal bowers, and whose triumphs
are not of war, — this is Robert Burns, the ploughman, the
minstrel of the people.

PART VI.

THE LAKE SCHOOL AND ITS CONTEMPORARIES.

1790 TO 1832.

INTRODUCTORY.

IN studying the progress of poetry from the earliest times, you will see that, like laws or government or religion, it is subject to many changes, and that there are revolutions in literature as well as in history. The poets of one period have all a certain likeness; even though each may be in his way original, his work will bear the mark of his own time, and follow the prevailing fashion. This continues till some man of great originality and power appears, who by his genius turns taste into new channels, and drawing after him a crowd who imitate him in his manner, founds what we call a *new school* of poetry.

We have seen how Pope had thus made a school, in which, as somebody says, " French taste was ruled by English understanding ;" and for almost a century his influence kept poetry in smooth, easy, flowing rhymes, but yet very artificial beside the naturalness of the earlier poets. Coleridge, of whom I am now going to speak, says, " The Pope school sacrificed the heart to the head ;" and that is, I think, as good a statement as can be made of it.

I pointed out in my last Talk that in Cowper there is an effort to make the head and the heart work together, and showed that in the Scotch poet Burns we have the first outburst of the real minstrel poet since the seventeenth century. But neither Cowper nor Burns was a man to found a school of poetry; they were only men who influenced it. Such work as Percy and Macpherson had done also aroused a taste for a new order of verse ; but the great departure from Pope, and the setting up of new ideas as the basis of poetry, was begun by what we call the *Lake School*. It is of this school that I am going to give you a brief account.

You remember I have said that Robert Burns began to write between two great revolutions, — the revolution of the people in America and that in France. In both these revolutions there was everything to stir up men's thoughts; and in the stirring up of thoughts there must always follow a stimulus to poetry, because poetry is only the highest thought of the most imaginative minds, inspired by the most stirring events. The thought underlying the American and French revolutions was that all men, even the poorest and lowest, have supreme rights, — rights to life, freedom, and to the largest amount of happiness possible. They were the same thoughts that the best minds in America put into our Declaration of Independence, — the same that Burns put into his *A Man's a Man for a' That*. It is plain — is it not? — that these thoughts, which in their birth shook governments, religion, and society as if they had been reeds in a tempest, must enter into and move the poet more than any other man of his time.

While these doctrines of liberty, equality, and brotherhood among men were being spread far and wide by the French Revolution, there were two young men in England in whose minds they took root. The first of these young men was WILLIAM WORDSWORTH, a student in Cambridge, who early in youth had felt himself consecrated as a poet; the other was SAMUEL TAYLOR COLERIDGE, who was in London at Christ's Hospital school, and who was also fired with a poetical ardor as intense as that of Wordsworth.

1770–1850

1772–1834

Of these two young men Wordsworth was the elder by two years. They had not met each other when the revolutionary fire broke out in them, although they afterwards became warm friends; but both had written verses on the French Revolution, and both were smitten with the same ardor for equal rights and human brotherhood.

Wordsworth left college in 1791 and went to France, then in the midst of her Revolution. I may as well tell you here that the horrors of bloodshed which followed the Revolution shook Wordsworth's faith in the ideas at work there, and led to a change in opinions which turned him from a violent democrat to a stanch English monarchist.

In the mean time Coleridge went to Cambridge, whence he ran away and came to London, with some vague idea of living by his pen. He soon grew so poor that, as a resource against starving, he enlisted as a private in the cavalry. He knew nothing of soldiering, and could not even sit a horse properly. When suddenly asked his name, he says, not wishing to give his real one, " I answered, Cumberback ; and verily my habits were so little equestrian that my horse, I doubt not, was of that opinion."

His friends found him out, and he was released from the service. Not long after, he met Robert Southey, a young man of nearly his own age, and of opinions after his own heart. Southey also was a radical, and a budding poet who had written in college a poem, *Wat Tyler*, which had been pronounced seditious and revolutionary. The two began a friendship natural to their age and their congenial opinions, — a friendship afterwards made stronger by their marriage with two sisters. They made a plan to emigrate to America and form a colony which should be established on the ideas of religion and government which they held sacred ; but this plan failed, and while Southey went to cool his youthful opinions in a tour in Europe, Coleridge went down to a little town in the south of England, where he met Wordsworth for the first time. They were both filled with the same ideas, and both had published a little volume of poetry ; it was natural that they should become warm friends, and that they should exert a great influence each on the other.

Their interchange of thought, their long rambles together in the lanes and woods of England, led to the publication of a little volume of poems, with a preface setting forth their theories about poetry, which finally gave them and those who agreed with them the name of the *Lake School*. They were given this name from the beautiful lake region of England in Cumberland and Westmoreland, where Wordsworth and Southey afterwards went to live. Coleridge never took up his residence there, although he was constantly going and coming, till, as Southey said, "his movements could no more be calculated than those of a comet."

The Lyrical Ballads — the first publication of the Lake School — was written on the theory that poetry might be the simple, natural language of men under the influence of strong feeling; that it should be free to treat the humblest incident of daily life; that the joys and sorrows of common men were the noblest motive for verse; and that a poet was no superhuman being, but "only a man speaking to other men." This statement of the poet's purpose was the keynote of the revolution in poetry; and you will see that it was a note in harmony with a spirit very different from, and more modern than, that of Pope, or any poet before his time.

To us there seems nothing very alarming or strange in this statement, and we have learned to love and reverence the poetry which it introduced. But the storm of criticism, of laughter, of contempt that was raised against these poets was tremendous. For nearly twenty years public opinion was dead set against them; and soon after the first little edition of five hundred copies was printed, the discouraged publisher gave Mr. Wordsworth his rights in the book as a worthless gift. But neither the men nor their poetry was to be crushed, and from year to year it grew more and more into favor, till at Wordsworth's death (he lived to be eighty) he knew himself judged by most as the great poet of his generation, and by many critics ranked as the sixth great poet in the line from Chaucer.[1]

Having thus given you, in as few words as I could, the story of the Lake School, let me say something of the poetry of the men who founded it.

[1] Chaucer, Spenser, Shakespeare, Milton, Pope, Wordsworth.

LI.

ON SAMUEL TAYLOR COLERIDGE.

OF Samuel Taylor Coleridge it is always to be said with regret that he did not accomplish as much or as good work as the world had a right to expect from such a man. He has left behind him comparatively little to prove that he might have been a great poet. I think this lack of accomplishment is due more to physical causes than mental ones. His father, a delicate, scholarly man, was over fifty when Coleridge was born, and from him came the inheritance of a weak body and nerves sensitive to pain. In very early childhood too much reading of fanciful stories filled Coleridge's brain with visions of spectres, and gave him a tendency to mope and dream. He was sent early to school, and was only ten when he went to Christ's Hospital, the famous Bluecoat School, where he gives, in one of his letters, this touching picture of his privations : —

"Our diet was very scanty, — every morning a bit of dry bread and some bad small-beer; every evening a larger piece of bread, and cheese or butter, whichever we liked. For dinner on Sunday, boiled beef and broth; Monday, bread and butter, and milk and water; Tuesday, roast mutton; Wednesday, bread and butter, and rice and milk; Thursday, boiled beef and broth; Friday, boiled mutton and broth; Saturday, bread and butter, and peas porridge. Our food was portioned, and, excepting on Wednesday, I never had enough. Our appetites were damped, never satisfied; and we had no vegetables."

In another letter he says, —

"Conceive what I must have been at fourteen. I was in a continual low fever; my whole being was, with eyes closed to every object of present sense, to crumple myself up in a sunny corner, and read, read, read, — fancy myself, on Robinson Crusoe's island, finding a mountain of plum-cake, and eating a room for myself, and then eating it into the shape of chairs and tables, hunger and fancy."

The penalty he had to pay for such an unwholesome and half-starved childhood appears early in Coleridge's life. He was hardly twenty-three when fits of torturing neuralgia seized him, for which he began to take opium, beginning with light doses, and increasing them till they grew into a habit of opium-eating which held him for years in its bonds, and was no doubt the cause that so many of his poetic designs were not carried out. We feel that if he had had the painstaking industry of Wordsworth, he too might have realized some of those glorious plans for poetry with which he fired the minds of his friend when they were wandering together over the fields and along the brooks of Somerset. As it is, Wordsworth took the place at the head of the school which Coleridge more than any other inspired. In literature we see Coleridge as one of the powers standing behind those who climb to the throne.

The Lyrical Ballads had been planned by the two poets to consist of two kinds of poetry: in one, the incidents were to be of a supernatural, imaginative kind; the other was to be on subjects drawn from ordinary life, such incidents and characters as are to be found in any village. It was arranged that Coleridge should take the supernatural, and Wordsworth the simple subjects. They wandered about the fields and lanes of Somersetshire, following the course of woodland brooks, laying their poetical plans. Already their radical opinions, their former sympathy with the French Revolution, had come to the ears of friends of the government, and a spy was sent down to watch these young men, who, strolling about, note-book and pencil in hand, were suspected of mapping out the land to give it to foreign enemies. But although the spy listened closely, he could hear nothing but a great deal of talk about a certain *Spynosy*, which the detective, who was blessed with an ample organ of smell, supposed was a name given to him. This was all the treason he could report on his return to London. The two friends had already lost their ardor for republicanism and the French Revolution, and were busy discussing German philosophy; and it was the great

Spinoza whose name the detective had taken to mean himself.

From what I have said of Coleridge's habits of work, you will not be surprised to find that when the *Lyrical Ballads* were to go to press, and Wordsworth had twenty-two poems ready, Coleridge had only the *Ancient Mariner* and a part of the weird poem of *Christabel*, which was never finished. Hazlitt says that the *Ancient Mariner* is the only one of Coleridge's poems which he should like to put into any person's hands whom he wished to impress favorably with his great powers. No doubt he is right ; and this one poem is great enough for one reputation. It is a unique poem in our literature ; and to those who feel its weird fascination it exercises a sway over the imagination which very few poems in our language can exercise.

Christabel remains a fragment, although Coleridge intended to finish it. He added a second part to it after it was first published, of which he said : " As in my first part I had the whole present to my mind, with the wholeness no less than the loveliness of a vision, I trust that I shall be yet able to embody in verse the three parts yet to come." It is characteristic of Coleridge that the mood for which he waited never came, and that to the last we have only the fragment. The poem of *Genevieve*, or *Love*, was written as an introduction to a longer poem, which was planned, but never written. It is, however, complete in itself, an exquisite little love-story in verse, and I quote it entire :—

LOVE.

All thoughts, all passions, all delights,
Whatever stirs this mortal frame,
All are but ministers of Love,
    And feed his sacred flame.

Oft in my waking dreams do I
Live o'er again that happy hour
When, midway on the mount, I lay
    Beside the ruined tower.

The moonshine, stealing o'er the scene,
Had blended with the lights of eve;
And she was there, my hope, my joy,
My own dear Genevieve!

She leaned against the armed man,
The statue of the arméd knight;
She stood and listened to my lay
Amid the lingering light.

Few sorrows hath she of her own,
My hope! my joy! my Genevieve!
She loves me best whene'er I sing
The songs that make her grieve.

I played a soft and doleful air,
I sang an old and moving story, —
An old, rude song that suited well
That ruin wild and hoary.

She listened with a flitting blush,
With downcast eyes and modest grace;
For well she knew I could not choose
But gaze upon her face.

I told her of the knight that wore
Upon his shield a burning brand,
And that for ten long years he wooed
The lady of the land.

I told her how he pined; and ah!
The deep, the low, the pleading tone
With which I sang another's love
Interpreted my own.

She listened with a flitting blush,
With downcast eyes and modest grace;
And she forgave me that I gazed
Too fondly on her face.

But when I told the cruel scorn
That crazed that bold and lovely knight,
And that he crossed the mountain-woods,
Nor rested day nor night;

That sometimes from the savage den,
And sometimes from the darksome shade,
And sometimes starting up at once
In green and sunny glade,

There came and looked him in the face
An angel beautiful and bright;
And that he knew it was a fiend,
       This miserable knight!

And that, unknowing what he did,
He leaped amid a murderous band,
And saved from outrage worse than death
       The lady of the land;

And how she wept, and clasped his knees,
And how she tended him in vain,
And ever strove to expiate
       The scorn that crazed his brain;

And that she nursed him in a cave,
And how his madness went away,
When on the yellow forest leaves
       A dying man he lay;

His dying words — But when I reached
That tenderest strain of all the ditty,
My faltering voice and pausing harp
       Disturbed her soul with pity!

All impulses of soul and sense
Had thrilled my guileless Genevieve, —
The music and the doleful tale,
       The rich and balmy eve;

And hopes, and fears that kindle hope,
An undistinguishable throng,
And gentle wishes long subdued,
       Subdued and cherished long!

She wept with pity and delight,
She blushed with love and virgin shame;
And like the murmur of a dream
       I heard her breathe my name.

Her bosom heaved; she stept aside,
As conscious of my look she stept;
Then suddenly, with timorous eye,
       She fled to me and wept.

She half enclosed me with her arms,
She pressed me with a meek embrace;
Then, bending back her head, looked up
       And gazed upon my face.

T was partly love, and partly fear,
And partly 't was a bashful art,
That I might rather feel than see
    The swelling of her heart.

I calmed her fears, and she was calm,
And told her love with virgin pride ;
And so I won my Genevieve,
    My bright and beauteous bride.

Coleridge wrote the dramatic poems *Remorse, Zapolya,* and the *Fall of Robespierre.* His finest dramatic work was in the translation of Schiller's *Wallenstein,* which is so well done that it has the value of an original drama in English.

Of all the Lake School, Coleridge seems to me to have been most of a poet by nature. "Logician ! Metaphysician ! Bard !" as his friend Charles Lamb addresses him, I can hardly limit my conception of what he might have been if, freed from the bondage of opium, he had only had the power of patient, persistent work in one direction. But it is work and patience against the world ; and without these, allied to genius, even genius itself can give nothing to the future.

LII.

On William Wordsworth and Robert Southey.

NEVER was the judgment of the critics more wholly overturned than in the case of William Wordsworth. He began by being laughed at ; he lived to see his name set among the great poets, and died at eighty with the full knowledge that his fame was waxing greater and greater.

No doubt he was helped, even in his darkest hour, by his belief in himself. He set out early in life to be a great poet ; he adopted it as a sacred profession, — one for which Nature had chosen him. He had fixed ideas about subjects for poetry, and the way these subjects should be handled.

It did not disturb him that his ideas were different from the poets who had come before him. It did not discourage him that his first poems were laughed at. There never was a poet who started with a clearer sense of what he meant to do as a poet, with a higher appreciation of his calling, or with a fuller belief in his own powers. This made it easy for him to wait till the world could see what he saw, and he waited without anxiety or trouble about the result.

Fortunately he was in the right path. He had chosen to be the poet of humanity; all that he wrote and felt was in harmony with the thought and feeling of the new age. Thus he could not speak far wide of his mark, and sooner or later he was sure to reach that heart to which he spoke.

His faults — and I think his best lover will admit faults in him — come from some of the very causes that make him great. Believing firmly in himself as a poet, working upon a theory which was exact and proportioned in his own mind, there is often something a little business-like in his manner as a poet. He finds poetical capital in all things : a tour on the Continent, a mountain ascent, a walk in the garden, — all furnish him song or sonnet. Having made up his mind that the natural, simple scenes of human life are the grandest themes for poetry, he finds nothing too trivial, and he sometimes tries to exalt things that cannot be lifted from the region of commonplace. It is well for genius when it is not moody, and can work patiently ; but we do not want to make it a common draught-horse.

I am sure that, with the best disposition to admire Wordsworth, the reader with a strong imagination will find him an unequal poet. After he has carried you away up with a flight like an eagle, he drops you like a stone. In reading his long poems you are constantly dropped thus. The divine fire in the poet never quite goes out ; that spirit which in youth whirled him about in such ardor of enthusiasm for liberty, equality, and fraternity, controls him in nobler fashion as he grows older and calmer ; but with all this there is a prosaic stratum in him, like underlying granite, which will crop out.

Thus, those who laughed at the *Lyrical Ballads* could always find reason for laughter. Sometimes the simplicity of these tales of sorrow or pleasure win the heart, but sometimes they touch the sense of the ludicrous. The long ballad called *Peter Bell* contains some beautiful lines. What a beautiful passage this is, which describes Peter Bell's dulness to all the sweet influences of Nature : —

> " He roved among the vales and streams
> In the green wood and hollow dell ;
> They were his dwellings night and day,
> But Nature ne'er could find the way
> Into the heart of Peter Bell.
>
> " In vain, through every changeful **year,**
> Did Nature lead him as before ;
> A primrose by a river's brim
> A yellow primrose was to him,
> And it was **nothing** more.
> .   .   .   .
>
> " In vain through water, earth, and air
> The soul of happy sound was spread,
> When Peter, on some April morn,
> Beneath the broom and budding thorn,
> Made the warm earth his lazy bed.
>
> " At noon, when by the forest's edge
> He lay beneath the branches high,
> The soft blue sky did never melt
> Into his heart, he never felt
> The witchery of the soft blue sky."

But to make the chief incident of this poem the sufferings of a jackass, is rather a dangerous experiment, even with readers of a very humane disposition. Here is a stanza or two where Peter has beaten the poor beast till it falls exhausted :—

> " As gently on his side he **fell,**
> And by the river's brink **did lie ;**
> And while he lay like one **that** mourned,
> The patient beast on Peter turned
> A shining hazel **eye.**

> "'T was **but one mild,** reproachful look,
> A look more tender than severe;
>   And straight **in sorrow, not** in dread,
>   He turned the eyeball **in his** head
> Towards the smooth **river** deep and clear.

> " Upon the beast the sapling rings,
> His lank sides heaved, his limbs they stirred;
>   He gave a groan, and then another,
>   Of that which went before the brother;
> And then he gave a third."

Now this rhyming, which lasts through twenty stanzas, is not poetry, although it is very good humanity.

Wordsworth's epic poem, *The Excursion*, has the' same **fault of inequality.** But it is **so** magnificent in its scope, **so** noble in its flights, that one skips the prosy places, almost unheeding them. **Here at last was** a grand epic which did not celebrate war, **nor the deeds of** Homeric heroes; **which** did **not dwell in realms peopled by imaginary creatures;** which neither soared **to heaven nor** dived to hell. In *The Excursion* the poet led into fields and villages, **among the** humblest abodes of men, learning lessons of human brotherhood in his course.

Wordsworth's shorter poems, many **of them,** are free **from** any of the faults I have hinted at. Some are nearly perfect; his sonnets, many of them, sound as if they had come from the bottom of the human heart, — as this, which he writes **on a** view of London at sunrise : —

> " Earth has not anything to show more fair :
> Dull would he be of soul who could pass by
> A sight so touching in its majesty :
> This city now doth like a garment wear
> The beauty of the morning : silent, bare,
> Ships, towers, domes, theatres, and temples lie
> Open unto the fields and to **the sky,**
> All bright and glittering **in the smokeless air.**
> Never did sun more beautifully steep,
> In his first splendor, valley, rock, or hill;
> Ne'er saw I, never felt, a calm so deep.
> The river glideth at his own sweet will;
> Dear God ! the very houses seem asleep,
> And all that mighty heart is lying still."

A fit tribute to Milton was this sonnet from Wordsworth :

> " Milton, thou shouldst be living at this hour ;
> England hath need of thee ; she is a fen
> Of stagnant waters ; altar, sword, and pen,
> Fireside, the heroic wealth of hall and bower,
> Have forfeited their ancient English dower
> Of inward happiness. We are selfish men.
> Oh, raise us up, return to us again,
> And give us manners, virtue, freedom, power.
> Thy soul was like a star, and dwelt apart ;
> Thou hadst a voice whose sound was like the sea ;
> Pure as the naked heaven, majestic, free,
> So didst thou travel on life's common way,
> In cheerful godliness ; and yet thy heart
> The lowliest duties on herself did lay."

Many of his short songs have the same purity and grandeur as these sonnets. And the simplest subjects, — a flower, a bird, an incident of humble life, — no one else has treated such with the sympathy Wordsworth shows.

And what shall I say of the ode, *Intimations of Immortality*, which is enough for any one poet to have written? This, in my mind, both in form and matter, is to be set far above that ode of Dryden's which he calls the best in the language : —

> " There was a time when meadow, grove, and stream,
> The earth, and every common sight,
> To me did seem
> Apparelled in celestial light,
> The glory and the freshness of a dream.
> It is not now as it has been of yore ; —
> Turn whereso'er I may,
> By night or day,
> The things which I have seen, I now can see no more.
>
> " Our birth is but a sleep and a forgetting :
> The soul that rises with us, our life's star,
> Hath had elsewhere its setting,
> And cometh from afar ;
> Not in entire forgetfulness,
> And not in utter nakedness,
> But trailing clouds of glory, do we come
> From God, who is our home.
> Heaven lies about us in our infancy !

" Shades of the prison-house begin to close
      Upon the growing boy,
But he beholds the light, and whence it flows, —
      He sees it in his joy;
The youth, who daily farther from the east
      Must travel, still is Nature's priest,
        And by the vision splendid
        Is on his way attended;
At length the man perceives it die away,
And fade into the light of common day.

  .   .   .   .

    " Oh, joy! that in our embers
      Is something that doth live,
    That Nature yet remembers
      What was so fugitive!
The thought of our past years in me doth breed
Perpetual benedictions, not indeed
For that which is more worthy to be blest, —
Delight and liberty, the simple creed
Of childhood, whether busy or at rest,
With new-fledged hope still fluttering in his breast;
      Not for these I raise
      The song of thanks and praise;
    But for those obstinate questionings
    Of sense and outward things,
    Fallings from us, vanishings;
    Blank misgivings of a creature
Moving about in worlds not realized,
High instincts, before which our moral nature
Did tremble like a guilty thing surprised:
    But for those first affections,
    Those shadowy recollections,
      Which, be they what they may,
Are yet the fountain light of all our day,
Are yet a master light of all our seeing,
  Uphold us, cherish, and have power to make
Our noisy years seem moments in the being
Of the eternal silence; truths that wake
      To perish never;
Which neither listlessness, nor mad endeavor,
      Nor man nor boy,
Nor all that is at enmity with joy,
Can utterly abolish or destroy!
  Hence in a season of calm weather,
    Though inland far we be,
Our souls have sight of that immortal sea
    Which brought us hither;
    Can in a moment travel thither,

And see the children sport upon the shore,
And hear the mighty waters rolling ever more."

A recent English philosopher, John Stuart Mill, says that in a period of great depression he tried poetry as a resource, and found most of all a balm and healing in Wordsworth. He afterwards says he believes Wordsworth to be the true poet of unpoetic natures, — for those of quiet, thoughtful tastes, without much cultivation of the imagination or the emotions.

Matthew Arnold, a modern critic and poet too, exalts Wordsworth much higher than Mill did. I am, myself, inclined to think that Wordsworth is not the poet for youth. One grows to love him. The ardor and fiery imagination of youth is rarely satisfied with him; he chimes in with the thoughts and aspirations of a maturer age.

ROBERT SOUTHEY, who is generally classed as the third in this trio of poets, hardly followed the theory of the Lake School in his choice of subjects, for they do not, as a rule, keep within the common interests of human life. His subjects are largely supernatural. His poem of *Roderick* is an old Gothic legend; *Madoc* was taken from British history; *Thalaba* is an Arabian tale; and *Kehama* is Hindoo in origin. Even his shorter poems, many of them tales told in verse, have a weird element which is more in keeping with the *Ancient Mariner* than anything Wordsworth wrote. I quote one short story in verse from Southey for the touch of humor in it, which gives variety to my Talk. It is not specially in illustration of Southey's style; that you must study in his long poems, *Thalaba* or *Roderick*. This is a simple ballad, called —

THE WELL OF ST. KEYNE.

A well there is in the west country,
  And a clearer one never was seen ,
There is not a wife in the west country
  But has heard of the well of St. Keyne.

An oak and an elm tree stand beside,
　And behind does an ash-tree grow,
And a willow from the bank above
　Droops to the water below.

A traveller came to the well of St. **Keyne,**
　Joyfully he drew nigh,
For from cock-crow he had been travelling,
　And there was not a cloud in the sky.

He drank of the water so cool and clear,
　For thirsty and hot was **he,**
And he sat down upon the **bank,**
　Under the willow-tree.

There came a man from a house hard by,
　At the well to fill his pail ;
On the well-side he rested it,
　And he bade the stranger hail.

" Now, **art thou a bachelor, stranger ?** " quoth he,
　" For **an** if thou **hast a wife,**
The happiest draught thou hast drunk this day
　That ever thou didst in **thy life."**

" Or has thy good woman, if one thou hast,
　Ever here in Cornwall been ?
For an if she have, I 'll venture my life,
　She has drunk of the well of St. Keyne."

" I have left a good woman who never was **here,"**
　The stranger he made reply ;
" But that my draught should be the better for that,
　I pray you answer me why."

" St. Keyne," quoth the Cornishman, " many a time
　Drank of this crystal well ;
And before the angel summoned her,
　She laid on the water a spell.

" If the husband, of this gifted well
　Should drink before his wife,
A happy man thenceforth is he,
　For he shall be master for life.

" But if the wife should drink of it first,
　God help the husband then ! "
The stranger stooped to the well of St. Keyne,
　And drank of the **water again.**

"You drank of the well, I warrant, betimes,"
    He to the Cornishman said ;
But the Cornishman smiled as the stranger spake,
    And sheepishly shook his head.

"I hastened, as soon as the wedding was done,
    And left my wife in the porch ;
But i' faith she had been wiser than me,
    For she took a bottle to church."

Like Wordsworth, Southey was very industrious; he worked in a great many fields, — history, biography, essays, and fiction. At the outset of his literary career he was poor, but by his work accumulated a fair fortune and collected a fine library. He was as much a radical as Coleridge had been in youth, but became more conservative than either of his friends, and bitterly criticised any difference from the opinions he learned to hold.

It is to be said of the Lake Poets that they were all men of pure lives ; strict adherents to principle, whichever way the vane of opinion was set ; good husbands, fathers, and friends. In bringing back some of the virtues of an early age of poetry, they brought back none of the vices of that day, and nothing in their career marks the literary man as a Bohemian or social outlaw.

LIII.

ON THOMAS CAMPBELL AND TOM MOORE.

JUST about the time the Lake Poets were making their first stir in the world of books, THOMAS CAMPBELL, who was a countryman of Robert Burns, first appeared in print. He was a youthful poet, — only twenty-two, — and his poem, *The Pleasures of Hope*, was written in that tiresome old rhyming measure used so continually since Dryden and Pope, which the Lake School did so much towards abolishing. *The Pleasures of Hope* proved a very popular poem, however, and while Wordsworth's

1777-1844

poems fell dead from the press, Campbell's **sold four** editions in less than a year.

There **are** strong passages in *The Pleasures of Hope*, although, as a whole, I think **it dull reading.** The best lines in it are those which burn with generous anger against the wrongs Poland had suffered when divided among her oppressors and crushed out of being as a nation. Campbell's best poems are his shorter ones, — *The Mariners of England, Battle of the Baltic, Hohenlinden, The Exile of Erin,* and the like. Every schoolboy knows these, as well as *Lochiel's Warning, O'Connor's Child,* and *Lord Ullin's Daughter,* which are founded on old stories of the Border. In these shorter songs he has escaped from the bonds of that see-saw rhyme, and his songs and ballads are full of spirit, **with a ring in the lines** which is like a bugle-sound. You can hear this **in** *Ye Mariners of England,* which begins, —

> " Ye mariners of England
>   That guard our native seas,
>   Whose flag has braved, **a** thousand years,
>   The battle and the breeze !
>   Your glorious standard launch again
>   To match another foe,
>   And sweep through the deep
>   While the stormy winds do blow ;
>   While the battle rages loud and long,
>   And the stormy winds do blow."

Still more **like** martial music is *The Battle of the Baltic :*

> "Of Nelson and the North,
>   **Sing the glorious** day's renown,
>   **When to battle fierce** came forth
>   **All** the might of Denmark's crown,
>   And her arms along the deep proudly shone ;
>   By each gun **the** lighted brand
>   In a bold, determined hand,
>   And the prince of all the land
>   Led them **on.**

> " **Like** leviathans afloat
>   Lay their bulwarks on the brine,
>   While the sign of battle flew
>   On the lofty British line :

It was ten of April morn by the chime;
As they drifted on their path
There was silence deep as death,
And the boldest held his breath
For a time.

" But the might of England flushed
To anticipate the scene;
And her van the fleeter rushed
O'er the deadly space between.
' Hearts of oak ! ' our captains cried, when each gun
From its adamantine lips
Spread a death-shade round the ships,
Like the hurricane eclipse
Of the sun.

" Again! again ! again !
And the havoc did not slack,
Till a feeble cheer the Dane
To our cheering sent us back;
Their shots along the deep slowly boom;
Then ceased, — and all is wail
As they strike the shattered sail;
Or, in conflagration pale,
Light the gloom.

" Out spoke the victor then,
As he hailed them o'er the wave :
' Ye are brothers, ye are men !
And we conquer but to save !
So peace instead of death let us bring;
But yield, proud foe, thy fleet,
With the crews, at England's feet,
And make submission meet
To our King.'

" Then Denmark blessed our chief
That he gave her wounds repose;
And the sounds of joy and grief
From her people wildly rose
As Death withdrew his shades from the day;
While the sun looked smiling bright
O'er a wide and woful sight,
Where the fires of funeral light
Died away.

" Now joy, Old England, raise !
For the tidings of thy might,

By the festal cities' blaze,
Whilst the wine-cup shines in **light**;
And yet, amidst that **joy and uproar,**
Let us think of **them that sleep**
Full many a fathom deep,
By thy wild and stormy steep,
Elsinore!''

Such pieces as these, vigorous and dramatic, are admirably adapted for recitation; and hence many of Campbell's minor poems have had wide circulation in reading-books and collections of poetry.

After publishing a volume of short poems, Campbell wrote his *Gertrude of Wyoming, a Tale of Pennsylvania.* It was written **on** a tragedy of the war of the American Revolution, **in which a savage** band, more **than** half of them Indians, **swept down on** a little settlement **in the** valley of the Wyoming, and **massacred the** villagers, men, women, and babes, without **mercy.** **It was** a shameful **and** bloodthirsty murder, **and** Campbell, whose sympathies were always passionately on **the** side **of humanity, put his** heart into the poem. The heroine is **Gertrude, who, mur-** dered by the enemy, dies in her husband's arms. **You will see** that the poem is in the Spenserian measure : —

"A scene of death! where fires beneath the sun,
And blended arms and white pavilions glow;
And for the business of destruction done,
Its requiem the war-horn seemed to blow;
There, sad spectatress of her country's woe,
The lovely Gertrude, safe from present harm,
Had **laid** her **cheek** and clasped her hands of snow
On **W**aldegrave's shoulder, half within his arm
Enclosed, that felt her heart and hushed its wild alarm.

"But short that contemplation, — sad **and short**
The pause to bid each much-loved scene **adieu,**
Beneath the very shadow of the fort,
Where friendly swords were drawn and **banners flew ;**
Ah! **who** could deem that foot of Indian crew
Was **near**? yet there, with lust of murderous deeds,
Gleamed, like a basilisk from woods in view,
The ambushed foeman's eye ; his volley speeds,
And Albert, Albert falls! **the dear** old father bleeds!

"And, tranced in giddy horror, Gertrude swooned;
　Yet while she clasps him lifeless to her zone,
　Say, burst they borrowed from her father's wound
　These drops? O God, the life-blood is her own!
　And faltering on her Waldegrave's bosom thrown,
　'Weep not, O love!' she cries, 'to see me bleed;
　Thee, Gertrude's sad survivor, thee alone
　Heaven's peace commiserate! for scarce I heed
These wounds; yet thee to leave is death, is death indeed!

"'Clasp me a little longer on the brink
　Of fate, while I can feel thy dear caress;
　And when this heart hath ceased to beat, oh, think,
　And let it mitigate thy woe's excess,
　That thou hast been to me all tenderness,
　And friend to more than human friendship just.
　Oh! by that retrospect of happiness,
　And by the hopes of an immortal trust,
God shall assuage thy pangs — when I am laid in dust!

"'Go, Henry, go not back when I depart, —
　The scene thy bursting tears too deep will move, —
　Where my dear father took thee to his heart,
　And Gertrude thought it ecstasy to rove
　With thee, as with an angel, through the grove
　Of peace, imagining her lot was cast
　In heaven; for ours was not like earthly love.
　And must this parting be our very last?
No! I shall love thee still, when death itself is past.'

　　　.　　　.　　　.　　　.　　　.　　　.

"Hushed were his Gertrude's lips, but still their bland
　And beautiful expression seemed to melt
　With love that could not die; and still his hand
　She presses to the heart no more that felt.
　Ah, heart! where once each fond affection dwelt,
　And features yet that spoke a soul more fair.
　Mute, gazing, agonizing as he knelt,
　Of them that stood encircling his despair
He heard some friendly words, but knew not what they were."

Campbell settled in Sydenham, and there edited for ten
years *The Metropolitan Magazine*, in which appeared many
of his own poems.　Another notable contributor to this review in its later days was a poet who had risen to fame just
1779-1852　about the same time as Campbell.　This was
　　　　　　Thomas Moore, a native of Ireland, whose *Irish
Melodies*, sung by himself to the airs of his own country,

were for many years the delight of fashionable circles in London.

There is something very winning about Tom Moore, although he had a great many vanities, and more faults than some men who are not so agreeable. He was always warm-hearted and affectionate; through all changes of scenes or fortune he never neglected his good mother in Ireland, nor failed in the midst of all his social triumphs to write to her letters as full of tenderness and spirits as if he were still a boy at her knee. He was always the loving husband of his " dearest Bessie," who was herself the most devoted and unselfish of wives; and these virtues cover much of the light-hearted selfishness and the eager vanity with which he sought the society of the rich and great, who petted him for his charming manners and accomplishments.

Moore was born in Dublin with no poetical surroundings, for his parents kept a grocery and liquor shop; but he took to poetry by instinct, and began to rhyme as early as Pope did. At nineteen he went to London with some translations from the Greek poet Anacreon, which he published by subscription and dedicated to the Prince of Wales. These made him at once known as a poet. A few years later he received an appointment of some kind at the Bermuda Islands, and went abroad, making a tour on his return through the United States and Canada. He was gone in all fourteen months, and published his poems soon after his return. Some of his American poems are among his best, — *The Lake of the Dismal Swamp* and *A Canadian Boat-Song.*

He was a little over thirty when he married his dear Bessy, and settled down in Wiltshire, far enough from London so that he could not be diverted from work by the constant call of society. Here he arranged with a publisher to furnish the *Irish Melodies* at five hundred pounds a year. Thus these songs, which of all literary productions sound the most spontaneous, were really made to order. The *Melodies* were written to national airs of Ireland, Moore writing the verses and adapting the music to

them.   His own feeling and taste for music helped him,
and one of their great charms was in the perfect fitness of
words to music; it must have been a treat to hear Moore
sing them.   Campbell said one could never appreciate
Moore's *Melodies* till he had heard Moore sing them.
They were sung everywhere, from the palaces of the English aristocracy to the highways of Ireland, where even the
Irish boy who drove the jaunting-car knew the best of them
by heart.   Moore was fêted and caressed by the great people in London, and wherever he went the doors of the best
houses swung open for him.   Holland House, the home of
Lord and Lady Holland, which for so many years was the
headquarters of literary men, artists, and agreeable people
of all sorts, was one of Moore's favorite visiting places in
London, and the walls of its drawing-rooms resounded
again and again to his voice as he sung his favorite songs.

The *Irish Melodies* are not all patriotic in sentiment,
although many of the best are so.   They are inspired by
various motives, and among them are love-songs, drinking-
songs, songs of country, songs of melancholy, and songs of
Nature.   *The Harp that once through Tara's Halls; Believe me, if all those Endearing Young Charms; Oh, blame
not the Bard*, are as familiar as household words wherever
our language is sung.   The following seems to me very
characteristic in its mixture of good-fellowship and real
feeling, which were a part of Moore's own nature : —

'Farewell! but whenever you welcome the hour
  That awakens the night-song of mirth in your bower,
  Then think of the friend who once welcomed it too,
  And forgot his own griefs to be happy with you.
  His griefs may return, not a hope may remain
  Of the few that have brightened his pathway of pain ;
  But he ne'er will forget the short vision that threw
  Its enchantment around him while lingering with you.

"And still on that evening, when pleasure fills up
  To the highest top sparkle each heart and each cup,
  Where'er my path lies, be it gloomy or bright,
  My soul, happy friends, shall be with you that night,
  Shall join in your revels, your sports, and your wiles,
  And return to me beaming all o'er with your smiles,

Too blest if it tells me that 'mid the gay cheer
Some kind voice had murmured, 'I wish he were here!'

"Let Fate do her worst; there are relics of joy,
  Bright dreams of the past, which she cannot destroy,
  Which come in the night-time of sorrow and care,
  And bring back the features that joy used to wear.
  Long, long, be my heart with such memories filled,
  Like the vase in which roses have once been distilled;
  You may break, you may shatter, the vase if you will,
  But the scent of the roses will hang round it still."

Another song, to his Country's Harp, is exquisite in its expression of the patriotic feeling which forms the basis of the *Melodies* : —

"Dear Harp of my Country! in darkness I found thee,
  The cold chain of silence had hung o'er thee long,
  When proudly, my own Island Harp, I unbound thee,
  And gave all thy chords to light, freedom, and song!
  The warm lay of love, and the light note of gladness,
  Have wakened thy fondest, thy liveliest thrill!
  But so oft hast thou echoed the deep sigh of sadness
  That e'en in thy mirth it will steal from thee still.

"Dear Harp of my Country! farewell to thy numbers,
  This sweet wreath of song is the last we shall twine;
  Go, sleep with the sunshine of Fame on thy slumbers,
  Till touched by some hand less unworthy than mine.
  If the pulse of the patriot, soldier, or lover
  Have throbbed at our lay, 't is thy glory alone;
  It was but the wind, passing heedlessly over,
  And all the wild sweetness I waked was thy own."

It was during his success with the songs, which appeared in numbers, that Moore was asked to write an Eastern poem, — a kind of work for which his lavish imagination and tropical style was very well fitted. He was a good student as well as poet, and studied India in her legends, poetry, history, and in the accounts of travellers who had journeyed thither. The result was *Lalla Rookh*, the best known of his long poems. It consists of four tales, — *The Veiled Prophet of Khorassan*, *The Fire-Worshippers*, *Paradise and the Peri*, and *The Light of the Harem*, — woven together by a tissue of prose which tells the love-story of *Lalla Rookh*.

Even in a subject so far away from Ireland as this poem of the East, we can see that Moore's national feeling was so strong that he was always most of a poet when that feeling was free to speak. In *The Fire-Worshippers* he puts his feeling for his own country into the guise of sympathy for a persecuted race, the last of the Persian Ghebers; and we can see that Iran[1] became Erin to him, by less than the change of a letter. Thus, of all the tales, *The Fire-Worshippers* has the most poetic fervor. Let us quote a few passages to show this: —

> "The morn has risen clear and calm,
>   And o'er the green sea palely shines,
> Revealing Bahrein's groves of palm,
>   And lighting Kishma's amber vines.
> Fresh smell the shores of Araby,
>   While breezes from the Indian sea
> Blow round Selama's sainted cape,
>   And curl the shining flood beneath,
> Whose waves are rich with many a grape
>   And cocoa-nut and flowery wreath,
> Which pious seamen as they passed
>   Had toward that holy headland cast, —
> Oblations to the Genii there,
> For gentle skies and breezes fair!
> The nightingale now bends her flight
> From the high trees where all the night
> She sung so sweet, with none to listen;
> And hides her from the morning star
> Where thickets of pomegranate glisten
> In the clear dawn, — bespangled o'er
> With dew, whose night-drops would not stain
> The best and brighest scimetar
> That ever youthful sultan wore,
> On the first morning of his reign.

> "And see, that Sun himself! — on wings
> Of glory up the east he springs.
> Angel of light! who from the time
> Those heavens began their march sublime,
> Hath first of all the starry choir
> Trod in his Maker's steps of fire.
> Where are the days, thou wondrous sphere,
> When Iran, like a sunflower, turned
> To meet that eye where'er it burned?

[1] The ancient name of Persia.

When from the banks of Bendemeer
To the nut-groves of Samarcand,
Thy temples flamed o'er all the land, —
Where are they?   Ask the shades of them
Who on Cadessia's bloody plains
Saw fierce invaders pluck the gem
From Iran's broken diadem,
And bind her ancient faith in chains,
And the poor exile, cast alone
On foreign shores, unloved, unknown,
Beyond the Caspian's iron gates,
Or in the snowy Mossian mountains,
Far from his beauteous land of dates,
Her jasmine bowers and sunny fountains!
Yet happier so than if he trod
His own beloved but blighted sod,
Beneath a despot stranger's nod!
Oh, he would rather houseless roam
Where freedom and his God may lead,
Than be the sleekest slave at home
That crouches to the conqueror's creed!
Is Iran's pride then gone forever,
Quenched with the flame in Mithra's caves?
No, — she has sons that never, never,
Will stoop to be the Moslem's slaves,
While heaven has light or earth has graves.
Spirits of fire, that brood not long,
But flash resentment back for wrong,
And hearts where slow, but deep, the seeds
Of vengeance ripen into deeds,
Till in some treacherous hour of calm
They burst, like Zeilan's giant palm,
Whose buds fly open with a sound
That shakes the pygmy forests round.

        .   .   .

" Yea Emir, he who scaled thy tower   . .
Is one of many, brave as he,
Who loathe thy haughty race and thee,
Who, though they know the strife is vain,
Who, though they know the riven chain
Snaps but to enter in the heart
Of him who rends its links apart,
Yet dare the issue, blest to be,
Even for one bleeding moment, free,
And die in pangs of liberty!

        .   .   .

" Yet here, even here, a sacred band,
Ay, in the portal of that land,

Thou, Arab, dar'st to call thine own,
Their spears across thy path have thrown;
Here, ere the winds half winged thee o'er,
Rebellion braved thee from the shore.
Rebellion! foul, dishonoring word,
Whose wrongful blight so oft has stained
The holiest cause that tongue or sword
Of mortal ever lost or gained;
How many a spirit, born to bless,
Hath sunk beneath that withering name
Whom but a day's, an hour's success,
Had wafted to eternal fame!"

Moore was so popular in his own time that it is not strange there has been a change in the feeling towards him. There is a disposition nowadays to think of him only as a poet of light fancies, rather fit for youth. But this is not altogether just. Besides his fancy and grace, he has much genuine feeling whenever his heart speaks, and his verse is so musical and flowing that it must always place him in a high rank as a poet. He worked conscientiously, and did a great deal of work. Besides many poems which I have not mentioned, he wrote several prose works of fiction and biography, and kept faithfully his own Memoirs, which are very entertaining gossip of the times.

LIV.

ON SIR WALTER SCOTT AND LORD BYRON.

IT is WALTER SCOTT the poet of whom I speak here. His work as novelist I shall consider later. Scott is the first poet whose name meets us as we cross the threshold of our own century. He published the *Lay of the Last Minstrel* in 1805. His first literary work was a translation of some German ballads, and a collection of ballads entitled *Minstrelsy of the Scotch Border*. He was always very fond of ballads, and it is thought that much reading of Percy's *Reliques* when a boy tended to make him a poet.

1771-1832

The *Lay of the Last Minstrel,* which was a weird sort of story in rhyme told by an old Border minstrel, made Scott known as a poet, and gained him admiring readers everywhere. We are sure that the critics who praised it, some of them the very men who had abused Coleridge and Wordsworth, never would have seen the merit of Scott so clearly if the writings of the Lake School had not opened their minds and made them more hospitable to what was new. In that half-finished story of *Christabel,* which Coleridge's mental indolence prevented him from finishing, Scott saw how effective such a measure might be made in a tale in verse, and set his Minstrel's Lay to a similar tune.

His poems followed each other quickly,—*Marmion, The Lady of the Lake, The Vision of Roderick,* and others, —till about 1817, when he ceased to write poetry. He had found a new gift in himself, and it is as Scott the novelist that he will be known longest and best. His poetry is vigorous, always pure and wholesome, like a breeze from his own Highlands. He is best in strong scenes, in battle descriptions, or in rough hand-to-hand encounters between sturdy foes. In the fight between Fitz-James and Roderick Dhu in *The Lady of the Lake,* or the description of the Battle of Bannockburn in *The Lord of the Isles,* which I give you here, you get an idea of his strength.

> " Now onward and in open view
> The countless ranks of England drew ;
> Dark, rolling, like the ocean tide
> When the rough west hath chafed his pride,
> And his deep roar sends challenge wide
>   To all that bars his way !
> In front the gallant archers trode,
> The men-at-arms behind them rode.
> And midmost of their phalanx broad,
>   The monarch held his sway.
> Beside him many a war-horse fumes,
> Around him waves a sea of plumes,
> Where many a knight in battle known,
> And some who spurs had first braced on,
> And deemed that fight should see them won,
>   King Edward's hests obey.

De Argentine attends his side,
With stout De Valence, Pembroke's **pride,** —
Selected champions from the **train**
To wait upon his bridle-rein.
Upon the Scottish foe he **gazed:**
At once, before his sight amazed,
  Sunk **banner, spear,** and shield.
Each weapon-point is downward sent,
Each warrior to the ground is bent.
'The rebels, Argentine, repent!
For pardon they have kneeled.'
'Aye, but they **bend** to other powers,
And other pardon sue than ours.
See where yon barefoot abbot stands,
And blesses them with lifted hands.
Upon the spot **where** they have kneeled,
These men **will die or win the field.'**
'Then prove **we** if they die or win;
Bid Gloster's **earl** the fight begin.'

"Earl Gilbert waved his truncheon **high**
Just as the Northern ranks arose, —
Signal for England's archery
  To halt **and bend their** bows.
Then stepped **each** yoeman forth **apace,**
Glanced at the intervening space,
  And raised his left hand high;
To the right **ear** the cords they **bring,**
At once **ten** thousand bow-strings **ring,**
  Ten thousand **arrows fly!**
Nor paused on the devoted Scot
The ceaseless fury of their shot;
  As fiercely and **as fast**
Forth whistling **came** the gray-goose wing
As the wild hailstones pelt and ring
  Adown December's blast.
Nor mountain targe of tough bull-hide,
  Nor Lowland mail, that storm may bide.
Woe! woe! to Scotland's bannered pride,
  If the fell shower may last!
Upon the right, behind the wood,
Each by his steed dismounted, stood
  The Scottish chivalry.
With foot in stirrup, hand on mane,
Fierce Edward Bruce can scarce restrain
His own keen heart, his eager train,
Until the archers gained the plain,
  Then, 'Mount, ye gallant free!'

He cried ; and vaulting from the ground,
His saddle every horseman found.
On high their glittering crests they toss,
As springs the wild-fire from the moss ;
The shield hangs down on every breast,
Each ready lance is in the rest,
   And loud shouts Edward Bruce —
' Forth, Marshal ! on the peasant foe ;
We 'll tame the terrors of their bow,
    And cut the bowstring loose.'

" Then spurs were dashed in chargers' flanks,
They rushed among the archer-ranks.
No spears were there the shock to let,
No stakes to turn the charge were set ;
And how shall yeoman's armor slight
Stand the long lance and mace of might ?
Or what may their short swords avail
'Gainst barbed horse and shirt of mail ?
Amid their ranks the chargers sprung,
High o'er their heads the weapons swung ;
And shriek and groan and vengeful shout
Gave note of triumph and of rout !
Awhile, with stubborn hardihood,
The English hearts the strife made good ;
Borne down at length on every side,
Compelled to flight, they scatter wide.
Let stags of Sherwood leap for glee,
And bound the deer of Dallom Lee.
The broken bows of Bannock's shore
Shall in the greenwood ring no more !
Round Wakefield's merry maypole now
The maids may twine the summer bough,
May northward look with longing glance
For those that wont to lead the dance,
For the blithe archers look in vain !
Broken, dispersed, in flight o'erta'en,
Pierced through, trod down, by thousand slain,
They cumber Bannock's bloody plain."

Scott was a warm patriot, and his poems have constantly occurring lines which speak his love of country, — his dear native Scotland. You all must know, I think, those familiar lines beginning, —

" Breathes there the man with soul so dead,
Who never to himself hath said,
' This is my own, my native land ? ' "

which open a canto of the first of his long poems, *The Lay
of the Last Minstrel.*

Another extract, from *The Lady of the Lake*, has this
address to his country's harp, which you may compare with
Moore's song to the harp of his native land, which we have
before read : —

"Harp of the North, farewell! The hills grow dark,
  On purple peaks a deeper shade descending;
In twilight copse the glow-worm lights her spark,
  The deer, half-seen, are to the covert wending.
Resume thy wizard elm! the fountain lending,
  And the wild breeze, thy wilder minstrelsy;
Thy numbers sweet with Nature's vespers blending,
  With distant echo from the fold and lea,
And herd-boy's evening pipe, and hum of housing bee.

"Yet, once again, farewell, thou Minstrel Harp!
  Yet, once again, forgive my feeble sway,
And little reck I of the censure sharp
  May idly cavil at an idle lay.
Much have I owed thy strains on life's long way,
  Through secret woes the world has never known,
When on the weary night dawned wearier day,
  And bitterer was the grief devoured alone.
That I o'erlive such woes, Enchantress! is thine own.

"Hark! as my lingering foosteps slow retire,
  Some Spirit of the Air has waked thy string!
'T is now a seraph bold, with touch of fire,
  'T is now the brush of Fairy's frolic wing.
Receding now, the dying numbers ring
  Fainter and fainter down the rugged dell,
And now the mountain breezes scarcely bring
  A wandering witch-note of the distant spell, —
And now 't is silent all! — Enchantress, fare thee well!"

Two years after *The Lay of the Last Minstrel* appeared
and was read with such delight, a little volume, called
Hours of Idleness, by GEORGE GORDON BYRON, a young
nobleman of nineteen, was reviewed in one of
1788-1824 the magazines with terrible criticism. The *Edinburgh Review,* the same which had so lashed the poets of
the Lake School with its criticism, now attacked this budding poet. It is true that the *Hours of Idleness* was not
a collection of masterpieces of poetry, but there was enough

of the promise of that genius which Byron showed afterwards to make us feel indignant that the critics could not
have been more generous to the young writer. If Byron
had been too sensitive to rally from the attack, his genius
might have been crushed by such severity. But he was not
a man to sit down in silence and take abuse, and had
a strong tendency to hit back again. He answered in a
satire in verse called *English Bards and Scotch Reviewers*,
which was so strong that nobody could doubt the ability of
the man who wrote it. In this satire he was himself severe
on the Lake Poets, gave Walter Scott some hard knocks, and
praised Campbell, Crabbe, and Rogers as the poets of the
classic school of Pope, whom Byron fancied that he thought
the greatest poet. In spite of this, Byron belonged by temper
and genius to the new school of poetry, and was much more
revolutionary in temper than any of the moderns.

In all he has written one sees that he was a child of the
age in which the French Revolution had raged. The tempests in his poetry would have torn to tatters the orderly
verses of Mr. Pope, or of any of the others whom Byron
praised so highly.

After his tilt with the bards and reviewers he travelled
on the Continent, and there wrote the first and second cantos
of *Childe Harold*. When he went to see his London
publisher, on his return, he showed him some translations
from the Latin poet Horace, as the great occupation of his
absence, the work of which he was justly proud. The
publisher, rather disappointed at this, asked if he had nothing original; on which he, rather unwillingly, produced the
first cantos of *Childe Harold*. The quick eye of the business man saw its merit; it was printed at once, and Byron
says, "I awoke one morning and found myself famous."
There was no doubt in the mind of critics of the old or
new order about such poetry as this: —

> "Clear, placid Leman! thy contrasted lake,
>   With the wild world I dwelt in, is a thing
>   Which warns me, with its stillness, to forsake
>   Earth's troubled waters for a purer spring.

This quiet sail is as a noiseless wing
To waft me from distraction.   Once I loved
Torn ocean's roar, but thy soft murmuring
Sounds sweet as if a sister's voice reproved
That I with stern delights should e'er have been so moved.

" It is the hush of night, and all between
Thy margin and the mountains, dusk, yet clear,
Mellowed and mingling, yet distinctly seen,
Save darkened Jura, whose capped heights appear
Precipitously steep; and drawing near,
There breathes a living fragrance from the shore,
Of flowers yet fresh with childhood; on the ear
Drops the light drip of the suspended oar,
Or chirps the grasshopper one good-night carol more.

" He is an evening reveller who makes
His life an infancy, and sings his fill;
At intervals, some bird from out the brake
Starts into voice a moment, then is still.
There seems a floating whisper on the hill,
But that is fancy; for the starlight dews
All silently their tears of love instil,
Weeping themselves away, till they infuse
Deep into Nature's breast the spirit of her hues.

" Ye stars! which are the poetry of heaven,
If in your bright leaves we would read the fate
Of men and empires, — 't is to be forgiven
That in our aspirations to be great,
Our destinies o'erleap their mortal state,
And claim a kindred with you; for ye are
A beauty and a mystery, and create
In us such love and reverence from afar,
That fortune, fame, power, life, have named themselves a star.

" All heaven and earth are still, — though not in sleep,
But breathless, as we grow when feeling most;
And silent, as we stand in thoughts too deep: —
All heaven and earth are still: from the high host
Of stars, to the lulled lake and mountain coast,
All is concentred in a life intense,
Where not a beam, nor air, nor leaf is lost,
But hath a part of being, and a sense
Of that which is of all Creator and defence.

" Then stirs the feeling infinite so felt
In solitude, where we are least alone, —

A truth which through **our** being then doth melt,
And purifies from self; it is a tone,
The soul and source of music, which makes **known**
Eternal harmony, and sheds a charm
Like to the fabled Cytherea's zone,
Binding all things with beauty; 't would disarm
The spectre Death, had **he** substantial power **to harm.**

    .   .   .   .

"The sky is changed; and such a change! O night,
And storm, and darkness, ye are wondrous strong,
Yet lovely in your strength, as is the light
Of a dark eye in woman! Far along,
From peak to peak, the rattling crags among
Leaps the live thunder! not from one lone cloud,
But every mountain now hath found **a** tongue,
And Jura answers, through her misty shroud,
Back to the joyous Alps, who call **to her aloud**!

    .   .   .   .

"Sky, mountains, river, winds, lake, lightnings! ye!
With night, **and** clouds, and thunder, and a soul
To make these **felt** and feeling, well may be
Things that have made me watchful. The far roll
Of your departing voices is the knoll
Of what in me is sleepless, — if I **rest.**
But where of ye, O tempests! is the goal?
Are ye like those within the human breast?
Or do ye find at length, like eagles, some high nest?

"Could **I** embody and unbosom now
That which is most within me; could I wreak
My thoughts upon expression, and thus throw
Soul, heart, mind, passions, feelings, strong or weak,
All that I would have sought, and all **I** seek,
Bear, know, feel, and yet breathe, into one word,
And that one word were Lightning, I would speak;
But as it is, I live **and** die unheard,
With a most voiceless thought, sheathing it as a sword.

"The morn is up again, — **the** dewy morn,
With breath all incense, and with cheek all bloom,
Laughing **the** clouds away with playful scorn,
And living as if earth contained no tomb,
And, glowing into day; we may resume
The march of our existence; and thus I,
Still on thy shores, fair Leman! may find room
And food for meditation, nor pass by
Much that may give us pause, if pondered fittingly."

This magnificent handling of Nature, **this** description **of** the breathless lull before the storm, the burst of the **clouds** on Jura's head, **the** passionate invocation to lake, river, and mountain, — all these, **beside the** poetry of the eighteenth century, **were like** a real thunder-storm beside a storm in a theatre.

Before Byron finished *Childe Harold,* he wrote a number of stories in verse, — *The Corsair, Lara, The Giaour, The Bride of Abydos.* These stories, nearly all with a hero who lived in revolt against law and order, **were** accepted as pictures of the poet's own **stormy nature.** Already, in respectable **English circles, there was** much horror felt at this strange, **original spirit, so lawless** and reckless ; and he made foes **as well as friends by** his poetry.

Going back to Italy a second time, Byron finished *Childe Harold,* and in his later years wrote several dramatic works. *Werner, Sardanapalus, Cain, The Deformed* **Transformed,** are among the best of these. These were dramatic in form, **but** not dramas in the sense of works fit for the action of the stage.

Byron's **shorter or lyric** poems **do not** match the longer ones in merit. His wings had a wide sweep, and he wanted plenty of room for his flights. **The** lyric poem was not his *forte.* **His best** short poems are to be found among **some** songs he wrote to Hebrew melodies. Here is one of the most familiar, — a **grand** piece of word melody : —

THE DESTRUCTION OF SENNACHERIB.

The Assyrian came down like the wolf on the fold,
And his cohorts were gleaming in purple **and** gold ;
And the **sheen** of their spears was like **stars** on the sea
When the **blue** wave rolls nightly **on deep** Galilee.

Like the leaves of the **forest when summer** is green,
That host with their banners at sunset were seen ;
Like the leaves of the forest when autumn hath blown,
That host on the morrow lay withered and strown

For the Angel of Death spread his **wings** on the blast,
And breathed in the face of the foe as **he** passed ;

And the eyes of the sleepers waxed deadly and chill,
And their hearts but once heaved, and forever grew still.

And there lay the steed, with his nostril all wide ;
But through it there rolled not the breath of his pride,
And the foam of his gasping lay white on the turf,
And cold as the spray of the rock-beating surf.

And there lay the rider, distorted and pale,
With dew on his brow and the rust on his mail ;
And the tents were all silent, the banners alone,
The lances unlifted, the trumpet unblown.

And the widows of Ashur are loud in their wail,
And the idols are broke in the temple of Baal ;
And the might of the Gentile, unsmote by the sword,
Hath melted like snow in the glance of the Lord.

There have been few poets who could handle language with Byron's ease and power. His rhyming is a marvel of facility. He wrote with a pen that played as freely as the lightning, and his thought never seemed to feel the bonds of rhyme.

In his poetry, Byron warmly took up the cause of Greece, which was then making an effort to free herself from the Turks. In *Childe Harold* and in other poems some grand passages are addressed to struggling Greece. The year before his death he entered into the plans of the Greek leaders in a war for their country's independence, and went to live at Missolonghi, where he mustered a band of soldiers in his own pay. Overwork and the bad climate threw him into a fever, and he was urged to leave the air of Missolonghi, which was malarious, and go elsewhere to recover. He refused, saying he would remain till Greece was either free or hopelessly subdued. He died soon after, at his post there, in the prime of life and genius. He used to say he had up to that time written only for women ; in the last of his life he would write for *men*. Would he had been spared to do even greater things than *Childe Harold !*

LV.

On Percy Bysshe Shelley.

BETWEEN Byron and PERCY BYSSHE SHELLEY, who were personal friends, there is a kind of resemblance in their lives, although they were men very unlike in charac-

1792–1822 ter. They were both of aristocratic birth, both held opinions very different from most young men in their position, and they won a similar reputation in their social circle, where their characters and their poetry were looked on by the conservative portion as dangerous and immoral.

Shelley had first drawn blame on himself in college, when he was barely twenty, by a publication which was condemned as atheistic; and he was expelled, finally, from Oxford. Much that he did later, confirmed the bad character this gave him in the eyes of respectable and well-ordered English society, which, like Byron, he seemed bound to set at defiance.

In character Shelley was a noble, pure man. The conduct for which he was blamed sprang from his own highest ideal of right. His mind had early formed radically different theories from those of most men of his class. Born of the aristocracy, he was an extreme democrat; in religious and social ideas he was a freethinker. Considered apart from his opinions, he was a shy, scholarly man, inclined to immerse himself in books, unselfish, full of humanity, keenly sensitive to all the abuses and distresses in the world, and eager to make the world better at any cost. Byron said of him after his death, "He was, without exception, the best and least selfish man I ever knew."

He began to write very early. When he was fifteen he had completed two novels. In college he began his poem of *Queen Mab*, which was condemned as an atheistic production; and after he left college his works followed each other rapidly. Although he died at thirty, he had written a good deal of prose, and tried his hand at all forms of poetic composition, — dramas, lyrics, blank verse, narrative poems, and several poems in the Spenserian stanza, which seems to have been a favorite form with him.

In 1817 he went to Italy, from which he never returned. He had written *Alastor, or The Spirit of Solitude*, and *The Revolt of Islam*, before his departure ; his other works, except a few shorter poems, belong to the five years in which he lived in Italy.

Among his dramas, *Prometheus Unbound* — a tragedy following the Greek models and with a Greek subject — was one of the first things written in Italy, during a residence at Rome. Afterwards he went to live near Lord Byron at Pisa, and here his mind and sympathies were so taken hold of by the sad story of *Beatrice Cenci* that he wrote on it his tragedy, *The Cenci*. It is the most painful and powerful drama written since the days of John Webster and Philip Massinger, and it would be, if the plot were not too revolting, a strong acting play.

In *Julian and Maddalo* Shelley put the characters of Byron and himself into a poem. At nearly the same time that this was written, he wrote also his lament for Keats under the title of *Adonais*.

Shelley's poetry is imaginative in the highest degree ; his was an imagination governed by high intellect. Of all the later poets he seems to me most of all a poet for other poets. No one who has not the imaginative quality in a rare degree can fully understand and appreciate Shelley. He also had the gift of writing verse of most musical quality, which seemed to flow without effort. Macaulay says, " His poetry seems not to have been an art, but an inspiration."

This musical quality shows most of all in his lyrics ; he wrote a great many of these, some long, others only a verse or two. I think there is no lyric of equal length in our language which is so perfect as Shelley's *Ode to a Skylark*. It is exquisite in melody, — the first requirement of a lyric ; the images it contains are poetic in the highest degree ; and it is full of an aspiration that upbears the thoughts, as if

borne aloft on the wings of the bird. Can anything be
more musical than this? —

> " Sound of vernal showers
>   On the twinkling grass,
> Rain-awakened flowers,
>   All that ever was
> Joyous and clear and fresh, thy music doth surpass."

Or more spirited than these? —

> " Higher still and higher
>   From the earth thou springest ;
> Like a cloud of fire
>   The blue deep thou wingest,
> And singing still dost soar, and soaring ever singest.
>
>   .   .   .   .   .   .
>
> " All the earth and air
>   With thy voice is loud
> As, when night is bare,
>   From one lonely cloud
> The moon rains out her beams, and heaven is overflowed."

And see how, without changing, the measure takes on deeper
meaning : —

> " Waking or asleep,
>   Thou of death must deem
> Things more true and deep
>   Than we mortals dream,
> Or how could thy notes flow in such a crystal stream ?
>
> " We look before and after,
>   And pine for what is not ;
> Our sincerest laughter
>   With some pain is fraught ;
> Our sweetest songs are those that tell of saddest thought."

The Cloud is another lyric, less subtle in thought than
The Skylark, but showing the wonderful music Shelley could
make by the interlinking of words.

Among his poems of a fit length to quote, I have chosen
The Sensitive Plant, because it seems to me a most characteristic poem, — in its melody, in its imaginative quality, and
in its very subject a poem in harmony with Shelley's own
nature : —

THE SENSITIVE PLANT.

PART I.

A sensitive plant in a garden grew,
And the young winds fed it with silver dew;
And it opened its fan-like leaves to the light,
And closed them beneath the kisses of night.

And the spring arose on the garden fair,
Like the spirit of love felt everywhere,
And each flower and herb on Earth's dark breast
Rose from the dreams of its wintry rest.

But none ever trembled and panted with bliss
In the garden, the field, or the wilderness,
Like a doe in the noontide with love's sweet want,
As the companionless sensitive plant.

The snowdrop and then the violet
Arose from the ground with warm rain wet,
And their breath was mixed with fresh odor, sent
From the turf, like the voice and the instrument.

Then the pied wind-flowers and the tulip tall,
And narcissi, the fairest among them all,
Who gaze on their eyes in the stream's recess
Till they die of their own dear loveliness;

And the naiad-like lily of the vale,
Whom youth makes so fair, and passion so pale,
That the light of its tremulous bells is seen
Through their pavilions of tender green;

And the hyacinth, purple and white and blue,
Which flung from its bells a sweet peal anew
Of music so delicate, soft, and intense,
It was felt like an odor within the sense;

And the rose, like a nymph to the bath addrest,
Which unveiled the depth of her glowing breast,
Till fold after fold, to the fainting air,
The soul of her beauty and love lay bare;

And the wand-like lily, which lifted up
As a Mænad its moonlight-colored cup,
Till the fiery star which is its eye
Gazed through clear dew on the tender sky;

And the jessamine faint, and the sweet tuberose, —
The sweetest flower for scent that blows,—
And all rare blossoms from every clime,
Grew in that garden in perfect prime.

.   .   .   .   .   .

And from this undefiled Paradise,
The flowers (as an infant's awakening eyes
Smile on its mother, whose singing sweet
Can first lull, and at last must awaken it),

When Heaven's blithe winds had unfolded them,
As mine-lamps enkindle a hidden gem,
Shone smiling to Heaven, and every one
Shared joy in the light of the gentle sun;

For each one was interpenetrated
With the light and the odor its neighbor shed,—
Like young lovers, whom youth and love make dear,
Wrapped and filled by their mutual atmosphere.

But the sensitive plant which could give small fruit
Of the love which it felt from the leaf to the root,
Received more than all, it loved more than ever,
Where none wanted but it, could belong to the giver, —

For the sensitive plant has no bright flower;
Radiance and odor are not its dower;
It loves, even like Love, its deep heart is full,
It desires what it has not, -- the beautiful.

The light winds which from unsustaining wings
Shed the music of many murmurings;
The beams which dart from many a star
Of the flowers whose hues they bear afar;

The plumèd insects, swift and free,
Like golden boats on a sunny sea,
Laden with light and odor, which pass
Over the gleam of the living grass;

The unseen clouds of the dew, which lie
Like fire in the flowers till the sun rides high,
Then wander like spirits among the spheres,
Each cloud faint with the fragrance it bears;

The quivering vapors of dim noontide,
Which, like a sea, o'er the warm earth glide,
In which every sound and odor and beam
Move, as reeds in a single stream; —

Each and all, like ministering angels, were
For the sensitive plant sweet joy to bear,
Whilst the lagging hours of the day went by,
Like windless clouds o'er a tender sky.

And when evening descended from Heaven above,
And the earth was all rest and the air was all love,
And delight, though less bright, was far more deep,
And the day's veil fell from the world of sleep, —

.   .   .   .   .

The sensitive plant was the earliest
Upgathered into the bosom of rest ;
A sweet child weary of its delight,
The feeblest and yet the favorite,
Cradled within the embrace of night.

PART II.

There was a power in this sweet place,
An Eve in this Eden, a ruling grace,
Which to the flowers, did they waken or dream,
Was as God is to the starry scheme.

A lady, the wonder of her kind,
Whose form was upborne by a lovely mind,
Which, dilating, had moulded her mien and motion
Like a sea-flower unfolded beneath the ocean,

Tended the garden from morn to even ;
And the meteors of that sublunar heaven,
Like the lamps of the air when night walks forth,
Laughed round her footsteps up from the earth.

She had no companion of mortal race,
But her tremulous breath, and her flushing face
Told, whilst the morn kissed the sleep from her eyes,
That her dreams were less slumber than paradise.

As if some bright spirit, for her sweet sake,
Had deserted heaven while the stars were awake ;
As if yet around her he lingering were,
Though the veil of daylight concealed him from her.

Her step seemed to pity the grass it prest ;
You might hear, by the heaving of her breast,
That the coming and going of the wind
Brought pleasure there, and left passion behind.

And wherever her airy footstep trod,
Her trailing hair from the grassy sod

Erased its light vestige with shadowy sweep,
Like a sunny storm o'er the dark-green deep.

I doubt not the flowers of that garden sweet
Rejoiced in the sound of her gentle feet;
I doubt not they felt the spirit that came
From her glowing fingers through all their frame.

She sprinkled bright water from the stream
On those that were faint with the sunny beam,
And out of the cups of the heavy flowers
She emptied the rain of the thunder-showers.

She lifted their heads with her tender hands,
And sustained them with rods and osier bands;
If the flowers had been her own infants she
Could never have nursed them more tenderly.

And all killing insects and gnawing worms,
And things of obscene and unlovely forms, •
She bore in a basket of Indian woof
Into the rough woods far aloof.

In a basket, of grasses and wild-flowers full,
The freshest her gentle hands could pull,
For the poor banished insects, whose intent,
Although they did ill, was innocent.

    .   .   .

And many an antenatal tomb,
Where butterflies dream of the life to come,
She left clinging ground the smooth and dark
Edge of the odorous cedar bark.

This fairest creature from earliest spring
Thus moved through the garden, ministering
All the sweet season of summer-tide,
And, ere the first leaf looked brown, she died.

PART III.

Three days the flowers of the garden fair
Like stars, when the moon is awakened, were,
Or the waves of Baiæ, ere luminous
She floats up through the smoke of Vesuvius.

And on the fourth the sensitive plant
Felt the sound of the funeral chant;

And the steps of the bearers, heavy and slow,
And the sobs of the mourners, deep and low.

The dark grass, and the flowers among the grass,
Were bright with tears as the crowd did pass;
From their sighs the wind caught a mournful tone,
And sate in the pines, and gave groan for groan.

The garden, once fair, became cold and foul,
Like the corpse of her who had been its soul;
Which at first was lovely as if in sleep,
Then slowly changed, till it grew a heap
To make men tremble who never weep.

Swift summer into the autumn flowed,
And frost in the mist of the morning rode,
Though the noon-day sun looked clear and bright,
Mocking the spoil of the secret night.

The rose-leaves, like flakes of crimson snow,
Paved the turf and the moss below;
The lilies were drooping and white and wan
Like the head and the skin of a dying man.

Then the rain came down, and the broken stalks
Were bent and tangled across the walks;
And the leafless network of parasite bowers
Massed into ruin, and all sweet flowers.

Between the time of the wind and the snow,
All loathliest weeds began to grow,
Whose coarse leaves were splashed with many a speck,
Like the water-snake's belly, and the toad's back;

And plants at whose names the verse feels loath,
Filled the place with a monstrous undergrowth,—
Prickly and pulpous, and blistering and blue,
Livid and starred with a lurid dew.

The sensitive plant, like one forbid,
Wept, and the tears within each lid
Of its folded leaves, which together grew,
Were changed to a blight of frozen glue.

For the leaves soon fell, and the branches soon
By the heavy axe of the blast were hewn;
The sap shrank to the root through every pore,
As blood to a heart that will beat no more.

For Winter came ; the wind was his whip ;
One choppy finger was on his lip ;
He had torn the cataracts from the hills,
And they clanked at his girdle like manacles.

His breath was a chain which, without a sound,
The earth and the air and the water bound ;
He came fiercely driven in his chariot-throne
By the tenfold blasts of the Arctic zone.

Then the weeds, which were forms of living death,
Fled from the frost to the earth beneath ;
Their decay, and sudden flight from frost,
Was but like the vanishing of a ghost.

And under the roots of the sensitive plant
The moles and the dormice died for want ;
The birds dropped stiff from the frozen air,
And were caught in the branches naked and bare.

  .   .   .   .

When winter had gone, and spring came back,
The sensitive plant was a leafless wreck ;
But the mandrakes and toad-stools and docks and darnels
Rose like the dead from their ruined charnels.

In Pisa Shelley's best poems were written, — *The Cenci,
Hellas, The Witch of Atlas, Adonais, The Hymn to Intellectual Beauty*, and nearly all the shorter poems of which I have spoken. The last thing he ever wrote was *The Triumph of Time*, which was left unfinished, and was published by his wife in as perfect a shape as she could bring it from his scattered papers.

In the spring of 1822 Shelley left Pisa and took a house on the west coast of Italy, near the village of Lerici. He was very fond of the sea, and had ordered a yacht built, in which he and a warm friend, Captain Williams, were going to spend many a day on the blue Italian waters close at hand. On the sixteenth of May the yacht arrived. Shelley was as pleased with it as a boy with a long-wished-for toy. They made several excursions in the boat, which was named "Don Juan," from Byron's poem, and finally came down to Leghorn in her. After a few days' stay here, Shelley and Williams started back in the boat for the town of Spezzia, on the Gulf of Spezzia, not far from their home.

This was the last ever seen of them. A sudden sea-storm came shortly after they started, with a dense fog. The little boat was probably run down by some larger vessel. After several days of waiting — terrible days for Mrs. Shelley and Mrs. Williams — the bodies were found washed up, wave-beaten and almost fleshless, on the shore. What was left of the two bodies was burned on a funeral-pile built on the sandy shore, and their ashes were buried in the cemetery in Florence. Byron was foremost in this strange burial rite, aided by Leigh Hunt and by Captain Trelawney, who was a friend of both the dead.

Thus, in the real opening of life, at the point where what was best in him seemed ready or fruition, Shelley died. Men of much less genius have gained a larger fame and held a higher place in the annals of literature. But as he is one of the most poetic of poets, he will always be loved by those of his own guild; his thought will take deep root in the hearts of other poets, and serve for their inspiration. For himself he died too young; the promise of his life was thwarted by his early death. Up to the time of his death he had been restless and unsettled in spirit. The seething waves of thought in his brain should have had time to cool and settle into tranquillity. Dying at thirty, he had not reached the serene heights where the poet ought to dwell. If he had lived longer, I feel sure time would have ripened him into a grand maturity, would have taught him trust and patience, and brought him to a calm which in his brief life he had not reached.

LVI.

On John Keats.

ONE of Shelley's most touching and beautiful poems is his *Adonais*, the lament for Keats. I wish it were not too long for me to quote it all; I can give you here only a few verses : —

" Oh, weep for Adonais !— The quick dreams,
   The passion-winged ministers of thought,
   Who were his flocks, whom near the living streams
   Of his young spirit he fed, and whom he taught
   The love which was its music, wander not, —
   Wander no more, from kindling brain to brain,
   But droop there whence they sprung ; and mourn their lot,
   Round the cold heart, where, after their sweet pain,
They ne'er will gather strength, nor find a home again.

   .   .   .   .   .

" One from a lucid urn of starry dew
   Washed his light limbs, as if embalming them ;
   Another clipt her profuse locks, and threw
   The wreath upon him, like an anadem,
   Which frozen tears instead of pearls begem ;
   Another in her wilful grief would break
   Her bow and winged reeds, as if to stem
   A greater loss with one which was more weak,
And dull the barbed fire against his frozen cheek.

" Another Splendor on his mouth alit,
   That mouth whence it was wont to draw the breath
   Which gave it strength to pierce the guarded wit,
   And pass into the panting heart beneath
   With lightning and with music ; the damp death
   Quenched its caress upon its icy lips ;
   And as a dying meteor stains a wreath
   Of moonlight vapor, which the cold night clips,
It flashed through his pale limbs, and passed to its eclipse.

   .   .   .   .   .

" All he had loved, and moulded into thought,
   From shape and hue and odor and sweet sound,
   Lamented Adonais. Morning sought
   Her eastern watch-tower, and her hair unbound,
   Wet with the tears which should adorn the ground,
   Dimmed the aërial eyes that kindle day ;
   Afar the melancholy thunder moaned,
   Pale Ocean in unquiet slumber lay,
And the wild winds flew round, sobbing in their dismay."

The tenderness Shelley shows for Keats in this beautiful
elegiac poem, which reminds me of Spenser's lament for
Sidney, is made more touching by the fact that when Shelley's poor disfigured body was found washed up on the
shore near which he had been drowned, one pocket of his
jacket had a volume of Keats in it, doubled back, as if

when death **clutched the** frail boat, the **reader** had hastily
thrust away his book, **in the middle of some favorite** line.

JOHN KEATS's life is sad **from first to last. He** was born
with the sensibility of a poet, which feels **a hurt**
at every pore. He lost his mother, **whom he** 1795–1820
loved most dearly, when a schoolboy; he was apprenticed
to a surgeon at fifteen, and the boy, who felt all sorts of
fancies flowering in his mind and asking for expression,
was kept for three years pounding drugs in a mortar and
putting up his master's prescriptions. During this time he
read *The Fairy Queen,* — that treasure-house for younger
poets, — and spent his spare time in imitating the Spenserian
stanza or in writing verses from his own heart. When he
was twenty-two **he** published his poem of *Endymion,* which
the reviews **pounced upon with** their usual savageness.
The leading reviews — **the *Quarterly* and the** *Edinburgh*
— remind one **in those days** of the giant in Mother
Goose's Melodies. **They seem to cry, —**

> "Fee! faw! **fum!**
> I smell the blood of a young poet.
> Be he alive or be he dead,
> In the street or in his bed,
> I must have some here in my can!"

On which they went to work and cut him up, heart, **blood,**
bones and all, in their pages. In Keats's case the process
of cutting up was fatal. He could not bear such treatment,
or, like Wordsworth, despise it, in **serene** faith in his own
power. **It is** generally believed that this severe criticism
was one cause of his death.

Nevertheless, in spite of the critics, *Endymion* was a
great poem, — a poem that **in** a short time the critics (who
are frequently very poor oracles till popular judgment comes
to set them right) were obliged to pronounce great.

Keats's disappointment at the way his poem was treated
was bitter, but it did not destroy his **power to** work. Already **a** blood-vessel had broken in his lungs, and signs of
consumption began to show themselves; but only two years
later he published another volume, containing *Hyperion,*
Lamia, Isabella, The Eve of St. Agnes, and other poems.

Among the shorter lyrics was that most exquisite *Ode to a Nightingale :* —

> "Thou wast not **born for** death, immortal Bird!
>   **No** hungry generations tread **thee** down;
> The voice I hear **this passing** night was heard
>   In ancient **days by emperor and clown;**
> Perhaps the self-same song that found a path
>   Through the sad heart of Ruth, when, sick for home,
>   She **stood in tears amid the alien corn;**
>   The same that oft-times hath
> Charmed magic casements, opening on the foam
>   Of perilous seas, in faery lands forlorn."

These were Keats's last words. His disease gained on him rapidly, and when only a little over twenty-five years he died. But his life as a poet was more rounded and complete than that of many older poets. I have not that feeling about his early death that I have for Shelley. Keats sang his songs and died; and they are so perfect in their way that we do not complain there are so few, nor feel that life could have added much to the richness of his genius. There are no signs of any conflicts in his spirit which needed to be outlived before he could write at his best, as in Shelley. His poetry is not a field on which ideas are at battle, or theories are displayed. They are beautiful fancies, or old tales woven into melodious, pictorial verses.

His poetry is the most perfect of word-painting. One can almost see colors in the printed lines of his *Endymion* or *The Eve of St. Agnes.* No poet could better use words whose sound fits the meaning, — such words as "lush," "murmurous," and others, in which the poet speaks to the sense as well as the thought. No poet since Shakespeare was more an artist in the use of the adjective words which give vividness and color. For example, — an "azure-lidded sleep," the "poppied warmth of sleep," "embalmed darkness," "the silver-snarling trumpet": his poetry is full of such instances. He is, however, much more than a mere word-poet, and has seasons of strength in which one feels as if a breeze from the sixteenth century had passed over

his pages. **As** you read some of his lines you are borne
over the artificial fields that lie between **to** the poetry **of**
Marlowe **and** Chapman; **you** hear a strain **in** *Endymion*
that resembles Marlowe's *Hero and Leander.*

But melancholy is most of **all** the mark **he set upon** his
poetry, — a mark which has been copied by so many later
versifiers that it has seemed as if grief and pining were the
poet's themes. In these later poets this is often affectation; in Keats it was genuine, — the note struck by the
sensitive spirit over whom hung the shadow of early death.

Before he died — and death **was** welcome as a release
from pain and weariness of living — he said: " I **can**
feel **the daisies** growing over me." And on his tomb he
ordered inscribed: " Here lies one whose **name was** writ in
water." **False prophecy !** Every year since his death has
set **him higher among the crowned** poets **of** the world.

It **is difficult to** quote **from** Keats. He has written few
short poems, and **his** longer poems will not bear taking by
fragments. His *Eve of St. Agnes* **is** one of the most **beau-**
tiful love-stories told in verse in our language. **I can give**
you only a few bits here and there, as it is too **long to quote**
entire.

The story opens with a scene of revelry on **St. Agnes'**
Eve, in which Madeline is the chief figure. Madeline's
heart has brooded all day on the stories of St. Agnes' Eve, —
how maidens who did certain charms might have a vision,
at **night, of** their true lovers, who would appear in their
sleep, offering **all** dainties **to** eat, —

> " **If** ceremonies due they did aright, —
> As, supperless to bed they must retire,
> And couch supine their beauties, lily white;
> Nor look behind, nor sideways; but require
> Of Heaven, with upward eyes, for all that they desire."

Meantime Madeline, gliding through **the dance, while**
her thoughts are elsewhere, is watched **by her** young **lover,**
Porphyro, with whose house her father and kinsfolk are at
war, and who, at peril **of** his life, has stolen here, hoping
only to get sight of Madeline.

The **old** nurse Angela, **who** is the young **lovers'** only friend in all **the hostile castle, tells** him of Madeline's **plan** **to try the** charm of St. Agnes' Eve ; and he persuades the dame to conceal him in **Madeline's** chamber, where, when she sleeps, he will spread **at her** bed-side the feast which **the** charm of St. Agnes promises to **her vision.**

The dame hides him there **and hobbles off,** half afraid of what she has done, **just as Madeline enters** her chamber.

"Out went the taper as she hurried in ;
　Its little smoke in pallid moonshine died :
　She closed the **door, she panted, all akin**
　To spirits **of the air and visions wide.**
　No uttered **syllable or woe betide ;**
　But to **her heart her heart was** voluble,
　Paining with eloquence her balmy side,
　As though a tongueless nightingale should swell
Her throat in vain, and die, heart-stifled, in her dell.

" A casement high and triple-arched there was,
　All garlanded with carven imageries
　Of fruits and flowers and bunches of knot-grass,
　And diamonded with panes of quaint device
　Innumerable of stains and splendid dyes,
　As are the tiger-moth's deep damasked **wings ;**
　And in the midst, 'mong thousand **heraldries,**
　And twilight saints, and **dim** emblazonings,
A shielded scutcheon blushed with **blood** of queens and kings.

" **Full on this casement shone** the wintry moon,
　And threw warm gules on Madeline's fair breast,
　As down she knelt for Heaven's grace and boon ;
　Rose-bloom fell on her **hands,** together prest,
　And on her silver **cross soft** amethyst,
　And on her hair a glory, like a saint :
　She seemed a splendid angel, newly dressed,
　Save wings, for heaven. Porphyro grew faint ;
She knelt, so pure a thing, so free from mortal taint.

" Anon his heart revives ; her vespers done,
　Of all its wreathed pearls her hair she frees,
　Unclasps her warmed jewels one by one ;
　Loosens her fragrant bodice ; by degrees
　Her rich **attire** creeps rustling to her knees :
　Half-hidden, like a mermaid in sea-weed,
　Pensive awhile, **she** dreams awake and sees
　In fancy fair St. **Agnes** in her bed,
But dares not look behind, or all the charm is fled.

"**Soon,** trembling in her soft and chilly nest,
 In sort of wakeful swoon, perplexed she lay,
 Until the poppied warmth of **sleep** oppressed
 Her soothed limbs, and soul fatigued away;
 Flown like a thought, until **the morrow day,**
 Blissfully havened, both from joy and pain,
 Clasped like a missal where swart Paynims pray,
 Blinded alike from sunshine and from rain,
As though a rose should shut, and be a bud again.

" Stolen to this paradise, and so entranced,
 Porphyro gazed upon her empty dress,
 And listened to her breathing, if it chanced
 To wake into a slumberous tenderness,
 Which, when he heard, that minute did he bless
 And breathed himself; then from the closet crept,
 Noiseless as fear in a wide wilderness,
 And over the hushed carpet silent stept,
And 'tween the curtains peeped, where, lo ! how fast she slept.

" Then by the **bedside, where the faded moon**
 Made a dim silver twilight, **soft he set**
 A table, and, half anguished, **threw thereon**
 A cloth of **woven** crimson, gold **and jet.**
 .   .   .   .   .

" And still she slept, an azure-lidded sleep,
 In blanched linen, smooth, and lavendered,
 While he from forth the closet brought a heap
 Of candied apple, quince and plum and gourd,
 With jellies soother than the creamy curd,
 And lucent syrops, tinct with cinnamon,
 Manna and dates, in argosy transferred
 From Fez, and spiced dainties, every one
From silken Sarmacand to cedared Lebanon.

" **These** delicates he heaped with glowing hand
 On golden dishes, and in baskets bright
 Of wreathed silver; sumptuous they stand
 In the retired quiet of the **night,**
 Filling **the** chilly room with perfume light —
 .   .   .   .   .

" Awakening up, he took her hollow lute,
 Tumultuous, and, in chords that tenderest **be,**
 He played an ancient ditty, long since mute,
 In Provence called, ' *La belle dame sans mercy !* '
 Close to her ear, touching the melody; —
 Wherewith disturbed, she uttered a soft moan :
 He ceased — she panted quick — and suddenly

Her blue affrayed eyes wide open shone :
Upon his knees he sank, pale as smooth-sculptured stone.

" Her eyes were open, but she still beheld,
   Now wide awake, the vision of her sleep ;
   There was a painful change, that nigh expelled
   The blisses of her dream so pure and deep.

   .   .   .   .

"' Ah, Porphyro,' said she, ' but even now
   Thy voice was at sweet tremble in mine ear,
   Made tunable with every sweetest vow ;
   And those sad eyes were spiritual and clear :
   How changed thou art ! how pallid, chill, and drear !
   Give me that voice again, my Porphyro,
   Those looks immortal, those complainings dear !
   Oh, leave me not in this eternal woe,
For if thou diest, my Love, I know not where to go.'

"' My Madeline ! sweet dreamer ! lovely bride !
   Say, may I be for aye thy vassal blest ?
   Thy beauty's shield, heart-shaped and vermeil dyed ?
   Ah ! silver shrine, here will I take my rest
   After so many hours of toil and quest,
   A famished pilgrim, — saved by miracle
   Though I have found, I will not rob thy nest,
   Saving of thy sweet self, if thou think'st well
To trust, fair Madeline, to no rude infidel.

"' Hark ! 't is an elfin storm from faery land,
   Of haggard seeming, but a boon indeed :
   Arise ! arise ! the morning is at hand, —
   The bloated wassailers will never heed.
   Let us away, my love, with happy speed ;
   There are no ears to hear, or eyes to see, —
   Drowned all in Rhenish and the sleepy mead,
   Awake ! arise ! my love, and fearless be,
Far o'er the southern moors I have a home for thee.'

   .   .   .   .

" They glide like phantoms into the wide hall ;
   Like phantoms to the iron porch they glide,
   Where lay the porter, in uneasy sprawl,
   With a huge empty flagon by his side ;
   The wakeful bloodhound rose, and shook his hide,
   But his sagacious eye an inmate owns :
   By one and one, the bolts full easy slide, —
   The chains lie silent on the footworn stones ;
The key turns, and the door upon its hinges groans.

"And **they** are gone : aye ! ages long ago
  These lovers fled away **into the storm ;**
  That night the Baron **dreamt of** many a woe,
  And **all** his warrior guests, with shade and form
  Of witch and demon, and large coffin-worm,
  Were long be-nightmared.   Angela the old
  Died palsy-twitched, with meagre face deform ;
  The Beadsman, after thousand aves told,
For aye unsought-for slept among his ashes cold."

With Keats, who died in 1820, we enter upon the fair field of modern poetry, and find ourselves among the poets of our own age and our own forms of thought.

Lowell, one of our most sympathetic literary critics, has said, —

"Three **men almost** contemporaneous **with each other** — Wordsworth, **Keats,** and Byron — **were the great means** of bringing back **English** poetry from **the sandy deserts of** rhetoric and recovering **for her her triple inheritance of simplicity,** sensuousness, and **passion. Of these, Wordsworth was the only** conscious reformer **and** the deepest thinker; **Keats, the most** essentially **a** poet; and Byron, the most keenly intellectual **of** the three. . . .   Wordsworth has influenced most **the ideas of** succeeding poets; Keats their forms; and Byron, interesting **to** men of imagination less for his writings than for **what his** writings indicate, reappears **no** more in poetry, but presents an ideal to youth made restless with vague desires not yet regulated by experience, nor supplied with motives by the duties of life."

LVII.

On Some Friends of the Lake Poets.

THERE are many interesting writers, in prose as well as **verse,** who wrote at the time the Lake School **was** rising **to fame.** They are worth better **and longer mention** than I **can** give in one brief Talk. The early **part of** this century saw gathered in London a group of men more interesting than any similar group since the days when the Scriblerus Club used to meet at Will's Coffee-house.

CHARLES LAMB, one of the sweetest and gentlest characters that the past keeps alive for us, was a school-
1775–1835
mate of Coleridge in Christ's Hospital school, and
they formed a friendship there which was never broken.
Lamb was a man of varied talents. He wrote poems and
one or two plays; but his merit as a writer is shown best
in his *Essays of Elia*, which are full of quaint humor, and
have a pathos entirely their own. No essays so fresh, delicate, and original had been written since the time of Abraham Cowley as these of Lamb, and I think I would rather
part with Cowley even than with the gentle *Elia*.

Lamb was a true Londoner, born and dwelling in or near
that great city all his life, and loving it as if it were a feeling and responsive being, conscious of his love. He went
to visit Wordsworth once, and enjoyed the beautiful lake
and mountain region among which his friend lived; but his
heart was always in London. In one of his letters to
Wordsworth he says, —

"Separate from the pleasure of your company, I don't much
care if I never see a mountain in my life. I have passed all
my days in London, until I have formed as many and intense
local attachments as any of your mountaineers have done with
dead nature. The lighted shops of the Strand and Fleet Street,
the innumerable tradesmen and customers, coaches, wagons,
play-houses, — all the bustle and wickedness round about Cov-
ent Garden, the watchmen, drunken scenes, rabbles,   the
crowds, the very dirt and mud, the sun shining upon houses and
pavements, the print-shops, old book-stalls, parsons cheapening
books, coffee-houses, steams of soup from kitchens, the panto-
mimes, — London itself a pantomime and masquerade, — all
these things work themselves into my mind, and feed me without a power of satiating me. The wonder of these sights impels
me into night-walks about the city's crowded streets, and I often
shed tears in the motley Strand from fulness of joy at so much
life."

Dr. Johnson also loved London as Lamb did, and preferred it to all the nature outside.

Lamb held for years a place as clerk in the India House,
and his slight, stooping figure, clad in clerkly black, coming

down Fleet Street to his **lodgings in the Temple, where he** lived many years, is one of the **most vivid pictures in** my imagination. His sister Mary, who **is the Bridget of** his essays, was his housekeeper. She was **subject to** fits of insanity, and he devoted his life to unfailing **care of her,** — a care repaid **on her** part by tenderest gratitude and love. **When** not under the influence of these melancholy attacks, she was a clever woman and charming companion.

When Lamb was about fifty he was pensioned by **the** East India Company, in whose service he had so long been **a** clerk, and for **the** rest of his days **he** lived in freedom. **One must read his own** account of his delight at his emancipation, **in his letters to** friends, to **see how keen and boyish was his enjoyment of** the liberation from **his daily** drudgery.

The *Essays of Elia* are **delightful reading.** Their humor is so quaint, **and yet so tender, that in** reading them one often laughs with **tears in the eyes.**

One series in the **essays on Popular Fallacies,** —*That handsome is that handsome does; That a man must not laugh at his own jest; That ill-gotten gain never prospers; That we should rise with the lark,* — are in Lamb's wittiest vein.

I quote for you from his *Essays of Elia* the greater part of his amusing dissertation upon *Roast Pig* : —

" Mankind, says a Chinese manuscript, — which my friend M— was obliging enough to read and explain to me, — **for the** first **seventy** thousand ages ate their **meat raw,** clawing it **or** biting **it from the living animal just as they do** in Abyssinia **to** this day. **This period is** not obscurely hinted at by their great Confucius, where he **designates** a kind of golden age by **the** term *cho-fang,* literally, the Cooks' Holiday. The manuscript goes on to say that the art of roasting, **or** rather broiling **(which** I take to **be** the elder brother), was accidentally **discovered in** the manner following. The swineherd Ho-ti, **having** gone out into the woods one morning, as his manner was, to collect mast for his hogs, left his cottage in the care of his eldest son **Bo-bo,** a great lubberly boy who, being fond of playing with **fire, as younkers of** his age commonly are, let some sparks escape into a bundle of straw, which, kindling, quickly spread the conflagration over every part of their poor mansion, till it was reduced to ashes. Together with the cottage (a sorry antediluvian makeshift of a building you may think it), what was of much more importance, a fine litter of new-farrowed pigs, no less than nine in number, perished. China pigs have been esteemed a luxury all over the East from the remotest periods that we read of. Bo-bo was in the utmost consternation, as you may think, — not so much for the sake of the tenement, which his father and he could easily build up again with a few dry branches and the labor of an hour or two, at any time, as for the loss of the pigs. While he was thinking what he should say to his father, and wringing his hands over the smoking remnants of one of those untimely sufferers, an odor assailed his nostrils unlike any scent which he had before experienced. What could it proceed from? Not from the burnt cottage, — he had smelt that smell before ; indeed, this was by no means the first accident of the kind which had occurred through the negligence of this unlucky young firebrand. Much less did it resemble that of any known herb, weed, or flower. A premonitory moistening at the same time overflowed his nether lip. He knew not what to think. He next stooped down to feel the pig, if there were any signs of life in it. He burnt his fingers, and to cool them, applied them, in his booby fashion, to his mouth. Some of the crumbs of the scorched skin had come away with his fingers, and for the first time in his life (in the world's life indeed, for before him no man had known it), he tasted — crackling !

"Again he felt the pig. It did not burn him so much now ; still, he licked his fingers from a sort of habit. The truth at length broke into his slow understanding that it was the pig that smelt so and tasted so delicious ; and surrendering himself to the new-born pleasure, he fell to tearing up whole handfuls of the scorched skin, with the flesh next it, and was cramming it down his throat in his beastly fashion when his sire entered amid smoking rafters, armed with retributory cudgel, and finding how affairs stood, began to rain blows upon the young rogue's shoulders as thick as hailstones, which Bo-bo heeded not any more than if they had been flies. The tickling pleasure which he experienced in his lower regions had rendered him quite callous to any inconveniences he might feel in those remote quarters. His father might lay on, but he could not beat him from his pig till he had fairly made an end of it, when, becoming a little more sensible of his situation, something like the following dialogue ensued : —

" ' You graceless whelp, what have you got there devouring ?
Is it not enough that you have burned me down three houses
with your dog's tricks, and be hanged to you, but you must be
eating fire, and I know not what: what have you got there, I say ? '

" ' Oh, father, the pig ! the pig ! Do come and taste how **nice**
the burnt pig eats ! '

" The ears of Ho-ti tingled with horror. **He** cursed his son,
and he cursed himself that ever he should beget a son that
should eat burnt pig.

" **Bo-bo,** whose scent was wonderfully sharpened since morning, **soon** raked out another pig ; and fairly rending it asunder,
thrust the lesser half by main force into the fists of Ho-ti, still
shouting out, ' Eat, eat, eat the burnt pig, father ; only taste ! '
with such like barbarous ejaculations, **cramming** all the while as
if he would choke.

" **Ho-ti trembled** in every joint while he grasped the abominable thing, wavering whether he should not put his son to
death **for an unnatural** young **monster,** when the crackling
scorching his fingers as it had done his son's, and applying the
same remedy to them, he in his turn tasted some of its flavor, —
which, make what sour **mouths he would for a** pretence, proved
not altogether displeasing to him.

" In conclusion (for the manuscript **here is a** little **tedious**),
both father and son fairly sat down to the mess, **and never left**
off till they had despatched all that remained of the litter.

" Bo-bo was strictly enjoined not to **let the secret escape, for**
the neighbors would certainly have stoned them for **a couple of**
abominable wretches who could think of improving upon **the**
good meat which God had sent them. Nevertheless, strange
stories got about. It was observed **that** Ho-ti's house was
burned down **more** frequently than ever. Nothing but fires
from this time forward. Some would break out in broad day,
others in the night-time. **As** often as the sow farrowed, **so sure**
was **the house** of Ho-ti **to be** in a blaze ; and Ho-ti himself,
which was **the** more remarkable, instead of chastising his son,
seemed to **grow more** indulgent to **him** than **ever.** At length
they were watched, the terrible mystery discovered, **and** father
and son summoned **to take** their trial **at** Pekin, **then an** inconsiderable assize town. **Evidence was given, the** obnoxious
food itself produced in court, and **verdict about to** be pronounced, when the foreman of the jury begged that some of the
burnt pig, of which the culprits stood accused, might be handed
into the box. He handled it, **and** they all handled it ; and burning their fingers as Bo-bo and **his** father had done before them,

and nature prompting to each of them the same remedy, against the face of all the facts, and the clearest charge which judge had ever given, to the surprise of the whole court, townsfolk, strangers, reporters, and all present, without leaving the box or any manner of consultation whatever, they brought in a simultaneous verdict of NOT GUILTY.

"The judge, who was a shrewd fellow, winked at the manifest iniquity of the decision ; and when the court was dismissed, went privily and bought up all the pigs that could be had for love or money. In a few days his lordship's town house was observed to be on fire. The thing took wing, and now there was nothing to be seen but fire in every direction.

"Fuel and pigs grew enormously dear all over the district. The insurance offices, one and all, shut up shop. People built slighter and slighter every day, until it was feared that the very science of architecture would in no long time be lost to the world. Thus the custom of firing houses continued, till in process of time, says my manuscript, a sage arose like our Locke, who made a discovery that the flesh of swine, or indeed of any other animal, might be cooked (burnt as they called it) without the necessity of consuming a whole house to dress it. Then first began the rude form of a gridiron ; roasting by the string or spit came in a century or two later, — I forget in whose dynasty. By such slow degrees, concludes the manuscript, do the most useful, and seemingly the most obvious, arts make their way among mankind."

A life-long friend of Lamb and an early admirer of Coleridge was WILLIAM HAZLITT, also a writer of essays **1778-1830** and one of the best critics of his time. He had set out to be a painter when a young man, but his success did not satisfy him, and he dropped the brush for the pen. His knowledge of art helped him as critic, and his essays on Hogarth's pictures, on Joshua Reynolds, on Vandyke, are all admirable reading. In the drama he was hardly less good as a critic, and in literature best of all. He was a student, as was his friend Lamb, of the sixteenth century poets, and a series of lectures which Hazlitt gave on the old poets of the Elizabethan age, and on Shakespeare's plays, are well worth reading. He also wrote on English comic writers, — the comic dramatists Congreve, Wycherley, Vanbrugh, and Farquhar; and besides all this critical work, he wrote a great many essays on all sorts of subjects, which are collected under the name of *Table Talks.*

It is not easy to select a specimen from Hazlitt's essays without quoting at too great length. Yet he is rich in strong, epigrammatic sentences, as this from the essay *On the Feeling of Immortality in Youth :* " No young man believes he shall ever die. There is a feeling of eternity in youth which makes us amends for everything ; " or this : " Perhaps the best cure for the fear of death is to reflect that life has a beginning as well as an end ; " or this grand sentence : " I can forgive the dirt and sweat of the gypsy under the hedge when I consider the earth is his mother, the sun his father." Among his essays is a series called *Spirit of the Age,* in which he gives, among many others, sketches of Coleridge and of Wordsworth, which I advise you to read, although it is to be kept in mind that Hazlitt held all through life the liberal opinions which Coleridge and Wordsworth held only in youth, and that there was in Hazlitt a little bitterness at what seemed to him their desertion of a cause.

An essay not to be omitted in reading him is *On my First Acquaintance with Poets,* in which he tells how, as a boy, he first met Coleridge, and describes the charm he held over him. And you must not miss another, *On Persons one would wish to have seen,* — an essay reporting a conversation on that subject, in which Hazlitt, Lamb, Leigh Hunt, and others took part. One feels quite sure that the conversation was held at Lamb's rooms in the Temple, on one of those charming evenings at which mirth and wit presided ; and one wishes, after reading, that it were possible to have been present.

Indeed, I do not know any of Hazlitt's essays which are not interesting ; and for my own part, I wish life were long enough to permit me to read every word he has written.

Leigh Hunt was a friend of Hazlitt and Lamb, as well as of Byron and Shelley. He was a writer of poems, **1784-1859** plays, stories, essays ; his pen was tried in every kind of writing. He began early to edit a newspaper, *The Examiner,* and made a brilliant paper ; but for a libel

against the Prince **Regent** which it printed, he was imprisoned for two years. He made his room in the jail **a bower
of taste, painting the** ceiling like the sky, cloud-covered, **and
papering** the walls in patterns of flowers; and with books,
piano, statuary, and all sorts of bric-à-brac made the visi-
tors who came to see him **feel as** if they had entered a
fairy-land. Here all the principal men of the time visited
him, — **Byron, Moore, Hazlitt, Lamb, William** Godwin,
Shelley, and many others, — till his cell seems like the meet-
ing-ground of the wits of that day.

His works **are too great in** number **even for the** titles to
be mentioned. **Some of his shorter** poems are very pretty;
among them I am sure you will know the little fable of *Abou
Ben Adhem.* **One of** his longest poems, *Rimini,* is on an
Italian subject. He was very fond of Italy and her poets,
and his translations from them, and tales paraphrased from
Ariosto, **Tasso,** and the other great poets, are **among his**
best works. **He was, like** Hazlitt, a good **critic of the**
drama and literature. He is a graceful writer, **with so much**
enthusiasm for that which **he likes in his favorite writers**
that he **makes his reader share his own pleasure** in reading
them.

His prose works, **such as** *A Book for a Corner, Imagination and Fancy,* and *Tales from the Italian Poets,* will outlive his reputation as a poet; **and it is** as prose-writer and
journalist that we shall best **remember** him.

WALTER SAVAGE LANDOR, **who was the friend** of Wordsworth, Lamb, and Coleridge, and the life-long and
1775–1864 intimate friend of Southey, was a man who outlived
his associates and companions by almost a generation of
time. He was born in 1775, and lived to be nearly ninety.

Like most of this group, he was poet and prose-writer
both, his first works in poetry proving too subtle in meaning for the ordinary **reader.** He took **up prose-writing in a**
style which, though **still remote** from common understand-
ings, found much **more** appreciation than did his poetry.
But his works have always found **warm** admirers among poets
and **scholars.** Shelley, **Lamb, Hazlitt,** all read his first

poem, *Gebir*, with delight; Southey hailed him as a great poet, and showed for him an admiration which Landor returned with interest; and in an essay on *Poetry that Poets Love*, Miss Mitford places Landor's poetry at the head of the list.

Landor's admirers stretch down through the century into our own time. Dickens loved him with enthusiasm, and has given some touches of his character in Lawrence Boythorn, in the novel of *Bleak House;* while Ralph Waldo Emerson, who has recorded a visit to Landor's home in Italy, in the *English Traits*, says: "Year after year the scholar must go back to him for a multitude of elegant sentences, for a wisdom, wit, and indignation which are unforgettable."

The best part of Landor's writing, indeed, is found in detached sentences in his prose, or short passages from his poetry. I think there are few writers in English whose works would furnish sentences for so large a book of aphorisms as his.

He was very much in sympathy with the Greeks and Romans. A good deal of his poetry is written in Latin, and many of his characters, in prose especially, are Greeks, drawn to the life. Of all his works, the general reader would be most interested in the *Imaginary Conversations*, which embrace several series of conversations between the historic characters of the past, — between Queen Elizabeth and Burleigh; Lady Jane Grey and Roger Ascham; Philip Sidney and Lord Brooke; Milton and Marvell. One of the most beautiful among all of these is the *Pericles and Aspasia*, in which appear the wonderfully life-like characters of Pericles, Aspasia, Anaxagoras, Alcibiades, and other Greeks of that time.

Landor had undoubted genius. A want of self-discipline seems to have hindered both his character and his work from coming to full perfection. It is a great deal to say of him that he is a poet for poets; it would be still better to be able to say that he touched the deep heart of humanity. One feels of him that he just missed a height he might have gained. **And yet** there are few books I would so unwillingly leave unread as the *Imaginary Conversations*.

THOMAS DE QUINCEY, who is most famous for his *Confes-*
1786–1859 *sions of an English Opium-Eater*, belongs among these men of the Lake School. He lived for years among the lakes of Westmoreland, and after Words-worth left his cottage at Grasmere to live at Rydal Mount, where the last of his life was passed, De Quincey took the Grasmere house, and lived there many years. In London his friends were, all of them, in the group of which I have just been speaking. Like Coleridge, he was many years an opium-eater, and his *Confessions* are tinged by the wonder-ful hues his fancy took on under the influence of this drug. There are passages from his prose which have few equals in the language for eloquence and imagination. And, not-withstanding the diseased state of mind which his habit of opium-eating induced, he did a great amount of work, and has left behind him many volumes.

This group of men of varied talents were contemporaries of the new school of poetry, and upheld its doctrines. They were all writers for the current periodical literature of the time, and the prose-writing of each has a distinct originality. But the master among prose-writers of this time, the magi-cian who cast his spell over his age and over future times, is Walter Scott, the publication of whose historical novels forms an epoch in English literature.

LVIII.

ON WALTER SCOTT AND THE WAVERLEY NOVELS.

FROM the time of Miss Burney's *Evelina*, in 1778, until the year 1814, I think it will be conceded that the best novels were written by women. Women had found their field, and they held it well. Among the masculine contemporaries of Miss Edgeworth, Mrs. Radcliffe, Jane

and Anna Maria Porter, and Miss Austen, were MATTHEW
LEWIS, whose lurid story, *The Monk*, followed in the track
of Anne Radcliffe; THOMAS HOLCROFT, the author both of
plays and novels which gained popularity in their day;
CHARLES MATURIN, an Irish clergyman, the author of romantic and improbable fictions, and the tragedy of *Bertram;*
WILLIAM BECKFORD, who wrote the weird Eastern story
of *Vathek*, a story to be classed in the group of fiction in
which Johnson's *Rasselas* belongs. But none of the works
of these authors are equal in interest to those of Maria
Edgeworth or Jane Austen.

If there is any exception to the pre-eminence of the
novels of this period written by women over those
of men, it should be given to WILLIAM GODWIN'S 1756–1836
Caleb Williams, which is to be noted, not only as a popular
novel, but as one of the first English fictions written for
a purely philanthropic purpose. Godwin had written a
work on *Political Justice* before he wrote this novel, and
no doubt saw he could reach more minds by a novel than
by a philosophic argument. He was one of the first who
used fiction to hold up to view social abuses and unjust
laws; but he has had many followers, and a large part of the
novelists of to-day have followed in Godwin's footsteps.

Caleb Williams is a book which every one ought to read
who is interested in the growth of the English novel. It is a
powerful book, and will hold the reader's interest from first
to last. That it is dramatic is proved by the fact that a
play-writer of the time, George Coleman, founded on it
his drama of the *Iron Chest*, still an acting play.

These names of men and women which I have just mentioned were the leading names in fiction when, in 1814,
an anonymous novel, called *Waverley*, appeared, — a novel
whose authorship for years was a subject of doubt and curiosity. *Waverley* was only the first of a series known as the
Waverley Novels, — a series appearing at rapid intervals for
sixteen years, till they numbered thirty-two novels. All
these tales were founded on historical facts, swarmed with
historical characters drawn with all the lines of truth, and

were placed among scenery and surroundings which seemed to be accurate studies from nature and life. The scenes of these romances are laid in England, France, Germany, the lands of the East, to the very door of the Holy Sepulchre; in time they cover a period which begins at the close of the eleventh century, and comes down to the opening year of the nineteenth; in action they enter upon almost every great historic field, from the wars of the Crusades in Syria, to the more peaceful scenes of the reign of George III. in England. Such a work, so wonderful in its scope, so varied in place, time, and action, was that of Walter Scott in the *Waverley Novels*.

The success of Byron as a poet turned Scott from a poet into a novelist. He printed his poem of *Rokeby* at the same time that Byron's *Giaour* appeared. Scott read the poem, whose popularity cast his own into the shade. When he laid down the book, he said, with the generosity which was natural to him: "Byron hits the mark where I don't even pretend to fledge my arrow."

Several years before this, Scott had begun the novel of *Waverley*, but had thrown it aside, and it had lain apparently half forgotten for years. Shortly after the publication of *Rokeby*, he took up this manuscript and went to work to finish it. In the evenings of three weeks in summer, when he was busy during the day with other affairs, he completed his first novel.

John Lockhart, who was his son-in-law, and after Scott's death wrote his life, relates that a party of young men, who lived in Scott's neighborhood at the time he was finishing *Waverley*, were having a jovial dinner together. They had adjourned to the library from the dining-room, and one of them, who sat opposite a large window which looked out upon the windows of an adjoining house, was observed to change in manner, and his whole face to become clouded and melancholy.

One of the party intimated a fear that he was not well.

"'No,' said he, 'I shall be well enough presently, if you will only let me sit where you are and take my chair; for there is a confounded *hand* in sight of me, which has often bothered me before, and now it won't let me fill my glass with a good will.'

"I rose to change places with him accordingly, and he pointed out this hand, which, like the writing on Belshazzar's wall, disturbed his hour of hilarity.

"'Since we sat down,' he said, 'I've been watching it; it fascinates my eye; it never stops; page after page is finished and thrown on that heap of manuscript, and still it goes on unwearied; and so it will be till candles are brought in, and God knows how long after. It is the same every night. I can't stand the sight of it when I am not at my books.'

"'Some stupid clerk!' cried one of the party. 'No, boys,' said our host, 'I know what hand it is, — it is Walter Scott's!'"

This was the hand which wrote *Waverley* in the evenings of three weeks in summer.

Scott's success as a novelist in his own time was immediate and complete. From the first publication of *Waverley* the fame and fortune it brought were like the wonders of a fairy-tale. He had always made money freely by his poems. One of the least popular of these had sold ten thousand copies in three months; but this success was nothing to the success of the novels. From one story alone he received in two months three thousand pounds. It was like the opening up of a gold mine. The ease with which money flowed in upon him was only equalled by the ease and rapidity with which he wrote. His pen seemed never to tire. And he said himself, "When I once get my pen to paper, it will walk of itself."

In spite of the great number of novel writers who have succeeded him, and whose works cover such a varied field of fiction, Scott's stories still hold over a large number of readers, old and young, a lasting enchantment. It is hardly to be expected that in this busy age, so full of books, we should read every one of his stories. But there are at least half a dozen which we cannot afford to leave unread. Each lover of Scott will have his favorites; I shall only give my preference when I name as the first half-dozen, *Ivanhoe, Quentin Durward, Kenilworth, The Fortunes of Nigel, The Talisman,* and *Woodstock.* There is perhaps something of accident in these preferences, and those who only read those I have named will miss many characters which have almost as much a place in the past as the characters of history, — the spirited Die Vernon, in *Rob Roy;* Lucy Ashton, in *The Bride of Lammermoor;* the quaint figure of Dominie Sampson, in *Guy Mannering;* and the original traits of Jonathan Oldbuck, in *The Antiquary.* It is said that of all his novels, Scott himself preferred *The Antiquary;* although an author's liking for any one of his books is not often a good criterion for a reader.

In so wide a range to choose from, it is difficult to settle upon an extract from Scott's novels which shall give an example of his style. I have finally taken a scene from *Ivanhoe,* the most widely read of all his books; and after that a scene from *Kenilworth.*

The scene from *Ivanhoe* is from the description of the grand tournament held by Prince John at Ashby, in which Robin Hood, under the disguise of Locksley, wins the prize for his skill in archery.

" The sound of the trumpets soon recalled those spectators who had already begun to leave the field, and proclamation was made that Prince John, suddenly called by high and peremptory public duties, held himself obliged to discontinue the entertainments of to-morrow's festival. Nevertheless, that, unwilling so many good yeomen should depart without a trial of skill, he was pleased to appoint them, before leaving the ground, presently to execute the competition of archery intended for the morrow. To the best archer a prize was to be awarded, being a bugle-horn mounted with silver, and a silken baldric richly ornamented with a medallion of Saint Hubert, the patron of sylvan sport.

"More than thirty yeomen at first presented themselves as competitors, several of whom were rangers and under-keepers in the royal forests of Needwood and Charnwood. When, however, the archers understood with whom they were to be matched, upwards of twenty withdrew themselves from the contest, unwilling to encounter the dishonor of almost certain defeat; for in these days the skill of each celebrated marksman was as well known for many miles round him as the qualities of a horse trained at Newmarket are known to those who frequent that well-known meeting.

"The diminished list of competitors for sylvan fame still amounted to eight. Prince John stepped from his royal seat to view more nearly the persons of these chosen yeomen, several of whom wore the royal livery. Having satisfied his curiosity by this investigation, he looked for the object of his resentment,[1] whom he observed standing in the same spot, and with the same composed countenance which he had exhibited upon the preceding day.

"'Fellow,' said Prince John, 'I guessed by thy insolent babble thou wert no true lover of the long-bow, and I see thou darest not adventure thy skill among such merry men as stand yonder.'

"'Under favor, sir,' replied the yeoman, 'I have another reason for refraining to shoot, besides the fearing discomfiture and disgrace!'

"'And what is thy other reason?' said Prince John, who, for some cause which perhaps he could not himself have explained, felt a painful curiosity respecting this individual.

"'Because,' replied the woodsman, 'I know not if these yeomen and I are used to shoot at the same mark; and because, moreover, I know not how your Grace might relish the winning of a third prize by one who has unwittingly fallen under your displeasure.'

"Prince John colored as he put the question: 'What is thy name, yeoman?'

"'Locksley,' answered the yeoman.

"'Then, Locksley,' said Prince John, 'thou shalt shoot in thy turn, when these yeomen have displayed their skill. If thou carriest the prize, I will add to it twenty nobles; but if thou losest it, thou shalt be stript of thy Lincoln green, and scourged out of the list with bow-strings for a wordy and insolent braggart!'

"'And how if I refuse to shoot on such a wager?' said the yeoman. 'Your Grace's power, supported as it is by so many men-at-arms, may indeed easily strip and scourge me, but cannot compel me to bend or to draw my bow.'

"'If thou refusest my fair proffer,' said the Prince, 'the Provost of the lists shall cut thy bow-string, break thy bow and

---

[1] This was Locksley, or Robin Hood, whom the Prince had noticed the preceding day applauding a Saxon triumph, which John interpreted as an insult to the Normans.

arrows, and expel thee from the presence as a faint-hearted craven.'

" 'This is no fair chance you put on me, proud Prince,' said the yeoman, 'to compel me to peril myself against the best archers of Leicester and Staffordshire, under the penalty of infamy if they should overshoot me. Nevertheless, I will obey your will.'

" 'Look to him close, men-at-arms,' said Prince John, 'his heart is sinking; I am jealous lest he attempt to escape the trial. And do you, good fellows, shoot boldly round; a buck and a butt of wine are ready for your refreshment in yonder tent when the prize is won.'

" A target was placed at the upper end of the southern avenue which led to the lists. The contending archers took their station, in turn, at the bottom of the southern access; the distance between that station and the mark allowing full distance for what was called a shot at rovers. The archers, having previously determined by lot their order of precedence, were to shoot each three shafts in succession. The sports were regulated by an officer of inferior rank, termed the Provost of the games; for the high rank of the marshals of the lists would have been held degraded had they condescended to superintend the games of the yeomanry.

" One by one the archers, stepping forward, delivered their shafts yeoman-like and bravely. Of twenty-four arrows shot in succession, ten were fixed in the target, and the others ranged so near it that, considering the distance of the mark, it was accounted good archery. Of the ten shafts which hit the target, two within the inner ring were shot by Hubert, a forester in the service of Malvoisin, who was accordingly pronounced victorious.

" 'Now, Locksley,' said Prince John to the devoted yeoman, with a bitter smile, 'wilt thou try conclusions with Hubert, or wilt thou yield up bow, baldrick, and quiver to the Provost of the sports?'

" 'Sith it may be no better,' said Locksley, 'I am content to try my fortune, on condition that when I have shot two shafts at yonder mark of Hubert's, he shall be bound to shoot one at that which I shall propose.'

" 'That is but fair,' answered Prince John, 'and it shall not be refused thee. If thou dost beat this braggart, Hubert, I will fill the bugle with silver pennies for thee.'

" 'A man can but do his best,' said Hubert; 'but my great-grandsire drew a good long-bow at Hastings, and I trust not to dishonor his memory.'

"The former target was now removed, and a fresh one of the same size placed in its room. Hubert, who as victor in the first trial of skill had the right to shoot first, took his aim with great deliberation, long measuring the distance with his eye while he held in his hand his bended bow, with the arrow placed in the string. At length he made a step forward, and raising the bow at the full stretch of his left arm, till the centre, or grasping place, was nigh level with his face, he drew the bowstring to his ear. The arrow whistled through the air, and lighted within the inner ring of the target, but not exactly in the centre.

"'You have not allowed for the wind, Hubert,' said his antagonist, bending his bow, 'or that had been a better shot.'

"So saying, and without showing the least anxiety to pause upon his aim, Locksley stepped to the appointed station, and shot his arrow as carelessly in appearance as if he had not even looked at the mark. He was speaking almost at the instant that the shaft left the bowstring; yet it alighted in the target two inches nearer to the white spot which marked the centre than that of Hubert.

"'By the light of Heaven!' said Prince John to Hubert, 'an thou suffer that runagate knave to overcome thee, thou art worthy of the gallows.'

"Hubert had but one set speech for all occasions. 'An your Highness were to hang me,' he said, 'a man can but do his best. Nevertheless, my grandsire drew a good bow —'

"'The foul fiend on thy grandsire and all his generation,' interrupted John; 'shoot, knave, and shoot thy best, or it shall be the worse for thee.'

"Thus exhorted, Hubert resumed his place; and not neglecting the caution which he had received from his adversary, he made the necessary allowance for a very light air of wind which had just arisen, and shot so successfully that his arrow alighted in the very centre of the target.

"'A Hubert! A Hubert!' shouted the populace, more interested in a known person than in a stranger. 'In the clout! — in the clout! A Hubert forever!'

"'Thou canst not mend that shot, Locksley,' said the Prince, with an insulting smile.

"'I will notch his shaft for him, however,' replied Locksley; and letting fly his arrow with a little more precaution than before, it lighted right upon that of his competitor, which it split to shivers. The people who stood around were so astonished at his wonderful dexterity that they could not even give vent to their surprise in their usual clamor. 'This must be the devil, and no man of flesh and blood,' whispered the yeomen to each other; 'such archery was never seen since a bow was first bent in Britain.'

"'And now,' said Locksley, 'I crave your Grace's permission to plant such a mark as is used in the North country, and welcome every brave yeoman who shall try a shot at it, to win a smile from the bonny lass he loves best.'

"He then turned to leave the lists. 'Let your guards attend me,' he said, 'if you please, — I go but to cut a rod from the next willow-bush.'

"Prince John made a signal that some attendants should follow him, in case of his escape; but the cry of 'Shame!' which burst from the multitude induced him to alter his ungenerous purpose.

"Locksley returned almost instantly with a willow wand about six feet in length, perfectly straight, and rather thicker than a man's thumb. He began to peel this with great composure, observing, at the same time, that to ask a good woodsman to shoot at a target so broad as had hitherto been used, was to put shame upon his skill.

"'For his own part,' he said, 'and in the land where he was bred, men would as soon take for their mark King Arthur's round table, which held sixty knights around it. A child of seven years old,' he said, 'might hit it with a headless shaft; but,' he added, walking deliberately to the other end of the lists, and sticking the willow wand upright in the ground, 'he that hits that rod at five-score yards, I call him an archer fit to bear both bow and quiver before a king, an it were the stout King Richard himself.'

"'My grandsire,' said Hubert, 'drew a good bow at the battle of Hastings, and never shot at such a mark in his life, and neither will I. If this yeoman can cleave that rod, I give him the bucklers, — or rather, I yield to the devil that is in his jerkin, and not to any human skill; a man can but do his best, and I will not shoot where I am sure to miss. I might as well shoot at the edge of our parson's whittle, or at a wheat-straw, or at a sunbeam, as at a twinkling white streak which I can hardly see.'

"'Cowardly dog!' said Prince John. 'Sirrah Locksley, do thou shoot; but if thou hittest such a mark, I will say thou art the first man ever did so. Howe'er it be, thou shalt not crow over us with a mere show of superior skill.'

"'I will do my best, as Hubert says,' answered Locksley; 'no man can do more.'

" So saying, he again bent his bow, but on the present occasion looked with attention to his weapon, and changed the string, which he thought was no longer truly round, having been a little frayed by the two former shots. He then took his aim with some deliberation, and the multitude awaited the event in breathless silence. The archer vindicated their opinion of his skill : his arrow split the willow rod against which it was aimed. A jubilee of acclamations followed, and even Prince John, in admiration of Locksley's skill, lost his dislike to his person. ' These twenty nobles,' he said, ' which, with the bugle, thou hast fairly won, are thine own ; we will make them fifty if thou wilt take livery and service with us as a yeoman of our body-guard, and be near to our person; for never did so strong a hand bend a bow, or so true an eye direct a shaft.'

" ' Pardon me, noble Prince,' saith Locksley, ' but I have vowed that if ever I take service, it should be with your royal brother King Richard. These twenty nobles I leave to Hubert, who has this day drawn as brave a bow as his grandsire did at Hastings. Had his modesty not refused the trial, he would have hit the wand as well as I.'

" Hubert shook his head as he received with reluctance the bounty of the stranger, and Locksley, anxious to escape further observation, mixed with the crowd, and was seen no more."

The novel of *Kenilworth* has for its main incident the visit of Queen Elizabeth to the Earl of Leicester at his castle of Kenilworth, and the festivities that were made to entertain her. The dramatic part of the story is the meeting of the queen with Amy Robsart, whom Leicester has secretly married, wishing to keep this marriage from the knowledge of his royal mistress. One of the most powerful situations in all Scott's novels is given in the following extract. The queen is walking in the gardens of Kenilworth, when by chance she enters a grotto in which Amy Robsart, who has come to the castle without the knowledge of her husband, has concealed herself : —

" Then the Queen became aware that a female figure was placed beside, or rather partly behind, an alabaster column, at the foot of which arose the pellucid fountain, which occupied the inmost recesses of the twilight grotto. . . . As she advanced, she became doubtful whether she beheld a statue or a form of flesh and blood. The unfortunate Amy, indeed, remained motionless, betwixt the desire which she had to make her condition known to one of her own sex, and her awe for the stately form which approached her, and which, though her eyes had never before beheld, her fears instantly suspected to be the personage she really was. Amy had arisen from her seat with the purpose of addressing the lady who entered the grotto alone, and, as she at first thought, so opportunely. But when she recollected the alarm which Leicester had expressed at the Queen knowing aught of their union, and became more and more satisfied that the person whom she now beheld was Elizabeth herself, she stood with one foot advanced and one withdrawn, her arms, head, and hands perfectly motionless, and her cheek as pallid as the alabaster pedestal against which she leaned. Her dress was a pale sea-green silk, little distinguished in that imperfect light, and somewhat resembled the drapery of a Grecian nymph, such an antique disguise having been thought the most secure where so many maskers and revellers were assembled, so that the Queen's doubt of her being a living form was well justified by all contingent circumstances, as well as by the bloodless cheek and the fixed eye. . . .

"From her dress, and the casket which she instinctively held in her hand, Elizabeth naturally conjectured that the beautiful but mute figure which she beheld was a performer in one of the various theatrical pageants which had been placed in different situations to surprise her with their homage, and that the poor player, overcome with awe at her presence, had either forgot the part assigned her, or lacked courage to go through it. It was natural and courteous to give her some encouragement; and Elizabeth accordingly said, in a tone of condescending kindness: 'How now, fair nymph of this lovely grotto, art thou spell-bound, and struck with dumbness by the charms of this wicked enchanter whom men term Fear? We are his sworn enemy, maiden, and can reverse his charm. Speak, we command thee.'

"Instead of answering her by speech, the unfortunate countess dropped on her knee before the Queen, let her casket fall from her hand, and clasping her palms together, looked up in the Queen's face with such a mixed agony of fear and supplication that Elizabeth was considerably affected.

"'What may this mean?' she said. 'This is a stronger passion than befits the occasion. Stand up, damsel: what wouldst thou have with us!'

"'Your protection, madam,' faltered forth the unhappy petitioner.

" 'Each daughter of England has it while she is worthy of it,' replied the Queen; 'but your distress seems to have a deeper root than a forgotten task. Why and in what do you crave our protection?'

" Amy hastily endeavored to recall what she were best to say, which might secure herself from the imminent dangers which surrounded her without endangering her husband; and plunging from one thought to another, amidst the chaos which filled her mind, she could at length, in answer to the Queen's repeated inquiries in what she sought protection, only falter out, 'Alas! I know not.'

" 'This is folly, maiden,' said Elizabeth, impatiently; for there was something in the extreme confusion of the suppliant which irritated her curiosity as well as interested her feelings. 'The sick man must tell his malady to the physician, nor are WE accustomed to ask questions so oft without receiving an answer.'

" 'I request, I implore,' stammered forth the unfortunate countess, 'I beseech your gracious protection — against — against — one — Varney.' She choked wellnigh as she uttered the fatal word, which was instantly caught up by the Queen.

" 'What Varney? Sir Richard Varney, the servant of Lord Leicester? What, damsel, are you to him, or he to you?'

" 'I — I — was his prisoner, and he practised on my life, and I broke forth to — to —.'

" 'To throw thyself on my protection, doubtless,' said Elizabeth. 'Thou shalt have it, — that is, if thou art worthy; for we will sift this matter to the uttermost. Thou art,' she said, bending on the countess an eye which seemed designed to pierce her very inmost soul, 'thou art Amy, daughter of Sir Hugh Robsart, of Lidcote Hall?'

" 'Forgive me, forgive me, most gracious princess,' said Amy, dropping once more on her knee, from which she had arisen.

" 'For what should I forgive thee, silly wench?' said Elizabeth; 'for being the daughter of thine own father? Thou art brainsick, surely. Well, I see, I must wring the story from thee by inches. Thou didst deceive thine old and honored father, — thy look confesses it, — cheated Master Tressilian, — thy blush avouches it, — and married this same Varney.'

" Amy sprung on her feet, and interrupted the Queen eagerly with, 'No, madam, no! as there is a God above us, I am not the sordid wretch you would make me; I am not the wife of

that contemptible slave, of that most deliberate villain! I am not
the wife of Varney! I would rather be the bride of Destruction.'

"The Queen, overwhelmed in her turn by Amy's vehemence,
stood silent for an instant, and then replied, 'Why, God ha'
mercy! woman,— I see thou canst talk fast enough when the
theme likes thee. Nay, tell me, woman,' she continued; for to
the impulse of curiosity was now added that of an undefined
jealousy that some deception had been practised on her,—
'tell me, woman,—for, by God's day, I *will* know, whose wife,
or whose paramour, art thou. Speak out, and be speedy. Thou
wert better dally with a lioness than with Elizabeth.'

"Urged to this extremity, dragged as it were by irresistible
force to the verge of the precipice which she saw but could not
avoid, permitted not a moment's respite by the eager words
and menacing gestures of the offended Queen, Amy at length
uttered in despair, 'The Earl of Leicester knows it all.'

"'The Earl of Leicester!' said Elizabeth, in utter astonishment; 'the Earl of Leicester,' she repeated, with kindling
anger. 'Woman, thou art set on to this,— thou dost belie him;
he takes no keep of such things as thou art. Thou art sub-
orned to slander the noblest lord and the truest-hearted gentleman in England. But were he the right hand of our trust, or
something yet dearer to us, thou shalt have thy hearing, and
that in his presence. Come with me, come with me instantly!'

"As Amy shrunk back in terror, which the incensed queen
interpreted as that of conscious guilt, Elizabeth, hastily advanced, seized on her arm, and hastened with swift and long
steps out of the grotto and along the principal alley of the
Pleasance, dragging with her the terrified countess, whom she
still held by the arm, and whose utmost exertions could but just
keep pace with those of the indignant Queen.

"Leicester was at this moment the centre of a splendid group
of lords and ladies assembled together under an arcade or por-
tico which closed the alley. The company had drawn together
in that place to attend the commands of her Majesty when the
hunting-party should go forward; and their astonishment may
be imagined when, instead of seeing Elizabeth advance towards
them with her usual measured dignity of motion, they beheld
her walking so rapidly that she was in the midst of them ere
they were aware, and then observed, with fear and surprise, that
her features were flushed betwixt anger and agitation, that her
hair was loosened by her haste of motion, and that her eyes
sparkled as they were wont when the spirit of Henry VIII.
mounted highest in his daughter; nor were they less astonished

at the appearance of the pale, attenuated, half-dead, yet still lovely female whom the Queen upheld by main strength with one hand, while with the other she waived aside the ladies and nobles who pressed towards her, under the idea that she was taken suddenly ill.

"'Where is my Lord of Leicester!' she said, in a tone that thrilled with astonishment all the courtiers who stood around; 'stand forth, my Lord of Leicester!'

"If, in the midst of the most serene day of summer, when all is light and laughing around, a thunderbolt were to fall from the clear blue vault of heaven, and rend the earth at the very feet of some careless traveller, he could not gaze upon the smouldering chasm which so unexpectedly yawned before him with half the astonishment and fear which Leicester felt at the sight that so suddenly presented itself. He had that instant been receiving, with a political affectation of disavowing and misunderstanding their meaning, the half-uttered, half-intimated congratulations of the courtiers upon the favor of the Queen; carried, apparently, to its highest pitch during the interview of that morning, from which most of them seemed to augur that he might soon arise from their equal in rank to become their master. And now, while the subdued yet proud smile with which he disclaimed those inferences was yet curling his cheek, the Queen shot into the circle, her passions excited to the uttermost, and supporting with one hand, and apparently without an effort, the pale and sinking form of his almost expiring wife, and pointing with the finger of the other to her half-dead features, demanded in a voice that sounded to the ears of the astounded statesman like the last dread trumpet-call that is to summon body and spirit to the judgment-seat, '*Knowest thou this woman ?*'"

From the publication of the *Lay of the Last Minstrel* in 1805, for twenty years Scott's prosperity was unbroken. Few literary men have had such continued fame and fortune. Early in his literary career he formed a business partnership, kept a secret, with two friends of his, James and John Ballantyne, the printers of his books. This firm was closely allied in interest with that of Constable, the publisher.

In the full tide of success, when he might have been supposed secure from pecuniary trouble, almost without warning, the firms of his publisher and printer failed. From the fact of his secret partnership, entered into so long before with Ballantyne, Scott found himself liable for the debts of the firm. At fifty-four years old he was overwhelmed with a debt of one hundred and twenty thousand pounds for the printing-firm, besides thirty thousand pounds of private debts. His private debt had been incurred in the fitting of his home, — the estate of Abbotsford. Although generally simple in his tastes, Scott had one pet extravagance. To create and beautify a home was the dream of his life. He had begun by buying some land on which he intended to build a tasteful house ; but by degrees more lands had been added, till the little estate grew into baronial acres, and the modest mansion became a castle. It was an ideally beautiful place ; as Miss Edgeworth said when she went from her home in Ireland to visit the author of *Waverley*, " Everything about you is exactly what one ought to have wit enough to dream."

When failure came, Scott accepted the position at once with characteristic courage, declared that he could and would pay all debts, and saying, " Time and I against any two," went at once to work. There were men noble enough to come to his aid. The young Duke of Buccleugh offered to assume alone the whole debt, but Scott refused all such offers. For answer, new novels began to appear at rapid intervals. In five years he had paid nearly half the debt, with interest. After his death the value of the copyrights on his books cleared Abbotsford, and it was preserved to his family.

But such work as this was too much even for such capacity for work as his. During his literary career he was author of many books other than the poems and novels which make his fame. He had edited the works of Dean Swift, with a biography, in nineteen volumes ; he had written a voluminous Life of Napoleon ; he was the author of a History of Scotland ; he had furnished articles for cyclopædias, magazines, and current literature : all these, with historical and biographical sketches, had come from this fertile pen. His was a life of almost unparalleled industry ;

and it is not strange that, while still in the vigor of age, the cord should snap by its strain, that the pitcher should be broken at the fountain. In the midst of his work he had a paralytic stroke, the natural result of such mental efforts.

After he was taken ill he would do prodigies of work, and often dictate from his bed while in pain and in mental weariness. In 1830 he had a stroke of paralysis. Even after this he finished his two last novels, *Count Robert of Paris* and *Castle Dangerous*. In the autumn of 1831 he went to Italy in the vain hope of restoration, but returned to Abbotsford in the summer of 1832 to spend his last days in his beloved home. He called one day for his pen; but the hand that had been so untiring could not hold it, it dropped from his grasp. The tears rolled down his cheeks as he bade farewell in that last effort to the work which was his life, and from that time he failed rapidly; and Sept. 17, 1832, at the age of sixty-one, he died.

His death and the close of his work seem to me to form a fit point at which to close the story of English literature. About the time that he passed off the stage there were entering upon it some of the men now foremost in the literature of to-day, — the living authors upon whom Time has not yet passed its verdict. With the death of Scott, therefore, I leave the history of the literature of the past. The history of the literature of our living writers belongs to the future.

INDEX.

ABBOTSFORD, home of Sir Walter Scott, 424.

Addison, Joseph, life and works, 264; publishes The Spectator, 266; essays quoted, 270.

Adonaïs, poem by Shelley, quoted, 393.

Akenside, Mark, poems of, 297.

Adhelm, poet of seventh century, 36.

Alexander's Feast, ode by Dryden, quoted, 236.

Alfred the Great, account of, 37; literary work, 38.

Alliteration, characteristic of Northern poetry, 33.

America, discovery of, its influence on literature, 84.

Ancren Riwle, quoted, 55.

Angles, their position in Europe, 20; name common to several tribes, 20; sold as slaves in Rome, 24.

Anglo-Saxon Chronicle, edited, 40.

Anne, queen of England, 243; clubs in her reign, 244.

Arabs, in Italy and Spain, 42.

Arcadia, written by Sir Philip Sidney, 109; extracts from, 110.

Areopagitica, Milton's, 197.

Arnold, Matthew, on Wordsworth, 362.

Arthur, king of Britain, 46, 47, 83.

Aryan, mother-race of European nations, 20.

Ascham, Roger, schoolmaster of Queen Elizabeth, 95.

Augustan age, The, 243.

Augustine, Christian missionary in England, 25.

Austen, Jane, novels of, 326, 411.

BACON, FRANCIS, life, 116; essays, 118; extracts from works, 119.

Bacon, Nicholas, 116.

Bacon, Roger, 56.

Ballads, Early English, 50; Robin Hood ballad quoted, 51.

Bards, among the Britons, 24.

Barrow, Isaac, eminent clergyman, 220.

Battle of the Baltic, poem by Campbell, quoted, 365.

Baxter, Richard, eminent divine, 220.

Beattie, James, 297.

Beaumont, Francis, life and works, 158; lyrics of, 161.

Beckford, William, author of Vathek, 11.

Beda, The Venerable, literary work of, 37; translation of Gospels, 37.

Bee, The, periodical published by Goldsmith, 314.

Beggar's Opera, The, quoted from, 253.

Beowulf, oldest English poem, 27; conjectures about, 27; quoted, 29-31.

Bible, first brought to England, 25; its influence on literature, 25; Wycliffe's translation of, 65; translated by Tyndale, 85.

Black-eyed Susan, ballad by Gay, quoted, 255.

Boethius, works of, translated by King Alfred, 38.

Boswell, James, biography of Dr. Johnson, 308.

Britain, first inhabitants, 21; its conquest by Romans, 21; invasion of, by English, 22.

British Museum, 27.

Britons, a Kymric people, 21.

Brittany, ancient books in, 46; tales of, 47.

Brut, The, poem by Layamon, 55.

Brutus, founder of the British nation, 46.

Bunyan, John, life and writings, 221; extract from works, 223.

Burnet, George, history of his time, 220.